A LARK'S RELEASE

A Regency Cozy

VERITY LARK MYSTERIES
BOOK IV

❧

LYNN MESSINA

potatoworks press • greenwich village

Copyright © 2024 by Lynn Messina

Cover design by Ann-Marie Walsh

ISBN (eBook): 978-1-942218-95-1
ISBN (Paperback): 978-1-942218-96-8
ISBN (Hardcover): 978-1-942218-97-5
ISBN (Jacketed Hardcover): 978-1-942218-98-2

This is a work of fiction. Names, characters, places and incidents either are the product of the author's imagination or are used fictitiously. Any resemblance to actual persons, living or dead, events or locales is entirely coincidental.

All rights reserved.

No part of this book may be reproduced in any form or by any electronic or mechanical means, including information storage and retrieval systems, without written permission from the author, except for the use of brief quotations in a book review.

Title Production by The Book Whisperer

Never miss a new release! Join Lynn's mailing list.

Prologue

Sunday, June 28
10:36 p.m.

When asked by Mrs. Ralston with an air of thinly veiled disgust if there was any sort of man with whom she would not consider consorting, Matilda, Countess of Abercrombie, replied that she was too liberal in her tastes to create a constraint where none naturally existed. Broad-minded and tolerant, she found herself attracted to a wide swath of physical traits and would never allow the color of an aspirant's hair or the line of his jaw to shape her opinion.

She welcomed all comers.

But only briefly.

If a contender failed to display an agile wit or an intriguing mind or a keen understanding, she immediately handed him his congé. The most interesting part of any romantic encounter was the conquest, the storming of the fortress walls, and there was no satisfaction to be had from overwhelming the feeble defenses of a vacuous Adonis.

Her unwillingness to submit to their exhilarating ministrations baffled these male beauties, who, with their limited intelligence, could make neither head nor tail of her resistance. Naturally, her bewildering indifference further inflamed their passions, and rejected suitors had a wearying habit of becoming relentless in their pursuit. To be sure, the number of disappointed admirers had fallen off in recent years as Tilly marked her fiftieth birthday and then her fifty-first, but the category remained robust enough to annoy her at varying intervals.

Among the most tiresome was Blandie.

A few years younger than she, he had lusted after her for decades.

Three, to be precise, for he had formed an attachment the very first time he had laid eyes on her—at some ball or another, or perhaps it was a rout.

It was impossible to recall the details after so long.

In an effort to be fair, Tilly acknowledged there was a rational theory underpinning his constancy, as she was quite the luscious bite, even now, so many years later, with her coquettish smile and adorable nose and generous bosom. Blandie's own appearance was notable as well, for he had windswept blond hair and brooding, dark eyes set in a square face with plush lips. And his form—it was quite pleasing, with powerful shoulders and thighs.

By his calculation, the countess and he were a matched set, and Tilly's inability to perceive how well they looked together was an indication of her own lack of mental acuity. As a man of integrity and honor, he could not in good conscience permit her to persist in her ignorance. It was incumbent upon him to show her the light.

Hence the decades of pursuit.

Although dogged, the quest had not been without its

distractions, and Blandie had taken a wife and two dozen mistresses during the long campaign. His marriage, by all accounts, was a satisfying one, with his spouse content to count her blessings rather than her husband's instances of infidelity. She had three well-behaved children, two modest-size homes, and one obscenely rich father-in-law whose excellent health could not continue indefinitely.

Sooner or later, the old reprobate would succumb to the ravages of time and there Blandie would be, dutifully mourning his beloved sire's passing with his hand held out demurely to collect his portion of the grand estate, which Blandie's wife assumed would be the largest, as her husband was the eldest of three sons and the only one to produce heirs.

One brother was without issue and the other had the grave misfortune of bringing four daughters into the world. The girls were presentable enough, with pleasing notions, affable visages, and pretty dispositions, but amiability could not overcome the inadequacy of their sex.

For these reasons, Blandie was just as sanguine about his future as his spouse, and although he had never been so gauche as to discuss his financial prospects with her, Tilly knew he had already begun to compile an extensive list of things he would do with the money once it was tightly in his grasp.

She always knew what Blandie was thinking because he was capable of only banalities. If he took her for a drive in Hyde Park, he would make mundane comments about the gentleness of the breeze or the confident hand of Hartlepool as he steered his mount across the path.

And he would laugh at his own sallies.

Watching Boggie fall off his hobbyhorse, which had been made to look more like a donkey by an unskilled craftsman, he would observe that his lordship was the true ass and then titter with deep appreciation at the display of astounding wit.

It was why she had begun calling him Blandie early in their acquaintance. He was entirely without interest, as bland as a piece of toast without butter or jam. The thought of spending more than a few minutes in his company bored her to flinders.

And yet there he was in her bedchamber, in her *bed,* his cravat unraveled, his shirt falling off his right shoulder, his hand stroking her calf before moving up her body. His eyes fixed on hers, he smiled with delighted complacency, his fingers eager to remove barriers, and she was struck by the vapidity of his gaze, astonished that something could be fathoms deep and blank at the same time.

Confident that he was judging his own performance, she assumed he gave himself high marks for deftly coaxing her to lie with him on the silken counterpane. All it had required was a flash of his gorgeous smile, those rows of even white teeth, that curl of bemused admiration, at the faro table at the Red Lantern, and she had yielded to the undeniable force of his presence.

Tilly knew it was not what he had intended for the evening.

Visiting the gaming hall in the company of his brother-in-law, he had planned to pass an hour or two testing his luck before retiring to his club for port. In all likelihood, he would be home by three, only slightly the worse for wear.

But then suddenly the lovely Countess of Abercrombie was standing beside him and chortling with giddy appreciation at all his remarks, even the ones that he did not mean to be humorous. He was genuinely peeved at losing the high bet, for his stake was not insignificant. But Tilly had laughed, murmured soothingly about the vicissitudes of fate, and pressed a hand to his shoulder.

It was the hand that settled the matter.

Within minutes, Blandie was bidding Elsmore goodbye and leading her ladyship to his carriage, which he directed to her residence in Grosvenor Square with all due haste.

The presumption of the command was breathtaking, and Tilly inhaled sharply, as though shocked by his audacity, which further emboldened him. He began his seduction the moment the carriage door had closed, and during the short drive to her home, she allowed him a few liberties. He lavished attention on her fingers, hailing them as delicate yet assured, and she responded with a faint whimper.

Arriving at her townhouse, he relinquished his claim to her hand and acquitted himself admirably in front of her butler, whose expression remained impassive.

Even so, Tilly detected a hint of curiosity in the servant's gaze.

Well you wonder, she thought in amusement, resisting Blandie's attempts to pull her through the first doorway he passed, which led to the dining room.

Ardently, his handsome features drawn into a frown, he said, "Come now, my lady, you have made me wait an age for this. Do not make me wait longer."

On a throaty laugh, she gestured to the stairs. "It is not long now."

Tightening his grip on her elbow, he climbed the steps to the landing and followed her to the bedchamber, which was opulent and plush, with rich fabrics in deep shades of blue, from the damask walls and velvet curtains to the silk counterpane, which was pulled back invitingly on one side. A dozen candles flickered from an assortment of sconces, which bathed the room in a golden glow, and a fire crackled warmly in the hearth, creating the sense that a stage had been set.

If something about the scene felt slightly off, he was either too distracted or too lack witted to notice it. He merely dove headfirst onto the bed, like a swimmer entering a pond, then flipped over to lean against the pillows and leer at her.

Presumably, he thought he was enticing her with a seductive grin.

Scornful of his technique, which lacked both finesse and skill, she nevertheless joined him on the mattress and purred encouragingly when he clutched a handful of her dress and tugged it up. For several moments, she permitted his fingers to roam freely over her body, her mind wandering as she marveled at how easily he had been maneuvered into this position.

Getting her own housekeeper to serve blancmange for dessert was more difficult.

Henry would be appalled by the display—and not because it would pain him to see his adored wife rolling around their marital couch with another man, although he would find that aspect of the experience extremely unpleasant. Rather, her dearly departed spouse knew from repeated exposure to Blandie that the man was a pompous ninny and well beneath her touch.

Even so, she demonstrated the correct amount of enthusiasm as she reached up to untie his cravat and undo the top two buttons on his shirt, revealing the honey gold of his torso. Although undeniably impressive, the definition of his muscles did nothing to stir her emotions.

If he had only possessed some small amount of intelligence, then she might be able to enjoy the physical aspect of the game.

Blandie responded to her ministrations in kind, heaving her dress over her head—with some effort, it must be noted, for the hem caught on her elbow—and tossing the garment onto the floor. Having removed one layer, he immediately focused on removing another.

"Oh, my, you are a wicked man, aren't you, sir," she said with a husky trill as he tried to draw up the hem of her chemise.

Releasing his grip on the lace trim, he slid up her body to lay a heated kiss against her neck. "You have not seen anything yet, my lady."

Shivering with high drama, she whispered, "I would never have believed you had it in you to be so ruthless. I must confess, it excites me to know what you are capable of."

His fingers danced along the edge of the bodice as he swore he was ruthlessness personified. "Just ask my tenants or sparring partners at Gentleman Jackson's. They tremble at the sight of me."

Naturally, he had resorted to an empty boast.

Blandie was as predictable as a clock; he would always chime on the hour.

On a breathy gush, she said, "The pure decisiveness of the action is thrilling. You always struck me as a milksop, cautious and fainthearted. That is why you could not secure my interest. An appealing face—and yours is significantly more appealing than most—was never enough for me. I crave resolve and authority. But now, I am transfixed by your manliness. I am overcome by it. It is all I can think about."

With anyone else, Tilly would worry about overdoing the extravagance of her praise, but in light of his meager gifts, she had decided that being too subtle presented the greater hazard, an assumption that was immediately confirmed by his preening response to her compliments.

Applying himself to her bodice with renewed vigor, he promised her that he was *all* man. "As you shall see presently, my dear."

She laughed in anticipatory delight and turned her shoulders coyly to the left to withhold the access he sought. "It is the hint of danger that arouses me, knowing that you tried to poison your own half sister. You are like a scoundrel from long ago, a Medici. I have always been fascinated by Lorenzino de' Medici, and being in the presence of a man just as powerful makes me feel small and helpless."

Confronted with the allegation of murder, Blandie barely reacted.

His fingers paused briefly.

Struggling to slip under her chemise to the warm skin beneath the silky fabric, they halted for a moment before resuming their invasion.

It was the only indication that he had heard her at all, and Tilly wondered if it was a testament to his ironclad control or an indication of his lack of it.

Assuredly, it was the latter, for even if he felt no horror at being accused of a heinous crime, the fact that she had been able to piece together his identity from the few descriptive traits Twaddle had included in his account should have alarmed him. Any prudent killer who remained in possession of his wits would have pulled back as if scorched, demanded a retraction, and asked to whom else she had shared her ludicrous supposition.

As he pursued none of these tacks, she pressed her advantage, cooing over the outrageous virility of his making not even a token effort to deny the charge. "Any other man would tell me I am mistaken, but you are not like the other men I have known. You know who you are and do not shrink from it. I find that wildly attractive."

Taking this tribute as his due, he said he had done what was required—no more, no less. "She was making trouble for me and I wanted her gone. It was as simple as that."

Tilly fluttered her lashes adoringly. "How commanding you are, sir!"

"Oh, I think we are beyond formalities now," he replied

chidingly, shifting his position so that she looked down at him, her hair falling in waves onto his chest. "You may address me by my given name, and I shall call you Tilly. And I must warn you that by the end of the evening you will say it with reverence and awe."

"Oh, my, yes, so very commanding," she murmured, owning herself astonished that his father's baseborn whelp could cause problems for a man of his standing. "You are so important, so consequential, and she is nothing. I cannot believe she had the cheek to threaten you. She should have realized she was outmatched by a superior opponent."

Blandie, chuckling with wry amusement, brushed a strand of hair behind her ear. "That insipid chit daring to take me on? I should like to see her muster the nerve. The problem is my father. He remains in robust health but knows his influence has begun to wane as he approaches his seventy-fifth year and makes periodic efforts to regain control by threatening to cut me out of the will and leave everything to the chit. It is a tedious gambit, which I know he will never follow through on, for he is too proud to admit his own by-blow into the family, however illustrious her connections may be. But after so many years of it, I am weary of the conversation and decided to bring it to a close once and for all. The plan encountered a hitch, which is unfortunate."

So it was a hitch, was it, Tilly thought cynically, amazed that he could be so dismissive of his scheme's tragic outcome. His inability to grasp the depravity of his conduct spoke more forcefully to his weak-mindedness than anything else.

Couching his failing as a virtue, she lauded his tenacity. "That is the Medici in you, allowing nothing to stand in your way. I find it so virile," she said softly, pressing her body languidly against his as she begged him to tell her what he intended to do next. "Will you let her live?"

He scoffed at the facile notion of mercy and pledged to see the problem through to its necessary conclusion, for his father was unlikely to stick his spoon into the wall anytime soon, which, to be sure, he did not want. "I bear him no grudge save for the infernal threats. I have already spun a new plot, and the issue will be resolved by this time tomorrow, I am certain of it."

"It is exhilarating to be in the presence of so much power," she fawned, lowering her shoulder in just such a way that her chemise slipped down a tantalizing inch. "Tell me how you will do it."

His eyes feasting on her cleavage, he said, "I must not."

"Oh, but you must," she insisted throatily. "I have a strong desire to know, and I never let my desires go unsatisfied. It is a point of pride me with me. I always follow through."

Practically drooling with anticipation, Blandie bowed to her demand. "A bottle of wine to be delivered tomorrow morning from the warden of Newgate. He is sorry for her wrongful imprisonment and eager to return to the Marquess of Ware's good graces. I gave him the bottle myself as well as the letter to include in the package advising the chit to raise a glass at once to the intoxicating rush of freedom," he added smugly before announcing that the time for talking was done. "As you yourself noted, my dear, I am a man of action and now I must act."

And act he did, reaching up with both hands to grab her breasts.

It was, Tilly thought, the most Blandie thing possible, which was to say trite, meager, boring, and predictable, and because it fell within the expected range of behaviors, she was able to dart out of the way before he could make contact with her flesh. Displaying the graceful elegance that made her a highly desired woman on three continents—and, yes, she was counting Australia, as it was where one of her most ardent former lovers had been sent after an unfortunate encounter with a pugilist—she swiveled her shoulders to the left and stood up in a single fluid motion. Directing her gaze to the blue-striped settee in front of the window and to the man crouched behind it, she said, "I trust that is sufficient."

Chapter One

※

Sunday, June 21
9:07 P.M.

If Verity Lark were to lodge a single complaint against the management of Newgate Prison—to which she was currently confined under the charge of murder—she would protest the staff's adamant refusal to issue coherent orders. Rather than make a request or even deliver a command, guards flung prisoners around as though they were sacks of onions, grabbing them by the arm to shove them forward or pull them backward or tug them to the side. If an inmate dared to object to the rough treatment, she was immediately subjected to further abuse.

And an objection, to be clear, did not even have to represent a fully articulated thought.

All she had said two days ago, when a turnkey jerked her to her feet to take her to the keeper's house, was *ouch*—a single word torn from her lips as her shoulder was scraped bare by a wall—and it was enough to ensure her arm was in almost constant contact with the jagged stones that lined the passageway.

The physical cruelty did not surprise Verity. It was what she would expect from the men who worked amid the squalor of England's most notorious prison. It was coarse and obvious.

But the lack of communication was more insidious because it created uncertainty, and the inability to understand what was happening at any given moment took a psychological toll on a prisoner. Tense with expectation, Verity had had no opportunity to prepare for the next blow, which was why she had been utterly dumbfounded when she'd entered the room in the keeper's house and found Her Outrageousness standing there, her brown hair curled in silken ringlets with a pink-colored ribbon arranged à la Montespan and her fingers encased in embroidered satin gloves.

Struggling to make sense of the bizarre sight, Verity had wondered if her mind had begun to deteriorate in the brief time she had been incarcerated.

It seemed unlikely that a brain could weaken so quickly.

How many hours had it been since her apprehension?

Twenty-eight.

It had been only twenty-eight hours since she had arrived at the Wraithe's house to discover the former headmistress of Fortescue's Asylum for Pauper Children dead from a bullet in her head.

And then the Runner arrived.

While she was still holding the gun in her hand, a Bow Street Runner named Cyrus Thimble had come upon her and arrested her for murder.

As those events were clear in her mind, Verity felt reasonably confident the duchess was not a hallucination. She was actually there, along with Marlow, an old family retainer, not Kesgrave.

She had looked around the room.

The duke was not present.

Either her half brother knew nothing of the duchess's visit or heartily disapproved of it.

The former, she had decided. Whereas a wife could blithely ignore a husband's preferences, a servant was obligated to obey. If Kesgrave had voiced his opposition to the undertaking, the butler would never have risked his position with open defiance.

Grappling for a response, Verity had silently cursed the vile turnkey for not recognizing that the greater torture would have been to inform her that the Duchess of Kesgrave awaited her pleasure in the keeper's house. The shame she would have felt while navigating the confusing maze of dark corridors would have been crippling.

For months, Verity had been hounding this woman, poking fun at her every action, from her bold examination of headless chefs to her love of rout cakes, and now she was there, at the fetid prison, to provide whatever assistance she could. Upon learning of Miss Lark's incarceration, Her Outrageousness had dashed posthaste to Old Bailey Street to offer her investigative skills to the scurrilous gossip known to all of London as Mr. Twaddle-Thum.

The duchess had no idea.

All her shrewd insights, and Her Outrageousness could not even begin to imagine the truth.

Verity declined her help.

It was painful enough occupying the same physical space as her victim. Availing herself of the very abilities she had repeatedly mocked was intolerable.

But her grace persisted, refusing to take no for an answer, and in the end, Verity accepted her help because she wanted her help. Although Twaddle's initial reports ridiculed the new peeress for her absurd presumption of styling herself as a lady

Runner, recent accounts displayed a growing respect for her proficiency. Somehow, inexplicably, the Duchess of Kesgrave possessed a genuine talent for solving murders.

Later that same day, it had happened again: Verity was grabbed, pulled, tugged, and flung down a series of near black corridors by a turnkey. His breath smelled like decay, and when they emerged into the fading light of day, she had fleetingly wondered if he was to be her executioner.

Exhausted and in pain, she could conceive of no other reason to be outside other than to mount the gibbet. An execution preceding the trial defied logic, but that was Newgate all over: Nothing made sense.

The guards and the turnkeys and the porters held their tongues, explaining nothing.

A conspiracy of silence.

It was how they controlled the inmates—with fear and confusion.

Despite her irrational terror, she was taken to a house on the far side of a desolate courtyard, led up two flights of stairs, and deposited in a small bedroom in the back of the house.

The warden's home, she had belatedly realized.

That had been Friday evening.

It was Sunday night now, and as Verity looked around her quarters, she felt profoundly grateful for the comforts they provided. The silence alone was glorious, for Newgate was a tireless cacophony, an endless scream, and being able to hear her own thoughts free of the suffering of others was a gift.

It was what enabled her to make a catalogue of her complaints.

Yes, complaints, plural.

Obviously, Verity would never confine herself to just one.

She knew her new accommodations had cost Hardwicke a small fortune because nothing in Newgate came cheaply. The outlay was in addition to the many other expenditures he had made on her behalf, including having her moved to the state side of the prison and engaging the services of a fellow inmate named Big Fist Johnston to oversee her safety, and it was a measure of her weariness that she did not begrudge any of it. She would repay every farthing without even a twinge of unease.

Verity did not believe in suffering for the sake of suffering.

She also did not believe in idle hands and had settled on the list as a way to keep herself occupied. One day, when she was far away from this horrible place, she would write about the inhumane treatment routinely meted out to inmates. From the way their own food was sold back to them at a premium to the turnkeys' predation, the degradations were manifold, and Robert Lark would detail every last one in a series of unsparing exposés.

The public knew in a general sense that the inmates suffered intolerable conditions and largely did not care because convicts forfeited their right to kindness and decency. But not everyone in Newgate was a miscreant or degenerate. Many of its inhabitants were innocent victims cruelly punished for crimes they had not committed or for which they had long since atoned.

And even if its walls had never confined a single blameless person, it was nevertheless incumbent on a civilized society to treat its most abhorrent members with charity as it befit *their* humanity, not the villain's.

Verity, deciding this thought captured the tone she wished to strike in her article, repeated it several times in an effort to commit it to memory and resolved to secure paper and a quill.

She assumed anything she required could be attained for a price, and as she already owed Hardwicke more money than she could reasonably return by the end of the year, she saw no reason to stint now.

When the footman came to collect her dinner tray, she would request the items.

She had no sooner made that decision than the door to her tiny chamber swung open.

Well, swung halfway, as its arc was blocked by the bed.

The footman, who was as rough and impatient as any turnkey, darted his arm into the room, snagged her by the shoulder, and yanked her into the corridor without explanation. Sneeringly, he told her to jump to it as he rammed her shoulder against the wall. "C'mon, c'mon, I don't got all day!"

Having been left to herself for almost forty-eight hours, Verity felt some trepidation at being forcefully removed from the safety of her room and to distract herself from darker thoughts she focused on the central thesis of her first story: Dignity to all creatures was what a moral society owed to itself.

Freddie would disagree.

Her lifelong friend and editor of the *London Daily Gazette* would inevitably take a harder stance, arguing that some people—the Wraithe, for instance—deserved nothing but the cruelty they themselves had inflicted. Agreeing, Verity would make no counterclaim except to add that was precisely her point: The punishment of a malefactor should not be placed in the hands of those seeking retribution. The process should be neutral and fair.

That observation would no doubt infuriate Freddie, and contemplating the robust discussion that would ensue, she felt a pang of sadness. She could not recall the last time she had gone three days without talking to him and felt his absence keenly.

Delphine's as well.

Nominally her companion, Delphine lived with her at

Bethel Street, provided vital editorial support, and sought to rein in her friend's wilder impulses. The dear girl was probably beside herself without Verity to chastise for her recklessness.

As these thoughts were no more conducive to a sanguine outlook than imagining the gallows, she wrested her attention back to the article she was mentally composing.

Annoyed with her for not bounding down the steps fast enough, the servant prodded her shoulder. "C'mon, then, stop yer dawdling!" he barked, thrusting her to the right when they reached the bottom and then along another corridor.

None of the house was familiar, as she had been led through a warren of dark hallways upon her arrival and delivered straight to her room, where she was directed to use a chamber pot for her needs. Consequently, she had only a vague sense of its size and was surprised to find herself in the threshold of a dark-beamed drawing room of gracious proportions.

"This way," he growled, heaving her roughly through the doorway and knocking her right shoulder against the frame. She bit her lip rather than cry out in pain, and when she would have reached out a hand to steady herself with the jamb, he tightened his clasp and shoved her forward. Only the bite of his fingers on her upper arm kept her upright, and as she regained her balance, she noted the contents of the room: settee, table, cabinet, warden, Hardwicke.

Hardwicke!

There he was, Lord Colson Hardwicke—England's greatest spy, the Marquess of Ware's dissolute second son—not ten feet away from her, his expression impassive as he observed her struggle against the footman's grip. Then he slowly and deliberately moved his gaze to the right, to the man standing next to her. As if stung, he released his grasp on her arm and muttered an apology as he stepped away.

The warden, who watched this exchange with a faint sneer on his face, opened his mouth to speak, but Hardwicke interrupted at once. "It is done," he said to Verity, holding out his elbow for her to take, as though escorting her to her box at the theater. "Come."

Her instinct was to protest.

Not only did it seem inconceivable to her that the thorny problem of the Wraithe's murder had been resolved so quickly but she also had things to collect.

In fact, she did not.

There was not a single item in the tiny room upstairs that she required.

She had no cause to linger in the dreary home a minute longer than necessary.

Even so, she wondered if she should thank her host for the cold gruel, sour milk, and harsh treatment, and then felt annoyed with herself for being uncertain.

Coolly, she laid her hand on Hardwicke's forearm, raised her eyes to meet the warden's, and declared herself grateful for his hospitality. "I will forget none of it."

She had not intended it as a threat, for what power did she possess to hurt him, but the warden flinched and glanced at Hardwicke with anxious concern.

"Well, yes, ah ... thank you for ... um ... visiting," the warden replied haltingly. "Do feel free to ... um ... call again."

As the drawing room was in the front of the house, it was a short walk to the door and only a few moments later they were outside and Verity took a breath of fresh air, noting that it smelled sweetly like leaves and rain. Hardwicke waited while she paused on the threshold of the home to inhale deeply, then led her to an elegant conveyance with a gilt frame, red curtains, and the Matlock family crest. Opening the door, he helped her ascend, and she could not articulate even to herself the utterly strange sensation of stepping from the warden's home into the Duke of Kesgrave's carriage.

Verity knew there was a rational explanation for the oddity, and a good portion of it was actually supplied by the vehicle itself. Presumably, Her Outrageousness had done it again, staring down an assortment of suspicious characters and properly identifying the guilty one. What she could not fathom were the details: whom she had interrogated, how she had located them.

Ordinarily eager to know everything, she found herself curiously indifferent to the particulars, and as Hardwicke settled on the bench next to her, she felt the inexorable comfort of his presence. Silently, she turned to him and laid her head against his chest, her arms circling his waist as she pressed against him like a small animal burrowing.

He was warm and solid and familiar and dear.

She held her tongue because she could not trust herself to speak. Her voice might quiver or tremble or break, and that would give Hardwicke the wrong impression.

Newgate had been an ordeal.

The smell was unbearable, the cries were intolerable, the despair that crept into every corner of her being felt like rocks dragging her under the sea. And yet the true agony came from having to relinquish control over her own fate. Trapped in that hellish pit, she could neither solve her own problem nor direct its resolution. All she could do was trust that others would handle it as competently as she herself, and if she had never been quite able to convince herself that vindication was inevitable, she had believed it was possible

Consequently, the relief she felt now was overwhelming. Her chest pounded with a painful ferocity and tears clogged her throat. She knew it was a good thing—the best thing—to be able to rely on others as assuredly as she could rely on herself, but something about it felt erroneous or wrong. Incapable of comprehending the reason for her inexplicable response, she sunk into the sadness, holding her position for the whole of the ride home, her ear pressed against the reassuring solidity of Hardwicke's heart.

※

Sunday, June 21
9:54 p.m.

If anything revealed the depth of Delphine Drayton's anxiety for her friend's welfare, it was the way she jumped onto the footboard of the duke's carriage before it came to a stop. Only the week before, she had chastised Verity for indulging in precisely that sort of rash behavior, a criticism she made with alarming regularity.

Nothing justified the heedless risk of life and limb!

The expression on Delphine's face as she suddenly perceived her own recklessness delighted Verity to no end, and as she climbed down from the vehicle, she felt the heavy sorrow she had carried since leaving the warden's home lift.

"You maniac!" Delphine chided as she crushed the former inmate in an embrace. "How dare you terrify us like that. You are a fool! I know it is not your fault, but you are a fool because it is all your fault. I will never, ever forgive you." But even as she pledged eternal resentment, she squeezed Verity harder. "Why would you go to her house alone? How could you not tell us the second the letter arrived? The Wraithe means trouble. She has always meant trouble. I would not be surprised to learn she arranged her own death just to make sure you were sent to the gallows. You think you are impervious to everything, but you are as human as the rest of us and more of a fool than Freddie and I combined. I hate you for what you have put me through."

Verity raised an eyebrow at her friend's erratic speech. "You have expressed the entire range of human emotion in less than thirty seconds, and *I* am the maniac?"

Delphine further tightened her grip. "You make me insane. And the poor orphans! I have been so beset with terror and fear that I haven't knitted a thing in days. The one time I tried to make a blanket, I tangled all the yarn and poked myself with the needles."

"Yes, dear, that is the problem with my being sent to Newgate for a murder I did not commit: the steep fall-off in blanket production at twenty-six Bethel Street. Mrs. Caffrey will have my head on a stick when she finds out," she observed wryly, submitting to her friend's ministrations despite a slight difficulty in drawing breath.

"As long as you have a head for Mrs. Caffrey to mount," Delphine replied sensibly as she lowered her arms to allow Freddie to also welcome Verity home. Then she launched herself at Hardwicke. "You gorgeous, gorgeous man, thank you!"

On a laugh, Freddie drew his friend into a hug and warned her to be careful. "Delphine is trying to steal your beau."

"She would never have him," Verity replied confidently, resting her head against his shoulder. "He jumps on more moving floorboards than I do."

"Ah, but he takes the squirrel problem in the garden seriously," Freddie pointed out as he gently pulled back to look at her and scowled at her bedraggled appearance: torn dress, blackened eye, mangled wrists. "Are you all right?"

"I am, yes," she said firmly, determined that they would all cease worrying about her at once. It had been a tribulation indeed, but it was over now and there was no purpose in fretting about what might have been. "Slightly worse for wear but nothing a warm bath, a hot meal, and an expert de-lousing will not fix."

At the mention of the parasitic insect, Delphine screeched, jumped back, and began brushing furiously at her clothes, which caused Verity to giggle. "Good lord, Delph, I was only teasing. I was not on the ward long enough to contract lice before I was whisked away to the state side of the prison."

It was, Delphine asserted, a specious argument, for there was no amount of time that was too short for the pernicious little beasts to take hold, and she insisted Verity have a good scrub while Cook prepared the meal of her choosing. "You may have anything you wish, anything at all. Name it and it is yours."

"Honestly, I have no preference," Verity claimed, adding that she would happily devour whatever food was placed before her on the table. "Cheese and bread, muffins, roast chicken, kippers—whatever is easiest for Cook."

Delphine, divining her friend's true desire from the order of the list, said she would arrange a tray of cheese and bread. "And meats, of course. I was served rosemary ham at dinner last night and barely took two bites. I am certain there is more. There are also some sausages, I think."

"My only criterion is that it not be gray and gluey, so you must not work yourself into a lather over me," Verity said firmly, threading her arm through Delphine's to lead her to the house, an act of amiable warmth that was instantly rebuffed by her friend, who could not allow her affection to supersede her concern about vermin.

Naturally, she could not, Verity thought, greatly amused as she entered the house, where Lucy was waiting to whisk her away to the bath, which had been prepared in anticipation of prison filth. Eager to join the others in the parlor to discover what had transpired during her internment, for she knew nothing other than what she had surmised about the Duchess of Kesgrave's investigation, she nevertheless lingered in the perfumed water. It was a luxury she rarely indulged, for there was nothing she could accomplish in the bath and it always felt indolent to remain unproductive for too long.

Arriving to the parlor almost an hour later, Verity found the company comfortably ensconced in the trio of armchairs across from the settee and Hardwicke rose to his feet to escort her to the sofa. As she sat down, Freddie held out a glass of wine, which Delphine intercepted with a shake of her head.

"If all you have eaten in the past four days is poorly prepared gruel, then your stomach must be empty," Delphine said reasonably. "Alcohol will go straight to your head, rendering you incoherent, and I would prefer that you remain lucid for the conversation."

As if on cue, Lucy entered with plates piled high with bread, cheeses, and meat, followed by Cook, who carried in a gaily decorated cake. Verity, delighted to see the confection, clapped in pleasure and announced that she had changed her mind.

"Cake," she said. "I wish for cake above all else."

As the servants laid the food on the table, Verity took her usual seat at the head and Delphine poured about half the wine from her friend's glass into her own. Graciously, she placed the diminished portion in front of Verity and said, "You may have a small cup."

"Yes, Mother dear," Verity murmured docilely, making no attempt to hide her mirth.

As Hardwicke cut the cake into several large pieces, Delphine sighed and begged her friend to bear with her. "I am not so woolly-headed as to believe my suffering over the past few days is equal to yours, but it was very difficult for me nonetheless. Freddie had his work to distract him, and Hardwicke had the consolation of running all around London, from the magistrate to the warden to the lord mayor. All I could do was sit here and mangle yarn. Inaction is the very devil."

Verity, who had made this exact lamentation to her friend on dozens of occasions during their long acquaintance, revealed no hint of smugness as she mildly agreed that it was painful to twiddle one's thumbs while there were problems to be solved.

Despite the bland response, Delphine felt the rebuke keenly and allowed that she might have been unfairly harsh in her judgment of Verity's impulsiveness. Clearly, the solution was to avoid situations requiring idleness.

"Yes, dear, I shall do everything in my power to refrain from getting arrested for murder again," Verity replied soothingly as she pressed her fork into the delicious smelling cake. "To that end, it would perhaps be helpful if I knew how I managed it *this* time. I assume it was a large conspiracy designed with the express purpose of ensnaring me? Who oversaw the plot and what score were they seeking to settle?"

Hardwicke tilted his head pensively to the side before admitting that the conspiracy was somewhat smaller. "Let us call it medium size. Your theory regarding a shadowy figure was more or less accurate, as there was someone influencing events, but her control was not absolute. She was following the action, not creating it."

Delphine, sliding the plate of ham closer to Verity, for cake did not constitute a nutritious dinner, looked up in surprise. "Verity's malefactor is a woman?"

Freddie, chuckling at her response, insisted there was no reason for astonishment. "The Wraithe herself was an extremely pernicious female."

Verity agreed that gender was not a reliable indicator of decency, then confirmed that the murderer was related in some way to Fortescue's. "As the Wraithe was the victim, it must be."

"Tangentially," Hardwicke said. "She is the daughter of a man whom Robert Lark exposed for his licentious interest in children. His generous donation to an orphanage near Spitalfields gave him the run of the place and unmediated access to its occupants."

Verity required no further information, easily recalling the details of the scandal, to which she had been alerted by one of Twaddle's informants. Georgie had been a former resident of the orphanage, and although he had escaped the wealthy patron's notice, several of his closest friends had not. "The miscreant killed himself, did he not?"

Unsettled by the reference to the repellent villain, who counted among the worst scoundrels the *Gazette* had ever written about, Freddie confirmed that he had indeed shot himself. "As soon as he realized society would not blithely overlook his molestation of vulnerable orphans, he decided to end his life rather than endure ostracism."

Delphine was likewise taken aback, for her complexion lost much of its color as she tried to understand why his daughter would resent Robert Lark. "Her father was a depraved monster. If anyone is to blame for his downfall, it is he, not the reporter who exposed it to the world. Or does she think it is all a hum?"

Verity was also confused. "I do not recall a daughter. There was a son who stomped around London for weeks, seething at the unfair sullying of the family name. He challenged his uncle to a duel in the middle of Oxford Street, I believe."

"It was Hyde Park," Hardwicke replied.

"Actually, now that I think about it, the sister visited the *Gazette*'s office requesting to speak with Robert Lark," Freddie said. "It was only a few times, two or perhaps three. As you can imagine, Robert had always just stepped away, having left to investigate one story or another, and I suppose she grew frustrated and stopped trying to meet with him. It was a few years ago so I cannot claim my memory is the sharpest, but I do not remember her being consumed with fury, not like the brother."

Hardwicke hazarded that she had not been unduly angry at the time. "Whatever ire Miss Hottenroth felt appears to have been tempered by practical considerations and was reignited by happenstance and opportunity. She discovered that Verity was Robert's true identity quite by chance, and the only reason she killed the Wraithe was she thought she could arrange for Verity to take the blame with no risk to herself. If she had understood the peril involved, I am certain she would not have acted."

Verity, duly spearing a thick slice of ham to placate her friend even as she eyed another piece of cake, marveled at the woman's hubris. No transgression was without danger, especially murder, for which a wrongfully accused killer would be highly motivated to find the correct one.

Perhaps her revenge had felt preordained, given Hardwicke's description of how she learned the truth about Robert Lark. If the information had fallen effortlessly into her lap years after it had ceased to matter, then clearly Providence wanted her to have it.

Ah, but how did she get it?

It was this question that preoccupied Verity the most, for it was a closely held secret and one that allowed her to move freely in the world as a reporter. If the truth was widely known, then she would have to come up with a new ruse to protect herself. Robert Lark was a fiction she had created from whole cloth and could do so again if necessary. Verity herself could disappear and reemerge as an entirely new creature.

"The dowager," Hardwicke said in response to the query.

In light of Verity's recent interaction with the Dowager

Duchess of Kesgrave, the answer was not a complete non sequitur, but nor did it follow any obvious logic. Her grace's interest in the child previously known as Mary Price extended only so far as finding out what had happened to the generous provision she had made for the girl's welfare—a process that had required a thorough investigation.

How had the dowager discovered what the former headmistress had done with the money? By asking the former headmistress what she had done with the money.

Appalled, Freddie gasped. "In conducting her investigation into the missing funds, her grace's representative unthinkingly alerted the Wraithe to Robert Lark's identity. At some point in the conversation, he must have called Mary Price Verity Lark, and from there it was an easy thing for the Wraithe to connect her to Robert. But I do not understand what any of this has to do with Hottenroth's daughter."

"They have a mutual friend," Hardwicke explained.

Delphine scoffed. "Impossible! The Wraithe did not have friends."

Hardwicke allowed that *friend* was overstating the case. "Rather than hand over a monthly payment of five guineas, one of the Wraithe's extortion victims managed to charm her into accepting her time, hospitality, and sympathetic ear in exchange for silence. This woman—her name is Alicia Beveridge—counts the former Miss Hottenroth as a dear confidant. It was she who gave Miss Hottenroth the information she needed to find out Robert Lark's identity. She also told her friend about the Wraithe's scheme to blackmail Verity, and that was what gave her the idea to incriminate Verity for the murder. The Wraithe had arranged for the Runner to arrive at her house a little before eleven, and all Miss Hottenroth had to do was delay his appearance for a few minutes so that he would come upon Verity with the gun in her hand."

While Delphine puzzled over the notion of inviting a law enforcement official to witness one's crime, Freddie repeated the name Alicia Beveridge several times before snapping his fingers in recognition. "She is one of the supervisors from Fortescue's. She resigned in disgrace with the rest of the board in the wake of our articles. So the Wraithe was blackmailing her as well. Well, that is certainly interesting."

Oh, but was it not, Verity thought, scowling fiercely as she realized she had missed something so patently obvious even a child would have noticed it. "Good lord, I am a ninny! The first rule of reporting is to look for the pattern! Of course the Wraithe had more victims. She was a blackmailer! A blackmailer blackmails! The moment I received a letter demanding silence in exchange for money, alarm bells should have sounded in my head, and failing that, I should have realized it as soon as I saw her body. My wits have gone begging!"

These self-recriminations, offered with so much derision, exasperated the other occupants of the room, who reminded her she had had more important things on her mind in recent days, such as surviving prison and fending off despair.

"And despite your determination to believe otherwise, the fact is you are only human and not invulnerable to fear," Delphine added peevishly. "If your wits had gone begging, it was just briefly, and I trust you are employing them enough now to realize how absurd you sound."

Chastened, Verity leaned back in her chair and permitted that the oversight might be understandable in the context of larger events. Even so, she was determined to hold herself to account. "If I had read the letter earlier in the day instead of a half hour before going to bed, it is likely I would have recognized the behavior of a habitual blackmailer and planned accordingly."

"Or if you had shown the letter to me rather than

pretending nothing was amiss and sneaking out of the house, I might have pointed it out," Delphine said.

"Or me," Freddie added.

Delphine smiled as she acknowledged the remark. "Or Freddie. The correct response was to summon us to the parlor at once so that we could pool our thoughts. But as I noted previously, you are not immune to fear and receiving a letter from that horrible woman after so many years must have distressed you greatly, so I will attribute your impetuosity to terror and hope you will remember this conversation the next time you are inclined to go haring off on your own."

Verity was tempted to argue, for she could not comfortably accept the charge of possessing ordinary human frailty, but knew the allegation was not without merit. It contained some measure of truth.

Nevertheless, she refuted *terror*.

In no universe did Verity Lark feel an emotion as extravagant as terror.

The most she would concede was *dread*.

Delphine rolled her eyes as she spread cheese on a piece of bread but otherwise refrained from commenting, and Freddie asked Hardwicke if he knew what Mrs. Beveridge had done to make herself vulnerable to the Wraithe's extortion.

"A dalliance with one of the gardeners," he replied.

As the sin was relatively benign, Verity could hardly believe the Wraithe thought it worth sixty pounds per annum.

"Apparently, Mr. Beveridge takes a hard stance on these things, as he has made his expectation of fidelity clear and his wife refuses to abide," Hardwicke said.

"And what about the other board members?" Verity asked, pursuing the line of inquiry now that she should have followed a week ago. "Were they also being soaked by the

Wraithe? And were their sins just as underwhelming as Mrs. Beveridge's?"

Hardwicke did not immediately reply. Instead, he reached over to grasp Verity's wineglass and filled it almost to the top. Then he laid it next to her plate.

As far as messages went, it was not particularly subtle, and Verity stiffened her shoulders in expectation of hearing something truly despicable.

Matter-of-factly, Hardwicke said, "Charles Wigsworth conducted scientific experiments on the children. He is convinced nitrous oxide can be used in conjunction with another gas to render surgical patients unconscious, which would make medical operations painless, and to figure out the ideal formulation, he enlisted the boys."

Verity felt dizzy.

Her head spun and her stomach quivered, and the word *enlisted* reverberated inside her skull as she grappled to comprehend how she had missed something so monumental.

She had investigated Fortescue's.

For months she had roamed the grounds and halls of her former home seeking evidence of the Wraithe's perfidy. Even as a young child she had realized there was something fishy about the way the headmistress managed the asylum because there was never enough money to buy milk or eggs and yet the Wraithe could afford silk nightdresses and a pair of new kid-leather boots every year.

That she was skimming funds from the operating budget Verity never doubted. Neither clever nor creative, the Wraithe took few pains to hide her thievery.

Even so, Verity could not lodge an accusation without proof, and after several days of evaluating her options, she decided to drop a few pointed words into the ear of the only board member who performed his duties with any semblance of diligence. Spurred by her gentle nudge, he examined the accounts with a critical eye and spotted the embezzlement. With further encouragement from her, albeit in a different disguise, he sent one of the old ledgers to the editor of the *London Daily Gazette,* whose apprenticeship with a printer he had arranged years before. With the book in hand, she and Freddie were able to identify a pattern, which led them to Lord Condon, Fortescue's patron, who had been placing children in wretched situations in exchange for cash, an arrangement that would never have been possible without the headmistress's cooperation and support.

The Wraithe, already the villain of every childhood story, turned out to be so much eviler than they had ever imagined.

Slowly, methodically, with the help of Delphine, Freddie, and Twaddle's network of spies, Verity uncovered every branch in their network and exposed it to public scrutiny.

And yet there, beneath her notice, obviously hiding in plain sight if the Wraithe was able to find it, was a depravity so horrible she had failed to conceive it.

Her stomach churned with guilt and sorrow.

Pressing one hand against her belly, she took a bracing sip of wine and glared at Hardwicke with flinty eyes. "Enlisted, did they? The boys had the option of refusing?"

It was, she knew, unfair to direct her anger at Hardwicke, but Wigsworth was not present in the parlor to grind under her heel.

"They were offered a crown to volunteer," he explained.

Somehow it was worse.

Wigsworth had put a price on their lives, and it was the cost of a Minerva Press novel.

An encyclopedia was worth more.

"Were any of the children harmed?" Delphine asked.

Hardwicke darted a look at her before returning his gaze to Verity. "One. He did not wake up as quickly as the others, although he did recover physically. But his mental faculties were diminished. None of the other boys suffered ill effects."

"That we know of," Verity amended.

With a curt nod, he acknowledged it was true. "We have only Wigsworth's word that just the one child was hurt, and he admitted it because it was the basis of the blackmail against him. He summoned his personal physician to examine the boy, and the doctor sent the bill for his services to Fortescue's rather than his residence, as requested. That is how the Wraithe learned of it."

"Presumably, he did not make that mistake twice," Verity said softly.

Freddie, whose mind had followed the same path as hers, insisted that once was all they needed if the physician agreed to talk to Robert. "I realize it does nothing to aid the boys on whom he experimented, but it is never too late to expose a grave injustice. And Wigsworth's reputation would suffer. I have read no reports about painless operations, which means neither Wigsworth nor anyone else has figured out the correct formulation. He may still be working on it."

Affirmatively, Hardwicke said he was.

"There, you see!" exclaimed Freddie. "Wigsworth is still working on his project and probably enjoys the respect of the scientific community at large. If we expose him now, he will be shunned, I am certain of it. The members of the Royal Society pride themselves on the ethical advancement of scientific knowledge, and even if they did not care about a parcel of orphans, they cannot be seen not to care. It will all be over for Wigsworth."

Over yes, but six years too late.

As if privy to these thoughts, Hardwicke observed that Robert Lark's reports on the corruption at Fortescue's ended the practice. "You might not have written about Wigsworth's degeneracy specifically, but the articles had the same effect.

All the supervisors were forced to resign over their egregious mismanagement and suffered for it socially if not materially."

"That is precisely right," Delphine said, rising from her seat to fetch her daybook, which was on the side table. "We did an excellent job routing the Wraithe and revealing Lord Condon's villainy, and now we will hold Mr. Wigsworth to account. You see, I am making a notation to begin researching him first thing tomorrow while you sleep late. You will allow yourself to sleep late, won't you, darling? You must be fatigued from your ordeal."

Verity swore she was not at all weary, then promptly undermined the claim by yawning widely. Laughing, she permitted that she might be a little tired.

"Here, do finish your ham and have some more cheese," Delphine said before announcing that she and Freddie would fetch some biscuits for dessert.

Startled, Freddie furrowed his brow. "Biscuits? But we just had cake."

Smiling tightly, Delphine tugged her friend by the collar until he pushed his chair backward and stood. "Cake was dinner."

"But when I wanted to have a muffin for dinner last week, you said the exact opposite," Freddie protested. "You said only children had pastries for dinner."

"No, I am pretty sure I said children had *only* pastries for dinner," she said, insisting that the distinction was not merely semantical, for the cake had been a side dish like roasted potatoes. "Regardless, it will take us ten minutes to fetch the biscuits. Then I will have to invite Hardwicke to leave so that Verity can get that much-needed rest."

Freddie, perceiving at this late juncture the purpose of the ruse, asked as they strode to the door if they were actually getting biscuits. "Or is the plan to loiter in the corridor? If it is the latter, then I would like to bring my slice of cake."

"Fetch biscuits! Obviously!" Delphine replied impatiently.

Chuckling as the pair left the room, Hardwicke pulled his chair closer to Verity's and grasped her hand. "I do not mean to imply that your arrest and imprisonment was in any way a positive development, but it does seem to have gotten me back in Delphine's good graces."

"Indeed, you seem to have risen in her estimation, for last time it took her only five minutes to fetch biscuits," Verity replied, shifting in her seat so that she could look directly into his fascinating eyes, which were a deep greenish blue in the candlelight. "Just imagine how long it would take her to tromp to and from the kitchens if you helped absolve me of a truly heinous crime, such as treason."

Amusement glittered in his eyes, now blueish green, as he dismissed the notion that Delphine had gone anywhere. "She is on the other side of the door counting the minutes until she can return and cluck over you like a mother hen."

Knowing it was true, Verity sighed. "The poor dear. I worried her dreadfully."

Hardwicke raised her hand to his lips and pressed a gentle kiss to her palm. "You worried all of us. I do not think I have slept more than five hours total since I received word of your arrest."

Something in the pit of her stomach fluttered at the warmth of his touch, and she could not discern if it was fear or excitement or both. All she knew was he felt too far away, which was absurd, for they were virtually sitting in the same chair.

Ah, yes, but there was a world of difference in *virtually,* she thought, lifting slightly and scooting closer until there was no space between them. Settled comfortably on his lap, she leaned forward and pressed her lips against his. He responded sweetly, deftly, his ardor matching hers but not exceeding it, and he raised his arms to embrace her only after she drew him closer and deepened the kiss.

Verity, who had spent her whole life thwarting the brutality of entitled men, could not fathom his gentleness. It was an unanticipated gift to be able to let down her guard a little and then a little more, and having lost all sense of time, she was startled and bereft when he pulled back.

Delighted by her bewilderment, he dropped a kiss on her forehead as he settled her on a separate chair. "They are just outside the door, which Delphine is asking Freddie in an unnaturally loud volume to open for her," he explained seconds before the pair swept into the room, the former clutching a tray of millefruit biscuits in two hands, although one would have been more than sufficient.

Placing the salver on the table, Delphine instructed Hardwicke to have as many biscuits as he would like in the next five minutes. "Then it is off to bed for Verity. You may return midmorning for tea, say, around eleven o'clock."

"By eleven o'clock Hardwicke and I will be well on our way to Montague House," Verity said. "He has an assignment from a man named Quartermaine, who works in the foreign office. It has something to do with the Elgin marbles. We were supposed to go on Thursday, but the Wraithe's murder disrupted our plan."

Delphine gasped at the ambitious proposal. "You cannot mean to do that tomorrow. You must take it easy and rest. I am sure Hardwicke understands."

Beseechingly, Verity begged her friend not to treat her as though she were infirm. "I have had four days of inactivity and shall go mad if I have to sit in front of a fire in my dressing gown for hours. You do not want me to go mad, do you, Delph?"

Freddie grinned and asked how often mad Verity jumped onto the floorboards of moving carriages.

Although Delphine did not appreciate the levity, she withheld her rebuke and conceded that it was better for Verity to be occupied than unoccupied. "But do not embroil her in any lethal affairs, Hardwicke," she added tartly. "Let us go one day without high jinks."

Hardwicke blinked innocently and swore he had nothing untoward planned. "It is merely a visit to gather information. There will be no jinks either high or low. That said, I feel compelled to state for the record that Verity has told me in no uncertain terms that she is perfectly capable of embroiling herself in lethal affairs."

Delphine, who required no reminder, thanked him for his circumspection and bid him a cheerful good night before leaving the room herself.

Even if Verity was not exhausted, she was.

Chapter Two

Monday, June 22
3:03 a.m.

As Verity had found it impossible to get a decent night's rest with the threat of the noose hanging above her, even in the relative comfort of the warden's house, she had expected to fall asleep the moment her head hit the pillow.

Alas, she did not.

To be fair, she dozed.

For several minutes at a stretch, sometimes as many as a dozen, her eyes would drift closed and she would drop off drowsily.

But it never lasted.

Something in her brain would ring or chirp or buzz, and various thoughts would clamor for attention, making it impossible to quiet her mind.

Eventually, she conceded the futility and padded downstairs to Robert's study to try to use the time productively. Perhaps if she jotted down the many ideas that swarmed in her head, they would cease plaguing her and allow her to sleep.

The first order of business: cataloguing her complaints about Newgate. Although she did not believe she would soon forget a single second of the miserable experience, she recognized the value of recording her thoughts as quickly as possible and began creating an annotated list. She was on number eighteen when she raised her head to turn the page and spotted Delphine hovering in the doorway. "Oh, dear. Do not tell me you could not sleep as well."

Yawing widely as she stepped into the room, Delphine assured her friend she had no trouble at all sleeping. "But since I was up to use the chamber pot, I decided to look in on you and saw the empty bed. I rather suspected this would happen. Are you creating a record of your stay in Newgate or making notes for our investigation into Wigsworth?"

"The former," she replied.

Delphine nodded wisely as she sat down in the leather armchair on the other side of the desk. "A three-part series exposing the worst abuses of turnkeys and guards?"

"Four part," Verity said.

"By Anon, I assume?"

"Well, I cannot write it under my own name, and attributing it to Robert would invite scrutiny," she explained, laying down her quill and leaning back in the chair. "I could have Robert relate the captivity of an unidentified source, but I think the story is most effective if it is told from my own perspective."

Delphine nodded in agreement, then gestured to the left side of the desk and observed mildly that she had never felt so much terror in her entire life as watching Her Outrageousness rifle through Mr. Twaddle-Thum's drawers. "And that is counting the moment I learned you had been apprehended for murder. For a fleeting second, I actually forgot you were in prison. Logically, I knew it would be fine because you keep everything Twaddle-related under the false bottom of the third drawer, for we can no more have Lucy stumbling across your secret identity than the Duchess of Kesgrave, but that did little to calm the shiver of fear that danced up my spine."

Verity, who could well imagine the moment, apologized for putting her through that anxiety as well as all the rest. "It was unavoidable. Once I agreed to accept her help, I knew she would have to come here to fetch the letter."

"It could have been avoided if you had shown the letter to me and Freddie rather than sneaking off to confront the Wraithe on your own," Delphine said.

Hanging her head in shame, Verity pledged she had learned her lesson and would never again hide a communication from a former nemesis. "You may be assured that getting arrested for murder and thrown in Newgate is a persuasive deterrent."

And yet her friend did not appear convinced.

Nevertheless, Delphine did not argue, noting instead how surprised she had been to learn that Verity had accepted the duchess's help. "I would expect you to refuse out of a mixture of embarrassment and pride."

Verity smiled faintly and admitted she had tried. "But the gravity of the situation was not lost on me, and I recognized the limits of my bravado. Despite what Twaddle may say, Her Outrageousness's record of success is impressive, and if she wanted to expend her energies on my behalf, I am not so foolish as to refuse."

"I am reassured to hear it," Delphine said, adding that it behooved her friend in the wake of the duchess's swift exoneration to send a note thanking her. "It does not have to be long, but it should be precise and sincere."

At the suggestion, Verity emitted a hefty sigh and lowered

her head to the desk. With her forehead pressed against the blotter, she muttered, "I have to give her shooting lessons."

Having expected some sort of dramatic response to her perfectly reasonable suggestion, Delphine was unsurprised by the reaction. Nevertheless, she had no idea what her friend was talking about. "Who?"

Verity raised her head only high enough to rest it against her palms. "Her Outrageousness."

Delphine giggled, certain she had misunderstood. "The Duchess of Kesgrave does not require shooting lessons from Mr. Twaddle-Thum."

"She is dissatisfied with her pistol instruction and seeks a new tutor," Verity replied, inhaling deeply as she dropped both hands onto the desk and sat back in the chair.

And still Delphine did not comprehend. "But her current one is Gerald Prosser, who is among the most accomplished marksmen in London. He once shot a calling card held by his wife at four paces."

"In fact, it was five paces," Verity noted mildly. "And I imagine the duchess would cite his eagerness to aim a gun at his wife as further evidence of his low regard for women. She claims he has barely allowed her to touch a loaded weapon in five weeks of lessons."

Delphine allowed that the span did seem overly cautious, as the duchess had shown herself to be competent on several fronts. "Where are you to conduct this instruction? In our garden or at Kesgrave House?"

Verity blanched and apologized for being unable to provide a useful response. "The details were not revealed to me at the time of the bargain."

"Then you must ask her in your missive," Delphine replied sensibly, earning a baleful glare from her friend. "I can see now why you are so cross. I am sure it will be fine. The duchess shall no doubt prove to be an excellent pupil."

"Well you laugh," Verity grumbled petulantly, not at all fooled by the pronounced gravity in the other woman's tone. "If I had an inkling of how much the visit to the Wraithe's house would cost me in terms of money and dignity, I would have eagerly sent you in my stead."

Knowing how her friend's mind worked, Delphine readily followed her line of thought and said Hardwicke did not begrudge a single farthing he had spent on her safety and comfort. "He would have happily expended double if necessary, and I hope you will not insult him by insisting on paying him back," she said, aware of the futility even as she made the statement. Verity would consider the notion that she should swallow the imbalance between them just as offensive. "He was as frantic as I was and grateful to have something useful to do to mitigate the situation. It would be quite uncharitable of you to take that away from him."

But Verity took no comfort in this thought either, for she did not want to imagine Hardwicke in a state of wild agitation on her behalf. She preferred to picture him cool and detached, calmly appraising a situation without the debilitating influence of strong emotion.

It made the thought of his feelings less unnerving.

And yet she was still unnerved.

"You poor darling," Delphine murmured softly, noting the expression on her friend's face. "It is too much to ponder at three in the morning. Come, let us get you to bed. You must rest up for your busy day of finding facts and avoiding mischief. We both know how hard it is for you to do the latter."

As Verity was too tired to protest the amused condescension in her friend's tone, she allowed herself to be led upstairs.

Monday, June 22
9:37 a.m.

Although in the course of Twaddling Verity frequently applied various types of blemishes, blotches, and bruises to her face, she had never been called upon before to hide a mark and had no established procedure for disguising the discoloration marring her left eye and upper cheek. In the days since she had sustained the blow to her face, its black and purple tint had faded to yellowish brown, but it still required concealment. A veil would never do. It was so dramatic and lacked narrative coherence: Why would a woman in deep mourning make a call to the British Museum in the company of Lord Colson Hardwicke?

She could don her familiar brown suit and present as an office clerk who had recently gotten into a scuffle with a colleague over a charge of inaccuracy in accounting. Or she could be the Turnip, whose overeagerness to please and imperfect coordination could easily lead him to stumble on the edge of a step and plant his face into a newel post or a door. As a rustic newly arrived to the capital, he got himself into all sorts of scrapes and quandaries, and it was truly remarkable that the poor young man was not constantly decorated with contusions of various shapes and sizes.

Verity aired these thoughts as she contemplated her wardrobe and turned to Delphine to ascertain her opinion.

Her friend sighed as if deeply aggrieved and insisted that not everything required a long, involved history. "Hardwicke invited Verity Lark to visit Montague House on an errand with him. Go as Verity Lark!"

Although Verity felt the level of her friend's exasperation exceeded the situation, she nevertheless took the suggestion seriously. "All right, but then why does Verity Lark have a black eye?"

Delphine, answering slowly as if speaking to a small child, said, "Because she was wrongly accused of murder and spent several days in Newgate, where she was violently attacked by an inmate."

"Oh, I see, you mean tell the truth," Verity replied with an amused lilt.

"Yes, I mean tell the truth," Delphine affirmed. "I know it seems like a radical idea to you. It might even feel wrong or unsettling. But I promise you other people do it all the time and suffer no ill effects. I think you should try it once and see how it goes."

As Verity did not consider herself "other people," she believed the scheme had little chance of succeeding but did not wish to quarrel with her friend.

Consequently, when Hardwicke arrived a half hour later to take her to the British Museum, he found her wearing a walking gown of deep cerulean blue, a poke bonnet, and pristine white gloves. If he thought the ensemble paired oddly with the bruise on her cheek, he refrained from making a remark, noting only that the wound was healing nicely. "I should expect it will be barely perceptible in a few days."

Although this prediction struck Verity as unduly optimistic, she allowed that he might have greater experience in this area and said nothing to the contrary as he offered his hand to help her board his curricle.

Taking firm hold of the reins as he directed the horses into the road, he asked whom he had the pleasure of addressing. "Miss Gorman, who had the grave misfortune of slipping on a bar of soap as she climbed out of the tub, or Mrs. Tyler, whose brute of a husband could not contain his anger at losing his monthly allowance at the hazard table?"

Delighted by how well he understood the situation, she admitted with a hint of embarrassment that she was neither. "I am Verity Lark, freshly sprung from Newgate, and I assure you it feels quite strange indeed. But Delphine was insistent, and as she has had a rough time of it lately, I did not want to upset her by quarrelling."

"Yes, *she* has had a rough time of it lately," he replied with pointed amusement.

As the remark referenced the matter she wished to discuss—namely, the comforts made available to her during her prison stay, which were directly attributable to his largess —Verity decided it was an excellent opportunity to discuss her debt and arrange a repayment schedule.

Before she could mention it, however, Hardwicke observed that the purpose of their visit had altered slightly from the original intent. "As I was otherwise occupied on Thursday afternoon, I sent an associate in my stead and he confirmed what I suspected, which is that there is no reason to think Richard Knight is in league with groups seeking to return the marbles to Greece. He is simply convinced that the sculptures are later additions by the Romans and therefore not worth what Parliament is willing to pay for them. Rather than conduct an investigation, we will simply assure the chief librarian that the foreign office does not anticipate trouble and that the sale will go through. A visit from me is not strictly necessary, as a letter with Castleheart's findings would have sufficed, but Grint will get word of it and be highly disgruntled that I am running errands for Quartermaine. I am petty enough to enjoy the thought of his displeasure."

At the mention of the government official, Verity smiled and asked how the functionary had received Twaddle's unmasking of Kingsley as the masterful spy known as Typhoeus. In fact, it was Hardwicke who had risked his life repeatedly in service to his country, but as it was the former under-secretary himself who had made Hardwicke's secret identity known in a drunken fit of pique, Verity had decided that it was only fair that Kingsley suffer the consequences of his revelation, which included dodging a horde of vengeful Bonapartists.

"Neither Grint nor Sidmouth took the news of Kingsley's newfound heroism well," Hardwicke admitted, darting a sidelong glance at her as he drew the horses to a stop to allow a cart to pass in front of them. "As you expected when you came up with the scheme, the Home Office could not leave one of its own dangling without inciting public outrage and promptly stepped in to provide protection. Currently, he is sequestered in his London home under military protection at the government's expense. As soon as Twaddle's report reached the home secretary, I was summoned to Whitehall to explain myself, but of course there was nothing I *could* explain, as I am just another of the wretched gossip's playthings. He is, I must confess, quite convincing in his disgust of me. I would not be surprised to find him outside my door with a pitchfork leading a pack of angry villagers."

"Twaddle has little use for dissolute second sons," she explained blandly.

"Does he not?" he asked with a roguish grin as the horses began to move again.

Struck by how handsome he looked, his expression mischievous as he tugged the horses back into motion, Verity felt her heart flip over. It simply did not seem plausible to her that any man could be so physically appealing. Even squinting in the glare of the sunlight, his eyes were fascinating.

"And where did you leave the matter with Sidmouth?" she asked.

"He seems to consider it a moral failing that I have not made it my singular goal in life to find out who this Twaddle scoundrel is, as I appear to be his favorite target," Hardwicke replied. "Naturally, I was compelled to point out that the

Duchess of Kesgrave receives far more attention than me and perhaps he should apply to her for information."

Verity winced.

It was impossible not to, for she still felt the shame deeply and could not conceive the mortifying ordeal of being in Her Outrageousness's company for the duration of a single shooting lesson, much less several.

If Hardwicke noticed her discomfort, he did not indicate it by word or deed.

But he had to be curious.

Even if he was too shrewd to broach the topic, he must have a dozen questions about her mistreatment of her half brother's wife.

Nevertheless, he kept his focus on Kingsley, speculating that the government official would enjoy the crown's protection for a few weeks. Then London would empty for the summer and the Home Office would ship him off to an obscure outpost in the country. "They will make him a clerk in a customs office, and he will be comfortable if not pleased with his situation."

Given Kingsley's many transgressions, the situation was still better than he deserved. But it was also less than he would like.

Verity would have to be satisfied with that.

"And am I right to assume the reason you wish to tweak Grint's nose is he declined to intervene on my behalf?" she asked, aware that he held his former superior at the Alien Office in much higher esteem than the occupants of twenty-six Bethel Street did. Delphine in particular harbored an intense dislike of the under-secretary, whom she had found officious and cravenly.

"I should like to do a great deal more than tweak it," he replied mildly.

"You cannot be surprised by his refusal," she said.

"Surprised by his refusal, no," he allowed amiably. "Surprised by his assumption of your guilt, yes. I have worked with him long enough to expect that he would trust my instincts, not lecture me on the inevitable deviousness of clever women."

"Oh, dear, Delphine will not like that," she murmured.

He chuckled at the understatement and said Delphine would not stop at Grint's nose. "She would bloody his whole face if given the opportunity."

As difficult as it was for Verity to imagine her gentle friend being riled to violence, she knew anyone could be driven to unusual behavior by extreme circumstances and was thankful Delphine would have little cause to cross paths with the under-secretary again.

Echoing this thought, Hardwicke led the curricle through the stone gate and drew the horses to a stop in front of the seventeenth-century mansion that housed the collections.

※

Monday, June 22
11:23 a.m.

Although Mr. Goddard could not fathom what interest a person of the female persuasion might take in classical sculpture, let alone the astonishingly complicated matter of international politics, he treated Verity with unfailing respect, insisting that she sit down for the length of his discussion with Lord Colson, for it was simply too much to expect a woman of her delicate sensibilities to stand for twenty consecutive minutes.

That he situated the chair next to the far window was merely further proof of his consideration, for the placement offered the best view of the room. If she was too far away to hear their conversation, then that outcome must be endured for the greater good. "I could not live with myself if I allowed our discussion to spoil your appreciation of the artifacts and their setting. Here, Lord Colson and I shall move into the corridor so that our chatter does not disturb you."

Naturally, Verity did not stay where she was put.

Her impulse, of course, was to irritate the insufferable librarian with a flagrant display of erudition, providing a lengthy treatise on the Greek government both ancient and modern before offering a detailed account of Knight's analysis of the marbles and reciting extensive portions of Lord Byron's scathing poetical critique of Lord Elgin, "The Curse of Minerva."

Several of her most beloved characters were ostentatious bores, and she could lecture with relentless tedium on an infinite number of subjects with the same pomposity as the most self-important member of Parliament.

Nevertheless, she restrained herself.

Mr. Goddard, who appeared incapable of holding a favorable opinion of the gentler sex, would inevitably conclude the exhibition of knowledge was a tantrum or perhaps an apoplectic fit and respond as though bothered or troubled.

By no account would he be impressed or chastened.

And obviously she did not want to make Hardwicke's work more difficult. It was not his fault the principal librarian was a sanctimonious prig who cherished an ardent dislike of women.

Stepping into the hallway and turning to the right, she ignored Mr. Goddard's cries of concern, for he seemed to think she had lost her way en route to the chair. The antiquities collection, if her memory served, was at the end of the north corridor.

It had been several months since Verity had visited Montague House. On that occasion she had arrived a half hour before closing, tucked herself behind a mummy coffin, and waited for the halls to empty before seeking out the Rosetta stone to confirm a recent report that an industrious librarian had filled in the inscription with chalk to make it easier to read. Her investigation did not entail discovering the identity of the overly solicitous vandal, but having met Goddard she assumed it was his work.

As noon was in the middle of visiting hours, Verity did not have the museum to herself and perused the galleries in the company of other interested parties.

The collection was, by and large, impressive and extremely interesting, and standing before the sculptures from the Temple of Apollo at Bassae, she could see the appeal of dragging the friezes back to London to be admired by the British public. The desire to show off items one found in far-flung corners of the world was a fairly ordinary impulse.

And yet possessing a deep admiration for something did not justify taking it.

Verity, for example, was not allowed to pocket a diamond pendant necklace at Rundell, Bridge & Rundell simply because she thought it looked better around her neck than in the shop's display case.

Such behavior was, in the common parlance, theft.

Naturally, the rules differed for Englishmen tromping through foreign parts enjoying their grand tour, but even if their standing allowed them to pilfer any item that caught their attention, larceny was still a gross violation of the rules governing the guest-host relationship.

Verity contemplated these thoughts as she examined a small statue of a black cat, its expression oddly alert as it sat upright on its hindquarters, its tail wrapped along the right side of its body and its ears perked. Resting on a five-sided base, the four-inch-tall feline bore a resemblance to a figurine owned by Delphine with a few significant differences, including a duller surface, sharper ears, and a collar on its chest. The similarities were not remarkable, as both statuettes appeared to be an expression of the Egyptian goddess Bastet, and yet the craftsmanship on Delphine's, while inferior to the work on the museum piece, was impressive. She had no recollection of where her friend had gotten the cat, having brought it to Fortescue's with her as a small child, and Verity wondered about its origins.

Hardwicke found her there.

"Done so soon?" she asked, affecting surprise.

Despite his confident assertion that the meeting would be brief, it had taken the better part of an hour and she wondered how many times he had endeavored to end the conversation before actually succeeding.

"In fact, yes," Hardwicke said soberly. "Goddard had several more concerns he wished to discuss regarding the safety and security of the marbles, and I perceive now that the only reason Quartermaine asked me to step in is he wanted a moment of peace and quiet for himself. Goddard is of a nervous disposition and cannot seem to stop himself from worrying about details that are beyond his control."

"Oh, dear, do not tell me he is irrational and emotional," she replied.

Whatever response he intended to offer was forestalled by the approach of a bespectacled man in a dark-colored suit. His manners impeccable, he displayed a familiarity with Hardwicke, who recognized him after a short pause.

"It is Owens, is it not?" he said.

On an enthusiastic nod, the man confirmed that it was indeed Owens. "Archibald Owens, my lord, younger brother to Harold Owens, with whom you attended university."

"How is old Harry?" Hardwicke asked fondly.

"Well, very well, thank you," Owens replied with a relieved air. "He will be flattered that you asked. If you will, my lord, there is something I would seek your assistance with. I understand if you must refuse, but I would not presume to ask if I did not consider it of the utmost importance."

Verity, who found this request highly intriguing, would not understand if Hardwicke refused. Fortunately for all involved, he agreed, and Owens led them down a series of corridors until they reached a large square room with tables lining the perimeters and statuary in varying stages of decay.

"Apologies for all the dust and grime," Owens said anxiously, wiping at the sleeves of his coat, which was pristine. "We are not accustomed to visitors here. This is where I work. It is my job to receive new items, evaluate their condition, and prepare them for display. It is interesting work and more engrossing than I had anticipated. When I accepted the position, I expected it to be dull and wretched for my asthma, but it is the very opposite. The only problem I have encountered is with the librarians. They tend to be very set in their ways and resistant to other perspectives."

"You mean Mr. Goddard," Verity said.

Owens winced dramatically and waved his hands in the air as though swatting away a bothersome fly. "Please, you must speak quietly. We do not know who is about."

As the door was closed and the room was otherwise occupied by ancient statuary, she thought they had a reasonably good idea of who was about. Even so, she recognized the benefit of demonstrating an excess of caution.

Owens, continuing in a near whisper, conceded that Verity was correct. "I do mean Mr. Goddard. He is an excellent principal librarian in that he ensures everything is where it belongs. The archives, for example, are orderly. Locating documents is easy and efficient. He also excels at securing donations and funds. Where his skills are less accomplished is in the study of antiquities. He has a basic understanding. For example, he could see the cat figurine you were looking at earlier and identify it as being from the Ptolemaic period in Egypt. But that is the extent of his ability—which brings me to this," he said meaningfully, his hand gesturing toward a relief about two feet square of a man in a conical hat leading a horse by the reins.

Verity, drawing closer, admired the level of detail in the depiction: the muscle definition in the horse's legs, the swirls of the man's beard. The man was carrying a staff and fish floated around his legs.

Or perhaps they were swimming.

"Is he meant to be in a river?" she asked, marveling at the precision of gills. "They are carved so neatly."

Gratified, Owens slapped his hand against the nearest worktable and said, "Precisely, Miss Lark. I am glad that *you* see the problem!"

With great reluctance, Verity confessed that she did not.

"You noticed the sharpness of the cut lines," he explained as he pointed to the fish in the bottom left corner. "All of the lines are clean. This relief is too freshly carved to be over two thousand years old. I would bet these cuts were made a few years ago at most. It is very obviously a forgery. It is not the worst one I have seen by far, but it certainly was not done by a clever hand—talented, yes, but clever, not at all!"

Intrigued, she took a step backward and scrutinized the beard again, noticing now that the outline of each curl was clean and distinct. Then she inspected another relief in the room, one that was twice as large and showed a horse pulling a cart. Although the image was clear enough there was a softness to it, a sense almost that she was looking at it through a pane of dirty glass.

The cut lines were dull.

"It is remarkable," she murmured, her reporter's mind churning with possibilities as she wondered how frequently the specialists at Montague House encountered forgeries. Did false antiquities come from a few skilled artisans or were half the craftsmen in London running around producing fake Assyrian tablets?

Most important: Would any of them be receptive to an interview?

"It is wretched!" Owens exclaimed. "I know it is a forgery, but I cannot say anything against Sir Thomas Soames without evidence, for he is a highly respected collector, and Mr. Goddard hopes to buy two more artifacts from him in the coming weeks. The thought of the museum spending additional funds on counterfeit items pains me to no end. And I do not know what to do. I tried to suggest to Mr. Goddard that this relief possessed troubling elements, but he would not listen. He had authenticated the piece and knew himself to be infallible. He refused to even discuss the cut lines!"

Although Verity had assumed Goddard held his underlings in higher esteem than the female sex, she was not altogether surprised to learn he regarded them with a measure of contempt. "And what is it you wish Hardwicke to do?"

"Visit Sir Thomas, look at his collection, and assess the legitimacy of his artifacts," Owens said, pivoting on his heel to make his plea directly to Hardwicke. "I know you have fallen on hard times, Lord Colson, and I cannot offer you compensation. But everything Harry has told me about your behavior at Cambridge leads me to believe you are a man of honor who will answer a call for help. You must consider it a favor to the people of England, not to me."

Verity was prepared to say yes.

If Hardwicke refused his services, then she would promptly offer hers—and not only because she was eager to discover more about the false antiquities trade. The prospect of knocking Goddard down a peg was irresistible.

Hardwicke, either because the assignment intrigued him

as well or because he had intuited her interest, agreed to call on Soames at once and take his measure.

Owens sagged with relief, grasping the edge of the table as if to hold himself upright. "Thank you, my lord. You are every bit as kind as Harry says. I have not seen the other fragments, so I do not know if they suffer from the same defect. It is possible that Sir Thomas himself was fooled by a dealer or he might be part of the swindle. For this segment alone, the museum paid him handsomely."

Verity assumed it was the latter.

If Soames was the longstanding collector Owens described him as, then he had to know the difference between the genuine article and a forgery. Even she had noticed the odd clarity of the fish gills and could claim no expertise in the subject.

After ascertaining Soames's direction, Hardwicke promised to send Owens a missive as soon as he had any information. Unable to express the depth of his gratitude, the specialist silently pressed his hand to his heart, then bid them good day.

Chapter Three

Monday, June 22
12:55 p.m.

Of all the days to try Delphine's audacious experiment!

There she was, Verity Lark, standing in the entry hall of the man who might very well turn out to be the premier antiquities forger in all of London and she was dressed as herself.

Not only as herself—as herself with a black eye.

And she was wearing a hat.

A pretty poke bonnet with ribbons!

In her lovely cerulean frock, she looked like a society hostess calling on Harding, Howell & Co. to purchase tablecloths for her next salon weekend. Soames would never believe she was an assistant in the accounting department at the British Museum.

Women were not assistants.

Women were not anything.

"Stop worrying," Hardwicke said, leaning slightly to the

left to speak softly in her ear as they waited for the baronet to appear. "All will be well."

Verity stiffened as she absorbed the full weight of the insult.

Worry?

Her?

To whom did he think he had the pleasure of addressing?

Mrs. Garret or her snide friend Lady Sophia?

Well, yes, probably, as that was precisely how she was attired.

If only she had had the foresight to bring something with her that would alter the cast of her appearance and add gravitas, such as an eye patch or even the veil.

Or argued more stridently for a detour to Bethel Street so that she could assume an appropriate identity for the outing. Hardwicke's assertion that they could readily overcome any reservations Soames might have about a female assistant by projecting confidence represented a particularly male view of the world, which she frequently shared—when she was dressed as a male.

Verity, unclenching her jaw with some effort, assured Hardwicke in the same hushed tone that she was not worried. Before she could add that she was concerned, their host swept into the room with a flurry of activity, a black poodle at his heels and a manservant at his side, asking when they could finish their discussion. As the dog barked, the steward explained that Mr. Cramp was waiting for his decision.

"I fear he is growing impatient," he added.

Sir Thomas Soames, a gray-haired man with rounded shoulders and ill-fitting buckskin breeches, waved his hand dismissively. "Cramp will wait as long as I require him to wait, and I do not want to hear another word about it, Travers. Now do excuse me as I send these lackeys from the British Museum packing. I cannot imagine what Goddard is about, subjecting me to questions in my own home. It is monumental!"

At these words, Verity abandoned the script.

With an abashed look at Hardwicke, she shook her head and sighed regretfully. "You were right, Parker, Sir Thomas *is* too clever. I should have listened to you instead of insisting that we engage in this facile charade," she said, turning to Soames and apologizing for lying to his butler. "You see, I thought you could be hoodwinked into believing that Parker and I were sent by Mr. Goddard of Montague House to examine the reliefs in advance of the sale to help arrive at an appropriate price. I was going to use all sorts of official-sounding terms such as 'calipers' and 'chisel.' You were going to be so impressed! But Parker said it would not work, and I can see now by the glint of intelligence in your eye that he was right and I was wrong. I must tell you, Sir Thomas, I do not appreciate having to concede that my father's steward is correct. It makes me quite petulant! But do not fear I will take my churlishness out on you. My manners are too pretty for that. Besides, I want to worm my way into your good graces so that I can convince you to sell the reliefs to my father, not the British Museum. I am Miss Hogan, Edna Hogan."

Soames stared first at her, then at Hardwicke, before finally aiming a flinty eye at his own steward, as if expecting Travers to understand what was happening.

Hardwicke, who did not require direction when assuming a new role at a moment's notice, immediately sketched a bow and stepped forward. "You are no doubt confused. Let me explain. I am David Parker and work as steward to Miss Hogan's father. He is a collector and seeks to acquire your Assyrian reliefs because he has heard that they are of excellent quality. Miss Hogan, being an avid reader of Ann Radcliffe and her ilk, devised an elaborate ruse that would allow us to examine the reliefs with an eye toward purchasing them without your knowing. She thought it would give her father an advantage when it came time to negotiate over price. I did not believe that such subterfuge was necessary. Furthermore, I argued you would not find it convincing. Miss Hogan, as is her wont, realized I was correct at the most inopportune time conceivable."

Verity fluttered her lashes. "It is true, Sir Thomas. I am always a few minutes too late in realizing the truth. La! What is done is done. And I hope you are not all out of sorts with me. I am only trying to protect my father's fortune. The old dear is so very rich and would spend all his money on antiquities if left to his own devices. I cannot rely on him to act rationally because of his passion, so I must do whatever I can to protect his identity. The second anyone finds out Amos Hogan is interested in buying an artifact, the price doubles. Remember the marchese in Rome, Parker, who suddenly demanded gold doubloons and Papa handed them over because he simply had to have the Venus statuette? You see, Sir Thomas, I thought I had no choice but to lie about our identities, but you are too discerning. Do say you forgive me and promise not to bleed Papa. He is like a day-old kitten for all the sense of self-preservation he has."

Far from making the promise, Soames repeated the collector's name softly as though he vaguely recognized it. "I believe I may have met him at one of Lord Kilverstone's evenings. I presented on pottery from the Song dynasty to an unusually large audience, and several men who were new to me came up to congratulate me."

Reluctant to commit her fictional sire to any social event with which she was not intimately acquainted, Verity said, "Possibly! Very possibly! Papa is so very eager and relishes any opportunity to discuss his favorite subject. If he was there, then I can assure you he talked your ear off. Poor Sir Thomas!"

With a condescending smile, Hardwicke said, "And now you can see where Miss Hogan gets her verbosity from."

Verity thrust her lips into a pout. "Parker, you naughty beast, teasing me in front of Sir Thomas. He will think you are serious and form a wretched opinion of me and never let us see his Assyrian reliefs. If that is the case, then you must tell my father, for I cannot bear to break the dear old boy's heart."

"I find you charming, Miss Hogan, utterly charming," Soames announced with a broad grin as he instructed one of his servants to deliver tea to the drawing room. "I will show them to you but only as a courtesy. As I said, they are promised to Goddard and I am a man of honor. I cannot break my word without great inducement. *Very* great inducement."

Although the meaning of his statement was readily available to his guests, Soames spent the next thirty minutes reaffirming his willingness to renege on his agreement in exchange for sufficient compensation. Without quoting a specific figure, he made it clear that he would accept no less than three hundred pounds per relief, and given the exploratory nature of his questions—trying, it seemed to Verity, to ascertain the exact size of Mr. Hogan's fortune—he appeared inclined to require quite a bit more.

"Your father has such a wide range of interests. That is highly unusual among collectors and so impressive," he added with fawning wonder. "Most of us find a period that appeals to us and acquire only those objects. It is a matter of economics. I, for example, cannot afford to buy important artifacts from all the great ancient civilizations, so I have focused primarily on ancient Greece, which is why I am selling my wonderful Assyrian reliefs, which I have enjoyed for several years. A contact found a stunning statue of Athena, and I need to raise funds to complete the purchase. How did your father make his fortune? Did you say it was in mining?"

"Diamond mines, to be precise," Verity said, deciding there was no point in being timid. If Mr. Hogan was to be a nabob, then he might as well have unlimited funds from an impeccable source. "In Brazil. It is actually a funny story. He went there to cultivate cacao trees and discovered diamonds instead. My mother was disappointed because she adores drinking chocolate and thinks jewelry that sparkles too much is vulgar. She has made do the best she can. I suppose it helps that Papa is so obscenely rich."

Soames acknowledged the compensatory benefits of massive wealth with a bow of the head and suggested they look at the reliefs. "If you are done with your tea, that is."

"We are, yes, thank you," Verity said, darting to her feet. "Your hospitality is delightful, but I am eager to see the artifacts. They must be of excellent quality if the British Museum is interested in acquiring them."

"Oh, they are, they are," Soames said as he led them into the corridor. He took them down a long hallway toward the back of the house and up a staircase to the first floor. "My gallery is in disarray, and I do hope you will excuse the mess. I was not anticipating visitors."

Verity gasped as she entered the room.

Well, Miss Hogan did, for she was taken aback by the treasures on display: the ancient slabs and statuary and tattered fragments of pottery and textiles. Reliefs hung on the walls with small plaques detailing each work's provenance, and tables and pedestals presented figurines, vases, and jewelry.

In contrast, Verity was underwhelmed.

Hardwicke, responding to his employer's enthusiasm,

urged her to remain focused on the purpose of their visit. "We are here to see the Assyrian reliefs and the Assyrian reliefs only. You cannot make an offer on everything in the gallery. Your father is wealthy but not *that* wealthy!"

"Oh, pooh, Parker, you are no fun!" Verity admonished with a pronounced frown as she strode across the floor to a counter that exhibited a pair of reliefs that resembled the one Owens had shown them. They were identical in style, indicating that they were from the same larger work. The one to the right was bigger and irregularly shaped, with one smooth side and three jagged edges like a torn sheet of paper. It was three feet at its widest and depicted a team of horses pulling a cart. The other showed a man on what could possibly be a throne waving to his subjects. Like the relief at Montague House, patterns decorated every inch of the stone, their edges sharp and crisp.

Going by Owens's parameters, these were fakes as well.

"How splendid," Verity said as she leaned forward to get a better view of the works.

"Here, let me help," Soames said, rushing forward with his candelabra to provide more light. "As you can see, they are in remarkable condition. I work with only the most cautious and respectful dealers in the region. They understand that we are involved in the project of restoration. I am not buying antiquities so much as preserving a culture for future generations. That is why I am determined to sell these to the British Museum. It will ensure that the greatest number of people can see and learn from them. If I sell them to your father, then only he and the coterie that surrounds him will have that pleasure. I do not know what it will take to appease my conscience on that score."

Gravely, Verity assured him she understood and lamented that money could not buy peace of mind. Even the largest sum could not quiet a guilty conscience. Then she called

Hardwicke over to marvel at the quality of the craftsmanship. "Just look at the fine detail on this horse's mane. It feels like you can see every single strand of hair. I do not know how you could even consider giving these up, Sir Thomas."

Soames beamed proudly as Hardwicke drew closer to the relief and Verity's eyes moved from the mane to the harness. It was, she thought, decidedly familiar, with one strap looping the horse's neck and another wrapped around its body behind the front legs.

Struck by it, she could not believe the design for a harness had not changed in more than two thousand years. The lack of ornamentation also felt off, and she swept her eyes around the room to find a comparable example.

Ah, yes, there, on the far wall, a much smaller relief with only a man's torso and the front half of a horse. As she had suspected, the harness was more elaborate, with a crescent-shaped headpiece and a tassel dangling under its neck from one of the straps.

Oh, dear, the forgers had made the rudimentary mistake of not sufficiently researching their subject before embarking on a scheme, she realized. In their defense, it was difficult to get all the details correct, especially when there was a historical element to the endeavor, for you could not know what you did not know.

Verity's solution to that exact conundrum was to assume total ignorance: She knew nothing and had to learn everything. At the same time, she rarely engaged in ruses that required deep historical knowledge.

Contemplating the situation, she changed course one more time and cried, "My spectacles! Dear me, Parker, I seem to have left the wretched things in the carriage yet again. I trust you will not mind the bother of fetching them for me? You know I cannot see anything up close without them, and I cannot arrive at a reasonable offer if I cannot examine the reliefs properly."

Hardwicke arranged his features into a moue of faint irritation as he lamented Miss Hogan's forgetfulness. "You are always leaving them in one place or another!"

"It is true, I am," she confessed with a sheepish grin at her host. "And that is why the obligation to remember falls to you."

If Hardwicke took exception to this nonsensical expectation, he hid it behind a bland smile as he murmured, "You are right, of course."

On an imperious nod, Verity waited until the ersatz steward had left the gallery, then turned abruptly to Soames. "That was a ruse to get Parker out of the room so that I could speak with you privately. My father's steward can be such an inconvenience! I have my spectacles right here, in my reticule," she said, patting the side of her small purse.

Startled by the communication, Soames opened his mouth to reply, but before he could speak, she said, "Sir Thomas, these are counterfeit."

He stiffened with outrage or insult or embarrassment or anger, and as he huffed defensively, Verity continued. "No, do not try to deny it. You will only mortify us both, and that will waste valuable time. Look at that harness, Sir Thomas. Just look! It is the very same one lashing my horses in front of this very establishment. It is shameful!"

But Soames refused to look!

Deciding the best response was to kick up a fuss, he damned her impertinence and swore he had never been more furious in his whole life. "That you would come into my home and make a slanderous charge! I do not care who your father is, young lady. I will not stand by and allow you to—"

"Yes, yes, you may be as outraged as you wish but do save it for later because we have not much time. Parker is probably searching the seat cushions as we speak. The truth is, I can talk all I want about Papa's money, but the pile has dwindled in recent years. He does have diamond mines, but it is just the two and they are almost empty. Plus, the cost to extract diamonds increases every year, and Papa simply cannot continue as he has been, buying every relic that catches his fancy. Certainly not at the prices he has been paying! I love the man dearly, but he is a terrible negotiator, always allowing sentiment to overcome sense. And that is why I desired a moment alone to talk. Do give me the name of your forger so I can satisfy Papa's demand for antiquities at a fraction of the cost. In exchange, I will not say a word to Mr. Goddard about your reliefs."

Soames hesitated.

Of course he did.

Only a fool would admit to a stranger that he had defrauded the British government.

"Please hurry up, Sir Thomas, and give me the name. Parker shall return in a minute and then it will be too late," she said, imbuing her tone with urgency. "You cannot be certain he won't notice the harness himself, and you may be assured he will not give you this opportunity if he does. He shall run straight to Goddard, for his principles are not as amiable as mine, most likely because it is not his inheritance that is at stake. Do make up your mind quickly. The seconds are passing. Tick-tock, tick-tock, tick-tock."

Pressing and pressing so that her target did not have an opportunity to think a matter through clearly was one of Verity's most productive tactics, and it worked now as Soames spouted the name and address of his contact.

Then he grew ashen as he realized what he had done.

"My good sir, you are a hero!" Verity said adoringly. "I would hug you in gratitude, but I know that is the moment Parker would return and he would get all stiff-necked and tell my father and cause a dozen problems for me. But know that I am clasping you in my heart. Now you must not worry about a thing. The moment Parker returns, I shall make our excuses and whisk him from the room before he can get a better look at the horse's harness. I should think you will want to fix that detail before you deliver the relief to Montague House, but you must do what feels right to you."

Verity was prepared to blather for another dozen minutes, but Hardwicke-as-Parker swept into the room then with surly annoyance and said the spectacles were not in the carriage. "Which means you must have left them at home again!"

Giggling self-consciously, she confessed that must be the case. "They are probably sitting next to the vase on the table in the entryway. It is appalling to be so forgetful. I suppose it does not matter, as our business here is concluded. Sir Thomas is determined to hold to his agreement with Mr. Goddard, and no matter how charmingly I plead with him to change his mind, he simply cannot bring himself to abandon his scruples. He is indeed the honorable man he professed himself to be. How vexing!"

Soames preened at the compliment, not at all discomfited by the wild inaccuracy of the praise. "I must abide by my conscience."

Cordially, Verity agreed, adding that she was a perfect beast for trying to convince him otherwise. "I did it out of love for my father, who will be crushed."

"I am sure you will find something more suited to his tastes soon," he said.

"My dear Sir Thomas, how sly you are!" she replied admiringly. "I appreciate your optimism and shall endeavor to adopt it. You have been lovely to allow us to barge into your home like this. Thank you again, and do give my regards to Mr. Goddard, as I have no reason to get in touch with him myself."

"I shall do just that, Miss Hogan, at the earliest opportunity," Soames said as he led them to the door and watched them leave from his perch on the threshold.

※

Monday, June 22
1:41 p.m.

Hardwicke, gathering the reins in his right hand, noted that eighty-two Cowcross Street was in Saffron Hill. Although he had been absent from the room when Soames gave Verity the address, she was not surprised to discover he had listened at the doorway. It was what she would have done if the situations had been reversed.

"You think Hell and Fury Hawes might have a hand in it?" she asked as the horses began to move. "Counterfeit antiquities seem a bit refined for his tastes, which run to brothels, opium dens, and gin parlors."

Cynically, he replied that there was money in the trade. "Money is always refined."

Verity conceded the accuracy of the statement as they arrived at the end of the road and Hardwicke directed the horses to the left. "Hardwicke, you've gotten yourself all turned around. Saffron Hill is that way," she said, pointing to the right.

He assured her he was well familiar with the geography of London. "I was returning to Bethel Street. It has been a rather eventful day."

"Eventful?" she repeated, thoroughly bewildered. "You mean all that very strenuous sitting and standing I did?"

"I mean mocking Goddard, questioning Owens, and hoaxing Soames," he replied.

"That is barely a full morning, let alone an entire day," she said, unable to believe *he* was not hoaxing *her.* "Indeed, we started late. Ordinarily, I am conducting interviews or surveillance by nine o'clock. If you are tired, then you must feel free to say so and not use me as a pretext. I will not judge you as inferior or weak if your spirits are so flagging."

Hardwicke, drawing his eyes from the road for a second, grinned. "And now *you* are hoaxing *me,* for you would most certainly render a harsh assessment."

"A harsh assessment, to be sure, but it would be reserved for your physician for allowing a man in the prime of his life to fall into decay," she said graciously. "You are but a victim of his mismanagement."

Soberly, he ignored the taunt and reminded her that she had been released from prison the evening before. "You do not have to jump back in with both feet."

Although it was on the tip of her tongue to snidely reply that she had not forgotten Newgate, thank you very much, she restrained herself, replying simply, "In fact, I do."

Considering her silently, he appeared on the verge of refusal, then he sighed and said, "Very well. But we will get the lay of the land only. Miss Hogan will not knock on the door and ask to peruse the merchandise."

"Naturally, not, for she is terrified of criminals," Verity replied primly as he directed the horses around the next corner, taking them toward Farringdon.

Hardwicke drew his brows together in disbelief, but he made no effort to refute the comment and reiterated that they would keep watch from across the street. Although Verity would have liked to add an interview or two with neighbors to the itinerary, she agreed without quibbling out of respect for his sensibilities. Like Delphine, he had been forced to stand by while she endured the horror of internment, and there was something about being outside of an experience that made it in some ways harder to endure. She could not pretend she had been unaffected by her ordeal—her inability to sleep for a significant stretch of time intimated that—but being engrossed in a mystery made her feel more like herself. She was genuinely excited to have a puzzle to unravel.

Consequently, she would abide by Hardwicke's request, return home to figure out the best way to introduce herself to Samson Kirks of eighty-two Cowcross Street, read the stack of tips from Twaddle's network, and go to sleep.

Hopefully, by then, she would be sufficiently tired.

Monday, June 22
2:09 p.m.

Arriving at the address, Hardwicke adamantly refused to allow Verity to draw closer to the building than thirty feet, citing her bright blue frock. As she was dressed far too conspicuously for any sort of stealthy investigation, she agreed to abide by his suggestion.

"And it *is* a suggestion, is it not?" she added immediately. "You are not *telling* me what to do as though you have authority over my actions."

"Let us call it an appeal to your good sense," he replied.

Said evenly, the statement nevertheless conveyed a hint of sarcasm, which Verity ignored, choosing instead to silently contemplate her options as she surveyed the various homes and businesses in the area. Directly across from eighty-two was a tobacconist with an assortment of clay pipes in the window.

Yes, that would do nicely.

"Come, you look as though you are in need of a reviving

puff," she said, threading her arm through his to lead him toward the shop. "Let us buy you a meerschaum."

Perceiving her plan, he readily fell in line, noting that he could in fact use a new pipe as the churchwarden his brother had given him years ago had recently snapped in half.

"Little wonder, with its absurdly long stem," she replied authoritatively. "I think you should purchase one that is short and stubby, but we can wrangle about it inside for ... I do not know ... about thirty minutes or so."

Dressed quite a bit finer than the store's usual clientele, they were besieged by an eager attendant the moment they stepped inside and Verity explained their quandary. Proposing a diplomatic solution, he recommended they purchase both types of pipes so that neither one of them would be disappointed. "If you will follow me, I can show you the selection we have at the counter."

But the counter was farther from the street and Verity had no intention of stepping deeper into the store. She picked up one of the pipes in the decorative display in the window and held it up. "I was thinking something like this."

The attendant, who had introduced himself as Mr. Strauss, hailed it as an excellent choice. "I have one just like it myself."

Furrowing her brows, Verity selected another pipe, almost identical to the one she already grasped, and owned herself uncertain. "Perhaps we should get something like this."

It was, Strauss assured her, another impeccable decision. His father had one that very size and often mentioned how pleasing the weight was.

"But dear Mr. Parker expressly wishes to have a long stem despite their being so impractical," she said regretfully as she examined the wares on display.

"The long stem gives a cooler smoke," Hardwicke replied.

Affirming this observation, the attendant said he had

more churchwardens in the back, near the counter, some of which were sturdier than others, and urged them again to follow him inside. These efforts were likewise rebuffed as Verity examined yet another pipe with a stub of a stem and marveled at its characteristics. Although there was clearly nothing different about this example, Strauss duly pointed out its features and praised each one as being distinct.

"And what about this lovely?" she asked, pointing to a meerschaum on a tray.

As the attendant heroically distinguished between virtually indistinguishable items, Verity kept one eye on the residence across the way. It was larger than the buildings around it, stretching about forty feet wide and rising three stories. The top floor had three dormer windows with curtains that were either dark gray or blackened with soot. The facade was likewise grimy, with streaks of dirt and cracked stucco.

During the thirty minutes it took for her decide on her purchases—and, yes, of course, she bought two to reward the man for his patience—she saw movement in the house only once. A figure in a box coat stepped outside and turned to the right. Although the day was not particularly cold, he had the collar turned up as if to ward off the chill, and a straw hat further obscured his appearance.

As Hardwicke handed the helpful Strauss a few extra coins for his troubles, Verity clutched the former's arm and said in an enthusiastic gush, "Oh, do look, Mr. Parker, at that house across the street. It has those charming dormers that I love so much. And it is the perfect size for our family! I wonder if the owners can be persuaded to sell. Tell me, Mr. Strauss, do you know who owns the home?"

"Kirks, Samson Kirks," he replied easily. "He patronizes the store regularly. He buys pipes here—he is a churchwarden man like yourself, Mr. Parker—and his tobacco. I sometimes run his purchases across the road for him, and he is generous."

"It is a large house for one person," she observed. "Does he live alone?"

Strauss colored slightly at the implication that he knew such an intimate detail about a customer, then admitted that it seemed as though Kirks was the sole occupant. "He has regular callers and gets several large deliveries a month, but as far as I can tell, he lives by himself, no family or servants."

"Thank you, Mr. Strauss, that is helpful to know," she said cheerfully. "Now I must convince Mr. Parker that it is time we moved homes. Although he knows our house is too small, he adores the neighborhood."

"We live around the corner from a leafy square," Hardwicke explained.

"That is true, and I visit it often with the children," Verity replied with a fond sigh. "They are a lively bunch and do love to run around."

Strauss offered up the garden behind St. John's on Bristol Street as compensation, then added that it was more of a place for quiet contemplation. "I am not sure excited children would be welcome."

"Important information to keep in mind," Verity said firmly before thanking the attendant for all his assistance.

He assured her it was his pleasure as he opened the door and bid them goodbye.

Chapter Four

❧❧❧

Monday, June 22
7:18 p.m.

Verity controlled herself for five hours.
Well, four hours and thirty-nine minutes.
So *almost* five hours.

After Hardwicke returned her to Bethel Street with instructions to rest, she had made every effort to follow his prescription. Finding Delphine in the parlor knitting quietly, she joined her friend on the settee, poured herself a soothing cup of tea, and discussed the various delights of Montague House while munching on buttery biscuits.

If she made no mention of counterfeit antiquities, it was only because she did not want to trouble her friend. She refrained from describing Goddard and his horrid opinion of women for the same reason.

An hour later, she moved to the table, where Delphine had sorted the many missives that had arrived from the Twaddle network during her absence into five piles. As usual, the largest stack pertained to Her Outrageousness's exploits, and Delphine was quick to point out that a Miss Lark appeared in several of the notices.

"Apparently, she is an unmarried woman of a certain age whose brother works at the same paper as Twaddle himself," Delphine added, making no effort to hide her amusement. "Mags assumes Twaddle knows the old girl personally. I think it is fortunate you stopped chronicling the duchess's antics earlier in the month or your restraint now might have raised some eyebrows. The lads are clever and do love a mystery. They would have eventually figured out the truth."

"I do not doubt it," Verity replied, sifting through the messages. Just because she had no intention of writing about her grace's most recent murder investigation did not mean she was incurious about the details her spies had uncovered.

"The letters in the next pile over relate the Leaky Fawcett's continued campaign to secure a principality," Delphine continued, employing Twaddle's epithet for the London hostess, whose talent for bringing young misses to tears was unmatched. "I think it is entering the final stages, for she has petitioned the foreign office to detain Prince Adriano on charges of treason so that he will be persuaded to remain in the country long enough to propose to her daughter. As Londonderry would not even design to consider it, she presumably will ask the prince regent next."

"Lady Bentham must be crowing," Verity replied.

Naturally, yes, for the two society matrons were fierce competitors and frequently sought to undermine each other with plots and schemes. Of late, the enjoyment had gone out of the rivalry for her ladyship, as her husband had been charged and convicted of a series of rather serious crimes. It was difficult to enjoy the season when one's husband was permanently incarcerated in Newgate.

Nevertheless, she had derived great joy recently in tolling her countdown clock.

"Countdown clock?" Verity asked, unfamiliar with the term.

"A recent innovation," her friend explained. "Every morning at ten she makes a great show of moving the hands of a clock backward one hour to denote how little time Mrs. Fawcett has left to nab her prince. She does it in front of her townhouse in Mayfair and a crowd has begun to gather."

Delighted by the nonsense, Verity decided it would be the topic of Twaddle's next column and excused herself to go to Robert's study to jot down some notes. She would not be able to write the whole account until she witnessed the spectacle herself, but she could compose a few paragraphs detailing the longstanding resentments between the two women and facetiously proposing various acts of Parliament to prevent the prince's departure from the country.

The Leaky Fawcett was excellent fodder.

Not the best fodder alas!

That distinction belonged to Her Outrageousness.

But all in all, she was a satisfying second best.

Sitting down at her desk, Verity resolved not to get up until she had settled on topics for the next two weeks. During her absence, Freddie published two stories from her file of perpetually relevant ideas, which she kept on hand for days when she was too busy with other matters to write an article. The eternals were perfectly fine as far as gossip reports went but lacked a certain titillation.

The Twaddleship loved titillation.

Despite being focused on her column, Verity's mind kept straying to the fraudulent reliefs and the house on Cowcross Street. She wanted to know what sort of man could be so industrious as to carve complex designs into alabaster, to patiently cut hundreds of swirls, and yet not bother to confirm the style of harness for the time period. Perhaps that lack of detail was at the heart of the forgeries trade and why it flourished: The administrators were just as careless as the counterfeiters.

Goddard certainly was.

But *did* the trade flourish?

Verity had no idea, and it was this question that she turned over in her head as she struggled to come up with an idea for next Wednesday's column, and by the time she was summoned to dinner she was ready to admit it was futile. She could not rest until she had gathered useful information about the occupant of number eighty-two.

Not a lot.

Just an intriguing tidbit or two.

And Verity would be careful.

She would poke around a little, maybe peek through a few windows and talk to some neighbors. It had been so frustrating earlier, to be across the road from the target and not make contact. Even in her blue dress, she could have devised a reasonable pretext to interact with Kirks as he was exiting his home.

And that was another thing—the empty home!

She and Hardwicke could have explored with impunity.

Obviously, she understood his reluctance. Her gown was so vibrant, and she had just been sprung from prison. Only one, however, was an actual obstacle—and it was the one she could easily fix.

Darting to her feet, she informed Delphine that she would take her dinner with her.

"With you?" echoed her startled friend. "What do you mean with you? It is lamb pottage. And where are you going?"

"To get some answers," she said, sweeping from the room.

Delphine sighed.

Monday, June 22
8:03 p.m.

Verity peered into Samson Kirks's house through the windows in his back garden, which she gained entry to by climbing over two fences and squeezing between a privy and a shed. In the process, she had torn the Turnip's best coat, which was a shame because he could ill afford to buy a new one, especially not of the same quality, as the garment had been a going-away present from his grandmother.

The damage was highly regrettable, of course, but sometimes sacrifices had to be made in the name of progress.

That progress, however, had been impeded by the panes, which were thick with grime.

Either Kirks was too remiss to clean the glass or he wanted the view into his home to be obscured.

From what she could see through the streaks of dirt, the room at the rear of the home was unremarkable. To the left, she spotted a hearth and a table; to the right was a wall of shelves with pots, jars, pans, and bowls. A large bucket sat on the floor next to a toasting rack, and moving slightly to the right to improve her vision, she spied what might possibly be a chisel on the seat of a chair.

If only the window were not so filthy!

Resisting the urge to wipe the glass with her sleeve, she pressed her head closer to see if she could discern movement or light in the corridor beyond.

She saw nothing.

Did that mean Mr. Kirks was away from home?

There was only one way to find out.

Leaving the garden by the same route she had taken to enter it—and doing no further harm to the coat—she approached the house from the front, knocked on the door, and took a few steps back to wait for an answer. When nobody responded right away, she tried again and stood up on her toes to see if she could reach the transom window. As she was stretching her torso, the door opened.

Kirks, who was younger than she had expected, barely thirty if even that, regarded her with a mixture of impatience and curiosity. "Can I help you?"

Ideally, yes, by inviting her inside so she could figure out where he fit in the counterfeit antiquities trade. Was he a forger or a dealer or a nondescript middleman?

Noting the pristine elegance of the fingers that held the edge of the door, she rather thought he was the dealer. Chiseling alabaster would mark the skin.

"Apologies for interrupting yer evening, sir," she said in the Turnip's eager baritone. "It is jest that I made a horrible mistake earlier and left a package for number twenty-eight Cowcross Street here, at number eighty-two Cowcross Street. And now I have to get it back before my uncle Justin realizes what I did. He is already cross with me for breaking two teacups while wrapping up the parcel for delivery. I swear it was not my fault! The paper was wet from water *he* spilled. But Uncle Justin got so mad and told me if I broke one more thing, he would send me back to Fanny Barks in disgrace. I couldn't bear that. Marcus—he's my older brother—he would be insufferable if I returned home, all smug and superior like the rat that ruined the grain. And I don't think delivering a package to the wrong place counts as breaking anything, but Uncle Justin can be unreasonable. He says I would try even the patience of a saint, which is not at all fair, because I would be nervous in the presence of St. Michael or St. Francis or St. Jude and almost certainly break something. So if you would be so kind, sir, please get the package that was meant for number twenty-eight and I will leave you in peace."

Despite the annoyed expression that had swept across his

face at this lengthy oration, Kirks smoothly denied all knowledge of a package.

"But it must be here!" Verity said, her voice rising with the familiar edge of the Turnip's panic. "It has to be! I left it right here, in front of yer door, because I was in a rush. Cowcross is a stupidly difficult street to find, and nobody would help me! I asked a dozen people on Farringdon where it was and they all shrugged. One told me it did not exist! So you had to have seen it, sir, you just had to have. Or maybe someone else brought it inside. Could I jest have a look around? Please?"

On this desperate plea, Verity brushed past Kirks and entered his home, her eyes frantically darting around as she took in the narrow entry hall, its walls white and bare save for a pair of sconces on each side.

Untroubled by her presumption, Kirks folded his arms across his chest and told her the package was not there. "You can look through the whole house, but you won't find a thing. I am afraid you're just going to have to confess your blunder to Uncle Justin and hope he shows mercy."

Verity, taking him at his word, rushed into the first open door. A parlor, it was occupied by a man in a linen shirt with his sleeves turned up and brown-and-beige-striped trousers. He was older than his host by several years, well past forty, judging by the droop of his jowls, and wider in the shoulders. Although he had a rougher quality about him, he did not glare or scowl at her when she bounded into the room. Having heard the entirety of the conversation, he seemed to expect her presence, "There is no package here."

But the Turnip had too much at stake to accept the word of a stranger and dashed around the room, looking behind the sofa and under the table. She drew the line at opening the cabinet, although she was sorely tempted to see if anyone stored relics or tools. "Are you absolutely sure *you* did not bring it inside?"

More amused than insulted, the man replied that he would remember carrying in a parcel. Kirks, however, was not as sanguine about her intrusion, despite having invited her to conduct a thorough search, and requested she leave at once. "I can't help you."

Instead of complying, Verity stood in the middle of the room and held her hands about six inches apart. "It was medium-sized and wrapped in brown paper, Maybe it got carried in with some other packages? Do you get many deliveries?"

"I have asked you to leave and now I am demanding it," Kirks said, glancing at the other man in the room as he took a threatening step forward. "Mickey, if you could grab his other arm."

Obviously, the Turnip cowered.

Threats of physical violence were abhorrent to the rustic, who had failed to develop any town bronze during his tenure in the capital, and Verity winced dramatically. "No, don't. Please! I'll go. I'll go. All I wanted was to find the package. Uncle Justin will be so disappointed," she lamented, rounding her shoulders as if to absorb a blow.

But she did not move, not immediately, and Kirks drew closer as his friend pulled his hands out of his pockets to help eject her. Verity saw at once that they were the hands of a workman: calloused palms, torn nails, and well-scratched fingers.

Could he be the forger?

She contemplated the question as she scurried to the door with apologies for exceeding her welcome. "But please forward the parcel to Hardison and Sons in Stamford Grove if you find it. Like I said, it is about so big and brown."

The slam of the door cut off her description, and Verity retreated several buildings down the road to wait for Mickey to leave. In no hurry to depart, he did not emerge until well after sunset, and although the darkness allowed her to disappear into her surroundings, it made trailing after him more difficult. She had to stay close in order to keep him in view, and she watched in relief as he entered the Lamb's Head, a tavern so boisterous half its clientele had spilled out onto the street. Squeezing between patrons, she slipped through the door and managed to find a spot at the counter. As she ordered a pint of ale, her eyes followed the man called Mickey, who went straight to the back of the establishment and had a word with one of the barmaids. She nodded several times, then left the premises.

While she was gone, he rested his shoulders against a pillar and drove his hands back into his pockets, a pose he held with little movement for fifteen minutes. When she returned, she had another man in tow—tall, slim, frosty blue eyes—and he spoke with Mickey briefly before scowling angrily, turning on his heels, and leaving.

Curious, Verity decided to follow him.

He did not go very far, turning into Grape Street and approaching a residence with an elegant pediment. He knocked and several seconds later the door was answered by an elderly woman in a mob cap. She accepted his greeting impassively and made him stand on the step as she disappeared to convey his presence to someone in the home. Returning more than a minute later, she admitted him to number fifteen.

Oh, but wait: 15 Grape Street.

That was where Hell and Fury Hawes lived.

She was standing in front of the home of the most infamous resident of Saffron Hill, which meant Soames's scheme *was* connected to the overlord of the underworld.

It was precisely as she had suspected!

Impatient to learn more, she resolved to wait until the tall, slim man reappeared, so she could follow him home. But it would never do, to stay there, so close to the house, and as she glanced around to find a spot where she could linger discreetly, her shoulder was rammed by a passerby.

Ye gods!

It hurt like the very devil, but as she was currently dressed as the Turnip, Verity dealt with the pain in his characteristically self-effacing way, swallowing a yelp and apologizing for standing in the wrong place. Cradling her injured arm, she realized all at once that she was tired and hungry and perhaps not as alert as the situation required.

Barely twenty-four hours ago, she had been imprisoned in Newgate and as she scowled at the departing back of the violently rude man, she conceded Hardwicke might have had a point after all: She needed to rest.

Given her sudden exhaustion, she felt confident she would have no trouble falling asleep.

Even so, abandoning a mission before achieving all of her objectives felt like defeat to her, but there was nothing to be done about it. Her failure to notice an approaching stranger indicated that her attention had begun to wane, and there was no telling what else she might miss if she remained.

Carelessness could be fatal.

Bowing to necessity, she rubbed her aching shoulder again and began the return walk to Farringdon, where she would wave down a hackney. Despite her disappointment, she allowed that she had accomplished several worthwhile things that day, including annoying a priggish librarian, outlining Twaddle's next three articles, and identifying several key members of a counterfeit antiquities consortium—and that was on top of eating half a dozen excellent butter biscuits.

All in all, it was a good first day back.

Tuesday, June 23
3:13 a.m.

Although Verity loathed not being able to sleep through the night, she much preferred enjoying four uninterrupted hours of rest to lightly dozing for the same period of time. Consequently, when she woke from an unsettling dream at three in the morning, she felt vaguely refreshed. Her mind raced with disturbing images—the helpful Mr. Big Fist Johnston hanging from a noose, the malicious grin of the warden—but they began to fade as soon as she lit a candle and her heart slowly returned to normal.

Fully awake, she pushed back the covers to slip on her dressing gown and visit Robert's study to attend to business. Having satisfied the immediate demands of Twaddle, she finally had time to turn her attention to Wigsworth, whose downfall would be swift and irrevocable. By the time she was done detailing his insidious behavior, he would not be able to show his face in society again.

She would begin by sending notes to the network to locate the physician who had treated the boy injured in the experiment.

But even as Verity rose to her feet, she knew it was foolish to mistake the brief spurt of energy for true wakefulness. It was merely the effects of the nightmare. Furthermore, if she allowed herself to become engrossed in an activity, she would inevitably grow tired sometime in the early afternoon, which would have a terrible effect on her productivity. Whatever work she managed to accomplish now would come at the expense of things she would try to achieve later.

The more effective tack was lulling her brain with something exceedingly dull, and to that end, she reached for the book on her night table. It was a novel of manners and courtship that Delphine had described as delightful. Verity, who shared none of her friend's interest in tales of romance and high drama, expected to be asleep by the end of the opening chapter.

ॐ

Tuesday, June 23
10:06 a.m.

Despite the elaborate meal Lady Bentham made of her countdown clock event—waving her arms with a flourish as two beautifully matched footmen carried the Thwaites & Reed over the threshold, having her butler pluck a few notes from a violin before proclaiming in stentorian tones the number of days left—the affair was underwhelming. There was only so much anticipation or showmanship one could instill in an announcement, and the crowd that had gathered seemed to feel the lack of pomp keenly. Approximately half of the thirty-two people in attendance milled about awkwardly for several minutes, as though expecting something more to happen.

It did not.

Lady Bentham smiled at her audience, sketched a curtesy, spun around gracefully, and disappeared inside her home. The footmen promptly followed, heaving the clock in their arms, and the butler shut the door with a decisive snap.

Verity, dressed as a flower seller, her arms holding a basket of peonies, glanced around in astonishment. "That is it? Is that the whole show? I came all the way from Covent Garden to see this because my daughter's husband's cousin said it was a laugh," she grumbled as she approached a woman in a pink walking dress and matching bonnet, whom she recognized as one of the season's Incomparables. "Is there really no more?"

Miss Melesville stared at her blankly, then confessed she did not know why the other woman was disappointed. "Did you not see the clock count backward from eight to seven? Those represent days, not hours, until Mrs. Fawcett will have to give up her hopes and dreams of having the prince of a mineral-rich principality as her son-in-law. She will be devastated and humiliated. That is exciting in and of itself. Oh, but maybe that does not mean anything to you if you do not know Mrs. Fawcett personally or if she did not point out to Mr. Charles that if one connected the four beauty marks on your cheek with a quill, they would create a very rude gesture. If you experienced the latter, then you would understand the significance. Plus, lemon ices, for we are just a few blocks from Gunther's."

Unfamiliar with the beauty mark incident, Verity leaned forward and said, "Gor blimey, miss, really? How did the gentleman respond?"

"He turned bright red, for he had just complimented me on the loveliness of my complexion and felt it was a rebuke of his tastes," she replied forlornly. "Later, when he asked me to dance, he apologized for not issuing a sufficient defense—as though he had issued any defense at all! I refused and told him that I had been wrong to think I was developing feelings for him. Clearly, he was a cad and a—"

However else Miss Melesville described her former beau, she did not get to share because her mother seized her arm and pulled her away.

Talking to flower sellers was not at all the thing!

Amused, Verity adjusted her grip on the basket and lingered as the other onlookers slowly dispersed. As Miss Melesville's comment implied, the majority of interest came from the Leaky Fawcett's victims, and as that was a rather large cohort, she imagined the crowd would grow only larger as the clock's hour hand drew down.

Given the dignified display she had just witnessed, Verity

had little expectation that Lady Bentham would increase the frenzy of her presentation, but on the return to Bethel Street, she amused herself with the possible embellishments her ladyship could add, such as hiring an orchestra or serving lemonade like at Almack's.

Amused, she decided that would be the perspective of Mr. Twaddle-Thum's report. He would own himself disappointed by Lady Bentham's restraint and then provide a few suggestions for increasing the drama of her presentation.

Yes, that was the perfect approach.

The Twaddleship would be vastly diverted.

Tuesday, June 23
3:43 p.m.

Verity had just finished slipping Twaddle's latest effort into an envelope when a knock sounded at the door and Delphine entered with an apology for interrupting.

"I know, I know, you are hard at work, and I promised not to disturb you until it was time to dress for dinner, but this intriguing package arrived for you over an hour ago and I am afraid my curiosity finally got the better of me," she explained with a wry smile as she held up a brown parcel wrapped in two brightly colored ribbons: one pink, one yellow. "It does not say whom it is from, which is unusual, and my first thought was Hardwicke. But then I decided it could not be because it is oddly coy to leave off the return address and it is impossible to conceive of him as being coy. And then I wondered if it could be a welcome home gift from the duke or the dowager? Did you send the thank you note as we discussed?"

Verity blanched at the reminder, for she had yet to do the minimum required of her.

A brief missive—gracious and sincere.

It was simple enough.

And yet the shooting lessons!

As she still had no idea how she would conduct those, Verity rose to her feet and noted dryly how much easier it was to imagine that pair of august personages as being coy.

Delphine laughed as she crossed the room to place the package on the desk. It was irregularly shaped, with a wide base that narrowed toward the top and stood about a foot tall. "Now you begin to perceive my impatience. No one we know would not include their name or deliver it in person. Presumably, there is a note inside."

"Presumably," Verity echoed softly as she untied the ribbons and removed three or four layers of silver paper to reveal a statuette of a cat.

The statuette of the cat from the museum.

The one she had been admiring the day before.

As Delphine murmured in appreciation, calling the figurine charming, Verity's mind raced with bewilderment and unease, as there was no benign explanation for the cat's sudden appearance in Bethel Street. Even if Goddard was inclined to send her the antiquity as a token of remorse for his rudeness, he did not have the authority. Everything in Montague House belonged to the British government. It was not the principal librarian's private collection for him to dispense items at his whim.

Its presence could augur only something truly dire.

"You know, this little creature looks a lot like Dilly," Delphine added thoughtfully, walking around the desk to examine it from the other side. "It is obviously older—that is, much older, something like centuries if not millennia—but it is the same size and color and the cat's expression is almost identical. Is there a note? It has to be from Freddie, right? No one else knows Dilly. But why would he send the statuette via messenger rather than give it to you himself when he calls later?"

"It is a trap," Verity said curtly.

Baffled by the announcement, Delphine inhaled sharply as though to argue with her friend. But then her features softened as she regarded her with concern. Gently, she said, "All right."

"If the parcel arrived over an hour ago, we may have only a few minutes," Verity continued as she contemplated what would happen next.

It was a snare, yes, but how would it be sprung?

A caller.

Someone would appear presently.

Soothingly, Delphine suggested they sit down in the parlor to discuss it.

She believes I am jumping at shadows. A few days in Newgate and now the poor girl cannot settle herself, Verity thought, taking no offense at the assumption. Instead, she told her friend to fetch Dilly.

Delphine, furrowing her brow in concern, started to object. "I really don't think—"

"Do it now! Go! There is no time to lose!" Verity ordered, urging her out of the room with a frantic wave of her hand. "Hurry, hurry!"

Deeply troubled now, Delphine scurried into the hallway, and Verity opened the bottom drawer of her desk. Then she raised its false bottom and slipped the figurine inside. It was not a perfect fit. The curve of the cat's behind lifted the deep right corner of the wooden cover, but the aberration was slight enough to escape all but the most intense scrutiny.

Whoever was coming to find the stolen artifact was not expecting a long and protracted search. They assumed the cat would be out in the open, either displayed on a shelf or tucked into a cupboard.

And so it would.

Verity had no sooner had this thought than a pounding knock sounded on the door and a booming voice demanded entry. "I am an official with the customs office and you will admit me at once."

Stepping out of the study, she waved at Lucy, who had darted to the entrance at the first loud clap, and called out, "Yes, officer. I am coming, officer."

Startled, the maid came to a halt in the hallway and darted back to the parlor, which she had been dusting when the visitor arrived.

Hearing the patter of footfalls on the steps, Verity ran toward the staircase as she assured the customs officer that she was almost there. "I just need to disentangle myself from all these ribbons," she yelled, holding out her hands as she looked up at Delphine, who tossed the figurine down the remaining steps. She caught it in her arms and then dashed madly to the study to envelop Dilly in the silver paper. Then, wrapping the ribbons around her forearms in a messy jumble, she shuffled to the door, which she just managed to open before everything slipped out of her grasp.

"Oh, dear, catch it!" she cried, scrunching her shoulders forward as if to cradle the parcel in her stomach. "Please!"

Responding to the strong directive, the custom's officer reached out with his hands and grabbed the package before it hit the ground.

Verity, her lashes fluttering with appreciation, cooed admiringly, "You darling, heroic man! You saved it from certain ruin."

The customs officer, sporting the traditional uniform— dark blue coat and trousers, plumed shako—smiled briefly in return before a scowl overtook his features and he handed the parcel back to her with an impatient snap. "I am Tillet. Officer Roger Tillet and I will search these premises freely and without obstruction, or if you make any attempt to stop me, I shall place you under arrest. Here is my writ of assistance. Now step aside!"

Although she had perceived the whole plan the moment she had heard the forceful rap of his knuckles on her door, Verity affected surprise and confusion. "I do not understand. Whose premises? You do not mean my premises!"

"I said, step aside, madam, and allow me to proceed according to my authority," he ordered sternly.

Clutching the figurine in its many layers of paper, she obeyed his command and stuttered an apology. "But I ... I d-do not un-understand. What is happening?"

Although Tillet was only an inch taller than she, he used his advantage to great effect, leaning forward as though to tower over her. "You are being subjected to the same swift hand of justice to which all smugglers in England are subjected."

Verity gasped. "Smugglers!"

A seasoned officer who had given at least twenty years of service to the profession, he paid little attention to this display and reiterated that he would begin his search for the contraband at once.

But this statement was as shocking as the last and she inhaled sharply again. "Contraband!"

Delphine, who had paused at the bottom of the staircase as Tillet entered the house, rushed forward and asked what contraband he imagined they had.

"Madam, I am an officer with his royal majesty's Customs service," he replied stiffly, grasping his hands behind his back as he approached Delphine. "I imagine nothing! The report I have conclusively states that you, Miss Lark—"

Timidly, Verity raised her hand and said that she was Miss Lark.

Tillet turned abruptly and continued, "That *you*, Miss Lark, stole an artifact from the British Museum yesterday morning at twelve noon and brought it here to your home. And you were quite brazen about it, too, according to the report."

Feigning utter shock, Verity gasped and sputtered, "But ... but that is a horrible lie!"

"I am sure it is, madam," the officer sneered doubtfully. "I am sure it is!"

"But it is!" Verity insisted, imbuing her voice with the sort of squeakiness that frequently accompanied panic. "I do not understand. How can your report say that I brazenly stole something when I did not do it? Someone is lying."

Unimpressed, Tillet said, "And I suppose now you are going to deny even being at Montague House yesterday at twelve noon."

Obviously, Verity could not and stared at him blankly, her mouth firmly shut.

"I did not think so, madam!" he stated tartly.

Appearing incapable of meeting his superior gaze for long, Verity glanced down at the parcel in her arms as Delphine asked the agent again to identify the illicit item supposedly in their possession.

He described it—a statuette of a black cat approximately four inches tall and made of a cupreous metal—and of course it matched the figurine delivered to the house only a little while before. Whoever had sent it to Verity had arranged for the customs officer. Tillet was supposed to discover the stolen antiquity and take Verity into custody for theft.

Only he had arrived too late.

Well, *possibly* too late.

A well-trained agent who had spent a significant portion

of his career rummaging ships for evidence of illicit brandy or lace during the war would know how to search a London residence. Finding concealed spaces was most likely second nature to him, and a false bottom on a desk drawer would be a minor impediment.

Delphine, who found nothing about the situation humorous, stomped over to where Verity stood, grabbed the package, and unwrapped the layers of paper with movements that could only be described as pointed in their contempt. "You mean *this* cat, Mr. Tillet?" she asked scathingly as she held it up for his inspection. "This lovely figurine that my employer gave me as a token of her appreciation at the conclusion of my fifth year of service? *This* is what you are here to confiscate? *This* is your excuse for terrorizing a pair of helpless women in their own home?"

Tillet was flustered.

Startled to find himself confronted with a statuette bearing a slight resemblance to the one he had been dispatched to find, he appeared genuinely uncertain of how to respond.

And the accusation!

Adding a tremor of fury to her voice as she reproached him for engaging in deliberate intimidation was a brilliant stroke.

Verity had often said that Delphine would make an excellent Twaddler if she could just bring herself to accept periods of physical discomfort. Nobody enjoyed hiding in a pile of dirty linens, but it was a fleeting condition. One endured the unpleasant smells, perhaps a few sticky substances, for an hour or two, and then voilà—one emerged into the fresh air in possession of vital information.

Taking advantage of the officer's unease, Delphine raised the cat higher so that it was almost pressing against Tillet's nose. "Here, seize Dilly if you must! It is only a cherished memento dear to an aging spinster's heart. I am sure your superiors will be very impressed with you!"

As Delphine had adopted an aggressive pose, Verity assumed its opposite, chastising her friend for being unduly hostile. "I am certain Mr. Tillet does not mean Dilly. Do you, Mr. Tillet?" she asked, looking at him with wide-eyed curiosity. "You would not come here and terrify me and my staff over a decorative figurine? You have it on good authority that the artifact you seek is here in my home, and although I think someone is making a May game of you, I would never dare to interfere with the customs office's business. Please do look as long and as hard as necessary to satisfy your duty. We have nothing to hide. If you decide in the end that you must confiscate little Dilly, I do hope you will be gentle with him. He is not a priceless relic from an ancient civilization, but he is very precious to me."

The generosity of these words did little to ease Tillet's discomfiture, and he snapped, "I do not need your permission, madam!"

Soothingly, Verity said, "No, of course not. Nevertheless, you have it."

Tillet opened his mouth as if to petulantly reassert his independence, but he held on to his temper and asked them to step aside so that he could conduct his search.

"Oh, but don't you want to examine Dilly?" Verity called after him as he turned right into Robert's study. "It looks like a charming bauble to us, but you are the professional. Maybe there is another statue hidden inside."

Tillet's response was to slam the door.

"Well, I am certain that is not standard procedure," Verity murmured softly to Delphine as she linked her arm through hers and drew her into the parlor. "Leaving the suspects alone provides them with an opportunity to hide or destroy the contraband."

But Delphine was in no mood for raillery and said sternly, "What did you do?"

Although Verity resented the assumption of guilt, she confessed that she might have stumbled across an illegal counterfeit antiquities scheme and one of its participants might have taken exception to her interest. "I am not saying it is Hell and Fury Hawes, but I am also not saying it isn't."

"Verity!" Delphine growled as they settled on the settee in the parlor, their heads close together to make sure their voices did not carry into the hallway.

"But it is not as you think!" she insisted. "I did only the barest amount of research, and the second I realized I might be tired, I came home rather than pressing on. I acted with all the responsible rationality you could wish."

"Well, obviously not *all*," Delphine replied scathingly.

Verity lowered her chin in shame.

"Did you really embroil yourself in Hell and Fury Hawes's business?" Delphine asked with an air of exhaustion and concern. "You always said Twaddle was too clever to involve himself in the immoral morass of systematized crime."

"The truth is, I do not think I did," Verity replied, launching into a report of yesterday's activities, which was interrupted by Tillet, who ordered them to remain seated as he searched the room. Then he commanded them to rise so he could look under the sofa cushions and examine the frame for secret compartments. After several minutes of silence, during which only the sound of his increasingly frenzied breathing could be heard, he stomped to the door. After he left, Verity resumed her account of the day before, calmly relating her conversations with Soames and Kirks as the knot of anxiety in her stomach eased. If Tillet was still bounding from room to room, then he had not discovered the false bottom in the desk drawer.

Aware that the customs officer could always return to

the study to search it a second time, she did not allow herself to relax entirely. Nevertheless, some of the tension left her shoulders, and she began to speculate as to how Hell and Fury Hawes had managed to organize a response so quickly. She had stood outside his house for only a few minutes the night before, barely enough time to learn any information. If she had not been bumped by the man who—

Oh, but she *had* been bumped, Verity realized, perceiving now the strike had not been the accident she had assumed.

The assailant was Hawes's man.

Even before she had arrived in Grape Street, the crime lord had been made aware of her interest in his forgery scheme, which indicated that his network passed along information at lightning speed. Twaddle's own web of spies was extensive and thorough, but all messages were filtered through the *London Daily Gazette*'s office, creating a delay that could be quite frustrating. The fact that Hawes targeted Verity Lark was especially troubling because his man had bumped into the Turnip.

So how did he get from Joseph Pope to Verity Lark?

The obvious answer was via Soames, who had found Miss Hogan so unconvincing he had immediately alerted Hawes to the threat of looming trouble.

It was a disquieting thought, for Verity prided herself on her ability to gull unsuspecting targets, and if her performance had been less than persuasive, then she had to wonder at its cause. Either she had been even more tired than she had realized yesterday or her sojourn in Newgate had dulled her abilities.

Disturbed by both prospects, she found the latter highly troubling, and she consoled herself by remembering that Hardwicke had been lulled as well.

Nothing about either their exchange with Soames or their

surveillance afterward caused him to worry that their true motives had been exposed.

As contemplating these thoughts did nothing to aid her current predicament, she pushed them aside to focus on sweeping Tillet out the door. Judging by the screeching she heard in the corridor, he had made his way belowstairs and Cook did not appreciate the invasion of her kitchens.

Good.

He was almost done.

Unless he decided to dig through Delphine's vegetable beds.

God help him if he looked for buried treasure *under* her potato plants.

The squirrels could tell him a thing or two about her wrath.

On this agreeable thought, she turned her attention to figuring out what to do with the statuette after the officer left. Having infiltrated the museum previously without difficulty, she knew she could slip inside and return the ancient artifact to its pedestal. But the last time she had broken into the building nobody had recently reported a theft and a writ of assistance had not just been issued in her name. If Hawes was as clever as she suspected, then he would make sure customs agents were watching the building to arrest her the moment she stepped inside.

It would be better, then, if Hardwicke sneaked the artifact back into the building. With his standing in society and relationship with the British government, he would have more recourse than she if he was apprehended. As soon as Tillet left, she would bring the artifact to him and let him dispose of it.

The sound of Cook's swears faded as Tillet entered the parlor again and explained that he had found no evidence of the stolen antiquity. His manner was stiff and formal, revealing a hint of bashfulness or embarrassment, and Verity wondered if his search had been more cursory than usual because of it.

If so, then everything had gone according to plan.

Delphine, responding snippily, said, "Of course you did not! I hope in the future you will think twice before scaring a pair of elderly spinsters half out of their minds."

As Tillet submitted to this reprimand, Verity smothered a smile at how rapidly she and her friend were maturing. Previously, they had been aging spinsters and now they were elderly.

"I was led to believe the information was impeccable, but I see now that a little more skepticism would have been appropriate," the officer said, vowing to be more cautious in the future. "I am sorry for the inconvenience and for any trepidation you might have felt."

As the officer had unbent enough to apologize—*and* as the information he had been given was actually correct—Delphine softened her stance and thanked him for making an unpleasant situation as painless as possible. "Once I recovered from my terror, I understood that you were merely here to do your job and did not bear us any personal animus," she said, stopping just short of offering an apology for inconveniencing *him*.

Appreciating the display of graciousness after so much anger and strife, Tillet smiled warmly and returned the compliment. "I have executed many writs of assistance during my career, and this is the first time I feel relief at not being able to locate the suspected contraband."

At this lavish tribute, Delphine simpered.

Tillet doffed his hat, and Verity firmly believed that if her friend extended her hand, the agent would kiss it.

"I do hope you find the missing statuette, Mr. Tillet," Verity said gently as she escorted him to the door. "If there is anything we can do to help, I trust you won't hesitate to let us know. Very good, then, goodbye!"

As soon as he crossed the threshold, Verity closed the door and pressed her shoulders against it with a sigh of relief. Then she smiled at her friend and said, "You were brilliant, Delph. Absolutely brilliant. Your ability to simulate outrage is a thing of beauty."

"Oh, my outrage was real," her friend assured her. "I do not care if the prince regent himself reported seeing you walk out of the museum with the figurine, Mr. Tillet should have approached his suspect in a more conciliating manner. He should ask to enter and respectfully present the writ, not storm about issuing orders. But that is neither here nor there. You were wonderful as well. Substituting Dilly for the artifact was a genius stroke. Thank goodness you thought of it so quickly."

Lucy appeared, then, peeking her head around the corner to see if Tillet was gone and calling over her shoulder to Cook that the coast was clear. "Lawks, miss, but that was terrifying! have never met a customs officer before, but if they are all like Mr. Tillet, I hope to never meet one again. He put his hand in the flour jar!"

"He put his hands in everything!" Cook exclaimed, her hands clenched in apprehension as she drew closer. "I have never seen anything like it."

"I thought he was going to arrest us all," Lucy added with a shiver. "And he refused to listen to a word I said. I swore there was nothing hidden in the pantry."

Calmly, Delphine replied that Tillet had merely been doing his job, as upsetting as it was to them, then suggested the women take the rest of the day off from their work to recover from the ordeal. "Verity and I can fend for ourselves. Why don't you take a walk in the park while the weather is good or visit the lending library? Please, do whatever you wish to take your mind off it."

While Cook made a token effort to object, Lucy ran off to fetch her spencer, and a few minutes later the pair of servants left the home. As soon as they were gone, Delphine retrieved the statuette from the bottom drawer, wrapped it in silver paper, and tucked it into a satchel. Handing it to Verity, she said, "I think it is safe, but perhaps you should leave through the garden as a precaution. Whoever sent you the artifact went through a great deal of effort to get you in trouble and will no doubt be disappointed by the outcome."

Verity, delighted by the thoughtful calculation on display, engulfed her friend in a brief hug and then swore they would make a Twaddler out of her yet.

Chapter Five

Tuesday, June 23
6:32 p.m.

Although the last time Verity had called on Hardwicke's residence, she had been sporting both a bloody dress and an oddly shaped, Bordeaux-colored stain on her upper right cheek that had devolved into a smear on her chin, the footman who answered her knock recognized her as Miss Gorman. He bid her good day, observed that it was a pleasure to see her looking so well—an observation she found plausible, given that a black eye was a vast improvement over a knife wound—and invited her to step inside with a sweeping gesture toward a parlor to the left of the door. "If you would wait here, Miss Gorman, I shall inform Lord Colson of your arrival. Thank you."

Readily, she complied, entering the receiving room, a cozy and small space on the ground floor, with dark gray walls and a pair of sunflower-yellow drapes. Adjacent to the window stood a tall bookshelf stuffed with leather-bound volumes, most of which were novels, although a few biographies were scattered among them. She was reading the titles on the top row when Hardwicke appeared in the doorway. Pausing on the threshold, he suggested they proceed directly to his study for the conversation. "Whatever you wish to tell me will no doubt go down better with a glass of brandy."

As he had not expected company, his dress was informal: unadorned brown trousers, white lawn shirt. In his shirtsleeves, he had not bothered to don a coat for her benefit, a decision she found equally delightful and unsettling because it implied an intimacy for which she was not certain she was ready.

On the other hand, he was quite striking in his casual attire, its austerity accentuating both the sharp angles of his face and the defined muscles of his form.

Aware of that, he could simply be preening for her benefit.

The male of the species was not above showing off.

Crossing the room toward him, she chided Hardwicke for his needlessly negative assumption. "How do you know this is not a social call? I might want to inquire about your health and chatter politely about social matters. My, my, Lady Bentham's countdown clock show is a bit disappointing. I wonder if she has considered hiring musical accompaniment and serving refreshments."

Grinning broadly, he stepped back to allow her to climb the stairs to the first floor, which housed his living quarters. "I am sure she will consider both options a few moments after Mr. Twaddle-Thum suggests them. But in regard to your first question, the reason I know it is not a social call is the distaste with which you imbue the words *chatter politely* makes it clear you would rather confront an army of brigands on a deserted road in the middle of the night than conduct small talk. But do not worry. We shall drink brandy, and you can tell me what has gone awry, and we shall figure out how to fix it. I trust Delphine is well?"

Although tempted to issue a stinging retort, she acknowledged the difficulty of mounting a high horse with a stolen antiquity in her satchel. Furthermore, Hardwicke had done her the compliment of using the passive voice—*what has gone awry*—rather than placing her at the center of the fray.

He did not perceive her as a small child who had gotten into mischief.

It was another point in his favor.

As if he needed more, she thought petulantly, unable to fully articulate why his preponderance of admirable traits peeved her.

He had already breached the citadel.

Despite waging a fierce battle, Verity had succumbed to her emotions, acknowledging that the fascination she felt for Hardwicke was in fact infatuation.

It was an unprecedented surrender.

And yet Hardwicke continued the assault.

He was already the shrewdest, most capable man she had ever met; he did not have to be kind and thoughtful as well.

Eventually, he would begin to reveal his other side, his darker side, the ugly qualities he endeavored to hide, and she would just as soon move along to that stage as quickly as possible.

Nobody was perfect, and she resented his pretending he was.

"Has she resumed knitting?" Hardwicke continued as they arrived at the top of the staircase. "Her inability to concentrate on her knitting worried her a great deal while you were in Newgate, but I suspect that was just displaced anxiety about your welfare. It made her feel a little less helpless to have something else to focus on."

Indeed, yes, the shrewdest man she had ever met, she

thought again as she assured him that Delphine had recommenced blanket production. "I believe she has already sent two to Mrs. Caffrey at Fortescue's in an effort to make up for lost time."

"Naturally, she has," he said affectionately.

This—fond sympathy for one's friends—was also what one wanted in a suitor, and yet it increased her churlishness. To forestall the snappish reply that rose to her lips, she looked around with frank interest. Although she had visited him twice before, both entries had been arranged covertly, with varying success, and this was her first opportunity to examine his home without fear of discovery.

It was, she noted, surprisingly lovely, with its inordinately high ceilings and subdued color palette. The drawing room walls were a bright white, the floor was a rich brown, and the drapes were a deep maroon that matched the settee and a quartet of armchairs in the center of a pink floral rug. Light poured in through the tall windows facing south, bathing the room in sunshine, and even as she admired the bright cheerfulness, she tried to calculate the dizzying cost of warming the space during the winter.

Even if the amount were not onerous, the effort would be.

All those high ceilings and drafty windows!

In contrast, the study was intimate and convivial with dark walls and intricately carved paneling. A mahogany desk anchored the room, adding a weightiness that Verity found comforting, and as she sat in a chair with angled sides, she felt the worst of her pique dissipate. In its place was a genial camaraderie.

Hardwicke retrieved a bottle from the bottom drawer and filled two glasses with brandy. He placed one on the desk in front of her and tightened his grasp on the second as he lowered into the chair next to her. Then he looked at her thoughtfully over the rim of his glass. "Now, then, Verity, what is the problem and how may I help remedy it?"

Dozens of words darted through her head as she contemplated the best way to explain the situation. It was not often one came into possession of a two-thousand-year-old statuette, and as she was a reporter, her instinct was to launch into a lengthy preamble so that her reader would not be startled by the revelation.

But Hardwicke was not one of her readers—he was a fellow conspirator and he was sitting next to her, his knees practically touching hers.

Silently, she opened the satchel, removed the figurine, and placed it on the desk.

Although he could not have anticipated the presence of the ancient cat in his study, he responded as though it were an everyday occurrence, examining it with mild interest to confirm its authenticity, Verity assumed. When he was satisfied with his inspection, he returned it to the desk and said, "It actually looks quite at home in this room, but I suppose we should probably put it back. If its absence has not been noticed yet, it will be soon."

Verity felt her heart trip at his response.

No arguing.

No swearing.

No wasting time with demands for a dozen insignificant details.

Just calm acceptance and ready action.

Well, of course he irritated the hell out of her.

His innate understanding of important business paired with the appealing figure he cut in his shirtsleeves—he was intolerable.

He was so intolerable she felt an almost irrepressible urge to lean across the brief space that separated them and press her lips against his.

Who is wasting time now? she thought.

But, oh, it made her giddy.

Desire was a rarity for Verity.

A woman alone in the world, she had spent much of her life evading the lascivious attention of predatory men. It had been particularly acute during her tenure as a scullion in an earl's establishment in Mayfair. Bearing a resemblance—slight, she had always thought—to La Reina, she frequently drew masculine interest and was repeatedly required to defend her virtue via deceit or brute force. In Mount Street, she had been forced to resort to sorcery, convincing Lord Stechford through various tricks such as cutting his hair while he slept that she had put a curse on him and would do much worse if he persisted.

After so many years of dodging these rapacious affections, she found it difficult to believe in an essential male goodness or an intrinsic code of honor. Both notions struck her as false as the spell she had cast on his lordship. If not for Freddie, whose very first act as the newly minted editor of the *London Daily Gazette* was to rescue her from the scullery in Mount Street, she would be unable to conceive of any decency in the world at all.

That she loved Freddie as much as she did still surprised her, but he had slipped through her defenses when they were little more than pointy sticks trussed together in a wobbly fence. Her battlements were mortar and stone now, and she had assumed that if any man managed to pierce them, she would feel the same sort of warmth. She could not conceive of trust without respect and respect without fraternal affection.

And there was Hardwicke, at ease in the middle of the fortress, inspiring admiration in the same breath as temptation. That she was capable of feeling both was a dizzying revelation to Verity, but even as she reveled in the novelty, she bristled with annoyance at Hardwicke's persistence.

It was over.

The battle was won.

He had to stop finding new ways to fascinate her.

Deliberately, she turned from him toward the desk, where the glass of brandy sat, and grasping it in her right hand, she stared into its golden depths for several seconds to regain her equilibrium. When she felt in control of her emotions, she raised her eyes and said its absence had not only been noted but also reported. "A customs officer named Roger Tillet, who arrived at the house about an hour after the figurine was delivered in a brown box with ribbons, conducted a thorough search of the residence."

A smile teased the corners of his lips as he said, "Well, obviously, it was not a *thorough* search, or we would not be having this conversation. I assume you have a secret compartment—well, several—that he did not bother to look for because you and your companion were so feeble he could not conceive of your having a secret compartment."

"Actually, Delphine was quite fierce, treating Tillet with the same surly contempt as she does Grint. By the time he left, I think he was ready to offer marriage," Verity said before conceding the general accuracy of his assessment. "We would never have squeaked by without Dilly. Dilly is a figurine that bears a notable resemblance to the cat. Delphine arrived with it at Fortescue's and has no idea of its origins."

He nodded as though something suddenly made sense. "That is why you were staring at it so intently yesterday afternoon."

Verity knew she should not be surprised by his level of attentiveness, for he had long demonstrated an ability to see things other people missed, and yet somehow she was. "I was struck by it and wondering if there could be a connection between the two."

"So you showed the customs agent Dilly and suggested it had been a silly mistake," he replied.

"More or less," she allowed. "Being presented with a statue that looked so similar to the one he had been sent to find was enough to make him wonder if he had embarked on a fool's mission."

"And that doubt made him careless," Hardwicke observed.

Verity took another sip of brandy as she nodded. "Fortunately for us. A man who spent years rifling through ships looking for hidden cases of brandy should have noticed a false bottom on a desk drawer. The compartment was designed to hide Twaddle's notes from Lucy, not stolen artifacts."

"If he had found it, you would have been back in Newgate by nightfall, and nothing I nor Her Outrageousness could do would make a difference," he said pensively.

Although she flinched slightly at the idea of the Duchess of Kesgrave riding to her rescue yet again, she smoothly replied, "Precisely."

Pressing his lips together, he contemplated her silently for several moments before noting that someone clearly wanted to eliminate her. "The question is who and why. Let us start with the latter and work forward from there."

"It is most likely related to the forged antiquity trade Soames is involved in," she said before launching into a description of her activities the previous evening. Although she expected a rebuke for investigating on her own after he had pointedly instructed her to rest, Hardwicke listened without comment, even when she mentioned that Kirks's associate had led her to yet another associate who had led her to 15 Grape Street.

He recognized the address.

There was no way Typhoeus did not know the location of

every crime lord in London, especially the most notorious one.

His next remark, however, pertained to Owens, the specialist who had identified the relief as a forgery. "We were looking at the cat figurine when he approached us about the forgery."

Yes, that was true, and she herself had noted the connection. Whoever sent the stolen artifact chose it because she had been spotted staring at it for several minutes. Any number of people could have seen her, not just Owens, and the idea that he would wish her ill after she had agreed to help him struck her as irrational. "My theory is that Soames was not convinced by our performance and had one of his men follow us. Recognizing us as a threat, he contacted Hawes, who took matters from there. Either he has spies in the museum or was able to buy the information, but he discovered my interest in the cat and concocted the scheme around it."

Hardwicke conceded the viability, adding that he would not be surprised if Soames or Hawes had targeted her because she was female. "Between the two of us, you would have appeared to be the easier target, a foolish assumption but more or less inevitable."

It was a lovely tribute.

Whether he intended it as such, she could not say, but something inside her dissolved at the certainty with which he spoke, and she succumbed to impulse, gently moving his drink from the chair's arm to the desk, so that the fine brandy would not spill when she slinked into his chair to kiss him. He responded without hesitation, his lips opening and searching, and although he never tightened his arms around her, she felt comfortably ensconced in his embrace.

Enraptured by the sensation, she protested softly when he

murmured against her cheek, "We should figure out how to return the statue and what to do about Hawes."

Verity agreed.

There was pressing business to address.

And yet she kissed him again.

Verity Lark rarely allowed herself to get distracted, and as Hardwicke trailed tantalizing kisses along her neck, she wondered how quickly the world would unravel if she permitted herself to do it more.

※

Tuesday, June 23
8:34 p.m.

As Hardwicke had agreed to accompany his mother to Lady Thackley's musicale, he could spare only fifteen minutes or so to discuss the situation with Delphine and Freddie, the latter of whom was still highly distressed by Hell and Fury Hawes's deft manipulation of the English Customs service.

"We do not know for certain it was Hawes," Verity reminded him, crossing her legs at the ankles as she settled comfortably in an armchair. "It is only speculation, so we should probably confirm it before the *London Daily Gazette* begins publishing daily articles lambasting the crime lord."

Freddie assured her the newspaper had no intention of taking such a wildly reckless course. "Furthermore, we do not lambast anyone. We report the facts, and the *facts* do the lambasting. Regardless, if it is not Hawes who is responsible for your unsettling near miss with Customs, then who is?"

Hardwicke replied that they could not rule out Soames, who would be extremely reluctant to allow word of his inept dealings to spread. "The horse's harness bearing an undeniable resemblance to the modern version reveals a worrying lack of attention to detail that I would be adamantly opposed to Hawes's finding out about if I were in business with him. Having Verity neé Miss Hogan apprehended for theft resolves the matter with a fraction of the fuss and bother kicked up by murder."

"That is true, yes," Verity said, adding that it was impossible to know what to think without more information, which she would begin collecting in the morning. "I will keep an eye on Soames's while Hardwicke puts the statuette back on its pedestal."

Delphine wondered if returning the figurine to its original location was perhaps a little too bold. "Maybe you found it outside the building tucked into a shrub? It caught your attention as you approached from the road, and you surmised that the thief had stolen the artifact and then panicked when he saw several members of the Eleventh Light Dragoons in the drive or some such."

Freddie, who thought the basic notion was solid, suggested that having an entire calvary regimen appear suddenly in the courtyard did not make narrative sense. "What if the thief panicked when one of the librarians entered the gallery and he tossed the cat into the first available sarcophagus, intending to come back for it later?"

Although Delphine had no objection to these alterations, she nevertheless felt compelled to point out that she had said "several members," not the whole battalion, which was, for the record, currently garrisoned in the Hounslow barracks—a distance, yes, but not prohibitively far.

"It is twenty miles away," Freddie replied.

Verity offered her support for the sarcophagus proposal, while Hardwicke explained that he would rather hand the statuette to Goddard, as it would give him an opportunity to question him about the forged relief. Then he rose with a regretful sigh and announced that he had to leave or he and the marchioness would miss the opening selection, which was an aria from *Orfeo ed Euridice*.

"That will be delightful," Delphine said, noting that Gluck was among her favorite composers.

Hardwicke assured her it would not be, as Lady Thackley's daughter lacked the range necessary for the role of Amore. "I would never be so discourteous as to describe her voice as a squawking chicken's, but if I were, I would mention the troubling resemblance."

Verity laughed at the disgruntled note in his voice and swore if he could bring himself to actually make the unflattering comparison, she could ensure that Twaddle would broadcast his egregious breach in civility so far and wide he would never be invited to a London social gathering ever again.

"Promises, promises," he murmured softly.

Delphine winced and begged him not turn a careless remark into a challenge. "Verity cannot resist a challenge."

"Yes, thank you, I have managed to figure that much out for myself," Hardwicke replied wryly before bidding them good night.

Verity, recognizing an opportunity to broach the egregious financial imbalance between them, rose to escort him to the door. As he was in a rush to leave, she would present the fact of her debt simply and succinctly. Hardwicke would perceive at once that it was a straightforward matter of pecuniary responsibility and not argue or take a pet.

He would agree.

Before she could introduce the subject, however, Hardwicke turned to her with a slightly apprehensive expression and reiterated that he had only been teasing. "You must not report that I compared Lady Susan's voice to a chicken. Lady Thackery is one of my mother's dearest friends, and she would have my head if I caused a rift between them."

It was, Verity decided, disconcertingly endearing to see the accomplished spy and inveterate wastrel genuinely anxious about his mother's disapproval, and finding herself unable to withstand the glean of amused anxiety in the depths of his teal eyes, she laid a gentle kiss on his cheek in reply.

※

Wednesday, June 24
10:36 a.m.

The flurry of activity that greeted Verity when she had arrived at the Soames residence two hours before had almost immediately subsided, leaving her with very little to observe. Although the front door had opened a few times, causing her to tense her muscles in expectation, the baronet had yet to emerge. On the first occasion it was the butler shaking out a dark blue rug; the second time, a footman trimmed the wicks on the lamps flanking the entrance. A pair of maids, who would ordinarily exit an employer's home via the servants' entry, slipped out with baskets over their arms, presumably on the way to the market, and Verity wondered if they were inordinately daring creatures or if Soames oversaw a lax household.

Verity hoped it was the latter.

Lax households were ideally suited for Twaddling.

Dressed in a simple pink muslin dress that had seen better days, she skipped down the steps to the lower entrance and rapped her knuckles against the door—once, twice, then repeatedly until someone finally answered.

Finally, of course, was a bit of an exaggeration because hardly any time had passed since the first knock, but that was Allegra Hodges all over: high-strung, impatient, incapable of moderation. She had been different as a young girl, but ever since her parents had died rescuing her and her sister from a fire that consumed the hostelry where they had stopped for the night, she had lost all sense of proportion.

Everything made her agitated.

Giving rein to her anxieties now, as the door opened, she introduced herself in a breathless rush and then demanded to see her sister. Disconcerted by the aggressive entitlement of the command, the housekeeper stared blankly, and Verity waited for the moment when the other woman seemed on the verge of answering to continue.

"You can't hide her from me," she said on a high-pitched wail. "I know she is here. I had a note from her yesterday. Your master is keeping her prisoner."

Stunned, the housekeeper repeated, "P-prisoner?"

"Don't pretend you have no idea what I am talking about!" she added angrily. "Your master is in league with thieves and murderers, and he has taken my sister hostage. You know it!"

The housekeeper shook her head, too shocked to do the logical thing, which was toss the madwoman from the house. Instead, she insisted there was some mistake. "My lord is decent and kind. He would never harm a hair on anyone's head."

"Bah! He pays you to say that," Verity cried dismissively.

"No, no, I swear it! He is decent and honorable," she returned, looking behind her to see if members of the staff were listening to the conversation.

Because she did not want anyone to overhear or because she wanted reinforcements, Verity wondered as she redoubled her attack, swearing that she knew the truth. "Your employer has dealings with dubious people, and he conducts business with criminals in Saffron Hill."

Remarkably, the housekeeper calmed down at this charge

and reiterated that something was decidedly off because that did not describe the master at all. "He collects antiquities, and I will allow that one or two of the men from whom he buys them do not have the best grooming habits. Mr. Cocker, in particular, always looks as though he has not bathed in weeks. But as far as anything nefarious happening, you are brainsick to even suggest it."

Although Verity knew how easily sincerity could be feigned, she was nevertheless swayed by the earnestness in the servant's voice. If there were rumblings about Soames's iniquity, they had not reached the ears of his housekeeper, and in any given household, very little failed to reach the ears of the housekeeper. Hiding secrets from his staff required a level of care he seemed disinclined to take judging by the maids' use of the front door.

Further investigation was needed to confirm these conclusions, but Verity felt it was unlikely Soames had overseen the customs scheme himself.

Hawes made more sense.

Having ascertained the information she sought, Verity aimed her darkest glower at the housekeeper and said, "The very fact that you can stand there and tell me that *I* am brainsick when you work for a degenerate like Milo Wilcoxson proves that *you* are the one who is daft. Now I will say it for the last time: Bring my sister to—"

But the housekeeper interrupted.

"Milo Wilcoxson doesn't live here," she said with a visible air of relief. "This is the home of Sir Thomas Soames. You have the wrong residence. You see, it is as I said, you made a mistake."

Verity gasped in horror, shrieked, "Curses!" and ran from the door to rescue her sister before Mr. Wilcoxson could do her grievous harm.

Wednesday, June 24
11:03 a.m.

Returning to Bethel Street, Verity found Delphine standing in the open doorway of the house, a brightly colored tin box in her grasp as she watched her neighbor's son-in-law engage in fisticuffs with a voluminous shrub. Her friend giggled, then started guiltily when Verity hailed her in greeting, an action that drew Mr. Muir's attention, and he briefly left off his tussle with the lively arborvitae to glare at them.

Delphine waved cheerfully in response, then smothered another chortle as one of the branches smacked Mr. Muir square in the nose. "I am a horrible person, laughing at the poor man. That oversize tree was put there deliberately to block the door, and it is cruel of me to derive pleasure from his struggle."

Verity respectfully disagreed, for they had nothing to do with the placement of the bush—that had been the work of Grint and the Home Office—and Mr. Muir was a self-important bore brimming with opinions about things that were outside his purview.

What business was it of his how inadequately Lucy scrubbed their windows? It was her employer's concern or lack thereof.

"If I were an officious didact like he, I would advise him to choose a less worthy opponent next time," Verity said softly, then flinched in sympathy as a bough walloped him on the cheek. Alarmed, she called out to ask if he was all right.

Mr. Muir glowered darkly.

Delphine swallowed a gurgle and held up the tin. "Would you like one, Mr. Muir?"

Verity, resisting the urge to grab her friend's arm, whispered, "What are you doing?"

"I am appeasing my conscience," Delphine replied softly as she removed the lid from the box to reveal an assortment of round, chocolate-flavored biscuits dusted with finely powdered sugar. "Aren't they lovely? They just arrived for you. That is how I happened to notice Mr. Muir. I answered the door to save Lucy the trouble. Here, there is a note. They are from the Earl of Goldhawk. He is delighted you are home safe and hopes you are recovering from your ordeal."

Uncertain if she was more horrified or mortified to receive a gift from Hardwicke's brother, she stared down at the floridly written note for several seconds. When she looked up, Delphine was a dozen feet away, kindly exhorting Mr. Muir to try one of the biscuits.

"They are chocolate puffs, and they are from a shop in Chelsea," she added encouragingly. "Are they not lovely?"

His scowl firmly in place, Mr. Muir stepped away from the shrub, looked inside the tin, and allowed that the confections appeared tolerably interesting.

"Please have one if you are so inclined," Delphine said, adding that it was a shame Mrs. Paisley had not had an opportunity yet to trim the arborvitae. "It is so very large, like something out of a fairy tale forest. I expect an elf to live in it."

Encouraged by this comment, for it confirmed precisely what he believed—that the tree was cursed—he selected a biscuit as he grumbled about his mother-in-law's refusal to prune it even a little. "Or get rid of it altogether, as I've instructed multiple times! She says she can't give it away because it's a tribute to her deceased relative. The woman was a third cousin twice removed whose existence was unknown to the family before the bush arrived," he said disdainfully before his expression grew marginally lighter and he deemed the puff adequate.

Delphine beamed at the faint praise. "Do feel free to have another."

Unbending slightly, Mr. Muir selected a second biscuit and looked past Delphine to Verity, who was still several feet away. "Did you get the bruise on your cheek last week when you were attacked by that coachman?"

As the event had happened in broad daylight, Verity was not surprised that the neighbors had taken note of it or discussed it among themselves. The assault itself was strange enough, but add in the other elements—a basset hound named Pinkie, a carriage belonging to the Dowager Duchess of Kesgrave, the ambassador to the Court of St. James—and it became incomprehensibly bizarre.

On the bright side, however, the neighbors appeared to know nothing about her imprisonment in Newgate, she thought, shivering with the sort of horror that was appropriate to a timid spinster. "Yes, I did, and it was horrible. I still can't sleep at night for picturing the wretched creature's terrifying face."

Munching on the puff, Mr. Muir owned himself baffled by the queer business. "It makes no sense that he would try to abduct you, when Mrs. Kendrick's daughter is across the road. She is of a child-bearing age and pretty," he said, drawing his brows together as he wiped chocolate crumbs from his chin. Then, as was his habit, he proposed various ways the assailant could have increased the likelihood of attaining his goal. "Everyone thinks they should approach from behind because it gives you the advantage of surprise, but then you cannot see what is happening behind you. An attack from the side gives the assailant a comprehensive view of his surroundings."

Verity trembled at the prospect of a more successful

assault and leaned on Delphine as though requiring extra support even to remain upright. "You must excuse me, Mr. Muir. I am suddenly lightheaded at the memory of the confrontation."

Delphine soothingly agreed to accompany her inside and held out the tin to offer him another. Although he professed reluctance, he snatched a third puff greedily, then bid them goodbye.

As she turned them toward home, Verity said, "You monster, giving away all my chocolate biscuits. I suffered for them!"

"And the worst is still to come, for now you must send Lord Goldhawk a lovely note thanking him for his consideration," Delphine replied with amusement. "And that is in addition to the note you have yet to send to the duchess."

Shuddering now with genuine terror, Verity offered her friend half of the remaining biscuits if she would write the missive for her. "Or the whole box. You can have them all."

On a laugh, Delphine selected one of the puffs, raised it to her nose, and inhaled sharply. "Ooh, they smell divine," she announced with anticipatory relish as Verity heard a squawk, as if from a large bird. She looked up to see if she could spot it as her friend sniffed again and murmured softly to herself, "Is that a hint of almond?"

It sounded again—the high-pitched screech, almost like a scream—and Verity, seeing nothing in the sky, looked over her shoulder and watched in horror as Mr. Muir dropped first to his knees, a putrid liquid streaming from his mouth, and then to his side as spasms shook his body.

Her heart stopped.

In the seconds it took for Verity to look from Mr. Muir to Delphine and confirm her friend had not eaten any of the puff, her heart literally ceased beating.

She thwacked the tin onto the pavement.

Stunned, Delphine swore at her friend, who grabbed her forearm and pulled her toward the neighbor's house, where Mr. Muir convulsed and convulsed and convulsed.

And then lay still.

※

Wednesday, June 24
1:54 p.m.

Verity did not know how much to argue with the coroner.

Arriving to find Mr. Muir's corpse on the dark blue settee in Mrs. Paisley's house, Mr. Quesnel swiftly assessed the situation and decided there was no need for an inquest. The deceased had clearly died of apoplexy.

"Fatal apoplexy," he added curtly as he rose to his feet, drawing the white sheet over the lifeless face. "It is an unfortunate turn but not one that requires either my attention or the resources of the English government. I am sorry for your loss, Mrs. Paisley. Good day!"

Mrs. Paisley nodded.

She had a vague air about her, her eyes darting all around the room, as though they could not bear to look at anything too long, and she appeared to have little understanding of what was happening. The sudden and gruesome death of her son-in-law was difficult enough to comprehend but having a representative of the crown in her home to ask questions about the sudden and gruesome death of her son-in-law—that was unfathomable.

Noting the older woman's frailty, Verity had gently urged her to sit down several times, but Mrs. Paisley remained resolutely on her feet. She had even insisted on helping Verity and Delphine carry the body inside, despite offers of help from the dozen other neighbors who had gathered outside to commiserate and gawk.

Mrs. Paisley, deciding that something more should be done, shook herself slightly and replied, "Ah, yes, thank you, Mr. Quesnel. Thank you very much for ..."

But here she trailed off, uncertain for what precisely she owed him her gratitude. To be sure, *she* had not sent her maid to fetch the coroner.

Why on earth would she?

The man had dropped dead of apoplexy.

It was obvious to anyone with eyes.

Verity, frustrated by how little consideration Quesnel had given Mr. Muir, explained that the victim had vomited. Pulling back the cloth, she gestured to the remnants on his mouth and clothes. "You can see it here and here."

Wincing, Mrs. Paisley dropped her eyes to the floor, and the coroner tugged the sheet from Verity's grasp and draped it over the body. Placidly, he replied, "I noticed that, Miss Lark, and although it can be unsettling to see, it is also fairly common. A variety of unseemly developments accompany death, and I do not perceive an advantage in further upsetting the deceased's loved ones by discussing them. We must think of the living."

The coroner was an older gentleman, somewhere north of sixty, with generous whiskers and a shock of white hair, who spoke with authority and command. He was clearly accustomed to having his word accepted without scrutiny, and when Verity pointed out how swiftly Mr. Muir had succumbed to his ailment—it was barely a minute from the first cry to the last convulsion—annoyance flitted across his face.

He knew his vocation, however, and rather than chide her for arguing, he assured her that this, too, was normal. "Death often comes before we know it."

"No," Verity said firmly, her patience beginning to wear thin at his determination to misunderstand her. "His whole body shook with the convulsions. It was not natural."

Quesnel nodded sagely, as if perceiving now the problem, and said she was correct. "Death *is* unnatural. It is the greatest unnaturality of all, and it is right that you are distressed by it. I advise you to have a glass of warm barley water and a rest, Miss Lark. Sleep does wonders to restore the spirit. Now, then, I shall take my leave," he announced, turning to Mrs. Paisley to again offer his condolences.

As Mrs. Paisley stepped forward to escort the coroner to the door, Verity made yet another attempt to clarify the situation. "What I meant was, he did not die of natural causes. He was poisoned," she said, glancing sympathetically at her host, for it was a horrifying notion and one she had hoped not to have to propose herself. Quesnel was the expert who had overseen dozens of inquests.

All the signs were there.

He just had to acknowledge them!

And as soon as he did, Verity would have to inform Mrs. Paisley that her son-in-law had been killed by mistake.

Verity was the intended victim.

It was she who was supposed to be lying under the sheet.

A chilling thought, to be sure, and yet it paled in comparison to the other image that swam endlessly through her mind: Delphine under the sheet.

If the traffic on Walton Street had been more severe.

If Mr. Muir had not brawled with the arborvitae.

If any number of random events had occurred only slightly differently.

And now the coroner was determined to brush off the murder.

Mr. Muir had been slain in the street as assuredly as if a

man with a pistol had shot him in the heart, and Quesnel would admit to none of it.

It was, Verity thought, a singular injustice for a man as devoted to correct methodology as Mr. Muir to have to endure a defective process without the ability to supply even one improvement.

At the mention of poison, Mrs. Paisley gasped and pressed a hand to her chest, and the coroner smiled kindly at her before shaking his head at Verity. "Oh, you girls, with your gothic novels and your mysterious black veils. I have a daughter a little more than half your age and she has a vivid imagination as well. She was convinced we had ghosts living in the attics, but it was just a nest of rats. There is always a logical explanation."

Hearing the testament to logic from a man remarkably inured to it was an infuriating experience for Verity, who nevertheless held up the tin of deadly chocolate puffs. "Mr. Muir had three of these biscuits before he died. They smell faintly of almonds and have a fine white powder on them that is almost certainly cyanide of potassium."

As this information was a little more than she could bear, Mrs. Paisley finally sat down, dropping like a stone onto one of the hard wooden chairs next to the hearth.

Quesnel regarded Verity with distaste and said with cynical disregard, "Then I suggest you be very careful with those biscuits, Miss Lark. Throw them away at once and do not allow anyone else to eat them, lest I be called back for a second apoplexy today."

Through clenched teeth, Verity pointed out that if a second person died of apoplexy after eating the biscuits, then it was obviously *not* apoplexy.

But the coroner's patience was at the end.

Having humored the distraught woman for almost fifteen minutes, he had no further interest in treating her kindly and called her an insolent chit. "How dare you stand there and question my expertise! What do you know about anything? Your head is filled with nonsense and drama. This poor woman is grieving"—here, he gestured to Mrs. Paisley, who whimpered—"and you are enacting the third act of a Shakespeare tragedy. Have some decency and leave her in peace!"

"She is overwrought," Mrs. Paisley murmured softly. "Miss Lark is usually a quiet thing. In all these years, I have scarcely heard her say three sentences, and now she is arguing with a man of superior intellect and experience. I do not know what to say other than she is overwrought. We should fetch her brother. He will know how to calm her."

Quesnel, owning himself relieved to hear that the wayward Miss Lark had a responsible male family member to restrain her worst excesses, applauded this proposal, and Verity, her fury exceeding anything she had ever felt before, offered the box of chocolate puffs to the coroner and invited him to try one.

Adamantly, he refused.

Chapter Six

❧

Wednesday, June 24
2:42 p.m.

Verity did not believe Hardwicke's brother was trying to kill her.

The Earl of Goldhawk was a peer with an excellent reputation, and although Mr. Twaddle-Thum's interest in him had been cursory at best, the only thing she had heard even remotely to his discredit was that he enjoyed keeping numerous mistresses at once.

As the wealthy aristocracy considered variety its birthright, there was nothing particularly remarkable about this excess, and the only reason Twaddle would have to include the information in a column was if it worked to Hardwicke's disadvantage. References to the Gold Son were reserved for underscoring the dross of the Coal Son.

It did not matter, however, what Verity believed.

The only relevant convictions were the ones that could be proved.

"Facts," she said to Delphine as she swept from the parlor

into the corridor, where she retrieved her spencer. "I need to establish the facts of the case before I do anything else. You know it is my number one rule."

Her friend scoffed dismissively. "Your number one rule is whatever is most convenient to you is your number one rule."

Verity ignored this cynical observation as she shrugged into the garment.

Delphine continued. "Before you go haring off to establish any facts, you must tell Lord Colson of the murder attempt. When he kept that exact information from you, I held a grudge against him for several days—as did you!—and we will both be perfect hypocrites if you now Holy him."

Amiably, Verity reminded her that she had sent Hardwicke a note apprising him of the situation. "You saw me write it! Indeed, you stood over my shoulder as I did and proposed minor modifications to the wording."

"Minor modifications such as do not send a message!" Delphine snapped, impatient. "You should call on him at once and state plainly what has happened because that is precisely the behavior you demanded of him. Your making vague allusions to a dire event that you have well in hand is a Holy tactic. You are Holying him."

"I am sparing him the troubling uncertainty of incomplete information," Verity replied. "Nobody wants to hear his brother is a murderer, especially when his brother is not in fact a murderer."

Delphine folded her arms across her chest. "More Holying."

But Verity insisted she was misusing the term. "In none of the various attempts made on Hardwicke's life was there an indication that a member of my family might be involved. If at any point in his investigation he suspected you or Freddie of foul play, then I would have appreciated his discretion.

Hearing him accuse either one of you of murder would have been highly distressing."

Unimpressed with the minute distinction, Delphine accused her of splitting hairs.

"I am a reporter," Verity said.

Delphine rolled her eyes. "Yes and ..."

"I have a finely honed respect for the precision of language," she replied as she opened the door to leave. She would call on the confectionary shop before deciding if an interrogation of the earl was necessary. "*Holying* means to withhold information from an interested party out of an excess of caution for his physical safety. I am withholding information from the interested party out of an excess of caution for his mental well-being. It is completely different. Now do stop fretting. I will call on Hardwicke as soon as I confirm that Goldhawk did not try to kill me. I promise you, he will thank me for my forbearance."

Delphine snorted.

Ignoring her, Verity cautioned her against opening the door for anyone but Freddie. "There have been two attacks against us in as many days. We have no idea if there will be a third."

"Freddie will agree with me," Delphine said fervently. "On the definition of *Holying*, he will agree that you are in the wrong."

"I shall look forward to a spirited debate on the topic when I return," Verity said with a delighted smile, then shut the door behind her to forestall further discussion. Turning to the left, she strode briskly to the corner and hailed a hackney to take her to Tiverton Road in Mayfair, where Marchesi Confectionary occupied a narrow lot between a haberdashery and a coffeehouse. Pausing outside, she admired the artistry on display in the window: various pastries piled on colorful plates resting on brass racks. Chocolate puffs mixed with Shrewsbury cakes, macarons, and rolled wafers.

Notably, the chocolate puffs were plain.

No dusting of finely powdered sugar decorated their smooth tops.

Intrigued, Verity opened the door and slipped into the shop, which was bustling in the afternoon with customers buying pastries for that evening or bread for the following morning. She approached the counter slowly, noting that the chocolate confection took pride of place on the center shelf with a sign reading, "The one and only chocolate puff — do not accept imitations." To the left, against the long wall, was a long table with chairs, and a pair of soldiers in bright red coats and epaulettes enjoyed pink ices. Next to them, a small boy joyfully devoured a chocolate puff while his mother talked to a shop attendant. As the biscuit was not sprinkled with cyanide of potassium, the boy suffered no ill effects from the treat, but with the memory of Mr. Muir's convulsions still fresh in her mind, the sight of his pleasure made her flinch.

When the mother stepped away from the counter to join her son at the table, Verity bid the attendant a cheerful hello and apologized for upsetting her.

Taken aback by this greeting, the attendant—a buxom woman with frothy blond curls under a white bonnet with a pink bow—frowned and insisted she was not upset.

"Not yet," Verity replied, looking around at the crowded interior and suggesting they step outside for their conversation. "But if you refuse, then I shall have to say something that will be deeply distressing to you and abhorrent to your patrons."

Her scowl deepening, the woman opened her mouth to tell Verity what she thought of her threat, then promptly closed it when a sparkle of gold from the guinea Verity had placed on the counter caught her eye. "Right this way, miss," she said agreeably, as she slipped the money into her apron and introduced herself as Mrs. Marchesi, the owner of the establishment along with her husband. "I can tell you are not a shopkeeper yourself or you would know that waving money around is sufficient. You do not need to make threats as well."

Following the proprietor outside, Verity murmured, "Duly noted," and held up another coin. Then she explained that she was seeking information about an assortment of chocolate puffs sold by the confectionary earlier in the day. If Mrs. Marchesi answered her questions honestly, then she could have the guinea.

Cautiously, the owner agreed.

"I appreciate it," Verity said, handing the woman the coin in a gesture of good faith. "The biscuits were packaged in a tin that said Marchesi and were a dozen in total."

On an eager nod, the woman said she recalled the order. "For the Earl of Goldhawk. He is one of our most reliable customers. He buys chocolate puffs at least once a week, sometimes twice."

It was not the answer Verity wanted to hear, and a knot formed in her belly. "He does?"

"Oh, yes, he gives them to his lady-loves," she affirmed succinctly.

Although Verity had been hoping to eliminate the earl cleanly, the information was not in itself a condemnation. It was alarming, to be sure, but not damning. A man with Hawes's extensive resources would be able to discover several of his lordship's most private habits easily enough.

Consequently, she sought particulars. "Does Goldhawk place the orders himself?"

"Goodness, no," Mrs. Marchesi replied with a shake of her head. "He sends a footman."

"*A* footman?" Verity asked, discouraged by the response because it did not put any distance between Goldhawk and the poisoned chocolate puffs. A trusted retainer could have carried out the deadly assignment on his lordship's orders or merely purchased the tin, which he blithely handed to his employer to adulterate and deliver. "Meaning it is the same footman every time?"

"Not every time," the owner clarified. "It is one of three footmen, although William comes most frequently. He is a lovely young man who always asks about my mother. She worked in the shop until it became too difficult to manage with her rheumatism. Now she stays upstairs in the house, bothering the maid of all work with her complaints."

Calmly, as though the answer did not matter, Verity asked, "Was it William today?"

"I don't know who it was today," Mrs. Marchesi said candidly.

The inconclusive reply did little to settle Verity's nerves, and she glanced into the shop, where two other women, both considerably younger, gathered biscuits from various trays on the shelves. "Would one of your associates know who came in today with the order?"

A fleeting smile crossed the owner's face as she shook her head. "You misunderstand me. I do not know who made the order because I've never seen the man before and he did not give his name."

As Verity considered any variation from a familiar pattern to be significant, she leaned forward. "Was he a newly hired footman?"

Mrs. Marchesi allowed that he might have been a new footman. "But he is definitely not new to the establishment."

The confidence in her tone unnerved Verity, for it further reduced the gap between Goldhawk and the poisoned sweets. Lacing a tin of pastries with cyanide was precisely the sort of task you reserved for a longstanding retainer. "How do you know that?"

"He paid for the puffs, which means he has earned the trust of the housekeeper," she explained. "William has been with the earl for more than two years and has never once provided cash upon receipt. None of the footmen have. They put the order on account, which his lordship settles at the end of the month. And consistently, too. He has never missed a payment and forced us to dun him like some of our other patrons."

Although Verity found the second discrepancy as meaningful as the first, she could not decide what it meant in terms of Goldhawk's guilt. If he had placed the order himself, then he would not want proof of it in the confectionary's ledger. But if a nefarious stranger hired by Hawes to kill her had made the purchase, he would also avoid leaving evidence of his visit.

Frustrated, she asked Mrs. Marchesi what the man looked like and received a description that was not particularly distinctive: blond hair, brown eyes, straight nose, sharp chin.

Then she added that he was older than William and the others. "And not quite as tall. I can see their chins over the display case next to the counter. But I couldn't see his."

Well, now, Verity thought, that was notable.

Footmen frequently came as a matched set.

"You are sure he was a footman?" Verity asked.

The proprietor shrugged and admitted she could not say definitely one way or the other. "But he was wearing the livery."

Ah, but was he sporting the actual uniform or merely the earl's colors?

To this query, Mrs. Marchesi could offer no definitive reply, as she had not looked that closely at the customer's clothes. The shop was always too busy for her to have time to notice such a specific detail.

Naturally, she did not, Verity thought as she withdrew

another guinea from her pocket and thanked her for being so helpful. "I appreciate your time."

Pleased, Mrs. Marchesi promptly accepted the gold coin and buried it in her apron. Then she complemented Verity on her speedy grasp of the shopkeepers' mentality and insisted on wrapping up some treats for her to take home. Instinctively, she reached for the chocolate puffs, as they were the confectionary's most requested item and the house specialty, but Verity recoiled and pointed to the Shrewsbury cakes.

※

Wednesday, June 24
3:49 p.m.

Unable to disguise the fading bruise on her cheek—and unwilling to waste time returning to Bethel Street to change clothes—Verity decided there was nothing for it but for poor Miss Chalmer's demanding employer to take a brutish turn. Lady Georgiana Puttlesmith had long been exacting in her requirements and prone to tantrums, but now she would respond to her maid's minor inadequacies with physical violence.

It was horrible, of course, for the blow stung, but Miss Chalmers really should have known better to than to respond to her mistress's query with the truth. Everyone in the household knew to lie to Lady Georgie, especially in situations pertaining to her appearance.

It was simple: Always reply in the negative.

No, your cheeks are not gaunt.

No, your nose is not stubby.

No, you do not have a large red spot in the middle of your forehead.

You see, it was as easy as falling off a log!

Although hesitant to discuss private Puttlesmith business with the other servants in the road, Miss Chalmers feared she had no other choice. She needed help, and the only way it would be supplied was by her asking for it.

Consequently, she stood in the doorway of the staff's entrance at the Earl of Goldhawk's home and explained her predicament to the housekeeper.

Naturally, she should have never asked Lady Georgie *which* chin hair she wished to be plucked! The only acceptable response was to furrow her brow and disavow all knowledge of chin hairs.

It was hardly surprising her ladyship had responded with a furious wallop, balling her hand into a fist and driving it into her maid's eye.

"Do not worry about me! I am fine," Verity rushed to add, although the slight crack in her voice suggested otherwise. "The bruise is already healed. You can barely see it! And my vision is impeded only a little bit. It is the statue! The one of Lady Georgie's grandfather. When she delivered her blow, I fell backward slightly. My own fault! I have never been graceful. But I bumped into the statue and toppled it to the floor. Thank goodness it did not break! I tried to put it back on the pedestal, but I couldn't lift it. I cannot ask any of the staff to help me because they are all a bunch of nattering gossips. You tell one person something before breakfast and it is the talk of the servants' hall by nuncheon. It makes working there ever so difficult."

Pausing in her lengthy tirade to take a breath, Verity suddenly got a pensive look in her eye as she tilted her head curiously and asked the housekeeper if her ladyship happened to be seeking to hire new servants. "I can get references!" she said excitedly before peevishly adding, "Just not from Lady Georgie."

Despite the placidness of the housekeeper's expression,

she was impatient with Miss Chalmer's rambling explanation and urged the lady's maid to arrive at the reason for her call. "And if this is merely a long-winded solicitation for employment, then I must disappoint you as we are fully staffed at the moment. As a personal aside, I would add that criticizing your current employer to your future employer is not a winning tactic."

Taking her critique of the overstepping Miss Chalmers to heart, Verity tilted her eyes down with embarrassment and quietly thanked the woman for her wisdom. Then she apologized for taking up so much of her time. "I need footmen!"

Baffled by the sudden announcement, the housekeeper frowned. "Footmen?"

"That is the reason for my call: I need footmen," Verity replied. "It is as I said: I can't lift the statue on my own and I can't ask anyone in the house for help. May I please borrow footmen?"

When the housekeeper did not immediately refuse, most likely because she was repeating the request in her head to make certain she heard it correctly, Verity inserted a wheedling note in her tone as she added she did not have much time. "I placed a counterpane over the fallen statue to hide it, but someone is bound to notice."

"This is highly irregular," the housekeeper said disapprovingly.

Verity hung her head in shame. "I know."

Nevertheless, the housekeeper asked how many footmen she required.

In response, Verity asked how many the house employed.

"Three," the housekeeper said.

"Well, then, I need three," Verity replied.

Finding this alignment a little too convenient, the housekeeper eyed her dubiously, and Verity rushed to explain that she actually needed four footmen. "It is a very heavy marble statue. But three footmen is better than no footmen and you *are* the fourth establishment I have asked and the first one not to slam the door violently in my face. The Puttlesmiths are new to the road, and I am making a wretched muck of their introduction. Still, I am desperate and grateful. Have I mentioned how grateful I am that you have allowed me to make my plea? Even if you refuse now, I will remember you kindly."

"Oh, for God's sake," the housekeeper muttered with a hefty sigh as she stepped back to allow Miss Chalmers to enter the corridor. "But you are to stay here, right here. Do you understand?"

"Yes, ma'am, right here," she replied soberly.

The housekeeper strode down the hallway, darting a skeptical look behind her as she disappeared around a corner. As her mistrust was well justified, Verity did not resent it in the least and thought the servant had been far kinder to the impertinent Miss Chalmers than she deserved. If the circumstance had been less pressing, she would have taken a subtler tack, tailoring her story to match each particular footman. The abused lady's maid in desperate need of a trio of footmen was a blunt instrument, but it had achieved her goal —fortunately.

In fact, it had not, Verity reminded herself as she waited for the housekeeper to return. Mrs. Fitzgerald could still throw her out on her ear and at that very moment could be fetching the butler to assist her in the endeavor. In that event, she would have to devise another way of getting a look at the Earl of Goldhawk's footmen, one that employed more stealth than announcing herself at the door. Climbing through a window in a dress was more difficult than in trousers but not impossible, and she had noticed an open pane in the back of the house.

Or she could dash to Bethel Street and return as something else, such as a collier.

Well, maybe not a coal delivery so late in the day.

Perhaps the Turnip could deliver a message.

As Verity imagined the chilly reception the Turnip would receive after Miss Chalmers's audacious request, the housekeeper returned with two footmen in tow.

"His lordship can only spare William and Jeffrey at the moment," Mrs. Fitzgerald explained. "If that is not sufficient, there is nothing I can do."

William and Jeffrey were sufficient.

Indeed, they were ideal, for two specimens were all Verity needed to establish a pattern—and what specimens they were: six feet tall, broad shoulders, blue eyes, black hair. Physical perfection was highly sought after in a footman, with advertisements frequently citing the required height, and she could not imagine the earl allowing a brown-eyed, blond-haired creature a few inches short to ruin the flawless presentation of his set.

Confident she had the information she needed to assure Hardwicke his brother had nothing to do with the attempt on her life or the murder of Mr. Muir, she shook her head back and forth with wild agitation as she observed that the statue was so very heavy.

Solid marble through and through!

Two footmen alone could never do it, and the prospect of making the enormous effort to bring them inside the house without anyone noticing while still risking almost certain failure?

No, Miss Chalmers simply did not have the nerve!

Muttering to herself, Verity ran from the house.

A LARK'S RELEASE

Wednesday, June 24
4:32 p.m.

Hardwicke apologized for the delay.

Climbing down from his horse, a sleek black thoroughbred with a white diamond on his forehead, he explained that he had intended to call on Bethel Street to make his report in person as soon as he had had something to eat. "I cannot say I have made considerable progress in solving the mystery of who sent the figurine, but I feel confident that Goddard is not involved. Far from being astonished at having the missing cat returned to him, he was startled to learn it had been missing. Nobody in the museum had noticed the empty pedestal. If he were part of the conspiracy to incriminate you, he would have handled the exchange with more aplomb. When I told him that Customs had been informed of the theft, he turned white and accused me of trying to discredit him with the Foreign Office. Then I mentioned my concern that one of the reliefs he had recently secured for the museum was counterfeit and he became totally incoherent. Eventually, he regained his senses, and we had a fruitful discussion about the relief from Sir Thomas. He agreed to hold off on purchasing further antiquities from him until I give him leave. I think he can be trusted, as he values his position and knows I have Quartermaine's ear. He does not want to do anything to imperil his employment. As nobody from the museum contacted the customs service, I decided it would be prudent to discover who did, so I visited their offices in Lower Thames Street. Tillet was not there, and his supervisor refused to talk to a man of my reputation. After that, I called on Grint and tasked him with finding out. And that is why I am returning only now."

He grinned as he said it, his eyes crinkling in the corners as he stepped toward her and asked if she thought he had run off with the precious artifact. "I assume that is why you are here—to make sure I did not sell the statuette to one of the dealers on Cistern Street? Once a dissolute gambler with crushing debts, always a dissolute gambler with crushing debts."

His cheerfulness unnerved Verity, who had spent much of the journey to his house contemplating the best way to justify her decision to withhold vital information. Delphine's understanding of Holying was unquestionably the correct one, and Hardwicke had every right to decry her hypocrisy in flouting her own rule. By rights, she should have promptly informed him of the attempt on her life.

True, yes, but what did *promptly* really mean?

"Immediately," sure, in many instances.

But also "in all due haste," which was the definition she had chosen to follow.

Dashing to Millman Street with incomplete information would have made a difficult situation worse by obligating her to tarnish the Hardwicke family name by saying the dreaded words out loud: It appears your brother tried to kill me.

In constructing her defense, she had never once considered the possibility that Hardwicke had not read her missive. Prepared to mollify his resentment, she found herself unwilling to pierce his good humor with talk of murder and betrayal.

As a result, she smiled in return and begged him to tell her more about these dealers on Cistern Street. "That is in Lambeth, is it not?" she asked, picturing a pit-ridden lane with dilapidated houses several blocks to the east of Fortescue's. "Is that where one takes one's father's pilfered signet ring?"

Despite this spirited reply, he perceived something amiss in her demeanor and his lovely teal eyes narrowed with concern. "Did something else happen? You do not mean to tell me that another artifact has been delivered to Bethel Street."

She did not, no.

But rather than explain there, amid the dust of the road, she gestured to the door and indicated with a wave that they should go inside. "Come, let us have some brandy."

"Verity," he said, an edge of warning in his tone.

She simply shook her head.

"All right," he replied softly.

As they entered the drawing room at the top of the steps, the housekeeper greeted them warmly and announced that she had prepared a plate of cheese and fruit. Hardwicke thanked her for being thoughtful as always and asked for it to be served in the study. While the servant carried in the tray and arranged the plates neatly on the desk, he withdrew a bottle from the bottom drawer.

Whiskey, Verity noted.

Either Hardwicke had instinctively comprehended the severity of the situation or he wanted something a little stronger after his own frustrating day.

Without comment, he filled two glasses with the amber liquid and handed one to Verity as she sat down. He closed the door after the housekeeper left the room, lowered into the chair next to her, and said, "All right, then."

Verity Lark was a nimble sparrer. Shifting effortlessly with the play, she could dart from a duel with swords to a bare-knuckle brawl without missing a step.

And yet the transition from defense to offense stymied her.

She had been so ready to jump into the fight in medias res, and now to have to go back to the beginning without a preamble tripped up her heels.

Slightly unsteady, she nevertheless leaped in, for she was nothing if not direct. Shilly-shallying was for the Turnip!

Matter-of-factly, she began the narrative with her return from Soames's residence. Disembarking from the hack, she discovered Delphine standing in front of twenty-six Bethel Street with a box chocolate puffs from a confectionery called Marchesi.

Did Hardwicke recognize the name?

He did not, no.

At least as far as she could tell.

But he *was* England's greatest spy.

If he did not wish his familiarity to be known, then it would not be known.

"Delphine was watching Mrs. Paisley's son-in-law tussle with the arborvitae Grint had deposited in front of her door to hide Morny last week," she continued.

"Mr. Muir," he interjected mildly.

Verity's heart twisted.

With a curt nod, she confirmed the name and suppressed the image of his lifeless features that darted through her mind. "Mr. Muir was annoyed at the shrub and batting at its branches, and Delphine could not help but giggle at the ridiculous picture he made. Naturally, she felt awful for laughing at him and held out the tin of chocolate puffs as penance. He took one, then another."

And there it was again: his empty eyes, his slack jaw, his soiled chin.

Ruthlessly, she thrust the image aside.

But the strangled gurgles—those she could not smother.

All the same, she continued with dispassionate precision, noting that Mr. Muir ate the three biscuits. "A few minutes later, he was dead."

Hardwicke's expression did not change.

It remained resolutely blank.

But his mind clearly churned with swift efficiency as he calculated the speed of the poison as well as the method of delivery and arrived at a reasonable conclusion. "Cyanide crystals ground into a fine powder and sprinkled onto the chocolate puffs?"

His composure was a balm.

Of course he had not cursed hotly and leaped to his feet, vowing vengeance or retribution or something equally fervent and unproductive. His approach to adversity was the same as hers: cautious, thoughtful, unruffled. Making a fuss solved nothing.

As she took her first sip of whiskey, Hardwicke continued to evaluate the information, supposing that the box had come with a note. "Who did it purport to be from?"

Purport, Verity thought.

Because he knew the difference. In his work for the Alien Office, he had probably affixed false names to dozens of letters. Grateful for his experience, she withdrew the card from her reticule, handed it to him, and waited.

It did not take long.

A few seconds later he looked up and regarded her anxiously.

Oh, but it was not anxiety.

It was deep distress.

Colson Hardwicke looked stricken.

And yet his voice was as smooth as silk when he said his brother had nothing to do with the murder attempt. "Alex is not an especially noble human being. He has the usual faults of a pampered aristocrat whose every desire has been satisfied. He is selfish and entitled and has never known a moment of adversity his entire life. But he is not a villain. He is not a vile scoundrel. Even if he harbored a violent dislike of you—which, I swear to you, he does not—he would not do this to *me*. He would never harm a single hair on the head of the woman I ... I ... of a woman of whom I am excessively fond. He simply does not have that sort of cruelty in him."

If the fingers holding the whiskey had not turned white from how tightly he was holding the glass, Verity would have been insulted.

To think she was so easily duped!

To assume she was as credulous as a babe still wet behind the ears!

But his fingers *were* white.

Hardwicke was incredibly worried that she believed his brother had arranged her murder, and that apprehension had clouded his ability to think rationally about the matter.

If he had retained his faculties, he would have proceeded logically to the next relevant query and asked if she had confirmed the delivery with the confectionery shop.

Briskly, she said, "Of course he has nothing to do with it. Your brother orders from Marchesi regularly but always sends one of three footmen, most frequently William, and puts the order on his account, which he settles at the end of the month. This morning, the order came from a footman the proprietor had never seen before and he paid in cash. These factors were different enough to convince me the earl had nothing to do with it, but before coming here, I visited his residence to confirm he did not employ a footman matching the description Mrs. Marchesi provided. I trust it goes without saying that I saw not even the vaguest resemblance."

Oh, but it did not.

The way Hardwicke loosened his grip on the glass made it quite clear to Verity that he needed to hear the words. Gently, he placed the drink on the table, and as he looked at her with gratitude mixed with surprise, she suggested Hawes as an alternative.

He dismissed it immediately on account of the method being too indiscriminate for a man of the infamous crime lord's experience and talents. "Even if all had gone according to plan, the likelihood that Delphine would have been poisoned alongside you, as well as Lucy, was extremely high. Three dead from excessive vomiting with a spilled tin of biscuits on the floor beside them would garner too much attention. Hawes has made a career of avoiding attention. Someone else is responsible," he said pensively, then noted in a seeming non sequitur that his sister-in-law harbored a dislike of drinking chocolate and would never condone a steady stream of sweets for the children. "Therefore, the puffs are for his mistresses. I know nothing of the arrangements he makes for them, as it is not something we discuss. He has several intimates, however, who would know about his habit, that is, aside from the women themselves. I cannot begin to speculate which among them wishes you harm."

Ah, there it was, the analytical mind she adored, Verity thought, grateful for the cogent reply, which suggested the next step in the investigation. Clearly, a call on the earl was in order to find out who among his friends or lovers—

And then her heart thudded as she heard it in her head: adored.

That was not quite true, was it?

She appreciated Hardwicke's analytical mind and sometimes sought to emulate it.

But adored?

Verity was not sure she even knew what the word meant.

Freddie adored his new carriage.

Delphine adored gardening.

The Duchess of Kesgrave adored rout cakes.

By that definition, meaning "enjoy greatly," the description was not without its validity—although *greatly* was perhaps stretching it a bit thin.

Irked by her own pedantry, she wrenched her thoughts back to the topic at hand and felt freshly annoyed at her failure to cultivate an interest in Goldhawk other than as a foil for his famously disreputable brother. If she had done her work properly, she would be able to list the earl's mistresses as well as his closest friends.

Now, of course, she would have to interview him to find out the information, and she wondered if Hardwicke would resist the idea. Men were notoriously prickly about their relations with the opposite sex, and a peer of Goldhawk's standing would consider his desire for privacy inviolate. Hardwicke, sharing this opinion, might argue that the business should be treated as a family affair.

It was nonsense, of course, and as the intended target of the attack, she had every right to press for the information, especially as a man had died in her stead.

Even so, the only thing that counted was the information itself, and if her stepping back allowed Hardwicke to get the answer more quickly, then she was happy to withdraw.

She trusted him to handle it correctly.

Verity, noting that it was almost five, suggested they call on the earl before it grew much later. "Ideally, we should conduct our interrogation before he and the countess sit down for dinner."

Taken aback by this comment, Hardwicke said, "Surely, you are not thinking of going."

Despite blithely resigning herself to the inevitable outcome only seconds before, she returned the glass to the desk with an angry thump and said, "Of course I am going! I am sorry if the prospect of discussing your brother's intimate relations in my presence discomfits you, but I will remind you that the man who murdered Mr. Muir was content to kill every member of my household. I trust you, Hardwicke, but I do not *trust* you, and if you deprive me of the opportunity to question Goldhawk with you, then I shall do it without you."

Hardwicke smiled.

The edges of his lips actually tilted up as he excused her outburst. "You are understandably on edge. But if you had allowed me to finish my thought, then you would know that your pique is unjustified. I was simply going to propose that you change before returning to Bedford Square. My brother met you previously, when you were driving with me in Hyde Park, and I assume you do not want him to recognize you now. My footman is your height and would be delighted to lend you a change of clothes."

No, he would not, Verity thought, imagining the servant's horror at having to provide Miss Gorman with one of his own outfits. By any measure, the charge exceeded the bounds of his office, and yet the footman would not utter a word of protest. Even if he was unaccustomed to the strange goings-on at the Hardwicke residence, he knew better than to air his dissatisfaction in front of a guest.

Vaguely embarrassed by her immoderate reaction, she thanked him for the practical solution, then advised him to summon the footman at once so she could assume the disguise. "It should not take me above a quarter hour to change."

"Very good," he murmured, rising to his feet and leaving the room for several minutes. While he was gone, Verity sipped the whiskey, enjoying its rich flavor, a sweetness tempered by smoky spices, and wondered if an apology was in order for assuming the worst, especially when he had remembered a vital detail she had momentarily forgotten. Hardwicke had been fair with her in all his dealings and had demonstrated a clear-sighted usefulness. If nothing else, he would comprehend the ineffectiveness of rousing her to anger by denying a patently reasonable request.

Savoring the whiskey, which was far better than anything they had at Bethel Street, she took another deep draw before returning the glass to the desk. She had eaten little that day, and it would never do to become tipsy before interrogating the Earl of Goldhawk.

To counter the effects of the alcohol, she chose a wedge of cheddar from the offerings provided by the housekeeper. Nutty and sharp, it pared well with the whiskey, and she had several more slices before selecting one of the strawberries, which were perfectly ripe, bright red and juicy. Marveling at how anything could be so delicious, she forgot her intention to apologize to Hardwicke for misjudging him and when he returned to the room with a pile of neatly folded clothes, she asked where his housekeeper purchased their produce. "Or do you grow these lovelies in your garden? If so, I must speak to the sorcerer who conjured them, for Delphine will want to know all their secrets, including how they handle squirrels. I am obligated to ask about squirrel management when engaged in any conversation that touches on an agricultural matter. I signed a contract."

Then she smiled to indicate she was teasing.

"It is only a verbal agreement," she explained, wiping a drizzle of strawberry juice from her chin as Hardwicke dropped the garments onto the empty chair, tugged her to her feet, and pressed his lips against hers with such feral intensity she felt almost dizzy, as though all the air had been drawn from her lungs only to be instantly returned in a heady rush. Bearing no resemblance to his usual response—careful and measured, attuned to her own fervor and aligned accordingly—it was unlike anything she had ever experienced before.

Verity had wondered about the depth of his passion.

She had sensed there was more than he allowed her to see.

But this ... this ferocity exceeded anything she could have imagined, and reveling in the way it pervaded her body, she was at once grateful for his restraint and maddened by it.

To think she could have experienced these glorious sensations all along!

But it was also too much, she thought, her sticky red

fingers clutching the pristine white of his cravat with a disquieting frenzy as desire dulled her brain, banishing everything but the feel of him.

In that moment, she cared nothing about Goldhawk or cyanide or Mr. Muir's horrible gurgle.

Verity, who never not cared, felt most alarmingly unlike herself, and when Hardwicke finally raised his head, releasing her from the almost primal need, she took the footman's garb from the chair and left the room.

Chapter Seven

❦

Wednesday, June 24
5:41 p.m.

Mrs. Fitzgerald displayed not a flicker of awareness.

Confronted with the sober features of Mr. Gorman, whose left cheek sported a bruise identical in shape, size, and color as Miss Chalmers, Goldhawk's housekeeper regarded Verity with bland indifference as she carried the silver tray to the table. The earl's study was a somber enclave, with damask curtains blocking the brightness of the sun, heavy furniture, and a scarce assortment of candles—all of which allowed Verity to hide in plain sight. If the interior of the room were brighter, then Mrs. Fitzgerald would have of a certainty recognized her as the desperate lady's maid seeking the assistance of three able-bodied footmen who had stood in the servants' entry two hours before.

Next to Verity, seated in a plush armchair in a deep wine-red shade, Hardwicke tightened his jaw as the housekeeper laid down the salver, then glanced at her employer to see if her service had been satisfactory.

Smoothly, Goldhawk dismissed her.

The moment she closed the door behind herself, Hardwicke darted to his feet, circled his chair, and gripped the leather trim with both hands. "Damn it, Alex, this is not a social call! I need information."

Goldhawk, who matched his brother in stature if not in appearance, his eyes a misty blue with none of the glints of green that made Hardwicke's so beguiling, replied. "So you said, yes. Nevertheless, I am determined to observe the proprieties. This is the first time you have introduced me to one of your associates from the Home Office, and I will not allow the occasion to pass without marking it in some way. Please do sit, Cole, as you will not get the intelligence you require any faster by looming over me. Now tell me, Mr. Gorman, do you like sugar in your tea?"

Hardwicke complied, regaining his seat without further protest, and although he did not heave a petulant sigh, Verity felt it in the way he thumped into the chair. "I do not have time to play your games. If you will just tell me who among your intimates know you routinely order chocolate puffs from Marchesi, you will be free to return to your evening."

"Who is to say this is not my evening?" his lordship asked.

Hardwicke growled in annoyance, and Verity, riveted by the exchange, leaned back in her chair as if watching a scene unfold on a stage. The earl clearly delighted in teasing his younger sibling, who appeared incapable of resisting the provocation, a development that charmed Verity. She had tried dozens of times to rile him and rarely succeeded.

Goldhawk did it with seemingly little effort.

The advantage of being an older brother, she assumed.

As she had failed to reply to his query, the earl tilted his head in her direction and inquired again about her preferences. "We also have honey. Mrs. Fitzgerald would be happy to bring it."

In Mr. Gorman's deep timber, Verity assured him that she liked her tea black. "Thank you, my lord."

Goldhawk, his light blue eyes amused, handed her the saucer with its delicate teacup and asked what she did for the Home Office. "Do you also work for Daniel Grint?"

As Hardwicke bristled at the needless chatter, Verity replied that she did not. "I do not work for anybody. Sometimes I work *with* Grint. It depends."

"How intriguing," the earl murmured. "Cole has told his family nothing about his work for the government despite our intense interest. Any attempt to garner information is met with arch resistance. For example, he would have replied to my query by denying all knowledge of Grint. Ignorance is his most frequently employed defense against curiosity."

"Alex," Hardwicke said warningly.

Unperturbed by the thread of anger in his brother's voice, Goldhawk smoothly replied that if he was going to share intimate details of his life, then he would know something about the man with whom he would share them. "Your question was oddly specific and personal, and I cannot fathom how you are even aware of my habit unless your Mr. Grint is investigating me now."

As much as she enjoyed observing the exchange between the brothers, Verity was as eager as Hardwicke to learn the name of the man who poisoned Mr. Muir, and returning the teacup to its saucer, she assured the earl that nothing of the sort was happening. "Mr. Grint does not know I am here, and although I am no more at liberty to explain the purpose of our questions than Lord Colson, I promise you the undersecretary has only the utmost respect for your privacy. By an unfortunate stroke of luck, your habit, as you call it, intersects with a larger issue threatening the security of our nation. If there were any other way to gain the information, I would not have dared to impose on you like this. Lord Colson made every effort to discourage me, as he knows you fear the marquess finding out about your extravagance and judging it harshly."

Goldhawk darted an amused glance at his brother. "Does he?"

Hardwicke shook his head. "I said your wife."

Now the earl smiled and allowed that the concern was justified. "Emily would send me to the country without my valet for a month if she knew how much I spend each week on confections for my mistresses—and it is the confections she would take issue with, not the expense. She would be perfectly sanguine if I sent something improving to one's health such as pork jelly, which does not rot the teeth, but one cannot woo a woman with pork jelly, not even to satisfy one's wife."

"The names, Alex," Hardwicke said, impatient with his sibling's nonsense.

Although the earl looked as though he would offer another teasing reply, his tone was solemn as he answered, "I do not believe this folderal about the safety of the nation for a minute, but I do know how little you enjoy this subject and would not raise it if you could avoid it. Andrew Brownell, Theodore Lamb, and Kevin Reedy. They are the three men among my intimate acquaintance who know of my habit. Reedy introduced me to Marchesi and I have recommended it to Andy and Teddy. I do not know if either one has taken the suggestion. Andy tends toward parsimony, as he believes his charms alone should be sufficient, and Teddy's pockets are frequently to let."

"Thank you," Verity said, conjuring two of the three gentlemen with ease, as both Andrew Brownell and Kevin Reedy had made appearances in Twaddle's column. The former, a blond-haired baron first in line for an earldom, was of modest height and fit the description given by the proprietress. A confirmed rake, he had seduced his brother's intended in order to secure her inordinately large dowry for himself. Shocking for a time, the affair had dulled into mundanity in the wake of other family scandals, such as his youngest brother having to escape to the Continent after accidentally shooting his mistress in a brawl. His other brother, the one from whom he had stolen the betrothed, had devised a scheme to sell shares in a fraudulent mine in Scotland.

And the father: Ralph Albert Brownell, Earl of Frimgallow.

He was associated with the worst excesses of the *ton,* gleefully seducing naïve misses from the schoolroom and even allowing himself to be embroiled in the Hottenroth molestation scandal at the orphanage near Spitalfields. As Robert Lark had been unable to confirm the rumor, he could not include them in the series of articles he wrote exposing the depravity of the institution's overseer. But Verity knew them to be true, and it required very little to imagine Andrew Brownell leaving poisoned chocolate puffs at her door even if the question of why eluded her.

Reedy, in contrast, had a shock of bright red hair.

She knew nothing of Lamb.

But Hardwicke did.

Verity could see it in the expression on his face, a supposition he immediately affirmed by cautioning the earl against saying a word of their conversation to anyone. "No mention at all, Alex. It is imperative. I am trusting you."

Taken aback by the severity in his brother's voice, Goldhawk exclaimed, "Good Gad, Cole, when have I not been worthy of your trust?"

As the query was rhetorical, Hardwicke did not bother to

respond, and rising to his feet, asked the other man if he knew which jeweler Brownell used.

Struck by the abrupt introduction of a new topic, Goldhawk raised his eyebrows as if trying to discern the connection to the previous one and replied after a moment of thought that he could only assume the baron frequented the usual spots: Rundell, Bridge & Rundell, Thomas Gray, Hamlet's. "Having said that, I do not believe he would be a regular patron of any, as bijoux are costlier than puffs, and those are already more than he can stand to pay."

Hardwicke thanked his brother for the information, which he hailed as helpful, and Verity, unable to perceive its relevance, wondered if he had begun to devise a scheme to entrap Brownell by exploiting his frugality.

"I trust that one day you will tell me what this is really about," the earl said as he rose to escort them to the door, the tea on the tray untouched by all three of them. "I know you delight in being mysterious, but you also have a sense of fair play and it is cruel to taunt me with such interesting tidbits. Now if Mr. Gorman would be so kind as to excuse us for a few minutes, I have a personal matter I wish to discuss with you, Cole."

Naturally, Mr. Gorman offered no objection, readily exiting the room to wait in the hallway and sliding her hands into her pockets as she rested her shoulders against the wall opposite the doorway. It was, she knew, a decidedly louche pose for an earl's establishment, but it was a necessary defense against her own curiosity, for she had an ardent desire to listen at the keyhole.

She could not, of course.

Eavesdropping on Goldhawk's private conversation was a terrible way to repay him for his assistance. Perhaps if he had not given them precisely the information they sought, she might have found it easier to overcome her scruples.

The exchange was brief, as promised, and scarcely five minutes later they were back in the carriage returning to Bethel Street to convene a council of war with Delphine and Freddie.

⁂

Wednesday, June 24
8:17 p.m.

Delphine, taking issue with the implied violence of the term "council of war," refused to participate in the discussion until they arrived at a more civil description of the exchange. She was sitting on the settee in a plain muslin gown, her hands deftly working a pair of needles as she knitted a blanket in the palest blue, and Verity, who had expected to find her friend anxiously peering out the window, was surprised by her calm.

"Am I calm, dear?" Delphine asked curiously, her eyes darting up to consider her friend as she strode deeper into the room. "Or am I simply exhausted from comforting a grieving widow, her fatherless children, and her guilt-ridden mother? She is blaming the arborvitae—Mrs. Paisley, I mean. She is convinced that if he had been able to exit her home without being provoked to fury by an unruly shrub, then his heart would not have given out. She is cursing the day it arrived, and I cannot blame her. The arborvitae *is* responsible, although not in the way she imagines, and yet I cannot help but be grateful for Grint's stupid contrivance, for without it, you would be dead, Verity, as would I, and possibly Lucy. Cook, I think, would have been fine because by the time she arrived upstairs to see what all the commotion was about, we three would already be dead on the floor. And that is what I keep thinking: that I am glad it was Mr. Muir rather than you or Lucy, and if that makes me damned, so be it. Nevertheless, it is quite fatiguing, reconciling oneself to perdition, and if it is all the same to you, I would choose not to have the specter of violence hanging over me as we discuss what is to be done about this wretched situation. It is enough to know the killer will strike again when he discovers his scheme failed."

Verity, who had been unable to banish the memory of Mr. Muir's gurgle and collapse from her own mind, sunk into the cushion next to her. Carefully dodging the knitting needles, she enfolded Delphine in her embrace and murmured soothingly. "I should never have run off and left you to handle everything else. I am a beast."

Delphine, laying her head on her friend's shoulder, let out a ragged laugh. "Goodness, no, you are terrible at coddling! You would have made everything worse by being so resolutely practical, pointing out all the advantages of being a widow to the devastated woman."

Verity shuddered at the description, swearing she had more empathy than that.

"You do, dear, yes, but when Mrs. Kendrick's daughter stormed into the house—"

Pulling slightly back, Verity interrupted to confirm the identity of the subject. "You do not mean Elizabeth? Little Lizzie Kendrick? What could she have to storm about?"

"Mr. Muir and she were planning to run off together to Dover, where he has family," Delphine explained. "It turns out, he had drained their accounts to pay for the journey, and Lizzie was convinced Mrs. Paisley found out about it and murdered him to prevent his leaving. It is impossible to say who was more shocked: Mrs. Paisley, Mrs. Kendrick, or Mrs. Muir. It was a desperate scene, and as I am certain you would have told the new widow she is better off without the useless bounder, it was for the best that you were not present."

Verity, who could not disagree with the general premise, insisted she would have made the statement to Lizzie. "The girl is barely out of apron strings. She is how old now—seventeen or eighteen? Far too young to ruin herself over any man, let alone a married father of two who would lecture her into an early grave."

On a wan smile, Delphine allowed that Miss Kendrick seemed to have benefited from her lover's untimely death. "If I did not know better, I would suspect Mrs. Kendrick of administering the poison."

"And she would have gotten away with it, thanks to that perfect clunkhead of a coroner, who refused to even consider the possibility of murder, I assume because he did not want to go through the bother of impaneling a jury for an inquest," Verity added with renewed aggravation. "I should not be surprised the crown employs so many useless men and yet somehow I am continually amazed by it. But that is neither here nor there. What do you think of calling it a round table?"

"Egalitarian, vaguely militaristic, and redolent of misguided quests," Delphine replied promptly.

Satisfied, Verity said, "Let us convene a round table, then. But only in the metaphorical sense, as I am too comfortable on the settee to relocate."

"It is a rectangle anyway," said Freddie, who crossed the room with a glass of wine, which he handed to Verity as he pressed a kiss against her forehead. "I am also very relieved you were not murdered by a poisoned chocolate puff, and if someone had to die in your stead, I am glad it was a hateful bore who seduces schoolroom misses."

"Freddie would not have improved the situation either," Delphine added with a hint of mischief as she laid her knitting to the side. "Very well, tell us what you discovered. I trust the confectionery shop confirmed that the Earl of Goldhawk did not place the order?"

Hardwicke, who was pouring himself a glass of Bordeaux, returned the bottle to the table and darted a grateful look at Delphine. "It was Brownell. Andrew Brownell."

Echoing the name in confusion, Delphine admitted that she was stunned. "What resentment could Baron Brownell hold against Verity? It makes no sense."

"Maybe he knows Verity is Twaddle," Freddie suggested pensively.

"Impossible," Delphine replied, refusing even to consider it. "Nobody knows she is Twaddle."

Owning himself equally confident in the security of their secret, Freddie wondered if they should allow some doubt in light of the dowager duchess's investigation. "We have no idea whom else her solicitor approached in the course of his probe. It is possible that through his inquiries Lord Brownell learned Verity was Twaddle and sent the poisoned puffs as retribution for airing his family's scandals."

Although Verity agreed that excessive certainty was to be avoided at all costs, Verity could not fathom what Twaddle could have reported about Brownell or his family that would spur him to revenge. "I aired nothing that was not already known to everyone. Two dozen people saw Rufus Brownell shoot his mistress in the lane behind the Duke's Head public house. There were so many witnesses that Delphine argued the affair was not worthy of the Twaddleship's attention. And the father, the Earl of Frimgallow, is brazen in his misdeeds, delighting in the attention, as if daring the beau monde to hold him to account, and I refrained from publishing the worst rumors because I could not locate a reliable source willing to corroborate them."

Freddie conceded the validity of the observation before reminding her that Mr. Twaddle-Thum had written three or four articles about Brownell in particular. "There was one when he took his wife's oldest friend as mistress, I believe."

Verity confirmed that was correct. "And when he took his oldest friend's wife as mistress. He also tried to seduce his brother Lewis's wife, which did not go as smoothly as he planned, according to the reports. Brownell fancies himself a Lothario, although he is somewhat clumsy in his execution and extremely limited in his imagination. If Rufus's mistress had not died from the gunshot wound to the belly, I do not doubt he would have attempted to take her to bed as well. Frimgallow succeeded in that goal, which is rumored to be the source of the argument that ended in the pistol discharging."

Hardwicke swirled the dark red liquid in the wineglass as he considered the evidence and deemed the motive inadequate. "Murder is too extreme a response for a few gossipy items in a newspaper, especially for a man who courts scandal to aggrandize himself. As Verity noted, Brownell is not especially creative, and his idea of a great lover follows almost a pattern card. He would not resent Twaddle, I am convinced, and certainly not enough to spur him to murder if he knew his identity, which, to be clear, I do not believe he does."

Persuaded, Verity asked Hardwicke if he had another theory.

He admitted he did not.

Freddie, his expression pensive, wondered if they were examining the situation from the wrong end. "The last time sometime tried to harm Verity, we assumed she was the target because the villain struck here. He broke into this house to abduct her. But it had nothing to do with her," he said, turning to look at Hardwicke. "It was about you and the enemies you made during the war. Could Brownell be among them?"

Hardwicke contemplated the notion, allowing that it was

possible. "Nothing comes to mind, but I was rarely given more information than required for my assignment. Grint will know more. I'll ask him tomorrow when I call to find out what he learned about the customs report regarding the missing figurine."

At the mention of the government official, whom she considered both disagreeable and cravenly for his refusal to help Verity during her imprisonment, Delphine scowled but otherwise held her contempt. Instead, she announced that she did not care why Brownell wanted to kill Verity. "As far as I am concerned, his motive is beside the point. All I want to know is how do we stop him from trying again. What about the confectioner? If Verity was able to identify Brownell based on that interaction, then presumably the shopkeeper can give evidence against him."

"It is not that simple," Hardwicke said. "For one thing, she did not see him sprinkle the chocolate puffs with poison, so her testimony would be of limited utility. Secondly, I imagine she would be reluctant to say anything against a member of the beau monde, which makes up a significant portion of her clientele. And even if she could be convinced, it would still be her word against a member of the aristocracy. In that case, the magistrate would defer to Brownell."

"All right, then," Delphine replied with a curt nod. "How do we gather more evidence? What about the poison? Based on its smell and how it was administered, Verity says it was cyanide of potassium. One cannot simply purchase cyanide of potassium from one's local apothecary. Where did Brownell get it? I do not believe he distilled it from bitter almonds himself."

Hardwicke assured her he did not, as cyanide of potassium was a highly lethal compound made by mixing prussic acid with potassium hydroxide. "The solution evaporates, and the potassium cyanide salts are left behind. It is incredibly dangerous to make, and if during the process you smell cherries or almonds, you are all but dead. It is most commonly used by jewelers to clean gold."

"Ah, so that is why you asked Goldhawk where Brownell purchased his baubles," Verity said with an air of comprehension. "He did not give a useful answer."

"Let me guess," Freddie said with a faint smile. "He said Rundell and Bridge."

"As well as the other two favorites of the Bond Street beaux," Verity affirmed. "But he was merely speculating, as Brownell is not known for bestowing jewelry on his paramours. We will have to pay calls to all the jewelers in London, and I suspect it will be one that is not favored by the *ton*. If he has any sense at all, he would buy his deadly poisons at a small shop on the outskirts of town. Finding it will require time and patience."

"Well, then, let us hope he has no sense," Delphine said tartly.

Hardwicke said he would ask Castleheart to help him make inquiries. "I agree with Verity's assessment, but due diligence requires us to tick the mainstays off the list. I will look into Rundell and company and assign the rest to Castleheart. It might take him a few days to find the right shop, but he will find it. You may depend on it," he added at Delphine's dubious look.

As the man in question was one of Grint's lackeys, Delphine had her doubts. Even so, Castleheart had acquitted himself competently during their previous affair. Charged with keeping an eye on the murderer while they implemented their scheme, he had ensured that no attempt was made on Verity's life before they were ready. "And what about the priceless cat figurine that suddenly appeared on our doorstep? Could that be related?"

"That is the good news," Verity replied cheerfully. "Hardwicke does not believe there's a connection, as Hawes would be far more precise in his attempt to murder me. He would never implement a scheme that might kill my neighbor or companion by accident."

Delphine, casting a withering glance at her friend, said, "There are two separate groups trying to harm you and *that* is the good news?"

As she could understand the cause of her cynicism, Verity made no effort to convince her otherwise, noting instead that they would know more about the antiquities plot against her after Hardwicke received Grint's report. Naturally, this information did little to appease Delphine, whose frown deepened as she acknowledged the debt she owed the under-secretary.

"To be eternally grateful to him for that blasted arborvitae!" she said angrily. "It is the very devil!"

Hardwicke, who shared the sentiment, ardently agreed. "That blasted arborvitae!."

Verity, who had expected neither Sidmouth nor his minion to intercede in the affairs of a woman of common stock, even if they believed she was innocent, bore the functionary no ill will. She was grateful for whatever assistance he could provide and dismissive of everything else. "To review, then, Castleheart will look for the jeweler who sold Brownell the cyanide of potassium, Hardwicke will look for the jeweler as well as find out what Grint has learned from the customs office, and I will keep an eye on Brownell so that we may know his next move before he makes it. All in all, an excellent first round table. If this continues, we shall have to get an actual round table."

"No," Delphine said firmly.

Duly respectful of her friend's opinion, Verity agreed that a table of those proportions was an impractical choice for the parlor. "It would jut out into the room too much."

"No, you are not 'keeping an eye' on Brownell," Delphine

snapped. "You are staying here with me until Hardwicke reports back. Or you may go to the *Gazette* office with Freddie. Those are your options. I would advise you to choose the former as Freddie provides very weak tea to his staff, but you are encouraged to make your own decision."

"Am I?" Verity asked with a lilt of amusement.

Determined to be fair, Delphine proposed a third possibility. "Or you may go with Hardwicke to visit jewelers and the Home Office. I am sure he would not mind your company."

Indeed, he owned himself delighted at the prospect.

But Verity refused to hear of it.

To not surveil the enemy—it was the height of imprudence!

"Given how little we know of Brownell and his motivations, it would be criminally irresponsible of me not to gather as much information about him as possible," she insisted. "You know it is true, Delphine. And you must not worry about my welfare. I can think of no safer place for me to be tomorrow than *behind* Brownell."

Glaring at Hardwicke, who had issued no objection to her friend's absurd plan, Delphine snarled, "And you are just going to let her do it, put herself in harm's way out of a reckless disregard for her own well-being just so she can prove to the rest of us that she is fearless? Truly, Lord Colson, I thought better of you!"

"Oh, dear, back to 'Lord Colson,'" Verity murmured with a sympathetic look at Hardwicke. "In a moment she will be foreswearing biscuits."

Delphine's frown deepened into a baleful glower. "You think this is funny! You think this is all a great lark! Narrowly evading a horrible death while an innocent man dies in our stead is just another opportunity to Twaddle about town! You care nothing of the risk because you believe you are too clever to die, which proves you are not clever at all."

Her anger was justified, Verity thought.

It had been a grueling day for all of them, with some aspects permanently entrenched in their minds, and sleep was the best thing for them.

A nice restorative slumber.

Delphine had already remarked on how exhausted she was.

Even so, Verity could not allow Delphine's misunderstanding to persist.

Gently, she said, "My stead."

And because she was so tired, Delphine stared blankly.

"An innocent man died in *my* stead," Verity clarified with concise emphasis. "Nobody is trying to kill you, Delph. You are not the target. I am the target, and *you* could have died in my stead. Investigating Brownell is not a Twaddle; it is a tactic. You cannot expect me to sit idly by while a murderer schemes against me. I did nothing in Newgate. I twiddled my thumbs while the Fates wove their threads. I cannot do that again, not when your life is at stake and Lucy's and Cook's and possibly even Freddie's. I am not a fool. I know how easily my life can be snuffed out. I saw it today in Mr. Muir's slack features. I will take precautions and tread carefully, and the advantage is mine because Brownell most likely believes his scheme succeeded."

Delphine, whose expression had turned stony at the mention of the squalid prison, regarded her friend with a mixture of regret and despondency. Then she expelled a hefty sigh, as though conceding the inevitable, and Verity, who found this surrender somehow more cutting than any reproach or rebuke, swore she was not as reckless or rash as her friend thought.

But Delphine knew it was not true.

No, not at all.

And she cited the irrefutable evidence: the Wraithe.

Well, yes, on *that* occasion Verity had been reckless and rash and stupid and imprudent and every other disparaging adjective Delphine cared to hurl at her. Confronted with a ghost from their past, she had allowed fear to overcome her good sense, and although she knew it would not happen again, for one had only so many long-vanquished foes from one's childhood whose sudden reappearance struck terror in one's heart, her friend would not be convinced. Delphine already knew everything about rules and exceptions because that was precisely *her* argument: Verity was human. She could not stand outside of her own existence, point to a single thing, and say, "That is the anomaly."

Constrained by the nature of reality, Verity could offer no refutation.

All she had was her intuition and confidence, neither of which Delphine found persuasive, so Verity avoided the topic entirely. Instead, she reiterated her determination to survive Brownell's fiendish plot if for no other reason than to fulfill her obligation to the Duchess of Kesgrave. "Being murdered by a morally bankrupt rakehell strikes me as an exceptionally cravenly way to avoid giving shooting lessons to Her Outrageousness."

As Freddie laughed at the absurd notion, Hardwicke tried to assuage Delphine's concerns by asserting that Verity's plan was sound. "She is a skilled stalker. She keeps her distance and hides readily. She will not put herself unduly in harm's way. I very much prefer it to the alternative."

Delphine furrowed her brow. "The alternative?"

"Breaking into Brownell's house and searching his belongings," he replied mildly.

Verity, seeking to smooth feathers before they ruffled,

promised her friend she intended nothing of the sort. "Hardwicke is teasing you."

In fact, he was not. "I am attempting to establish parameters to minimize my own anxiety because I have the same concerns as Delphine and I would love nothing more than to confine you to the house until the threat has passed," he said, then darted an apologetic look at Delphine as he added that he could not control Verity's behavior. "Any attempt to do so would be Holying, and I have been told by every person in this room that Holying is not an acceptable option."

And yet there was an archness to the statement, a slight ticking up in his intonation, as though uncertain if a reevaluation of the rule was underway.

There was not, no, although Delphine thought there was a distinction to be made between withholding information and adopting a new opinion based on a well-reasoned argument.

Verity owned herself receptive to hearing it, but Delphine was too tired to do anything other than yawn and shake her head.

Chapter Eight

Thursday, June 25
8:11 a.m.

Positioning herself in the garden square across the road from Andrew Brownell's residence in Penfold Street, Verity noted how well the tepid drizzle befitted the home's gray exterior. The houses to its right and left had been recently scrubbed, revealing the warm cream of Portland stone, and the contrast was startling for the refined district. She imagined the neighbors complained incessantly, either to the owner himself or to each other.

The condition was surprising, given the size of Brownell's fortune, which had increased significantly with the addition of his wife's hefty dowry, and she wondered what the baron spent his money on if not the care and upkeep of his London residence.

Like most gentlemen of his standing, he was fond of the gaming table but no word of profligate losses had reached her ears. Instead, the gossip centered on his determined pursuit of women whose spouses he counted among his acquaintance.

As he seemed singularly interested in wives, Verity could not help but wonder if he was trying to avoid his father's worst excesses or if the true appeal of the female sex for him was the seething rage drawn from emasculated husbands.

He would not be the first to delight in the perverse power of cuckoldry.

As the rain increased, Verity tucked herself under the branches of a sycamore tree. She did not expect a man of Brownell's habits to emerge from his home before ten o'clock, but she knew better than to risk missing him on his first outing of the day. In more clement weather, he might enjoy an early run in Hyde Park or a stroll around the square. In her experience, the gentry were receptive to taking exercise to ensure their well-tailored clothes continued to show them to advantage.

Verity expected nothing less of Brownell.

On a wretched day like this, however, the house was slow to wake up, and the only signs of life she had seen in the half hour since she had arrived were from the servants. A maid opened the window on the first floor to allow in fresh air, and a flower seller was turned away from the servants' entrance, the bright red blooms in her grasp starting to wilt from the rain and cold.

Feeling the effects of the chilly day, Verity folded her arms across her chest for warmth and rested her shoulders against the trunk of the sycamore tree.

Thursday, June 25
10:32 a.m.

Although Verity had been a regular patron of Addison's coffeehouse for several years, she had little expectation of being recognized. Rarely did she call enough attention to herself to be memorable, and she made a point of frequently changing her identity: Sometimes she was a young sprig from the country eager to soak up the wisdom of his elders and other times she was an old man with too many opinions he was determined to spout. Most often, she was a sober-minded clerk seeking an hour of repose before returning to the office.

Mr. Bloom, the man who had tended the counter for the past few months, barely looked at her now as she handed him her penny. She thanked him in a Scottish brogue as she picked up her coffee and examined the seating options. Brownell had joined a group of men in the back right corner, and sitting at the table, he presented his back to the room.

Perfect, Verity thought, taking a chair at the table opposite.

Although intellectual rigor was not something she associated with a man of Brownell's temperament, she was not surprised he had led her there. Coffeehouse chatter was de rigueur for men of his cohort, and he would want to make sure he was seen preening in all the right places even if he did not have much to contribute.

The topic, she noticed as she quietly sipped her coffee, was the unrest in the north among the textile workers who objected to the new machines that performed their trade. There was a general sense of impatience for the factory owners who did not immediately stifle dissent, and Verity recognized a few of the most ardent orators. The loudest voice among them belonged to Merrill Cosway, proprietor of the successful hosiery concern bearing his name, who called for hanging a noose around the neck of every Luddite, regardless of age, gender, or history.

A lively cheer greeted this suggestion, and someone asked if the price of cotton was expected to rise in the next three months.

Tilting her head slightly to the left, she saw the speaker was Brownell.

His lordship wanted to know about the price of cotton.

Perhaps he had made a large investment in the industry and was worried about his return. Although he should be flush enough from his quarterly income and interest on his wife's dowry, Brownell would not be the first man to drain his accounts. His own brother, Lewis, had gotten himself into such a fix he had no choice but to fleece his acquaintance with a false mining scheme.

Naturally, Verity was being facetious.

One always had a choice.

Nevertheless, their father—the Earl of Frimgallow—kept them on a tight leash, either because he did not trust them with the family coffers or he had need of the money himself.

Tilting her head closer to hear the response, she recalled Freddie's theory that Brownell had learned of Twaddle's identity via some random and circuitous route and now sought to punish her for her columns about his family. Putting aside the implausibility of discovery, she could not believe the stories were enough to incite the baron to murder. As much attention as she had paid to his lordship's romantic entanglements, she had recounted them with a light hand, finding them more ridiculous than malicious. The women with whom he tangled were well past their first blush of youth and sophisticated enough to know better. His brother Lewis's swindle, however—that Mr. Twaddle-Thum had treated with deep derision, for the younger Brownell had exploited his victims' trust, relying on their longstanding relationship with his father to pick their pockets.

Perhaps Brownell objected to how concisely she had called a spade a spade or the way her articles had drawn out the scandal. What would have been a nine days' wonder was extended to a full two weeks, prolonging the public humiliation and making things awkward for Brownell at his club.

Discomfit at Brooks—it simply did not strike Verity as sufficient cause for murder.

Regardless, she could not conceive of any line connecting Dowager Duchess of Kesgrave to Andrew Brownell and decided Freddie's other suggestion was more likely: Hardwicke might be the true target. His activities during the war were varied and abundant, and there was no telling what enemies he had made.

Brownell asked next about the price of wool, and Verity, leaning back in her chair, took another sip of coffee as she listened to the answer.

※

Thursday, June 25
12:14 p.m.

Soaked from the persistent rain that fell in St. James Street, Verity watched in envy as a groom pulled a silver flask from his pocket, tilted his head back, and drank deeply. Whatever the vessel contained—brandy, port, sherry, even ratafia—would be a blessedly warming treat on such a miserable afternoon.

The clever groom had not even been subject to the weather for very long. He had arrived only ten minutes before, presumably to pick up his employer, who had yet to emerge from White's. Verity, in contrast, had been loitering in the general vicinity of the establishment for almost an hour and had no idea how long Brownell would be inside. Some gentlemen passed entire days in their clubs, but if that was the intention here, she would hope he would have the decency to allow his driver to return at an appointed time.

Although the baron did not have a reputation for treating women with decency nor men with respect, Verity assumed he had the sense to extend a particular courtesy to his servants, whose indisposition would be a great inconvenience to himself.

Surely, Brownell had not meant to linger this long.

Shivering, Verity watched as the groom took another sip and contemplated the irony of her expiring from a vicious chill while surveilling the man who had tried to murder her. Delphine would most certainly not be amused.

The waiting would not be so excruciating if she had brought an umbrella with her, but she had forgone the protection out of concern it would make her too recognizable. Some men still considered the device too French to be worthy of an Englishman. Brummel, for instance, would not be caught dead with one, although perhaps being forced to take up residence in the hated country would inevitably compel him to reconsider his position on what was too Gallic for his liking.

Brownell's driver, who appeared no more pleased with the situation than Verity, shook his head, dislodging a rivulet of rain from the brim of his hat. He probably also wished his had brought an umbrella.

Or a flask of whiskey.

On that thought, she approached the wily groom, complimented his ingenuity in preparing for the downpour, and offered several pence in exchange for the flask. Although startled to find himself in the middle of a negotiation, he cheerfully countered with a much higher figure before agreeing to a shilling. Then he doffed his hat as though delighted with the bargain and asked if he could interest her in a slab of roast beef for only four pence.

"And it's wrapped in oilcloth, so it's not soggy or nothing," he added.

Firmly, Verity declined and opened the container to identify its contents.

It was brandy, as suspected.

Holding the flask aloft, she strode past several carriages to where Brownell's driver was staring at a puddle and said, "Here, mate, help yourself to some warm relief. You've been here almost as long as I have."

The groom was older than Verity had expected, not wizened or withered but well past forty years of age with several decades of experience to his credit. As such, he would be less inclined to grumble about his employer.

Nevertheless, Verity stayed the course. "Don't be shy. I can't pretend it's from Lord Colson's private stock, but it's decent brandy. I poured it myself from the decanter in his study. He'll never notice. Have a taste! I promise it will warm you right up."

Stiffly, the driver refused, foreswearing the need for any reinforcements.

Verity nodded knowingly. "Oh, I see, sure, your bloke will be out any second now and it would not be professional to be seen imbibing. I understand, sure. I envy you, mate. Lord Colson will be here for hours. He will make me stand out here and shiver for half the day and never give me a thought. That's why I sometimes help myself to a tipple. But never the best stuff, as I said! I know my place! Only the brandy from the study, and it's not a problem because Lord Colson isn't very attentive. He's too busy losing his father's money gambling. You know how it is with the"—here, she paused to look around and then lowered her voice—"Coal Son. If he were the clever one, he would wonder where all his brandy is going. But I say it's what he deserves for keeping me out here in the rain and the cold for hours. My toes have started to go numb! I don't know how you do it, mate."

Although his demeanor remained taught, Brownell's

groom admitted that he might be a bit chilled. "The wind is biting."

"Oh, go on, have a sip," Verity urged softly. "Nobody needs to know."

A gust swept through the elegant lane and, wincing, the groom tightened his shoulders before accepting the flask. He took a deep gulp and immediately coughed at the drink's shocking sting. Sputtering, he said, "*That* is Lord Colson's best?"

"Second best," she reminded him. "But you know how it is with men like him, gamblers who live close to the ground. He is always trying to shake coins loose from his father's pockets. Humiliating for a grown man, I say, but Quality are different. You know nothing about that 'cause you work for a good one. Your bloke won't keep you out in the rain all day, will he?"

The groom raised the flask to his lips again and swallowed the brandy smoothly this time, then he admitted he had some idea what it was like. "I'm stuck here all day too, and if I were to seek shelter inside the carriage, I would be turned off without a notice. It happened just last month to his tiger. And his nibs isn't so comfortably set that he doesn't worry constantly about being cut out of his father's will."

Well, now, Verity thought, wasn't that a riveting tidbit?

Coolly, so that she did not overplay her hand, she said, "Quality are the same all over. The Coal Son worries about that too. It seems like every other month, the marquess threatens to cut him out unless he reins in his gambling and drinking and wenching. He usually falls in line for about a week or two and then he's back at the Red Lantern betting everything he has on the turn of a card. But your employer married well, did he? He has his wife's money too."

With a dismissive scoff, he took another sip. "Enough is never enough, is it, for some people. And his father is a mean one. He likes watching his son twist in the wind, which his nibs puts up with because he wants the money. He pesters the lawyer constantly for information, but he is closemouthed. Won't tell him a thing!"

"The marquess's solicitor too," Verity replied with a hint of excitement. "McNeill over in Tuck's Court? Tall man with curly brown hair and a dimple in his chin? Always looks like he's about to yell at you for dragging mud into the parlor?"

"Hamilton Fisk, at Lincoln's Inn," the groom replied. "Barely five feet tall with ginger hair. But with the stern look. He does not like it when his nibs comes to call."

"Quality," Verity said again, shaking her head with an air of confoundment, as though she would never understand the behavior of her betters even if she lived to be a hundred. Then she shivered as though unbearably cold and announced she was going to take a turn around the block to warm up. "See if I can get the feeling to return to my toes. Tell you what, mate, why don't you keep the flask. I can always get another—the Coal Son will never notice."

Although his eyes lit up at the offer, he demurred, insisting that she had already been generous enough. But it was he who had been generous, supplying her with vital information, which was several times more valuable than a few gulps of inferior brandy, and Verity waved off his concern with a flick of her hand as she strode away. Having promised Delphine that she would do nothing to endanger herself further, she believed abandoning her surveillance of Brownell in favor of investigating his father's lawyer fell within the confines of their agreement. If anyone had cause to complain about her behavior that morning, it was Hardwicke, whose good name had been abused in the pursuit of evidence. She had revealed nothing truly shocking, drawing on many of the tropes Twaddle had used in his various accounts of the wastrel second son's antics, and she did not think any lasting harm had been done.

Indeed, it was to the good, for they did not want Hardwicke's reputation to be rehabilitated too much, lest it make him a target again for rabid Bonapartists.

Pulling her coat more tightly around her shoulders, Verity made a right onto Piccadilly and raised her arm to hail a hackney.

She could not wait to get out of the rain.

※

Thursday, June 25
2:44 p.m.

Hamilton Fisk's clerk towered over him.

Although the solicitor exceeded the groom's assessment by several inches, he still appeared quite diminutive in comparison to Mr. Smeaton, who easily topped six feet, and Verity assumed he wore vibrant colors in a bid to add to his consequence. The bright blue of his waistcoat, adorned with pink florets and offset by green pantaloons, stood in marked contrast with his assistant's dour attire, signaling his significance.

Whatever his height, he would not hide his light under a bushel.

At the moment, however, his cool command of his profession was undermined by an air of panic as he pawed through the contents of his leather bag. "The codicil!" he cried, his expression harried as he raised his eyes. "Quick, Smeaton, get the codicil!"

Leaping to his feet as though scorched by fire, the clerk dashed across the threshold into Fisk's office to fetch the document.

"No, no, the table by the window!" Fisk called out crossly.

"It is on the table by the window, where all the wills are kept. You *know* that!"

"Sorry, sorry, I know!" Smeaton said in a plaintive whine as he returned with the paper in hand. He stuffed it into the case. "I just got confused for a second."

The lawyer replied with a grunt as he pressed a black hat onto his head. "Right, that is everything! If the traffic behaves, I should be able to make it to Bedford Square just in time. I do hope I do. I would hate to offend Lord Kidlington with my tardiness. I knew I should never have scheduled an appointment with Toynbee immediately before. They always run long!"

Confidently, the clerk assured his employer that he would arrive to his meeting in plenty of time. "The rain is letting up. But do not forget your umbrella, sir."

Grateful for the reminder, Fisk grabbed the implement from where it rested in the corner beside the door and clutched it tightly in his left hand. "Very well, then, I am off!"

The moment the lawyer darted from the room into the corridor, Smeaton's sunny smile crumbled into an anxious moue, and he tugged on his watch fob to consult the time.

Oh, dear, the clerk did not believe Fisk would make it.

Nor did Verity.

Perhaps if the weather were less soggy.

Consolingly, she said, "You did everything humanly possible to move Toynbee and his daughter along."

Smeaton, startling at the sound of her voice, turned his head sharply to the right, where she was standing next to an office door across the hall, a wet coat balled awkwardly in her grasp. "Excuse me?"

Verity sauntered toward him as she explained that she had watched his interaction with the clients. "You pointed out the time on three separate occasions, but they were determined to linger. And that was after they had arrived ten minutes late themselves."

His brow furrowed at this presumption, and he asked, "Who are you?"

"Robby McNeill," she said, tilting her head toward the other side of the hallway. "I have an appointment with my solicitor. Well, *had* an appointment. It was supposed to be at one-thirty, but I am still waiting."

Smeaton regarded her with amazement. "Mr. Danson is away for the week. He had to address an urgent family matter. It's all there, in the note on the door. Can't you read?"

Verity hung her head in shame and mumbled, "No, I can't read."

"Oh, I see, well, yes, then the good news is you don't have to wait anymore. Mr. Danson isn't coming," he replied cheerfully, then grimaced as he realized he sounded unduly merry. "Thank you, Mr. McNeill, for your observation. I did make several attempts to encourage his lordship to leave after the conclusion of his business, but he loves to chatter. He is a great gossip. And Mr. Fisk has too much respect for his client to interrupt. It often falls to me to remind him of his schedule, but there is only so much I can do."

"The daughter is lovely," Verity said coolly, then watched as a blush crept up the clerk's cheeks. From her perch in the hallway, she had noticed how flustered he grew every time Lady Blanche fluttered her long lashes in his general direction and had begun to concoct a scheme to exploit his vulnerability.

Naturally, she would need to change first.

Mr. McNeill could not hope to induce Smeaton to indiscretion by flirting.

But after she heard where Fisk kept the wills, her plans underwent a slight revision and she considered how to gain access to the table by the window so she could see how the

Earl of Frimgallow had decided to divide up his worldly goods. She could wait until after the office closed and then sneak in, but that was still hours yet and the opportunity seemed ripe now. She just had to lure Smeaton away.

Her options for doing that were limited.

Fisk had been gone too long to create a crisis involving another forgotten document, and Toynbee and his daughter had left nothing behind.

The threat of vermin was always effective, she thought, picturing Dudley Tiffin's austere uniform and daunting equipment. Even the most impervious porter began to twitch when he described flesh-eating parasites with long Latin-sounding names.

But donning the disguise of the official bug destroyer to his majesty and the royal family required her to return all the way to Bethel Street to change clothes, which would take at least two hours, perhaps three in the rain.

No, she wanted to strike now.

Smeaton, responding to her observation regarding the young lady, replied that Lady Blanche's disposition was as lovely as her appearance. "Not that I would presume to discuss either with a stranger! I am sorry about your misunderstanding with Mr. Danson. Now I must bid you good day. I have work to do."

"Yes, of course," Verity murmured graciously, then apologized for the thoughtless interruption. She had seen for herself just how busy he was!

The clerk smiled at her absently, then firmly shut the door. He clearly did not appreciate being observed without his realizing.

As she took the stairs to the ground floor, she continued to turn the challenge over in her mind. There had to be some way to convince Smeaton to leave his office for a few minutes that did not involve a change of clothes.

And he did not even need to leave the office.

If she could create enough chaos, then he could remain.

Ah, yes, as though pandemonium were a simple thing to conjure, she thought as she stepped outside into the rain, which had lessened to a drizzle. The wind immediately cut through the wet clothes to her skin, and as she unfurled her coat to shrug into it, a small animal darted across her path.

It was a squirrel.

※

Thursday, June 25
3:09 p.m.

Despite Delphine's longstanding crusade against the tyrannical squirrels who invaded the garden at twenty-six Bethel Street, Verity had never tried to catch one before and was delighted to discover it required only three plucky children, two burlap sacks, and a handful of seeds. Although capturing the wily little creature took longer than she had anticipated and resulted in several mud stains on both her clothes and her person, she was satisfied with the outcome.

The squirrel had some objections, as it did not appreciate being held in the folds of her thick wool coat, and squirmed fiercely.

Sympathetic to its plight, she cooed at it softly as she strode down the corridor, promising that it would be just one more minute. "Just hold on a little longer," she added softly as she arrived at Fisk's office. Redoubling her grip on the writhing animal cradled in her right arm, she knocked briskly on the door before opening it. Then she stepped inside the clerk's vestibule and promptly closed the door behind her.

Allowing the surprised clerk no opportunity to protest, she began to speak immediately, apologizing for the interruption. "It is just that I should have asked before I left if the note on Mr. Danson's door said anything about when he would return."

Smeaton stared at her aghast, and she wondered what appalled him more: her disheveled appearance or bold presumption. Rising from his table, he replied that the note gave no specifics, and he reached for the door to sweep her out again. "I would advise you to call again in a week."

Verity lurched to the right to block his access to the handle and then let out a violent screech. "Oh, my lord. What is *that*?" she asked in shrill horror, her hand darting upward to point at Fisk's office and the clerk's eyes followed the direction of their finger, seemingly of their own volition. As soon as he turned away, she loosened her grip on the coat, and the squirrel dropped out, landing on its back for barely a second before flipping over and running toward the daylight entering through the windows in the other room.

Even as Smeaton turned to glare at her with astonishment, he caught sight of the movement out of the corner of his eye and howled in distress.

"Goodness, it is huge!" Verity exclaimed.

In fact, it was not.

If anything, the squirrel was on the small size, perhaps a juvenile, which might explain why it had been so easy to catch, but the clerk agreed with her assessment, jumping onto the table with a fearful cry. "Is it a rat? Please don't tell me it is a rat. My grandfather used to lock me in the cellar with the rats as a toddler whenever I ruined my sheets, and I can still remember what they felt like crawling up my leg."

Verity had not expected to inflict undo trauma on Mr. Smeaton.

Unsettle him, fluster him, perhaps encourage him to run out of the room to find a broom for proper pest removal—certainly, yes.

But she had not intended for him to relive the waking nightmares of his childhood, and when she leaped in front of him, pledging to protect him from the critter, she meant it. Valiantly, she instructed him to stay where he was. "I shall dispose of it!"

Smeaton whimpered in reply.

Before the squirrel could dart out again, Verity ran into the other room and slammed the door behind her. At the crack, the rodent scurried under the desk. "I see him," she called out reassuringly as she ran to the table with a high stack of papers and began looking through the wills: Addleton, Aspenlea, Beryl.

They were alphabetized!

Excellent, she thought, zipping through more letters: C, D, E.

Frimgallow was after Farber.

"This won't take a minute. I've almost got it!" she yelled as she pulled the document from the pile. Then she stamped her feet three times and let out a frustrated grunt. "Damn it! He is a cunning beast!"

Verity's eyes flew across the page, noting not so much the distribution of his lordship's property as the dozens of comments in the margins, a seemingly endless set of amendments recorded in the solicitor's steady hand. Judging by the dates that accompanied each instruction, the earl changed his mind about the estate's dispersal on a fortnightly basis, and although she knew the version she held had too many names crossed out to stand as official, the document provided useful insight into how the family functioned as a unit—which was to say, it did not function as a unit at all.

Among the Brownell clan, it was every man for himself.

Worried that she had been silent for too long, Verity grabbed a brass candleholder and threw it onto the floor, where it clattered loudly.

"Everything all right?" Smeaton called out anxiously. "What is happening?"

"It is hiding under the desk," she said as she returned the pages of the will to their proper order. "I can almost reach it. If I just stretch ... a ... little ... more."

As she broke up the sentence to make it sound as though she was straining, she slipped the document back into the stack, then looked around the room for the squirrel.

She had no idea where it was.

Crouching on her hands and knees, she looked under all the furniture—desk, table, bookshelves—and spotting it under the cabinet, she said, "Oh, it is not a rat. It's a squirrel!"

At once, the door opened and the clerk marched across the threshold with an air of determination. "A squirrel! That is madness. How did a squirrel get into our office?"

Owning herself as bewildered as he, Verity asked him to fetch some books from the shelves so they could trap it under the cabinet.

Ten minutes later, Smeaton deposited the miscreant outside.

Chapter Nine

Thursday, June 25
6:19 p.m.

Before entering the Queen's Nook, Verity tugged the sleeves of her silk gown down another half inch, inspected her décolletage, and made eye contact with the burly fruit seller to whom she had paid one shilling. When he nodded in confirmation, she inhaled sharply several times in rapid succession to make herself sound vaguely out of breath and entered the tavern with a hesitant step and a cautious look behind her. Then she scurried across the room in a dozen anxious strides and sat down next to Hamilton Fisk's clerk.

All Mr. Smeaton wanted was a quiet pint of ale to enjoy after a trying day in the office and now Verity Lark was there tormenting him again.

She ordered him to laugh.

Her voice low and seductive, as if airing a secret she wanted only him to hear, she added, "Laugh uproariously as though I have just said something extremely funny."

Smeaton complied.

Too startled to do anything else, he giggled with self-conscious confusion, his cheeks turning bright red as he tilted his eyes down to look at the table and unexpectedly encountered her bosom.

"Very good," she said approvingly. "Now glare at the door."

His eyes flew to her. "What?"

"No, not at me," she chided gently as she widened her smile and looked at him adoringly. "At the door. At the man there, you see him, in the white apron with the streak of dirt? Glare at *him*. Imagine he has come this close to knocking you down with his carriage and you cannot believe he is allowed to drive a team with his inferior skills. Glare at him like that!"

Smeaton tried.

He narrowed his eyes and puckered his lips, which made him seem more like a petulant child than a furious man.

Nevertheless, it worked.

The fruit seller's own expression turned pugnacious for a moment—believably so, she noted, impressed by the ability of the random stranger she had hired to play the part—before he turned and left.

"You wonderful man!" she said on a squeal of delight. "You have no idea the service you have done me. That horrible brute followed me here all the way from Covent Garden."

As the flush in his face deepened to bright purple, Smeaton insisted he had done nothing. "I was just sitting here."

But Verity would not permit a display of modesty. "Your ferocious glower scared him off! And I am so grateful. You must allow me to hail you as my hero. And thank you as such. Please, let me reward you," she said, sweeping her eyes around the room until she spotted a barmaid, whom she summoned with a wave. After she ordered two pints of ale, she turned to the clerk and promised to leave him in peace shortly. She just wanted to wait a little while to make sure the brute was not hovering outside. "I hope you can stand my company for fifteen minutes."

"I *can* stand it for fifteen minutes," Smeaton replied eagerly, then immediately added that a quarter of an hour was the bare minimum. "Please do not feel as though you have to run off on my account. The longer you stay, the safer you will be."

She fluttered her lashes in her best imitation of Lady Blanche. Toynbee's daughter was younger than her by fourteen years, but Verity's gown was lower cut and she regarded him with an air of adoration, both of which were enough to overcome the disadvantage of age. "I had a good feeling about you. The moment I saw you, I thought, There is a decent man who will help me."

Smeaton, his chest seeming to swell with pride, reiterated that he had done nothing remarkable. "Any other man in the tavern would have gladly helped a damsel in distress. It is our nature to be chivalrous."

But his demurral lacked conviction and his eyes swept the room, narrowing with calculation, as though he was trying to decide which patrons would have risen to the challenge and which ones would have left her to her fate.

The barmaid delivered their ale, and Verity raised her glass in salute to his bravery, insisting that he must do something very courageous in his employment. "Are you a Runner or a soldier?"

His frame, already slim, seemed to shrink at her outsize expectations, and when he replied, his tone was almost apologetic. "I am a clerk in a solicitor's office."

"The legal profession!" she gushed appreciatively. "I knew it was something noble."

Smeaton blushed again and said copying contracts and

scheduling meetings for his employer did not quality as noble. "But it is important work," he added defensively.

Ardently, she agreed. "Lawyers are essential to a civil society. Without them, we would be at each other's throats. I sincerely believe that. Inheritances, for example. If we did not have a way to ensure the orderly passage of property from one general to the next, England would be chaos. My father had only a few possessions of any significant value, and my siblings and I fought over them viciously. It almost descended into open warfare, which was what my father wanted. He believed setting us against each other would make us stronger, so he changed his will constantly. One day I was to inherit his mother's acrostic ring and the next it was to go to my eldest sister. But that is a rare case. Gentlemen of wealth and standing are more elegant than my father. They would never be so ill bred as to change their will every month."

Smiling enigmatically, he said, "I would advise you not to be so certain of that."

Verity gasped and clutched his forearm, which rested on the table. "Do tell!"

He flinched at the contact but otherwise remained still. "I cannot say anything. A client's privacy is sacred."

"Of course it is," she said with a reassuring squeeze of her fingers as she slid her chair an inch closer to his and lowered her voice. "You are a man of honor and would never break a confidence. But you can tell me a few interesting details without revealing anything sensitive, can't you? It is not as though I would have any idea who you meant if you said Gentleman A or Lady B. I do not know the names of your clients. I do not even know *your* name!"

Poor Mr. Smeaton!

He was so uncertain how to proceed.

Obviously, he could not say a single word about a client.

To even consider it was a gross dereliction.

And yet how would it harm anything if he offered a few tempting morsels?

All he had to do was withhold identifying characteristics, which would be child's play for a man of his intellect and experience.

To push him toward the decision she required, Verity started suddenly, released his arm, covered her face with both hands, and owned herself mortified by her behavior. "I have overstepped! You heroically come to my rescue, and I repay you by pressing you into an indiscretion. I am horrible. My only excuse is I am still rattled by my earlier encounter with the brute. But that is not your problem. Here, let me finish my drink and remove myself from your presence," she said, grabbing the glass and taking a deep gulp. Then she lowered it and assessed her progress. "Almost halfway there!"

"No, no, please," Smeaton said, reaching out his hand as if to clutch her wrist, then letting it drop to the table. "You are going to choke if you drink too quickly, and you have done nothing wrong."

But Verity shook her head and said she had displayed a vulgar amount of interest.

The clerk insisted it was his fault for provoking her with an intriguing tidbit. "And if you will draw closer again, I shall tell you a little something about it."

"Are you certain?" she asked, holding herself stiffly as she stared down at her fingers, too embarrassed to look him in the eye. "I really should allow you to enjoy your drink in solitude. You have already been so kind to me."

Earnestly, he asked her to stay. "I appreciate the company."

Verity smiled hesitantly and agreed.

Thursday, June 25
7:56 p.m.

Having consented to discuss the private affairs of his firm's clients, Smeaton could not bring himself to actually broach the topic, at least not right away. First he needed to explain to her what it was like to work under the direction of Mr. Hamilton Fisk, a fastidious man with very precise notions about how things should be done.

Bottles of ink must be filled three quarters of the way to the top.

Quills must be lined up in descending order of sharpness.

Edges of folded cards must be neat and crisp.

"He is relentless about details and is so easily riled when his expectations are not met fast enough," he said morosely, swallowing the last sip of his ale, then returning the glass to the table with a resounding thump. "I would not object so stridently to his particularity if he held himself to the same standard. But he is free and easy in his ways. Do you know what he does with the tea?"

"He spills it," Verity replied as she drew the attention of the barmaid and indicated she should bring them more drinks. After three pints, Smeaton was already rather tipsy.

"That is right!" the clerk exclaimed. "He spills it. Every time I bring him a cup of tea at his desk, he spills it on the documents. There I am, lining up quills and sharpening edges, and he is splashing tea all over the wills and contracts. Do you know how that is?"

Indeed, she did, for Smeaton had made the very complaint four times before.

At first she had assumed his tirade against Fisk was a delaying tactic to forestall the moment when he would have to deliver on his agreement to reveal confidential information. Obviously, he had regretted his rash promise the moment he had made it and sought to distract her with the tedious minutia of his job, a supposition seemingly confirmed by the fact that he had repeated the litany several times.

But with each retelling he added more particulars, some of them poignant, and as he described how his fingers ached from copying documents late into the night, she had realized he was venting his spleen to the first person to show interest in his work in a long time or perhaps ever. His family lived in Plymouth, and it had been many years since he had seen them. He had hoped to visit for a month last July, but Fisk could not spare him.

"It is unfair," she replied now to his query.

"It is bloody unfair!" he sneered, gratefully accepting the fresh pint of ale when it was delivered to the table. He took several eager gulps, then belched loudly and without any self-consciousness, the latest indication that he was already several sheets to the wind. "If Fisk is allowed to make mistakes, then I deserved the same opportunity. Instead, I get reprimanded for the slightest infraction. If I splattered tea all over one of Frimgallow's half dozen codicils, so that half the words are illegible, I would lose my pay for a week. But when Fisk does it, all that happens is I have to copy the page again. Oh, right, that reminds me. I said I would tell you a little something about Frim—"

Abruptly, he shut his mouth, then looked around as though to make sure nobody had seen how closely he had come to making a huge faux pas.

More softly, he said, "Let us call him Lord Firm Grip. That way nobody will be the wiser, and I will keep all identifying details out of the story. You will never know that Lord Firm Grip has three grown sons. When I say 'his children,' you will wonder how many they are and whether they are boys or girls, but please do not ask. You are a lovely woman, Miss Farnaby, and I should hate to refuse you anything. But I cannot tell you that Lord Firm Grip has three sons and that they are all boys."

Solemnly, Verity pledged to abide by his conditions.

Smeaton smiled brightly at her ready acquiescence and murmured, "Good girl." Then he wondered what his point was in introducing Lord Firm Grip to the conversation. "Oh, yes, aged men and their capricious manipulations to hold on to power. Lord Firm Grip is Machiavellian in his schemes, and he has kept his three sons at each other's throats for a decade now. Well, his two sons, for the third had to run off to the Continent following a scandal—I cannot say anything more so do not ask!—and has been disowned. But Lord Firm Grip plays the remaining two against each other like they are horses at Ascot, and of late has begun to threaten to leave his entire estate to his daughter. Lord Firm Grip does not have a daughter, you understand, and I must admit that I am not sure if he invented one to further torment his sons in a new way or if he has begun to lose his grip on reality. I suspect it is the latter because he is quite old now. I asked Mr. Fisk if it was legal to put a fictional child in a will, and he said it depends on what she is inheriting. I think he was teasing me, but before I could ask, he tipped over a steaming hot cup of tea and gave me a ferocious burn," he said, holding up his left hand and wiggling his pinkie. "You can see it is still red."

In the dim light of the Queen's Nook, Verity saw only darkness and shadow as he fluttered his finger, but she acknowledged the injury with a nod to encourage him to keep talking. Distracted by the notion that had occurred to her at the mention of Frimgallow's claim to having a daughter, she was nevertheless paying close attention, and even before the clerk added, "So you see, your father is not especially remarkable in the cruelty of his tactic," she had already thought: My father.

A LARK'S RELEASE

Thursday, June 25
8:22 p.m.

Verity could not in all good conscience allow Mr. Smeaton to find his own way home. Jug-bitten, he could barely locate the entrance to the tavern, let alone Villiers Lane, and as she was directly responsible for his condition, abandoning him to his fate seemed unduly callous.

Fortunately, he was able to hold himself upright.

His gait was unsteady and holding to a straight line was beyond whatever meager resources he had left, but he required no assistance to stand. Staying on the pavement and not stepping in front of a carriage—well, that was a different matter. If left to his own devices, he would immediately veer into traffic.

Still, guiding him four blocks was far easier than lugging his weight.

Smeaton made an effort to protest.

A man of strong moral fiber, he could not sully Miss Farnaby's fine character by allowing her to be seen publicly in the clutches of a man who was neither her husband nor her intended. That was the behavior of a cad!

As a remedy, he proposed marriage.

His salary was enough to cover the expense of a wife—as long as she was not too fancy in her notions—but children presented a problem, as Fisk did not compensate him enough to support a family and he had only the two rooms. It would be so cramped and where would all the baby things go? Certainly not in the hearth. They would need that for heat and to make tea.

Gently, she declined the offer, and although he professed deep disappointment at her refusal, he forgot it a minute later, when he stumbled over a crack in the pavement and fell, landing on his wounded pinkie. He yelped in pain and started to cry.

Verity heaved him to his feet and led him to his boardinghouse, where she knocked firmly on the door and slipped away as it was opening to evade the proprietor's interest. Returning to the main road, she summoned a hack, instructed the driver to take her to Bethel Street, and boarded the conveyance. Once she was settled, she turned her thoughts to the revelations regarding her father.

No, she corrected herself: her suspected father.

The only thing she knew for certain was that Andrew Brownell believed she was a threat to his inheritance. Whether he had reached that conclusion based on a statement his father explicitly made or via a misunderstanding was yet to be determined. In either event, her name had been mentioned in connection to the Earl of Frimgallow's estate.

It was a remarkable development because Verity Lark barely existed.

She was, at most, an appendage of her brother, for whom she provided a comfortable home with a minimum of fuss. Shy, dull, and clumsy, she did not bother the neighbors or beggar the shopkeepers. She was a polite nonentity, softspoken and self-effacing, and nobody who interacted with her on a regular basis could describe a single striking thing about her, not even the butcher, whom she visited with increasing frequency in hopes of understanding the smuggling ring he oversaw from the backroom of his shop.

Having made herself all but invisible, she could not believe she had caught Frimgallow's eye. Even among the rarefied company of the *ton,* whose pleasures were often esoteric, he had a reputation for depravity, and if he knew of Verity Lark, then it was because he had a very specific reason to know of Verity Lark.

Obviously, that reason was her mother.

Was he one of her lovers?

He met the criteria in that he was rich and titled.

And his age—it aligned with La Reina's heyday.

Without knowing precisely how old he was, she calculated he was probably around forty when she was born thirty-five years ago.

In that case, he *could* be her father.

The fact that he was an infamous scoundrel lent further credence to the speculation, as it conformed with the Dowager Duchess of Kesgrave's statement implying that Verity's father was as irredeemable as her mother.

Allowing it was possible, Verity contemplated what accepting Frimgallow as her father gained her in understanding the current predicament.

For one thing, it provided a motive.

Killing her preserved Andrew Brownell's inheritance.

Oh, but surely that notion was too ridiculous to take seriously. There was no way a man of the baron's education and breeding could actually believe his father would leave the family's vast holdings to his former mistress's bastard. No man, no matter how disgusted he was by his own rightful heirs, would make such an outré decision. Even legitimate daughters were deemed unworthy of inheritance. Money, lands, and titles passed through the male line, and entails were created to ensure women did not disrupt the system.

Brownell knew that.

His father was a rakehell, not a reformer.

In order to think otherwise, the baron would have to be an utter lackwit, which was not impossible, as a daunting number of nobles were soft in the head.

To that point, nothing about the murder scheme indicated a great mind at work.

Anyone with a bit of sense would have realized that

sending a tin of cyanide-laced biscuits risked failing to achieve its goal by killing the wrong person. Presumably, no servant among his staff would dare open a box addressed to him, let alone sample its contents, and his inability to wonder if her household functioned differently from his own spoke to the limitation of his imagination—a limitation that allowed him to believe his father would leave his entire fortune to an unwanted by-blow.

Verity was not entirely persuaded by the theory, which depended too much on Brownell's stupidity. The practice of primogeniture was deeply ingrained in the aristocracy, dating well back to the Middle Ages. It was the backbone of the nobility. Brownell would not resort to murder without sufficient provocation.

Something else had to be in play.

The challenge, of course, was finding out what, and as the carriage rolled to a stop in front of number twenty-six, she considered the various disguises she could adopt to draw closer to Brownell and possibly interrogate him.

As she had promised to keep her distance from the man who murdered Mr. Muir, she would have to gain Delphine's permission before proceeding with a more direct plan. Once her friend knew who Baron Brownell actually was, she would agree a new stratagem was in order, and if she continued to resist, then Freddie would help convince her.

Freddie! Verity thought suddenly, annoyed that it had not occurred to her to stop at his residence on the way home. She could have no conversation about her father that did not include Freddie. Like Delphine, he had long been fascinated by the great mystery of her sire and could not fathom her indifference to his identity. He was, as far as she was concerned, the provider of necessary organic material—no more, no less—and scoffed at Freddie's argument regarding what he called the information gap.

Did it not worry her not to know everything about herself?

The answer was no.

It did not trouble Verity at all not to know that minor detail of her parentage because she could not think of her father as anything but a faint smudge in the very far background of a vast landscape. Even before the dowager duchess had hinted at the gross deficiency of his character, she had assumed he was of a dastardly bent, as there could be no other explanation for the way he allowed her to languish at Fortescue's. If he had any courage or decency, he would have removed her to a family on one of his estates as was generally the custom for the baseborn daughters of noble men.

She refused to believe he knew nothing of her existence.

The dowager duchess had learned of it easily enough, and Verity assumed there were other members of the beau monde who had briefly followed the fortunes of Mary Price.

So no, her father held no interest for her.

And yet now, it seemed, Freddie's understanding had been the correct one: Mr. Muir was dead because of the gap in her education. If she had bothered to learn the identity of her sire, then she would have known her usefulness to him and taken steps to insulate herself from it.

Sighing, Verity unlatched the door and resolved to send Freddie a note at once. While she waited for him to arrive, she would have a late dinner.

She hoped Delphine would not be too cross with her for returning so late. When she had dashed home to change into Miss Farnaby's favorite gown, she had promised to be back by nine—and she would have had Smeaton not required an escort.

With this thought in mind, she was not at all surprised to find her friend waiting in the hallway when she entered the house. Clearly, she had been watching for her.

It was just like Delphine to fret herself into a lather for no reason.

Before Verity could offer a defense, Delphine hailed her timing as excellent. "We were just about to get started. Are you hungry? Cook made mackerel with fennel and mint. I could have her send up a plate."

Disconcerted by the cheerful reception, Verity foundered for a reply, which immediately became unnecessary when her stomach growled.

Delphine, laughing lightly, said, "I shall take that as a yes. Do go sit in the parlor while I pop downstairs to sort out a meal. There are also rolls and buttered peas."

"That sounds wonderful, thank you," Verity replied, hungrier than she had realized. "And please ask Lucy to deliver a note to Freddie. He will want to hear what I discovered."

Nodding amiably, Delphine stopped abruptly and darted a sharp look at her friend, for there was just enough portentousness in the statement to alert her to trouble. "What have you discovered?"

Verity insisted that they wait for Freddie.

"Freddie is here," Delphine announced. "Hardwicke as well. They are both in the parlor. We were about to convene a round table, so there is no reason to delay. You may tell us all the bad news at once."

Amused, Verity asked her friend why she was so confident the news was bad. "I said *discovered*, which is a neutral term."

"It is always bad news," Delphine replied with dispiriting pessimism as she strode to the parlor door, all thoughts of dinner forgotten.

Verity, her stomach rumbling ravenously, said she would join them in a minute. "I will just fetch that plate of food first."

In fact, she would not. Delphine would summon Lucy after Verity told them the worst. "And not a minute sooner."

Muttering under her breath about tyrants, Verity followed her friend into the parlor, where Hardwicke and Freddie were gathered at the table. Set before them were several editions of the *London Daily Gazette* opened to the middle spread. As Hardwicke rose to greet her, Delphine announced that they could stop scouring Twaddle's old columns for the source of Brownell's antipathy. "Verity has discovered it, and it is something awful."

Smothering an urge to stamp her foot like a small child, which she felt only because she was so famished, Verity replied that she had said nothing of the sort.

Delphine conceded the accuracy of the statement. "But you implied it heavily."

"There was no implication, heavy or otherwise," Verity insisted, lowering to the settee. "All I said was I discovered something that Freddie would find interesting as well."

But sitting felt wrong.

It was too static, she decided, and stood up.

Freddie, deeply unsettled by the sight of his friend rising to her feet, exclaimed, "Good God, Verity, you are fidgeting. What on earth has happened?"

Insulted, she swore she was not fussing. "I am merely too hungry to settle because *someone*"—here, she looked meaningfully at Delphine—"refused to provide sustenance."

But it was no good.

Verity *was* in a fidge.

The evening's revelation had unnerved her, although not in the way Delphine or Freddie would expect. Truly, Verity did not care about her father's identity. He could be the prince regent himself and she would still yawn with ennui.

No, she was disquieted by a deep and profound awareness of her vulnerability.

Verity had constructed her life on the assumption that control was possible. To ensure a positive outcome for herself and her friends, all she had to do was pay close enough attention to the events and people that impacted their lives.

She would not be buffeted by fate.

But Mr. Muir's horrible gurgle sounded the truth: She controlled nothing. With all her schemes and plans and networks of spies, she was still subject to cabbage heads like Brownell. Any pig widgeon anywhere could jump to an outrageous conclusion, and all of a sudden Delphine was a hairsbreadth away from swallowing cyanide of potassium.

Verity had glimpsed it last week.

In trying to understand how she had landed in Newgate, she had imagined a shadowy figure orchestrating a vast conspiracy.

And yet it was only the dowager duchess trying to right a wrong.

What looked on the wall to be a terrible monster was only the shadow of a mouse.

It was actually very funny, Verity thought, as she walked to the bell cord and gave it a tug. Then she tossed herself onto the sofa, rested her head against the back cushion, and said, "The Earl of Frimgallow is my father."

Chapter Ten

❦

Thursday, June 25
9:19 p.m

Delphine gasped.
No, not gasped.
It was more of a convulsion, with her whole body seeming to tighten at once as the air caught in her chest and she pressed a hand against her breast. Her eyes flying open, she turned to Freddie, as if seeking his confirmation.

Alas, he did not provide it.

Instead, he tipped his own gaze downward to studiously examine his fingers, as though an explanation for the confounding news could be found in his grasp.

Only Hardwicke received the information with any semblance of equanimity. Raising a glass of wine to his lips, he murmured, "Of course he is."

His complacency was infuriating.

Naturally, it was!

Verity herself had never considered the connection, and

for him to blithely imply he had known it all along—she would not allow it. Lifting her chin to regard him with a flinty eye, she warned him against a display of omniscience. "If you dare to pretend to have long suspected it, then tomorrow Twaddle shall report that you are training a ladybird to unseat Viscount Ripley's champion. And it shall contain so many details of your rigorous methods for increasing speed and agility that even your mother will not be able to look at you without wincing in embarrassment."

It was a terrible threat, and Hardwicke shuddered accordingly. "You are right but wrong. She would be horrified by my gratuitous abuse of innocent insects and lecture me on the dignity of all living creatures," he said as he sat down next to her. "Fortunately, it shall not come to that because I had no intention of making any such claim. I merely meant that the resemblance is obvious once one knows of the relationship. You have his height as well as some features, such as his eyes and lips. He is also the right age for a liaison with your mother, and abandoning a child conceived out of wedlock is precisely what one would expect of him. Indeed, I am reasonably certain he abandoned the children he conceived *within* it, as it is my understanding that he did not show any interest in his sons until they were sent down from Eton, which they all were in their turn."

Although she did not relish the prospect of sharing any qualities with Frimgallow, Verity knew from experience that the similarities were not significant. If lineage were destiny, she would be as cold and brittle as her mother by now. "Thank you for your restraint. I know how much you enjoy impressing others with your clairvoyance."

With a modest shrug, he said his gift for divination was merely preparation plus observation. "Anyone can do it. They just have to apply themselves."

Despite herself, Verity smiled, amused by the tidy maxim,

which was in no way accurate. Preparation and observation were useless without acuity and intelligence.

A knock sounded on the door, causing Delphine to gasp again.

Gently, Verity reminded her it was Lucy.

"Oh, right, yes, Lucy," Delphine said with a shake of her head as she crossed the floor to arrange for a plate of food to be prepared for her friend. "Silly me, jumping at shadows."

Attending to the minor domestic matter, however, restored her composure, and when she returned to the room only a minute later, she asked Verity to elaborate. "You may start by telling us how you came by the knowledge that Frimgallow is your father—not that I think it is wrong. Like Hardwicke, I can see the resemblance now that it has been pointed out to me. But it is such a remarkable thing to discover after all these years and I cannot fathom what it has to do with Brownell's plot against you. The notion that he wants to eliminate you because he perceives the existence of an illegitimate half sister as a threat is confounding. It is not as though you can inherit any of his—"

And then she did it again: gasped with her whole body.

Agog, she looked at Verity. "*You* are Frimgallow's heir!"

Freddie insisted it was impossible. "Frimgallow would never leave his fortune to his by-blow, but that does not mean that Brownell does not believe it. Somehow he convinced himself that Verity is a threat to his inheritance. It is a wild notion!"

"He believes it because Frimgallow said it," Verity replied. "According to the clerk for the solicitor who oversees his affairs, Frimgallow has threatened on several occasions to leave his fortune and estates to me. Threatening to cut one son or the other out of the will is his modus operandi. He has been doing it for years. The latest version of his will is marked up with all sorts of changes. One notation in the margin says to find an organization that cares for injured soldiers to which to give the Sussex property. As Freddie said, it is utter nonsense. But Brownell is either too gullible or stupid to realize it."

Hardwicke, his brow drawn close, observed that Brownell had been in Hyde Park when he introduced Verity to his brother.

Although this was not a detail Verity recalled, she did not doubt its accuracy.

Its relevance, however, escaped her.

But Delphine perceived it immediately. "Then only a week later your father interceded on Verity's behalf when she was in Newgate. He made a direct appeal to the Lord Mayor of London to meet with you to discuss a trial date, which Frimgallow would have known about if he, like Hardwicke, greased enough palms. Any information can be had for a price."

"And all of a sudden the threats did not seem so implausible after all," Freddie murmured pensively. "While Frimgallow would never cut out his good-for-nothing sons for a harlot's daughter, he would for the Marquess of Ware's daughter-in-law."

"He must think an announcement is imminent," Delphine added.

With a firm shake of his head, Freddie insisted that what the earl did or did not think was beside the point. "It is what Brownell believes that matters, and he believes his father would leave some part, if not all, of his fortune to Verity."

"Of course he does," Delphine affirmed with an airy confidence. "He knows that Lord Frimgallow is a vile reprobate who would delight in knowing that his final act shocked society and beggared his children. He would consider it a brilliant stroke. And then there is the marquess factor!"

Freddie enthusiastically agreed, noting his lordship would

never have dared to look so high for even a legitimate daughter, and Verity, who had not realized that the Marquess of Ware had been dragooned into helping her, felt discomfited to discover her debt to Hardwicke exceeded her own modest calculation. It was one thing for him to exert his influence on her behalf; it was quite another for it to be a family effort.

There was no dressing it up in pretty linens: It was humiliating.

For her introduction to the powerful lord to be as a suspected murderess and prisoner of Newgate—Verity could not fathom a greater mortification.

Even so, she calmly accepted the necessity.

In retrospect, Hardwicke's concern about the date of her trial was unwarranted, but he could not have relied on the Duchess of Kesgrave's finding the real murderer as quickly as she did. Her investigation could have continued for weeks, and Verity's ultimate exoneration would have meant little if her neck had already been stretched by a noose.

Securing the lord mayor's goodwill had been vital, and she was grateful to the Marquess of Ware for his assistance.

Truly, she was, and when she ascertained from Hardwicke the precise amount she owed him for money expended on her behalf, she would ask him to convey her gratitude to his father as well.

Delphine, of course, would have her write a note.

Insisting that the circumstance demanded a personal response, her friend would assert that a graciously composed missive was the only acceptable way to thank the marquess, as though *Mrs. Chrisman's Manual for Etiquette and Civility* had an entire chapter addressing prison decorum.

Verity resolved to raise the subject of her debt to Hardwicke just as soon as they settled on a course of action. She had already left it too long.

Freddie wondered if the others were involved in the

murder plot—they had no proof that the youngest brother, Rufus, was still on the Continent—just as Lucy returned with the tray, and they all waited in silence as the servant set down the plates. After she left, they reconvened around the table, and in between bites of mackerel, Verity proposed the only logical solution: exploit Brownell's fears to goad him into making another attempt.

"According to Delphine, all it would take is an announcement in *The Times*," she continued, pressing her fork into the flaky fish. "It publishes on Saturday, Brownell tries to kill me on Sunday, the Runners cart him away, and on Monday we can return to our forged antiquities investigation."

Delphine said no.

"He is going to make another attempt regardless," Verity pointed out reasonably. "All we can do is control as many elements as possible. I think having him try to kill me on our schedule is the best we can hope for."

"How is it that making yourself the target is your solution to everything?" Delphine asked, drawing her fingers through her hair in frustration. "How can it be that no other ideas ever occur to you?"

Frowning, Verity swore her friend was being decidedly unfair. "Just this morning Cook was complaining about mice in the flour stores and I suggested we put out poison."

Unamused, Delphine looked at Hardwicke and said, "I trust you will make a sensible argument that will convince her her idea is stupid."

But Hardwicke demurred, noting that instigating a quarrel was not the most auspicious way to begin a betrothal.

Delphine responded to his mocking reply with a steely glare.

"Oh, dear, you shall be Lord Colson again if you are not careful," Verity said.

Although she appeared on the verge of snarling at her

friend, Delphine restrained her temper and asked about their efforts to identify the source of the poison.

Soberly, Hardwicke explained that he and his associate had had no luck yet locating the jeweler from whom Brownell purchased the cyanide of potassium. "Castleheart visited a dozen jewelers, workshops, and goldsmiths. After meeting with Grint, I called at all the beau monde's favorites. They all claim not to have sold cyanide to anyone in the past month, and given they were offered a great deal of money in exchange for a name, I do not believe they are lying. Castleheart will widen the search tomorrow. I am confident we will find the jeweler eventually, but I am surprised it is not someone in the immediate vicinity. 'May I buy some highly deadly poison from you?' is not the sort of question one generally feels comfortable asking a stranger."

"Perhaps Brownell did not ask, then," Freddie said. "He might have assigned the task to one of his footmen or stableboys or a groom. Maybe one of them has a connection to a goldsmith or a jeweler, such as a family member or a neighbor."

Hardwicke allowed it was possible. "But the issue of proximity remains. If we date the beginning of Brownell's true anxiety about his father's threats to the day he saw me introducing Verity to my brother in Hyde Park, then we are looking at a period of approximately two weeks. It was the eighth, I believe, so seventeen days ago. But it is unlikely he went home from Hyde Park, concocted a murder scheme, and put it into action. The plan would have to brew for a couple of days. Given the time constraint, I would imagine the seller is either in London or within two days' ride of London. It might take a little while to find the source, but we'll find him. And if Brownell used an emissary, then that is one more conspirator who can testify against him."

Heartened by this optimistic assessment of the situation,

Delphine said amiably, "Ah, there, you see, darling, you not have to incite Brownell to murder you after all."

It was fascinating, Verity thought, how two people could hear the exact same words and extract diametrically opposed meanings. "If we can do nothing but mark time while Castleheart searches for the origin of the poison, then I am a target either way—in which case, it is better that we control the pace of the play rather than sit in our parlor and watch the door for an intruder."

"Verity is right," Hardwicke said with a consoling glance at Delphine. "Everything we know about Brownell, including his motive, gives us the advantage, and we should use it to end the threat as quickly as possible. His first attempt was bold and cruel. He did not care whom else he hurt in his pursuit of his target, and we cannot assume we will be so lucky next time that only one person is killed. He might injure three or four."

Aware that he was making a genuine concession, Verity quietly thanked him. "I know you do not like the idea any more than Delphine and Freddie."

"I am not endorsing your plan," he added with a genial grin. "I am suggesting my own and marshalling my forces for a vigorous debate on the merits."

Now Delphine thanked him. "Inauspicious beginning or not, I knew you would not disappointment me."

"It involves Lady Abercrombie," Hardwicke said.

At the mention of the notoriously feather-brained countess whose current occupations included rearing a lion cub and juggling three younger lovers, Delphine's expression lost some of its sanguinity. "Or perhaps I spoke too soon."

Hardwicke made no attempt to deny it. "Having met her ladyship recently, I can confirm she is exactly what you think she is: flighty, flirtatious, egotistical. But Brownell desires her. He has spent years pursuing her, and I believe he could be persuaded to confess to the murder if he believes it would burnish his reputation with Lady Abercrombie."

Verity laughed.

How could she not?

She had proposed dangling herself in front of an unscrupulous killer to draw him out, and Hardwicke countered with a capricious bit of fluff whose greatest accomplishment was decorating her drawing room in an astounding amount of red silk.

No, but truly astounding.

Mr. Twaddle-Thum devoted three columns to the various shades of rose, rouge, scarlet, vermillion, ruby, and cerise that festooned the room, whose aesthetic could only be described as the Chinese style run amuck.

There was a bamboo canopy hanging over the side table.

And gilded serpents—they were everywhere, coiling around the coved ceiling and lotus-shaped chandeliers.

"You are teasing Delphine, and I think it is unkind," she said tartly. "If you do not apologize for getting her hopes up, then *I* shall start to call you Lord Colson."

"Oh, but I am not teasing," he replied, looking at Delphine to convey his sincerity. "Brownell has been trying for decades to get the countess into bed. He has received no encouragement, as he has gone about it in a particularly inexpert fashion, but the fact is he remains hopeful of success to this day."

Verity regarded this revelation with deep suspicion, as Twaddle had heard nothing of Brownell's interest and her ladyship was not the sort of woman who respected privacy, either her own or anyone else's. She reveled in attention, and her sumptuously appointed drawing room was meant to shock the beau monde with its extravagance.

The lion cub with whom she shared the Grosvenor Square address had been adopted with the same purpose in mind, but where the drawing room was an essentially harmless affectation, coddling a wild beast would soon present difficulties that would not be easily resolved.

Viscount Ripley, at least, had the good sense to limit his eccentricities to harmless insects.

"And how did you come by this information?" Verity asked.

"Lady Abercrombie mentioned it," he replied.

Verity narrowed her eyes doubtfully. "You met her for the first time only recently, and yet the topic of Brownell's repeated seduction attempts somehow just worked itself into the conversation?"

"Correct," he said firmly. "Although I would say the *somehow* of it is the countess's desire to be perceived as slightly disreputable by society. Regardless, she was at Kesgrave House when I called there on the day of your release, and when the topic turned to the Hottenroth scandal, she mentioned Frimgallow's connection to it. He was among the men to whom Hottenroth granted access to what is generally described as his private harem, and Brownell told her about it on the assumption she would be titillated by the information. She called him a lecherous puppy who sees himself as a dangerous rakehell. Despite what you may think of her, her ladyship is a clever woman, and I think she could use what she knows about Brownell to extract an admission of guilt."

Unconvinced, Freddie wrinkled his forehead dubiously and owned himself reluctant to entrust any scheme to the famous scatterbrain. "She would forget herself and prattle about it to one of her lovers or Lady Jersey. I am sure she is a lovely person, though."

"It is a strong argument. I am persuaded," Delphine announced, altering her opinion of the scheme based on

Hardwicke's explanation. "Freddie is just being cattish because he thinks the countess is too free with her favors."

"I think nothing of the sort!" he exclaimed. "As editor of the *London Daily Gazette,* I have read a dozen articles detailing her love of attention, and I cannot believe she would enter into an intrigue without an eye toward how she could turn it a daring escapade she could share with fifty of her closest intimates."

"Cattish *and* insulting to women," Delphine said with a hint of disgust. "Well, *I* think she could do it precisely because she has a reputation for being a peagoose. Brownell will underestimate her. She will coo over his roguish turn and tremble at the newfound air of danger about him, and he will confess everything. And then the Runner will pop out from behind the drapes to arrest him and take him away to Newgate for the murder of Mr. Muir."

Verity, who was far from convinced, said they would have to tuck a magistrate behind the curtain. "The confession would not be ironclad. Brownell will immediately claim he had been lying to impress her ladyship, and it would be harder for him to slither free if the magistrate himself heard the confession. But even then, I do think it is likely he slithers free by claiming he had been lying to impress her ladyship."

"It is a concern," Hardwicke granted. "But his confession alongside the eyewitness account from the confectioner who sold him the chocolate puffs will be sufficient to warrant a trial, giving Castleheart time to find the jeweler or goldsmith who sold him the cyanide of potassium. And *that* will be enough to convict him of Muir's murder."

"Twaddle could write about the arrest, which would allow us to have a measure of control over the story that is bandied about," Freddie suggested. "If he told the *ton* that Brownell killed Mr. Muir because he mistakenly believed the victim was a threat to his inheritance, that is all anyone will discuss. It is a minor fiction and will allow Verity to preserve her anonymity, which is of the utmost importance."

As Delphine reminded him that their friend had been prepared to announce her betrothal to the Marquess of Ware's wastrel son in *The Times* not fifteen minutes before, Verity silently conceded the inaccuracy of Freddie's observation. Her anonymity could not take precedence over justice. The most important thing was making sure Brownell paid for his crime. If in the pursuit of that goal her identity could be obscured, then wonderful—everything would proceed as it was.

If it could not, she would assess and move on.

There was always another scheme.

Hardwicke, raising a glass of wine to his lips as he sought out Delphine's gaze, said, "I trust it goes without saying that I accept."

Verity ignored this particularly provoking aside and turned her attention to Hardwicke's plan, examining it for weak points. How, for example, would Lady Abercrombie know about Muir's murder in the first place or Brownell's part in it? The information was not public, so it did not make sense that the countess would magically know of it.

Freddie, pondering the query, noted that Twaddle could help them out there as well. "He already knows everything by seeming magic, so it would not be strange if he knew about the murder. And he could structure the account as a series of questions about the poisoning itself, things he does not know the answer to but her ladyship does. Her knowledge could rest on an obscure fact that we arrange with her in advance. That could work, could it not?" he asked, darting his eyes around the table.

"Of a certainty," Delphine said with an approving nod. "If

Brownell thinks that he and the countess share an illicit secret, he will not be able to resist confessing all."

"And basking in Lady Abercrombie's approbation," Freddie added, turning to Hardwicke to ask if he really thought the widow would consent to participate. "As I said, I do not think it is something she would take an interest in if she could not preen about it to her coterie of admirers."

It was, Hardwicke conceded, a fair assessment of her character. "And I would not be surprised if she commissioned a play afterward to dramatize the events from her perspective. But I also believe she is a highly intelligent woman who shrewdly calculates the effect of every word she says before she says it. She will agree because she loathes Brownell, appreciates a challenge, and recognizes a wildly entertaining anecdote when she hears it."

Although Verity held pretty much the same opinion of Lady Abercrombie as Freddie, she allowed that Hardwicke's understanding of the woman might be more complete. None of Twaddle's dozen reports on the countess delved beneath the surface.

It had not been necessary.

The gossip's objective was to present the Twaddleship with gaily wrapped absurdities, and her ladyship's romps came adorned with their own vibrant bows.

Whereas she had to rummage through Lord Hartlepool's cupboards to find a way to make him appear ridiculous, such as inventing a horse alter ego who neighed with disapproval at the antics of the younger pony set, Lady Abercrombie's life was laid bare in her drawing room.

Or so Verity thought.

Twaddle had misjudged the narrative of the Coal Son.

Perhaps he made a habit of it.

Disheartened by the prospect, Verity suggested they call on the countess in the morning, and Hardwicke advised her to be ready to leave starting at nine. He would apprise her of the exact time just as soon as he arranged it with her ladyship.

With the most pressing matter settled, she asked what Grint had discovered from the customs service and was unsurprised to hear he had learned little from the official, who insisted in the strongest possible terms that nothing untoward had occurred. An employee of the museum noticed the empty pedestal, reported the figurine as missing to the customs office, and an agent was dispatched to investigate based on the information provided. Satisfied that the paperwork was in order, the under-secretary thanked the fellow government official for his time and left without making any effort to ascertain pertinent details about the individual in question other than his name.

Horrified by the display of ineptitude, Verity cursed in frustration and marveled that they were not all speaking French right now with Grint overseeing the Alien Office during the war. "Good gad, the man had the brazen audacity to call himself John Smith! Is there a greater indication that something devious is afoot than the use of such a bland name? How could he leave without getting a description of Mr. Smith? It is shocking to me that he allowed Sidmouth to sack Kingsley because, with that imbecile gone, Grint's own incompetence is on blatant display."

"It was probably a matter of professional courtesy," Delphine said with a sneer. "He did not want to discomfit the customs agent with questions that might have implied he had been less then exemplary in the performance of his duties. You know how government officials are, so full of respect for each other and contempt for everyone else."

Hardwicke, making no attempt to correct this assumption, surmised that Grint wanted to confirm that there is nobody by the name of John Smith employed by the British

Museum before pressing the issue. "I realize he is showing an undue amount of deference, and I am no more pleased with it than any of you. But the truth of the matter is we have more than enough to contend with, with Brownell's murder plot. The forged antiquities scheme can wait until Monday, as Verity said."

Delphine rolled her eyes at the notion that Grint would be able to attain useful information in only a few days. "Maybe by next Thursday."

"Even better," Hardwicke replied. "That would allow you an opportunity to do some gardening before the next debacle."

"It is true," Verity said, washing down the last bite of mackerel with a generous sip of wine. "Between my imprisonment and Mr. Muir's murder, poor Delphine has had barely ten minutes to scold the squirrels."

Curtly, Delphine announced that the squirrels were going nowhere. "Unlike my beetroot seeds, which the vile beasts have devoured entirely. I wonder if Grint's time would be better spent planting my vegetable plots while I oversee the Home Office?"

Hardwicke, rising to his feet, promised to propose the job exchange at the earliest opportunity. "A little gardening is no doubt precisely what he needs to renew his spirit."

Freddie smiled faintly as he stood as well and bid them goodbye. It was almost eleven, and he still had two articles to edit for the next day's edition. "I trust you will inform me of the countess's answer as soon as you have it."

Verity agreed, and as Hardwicke followed her friend to the door, she asked him if he would mind delaying his departure by a few minutes. It had been five days since her release from Newgate, and she still had not broached the subject of her debt, despite making several attempts.

Ah, but they had been half-hearted attempts that reflected her reluctance to raise the issue.

As Delphine had intimated, Hardwicke would initially resist.

Irritated by what she perceived as a weakness, she added, "There is something I have been meaning to discuss with you."

Naturally, Hardwicke did not mind staying longer, and it was a sign of Delphine's fatigue that she left them alone without issuing her usual warning to return in five minutes.

Her friend, she suspected, would head directly upstairs to her bedchamber.

Once they were alone, Hardwicke pressed a soft kiss against Verity's forehead and ran his fingers through her short curls. "I know you are disappointed not to be throwing yourself into the line of fire, but I share Delphine's concerns. Even though you were prepared for Beaufoy's attack, he moved with so much speed and agility he knocked you to the ground in a matter of seconds. You knew it was coming and still he had the advantage. You were never in danger because even if the dowager had not bashed him over the head with her cane, Grint or I would have interceded, but it's a salutatory reminder that things rarely go according to the way we plan them."

Graciously, Verity granted that the countess's scheme was a worthwhile endeavor. "I am not as confident as you that she will agree to participate, and in an effort to be fair, I do think you and Delphine should admit that your plot is more outlandish than anything I have ever proposed. But those caveats withstanding, it does seem to have a reasonable chance of succeeding. And you are right in regard to Beaufoy: He did come for me with more force than I anticipated, and I have every intention of learning more about the technique he employed, which I believe Grint called jitsu. I will have to ask him for more information about it. However, the subject I wish to discuss is my debt."

Startled, Hardwicke raised an eyebrow inquiringly. "To Grint?"

A ghost of a smile appeared on her lips. "No, to you."

But this reply failed to clarify the matter, and he professed to have no idea what she was talking about. "You do not owe me anything."

"For getting me out of Newgate," she explained.

And still comprehension eluded him. "The Duchess of Kesgrave is the one who got you out of Newgate, and quite handily too, I might add. And if I understand it correctly, you are to repay that debt by teaching her how to shoot a pistol," he said, highly amused by the prospect. "Will you scowl at me some more if I confess that I should like to be a fly on the wall during your lessons?"

Irked by his obtuseness, which she felt certain was deliberate, she peevishly added, "For arranging my removal to the warden's house. That is what I meant by 'out of Newgate.' And for securing a room for me on the state side of the prison before that. And for arranging the services of Mr. Johnston, which I cannot believe came free of charge. And paying bribes to various turnkeys and guards to ensure they treated me less harshly than other prisoners. You paid for all of that, and now I should like to reimburse you for your outlay."

As she ran through her tally, his expression smoothed and confusion was replaced with mild curiosity. "You wish for me to add up all the funds I expended ensuring your safety while you were wrongfully incarcerated in the country's most vile prison and inform you of the total?"

"Yes, down to the last farthing," she said.

Hardwicke regarded her silently for several seconds

before repeating with unnerving quiet, "Down to the last farthing?"

"Correct," she said, aware that he was not entirely pleased by the request but determined to stay the course. "You do not need to round down to the nearest pound on my account."

Calmly, he refused.

Although he did not raise his voice an iota or imbue his tone with even the faintest hint of emotion, the single word felt swathed in anger: no.

His pique was expected, Verity reminded herself as she felt a tremor of alarm at how forcefully he spoke despite the brevity of the response. "I know you spent the money without sparing a thought for the amount and I would hate for you to think I do not appreciate your generosity. I am extremely grateful for it. Although I was making a reasonably good show of it before Mr. Johnston intervened, I would have sustained many more injuries if he had not provided his assistance. But the fact that the money means little to you underscores how important it is that I pay you back for expenses accrued on my behalf."

"No, Verity, I will not present you with a bill for expenses accrued on your behalf," he said easily.

Too easily.

Hardwicke could mask his anger with all the bland insouciance he could muster, but she knew he was offended. He considered being reimbursed by her a personal affront and was prepared to argue about it.

Only he did not want to appear as though he were arguing about it.

His response was hardly surprising.

A man of his ilk—raised in comfort and privilege, wanting for nothing save purpose, which he had eventually found—would inevitably disdain any attempt to reestablish balance. The very notion of a ledger was an insult to him, for he saw the world as a single entity, not a series of narrow columns counting guineas and farthings.

Noblesse oblige demanded it.

Money must be perceived as so valuable as to be essentially worthless.

What? Oh, this old pile of gold coins? Do be a dear, peasant, and cart it away.

Hardwicke had no idea what it was like to live on sufferance.

To be so bloody *grateful* for everything you managed to scrape together.

Hoping to avoid a quarrel, she tried presenting the problem in terms he would understand. "It is a debt of honor."

If anything, this new positioning seemed to amuse him. "A debt of honor?"

Encouraged, she nodded. "As if I had lost a wager at Brooks or a hand of cards."

"A civilized wager among gentlemen," he added affably.

"Precisely, yes, a debt of honor. It would be churlish of you not to allow me to discharge it in a timely manner," she said.

His demeanor did not darken.

Indeed, it grew lighter, and yet she could feel his irritation in the smooth curve of his lips and was not surprised when he reiterated his refusal. "If that is all, I should probably be on my way before Delphine returns with a plateful of biscuits. I do not have an appetite for that at the moment. I shall send a message in the morning as soon as I hear from the countess. Good night, Verity."

And then he kissed her on the forehead again.

As though they had peacefully resolved a disagreement.

Or had had no disagreement at all.

The arrogant superiority of his attitude infuriated her.

How dare he treat her concerns as though they were inconsequential!

She knew a turnkey's compliance did not come cheaply. It had cost her fifteen shillings just to find out that Francis Altick was not being kept at Newgate.

Hardwicke must have spent a hundred times that to ensure her welfare.

And that was only in regard to material expenditures.

He had pressed his father into service as well.

The Marquess of Ware begging a favor of the Lord Mayor of London in aid of the murderous by-blow of the England's most grasping courtesan.

Overwhelmed by how much she owed him, Verity felt her restraint snap and a wave of hot rage swept through her. He would leave as smugly confident as he arrived.

The thought choked her.

Ah, but she had not spent seventeen years under the heel of the Wraithe and learned nothing about self-control.

Consequently, her tone was cool if a little snide as she apologized for not fully comprehending the limitations of his situation. "Obviously, a man in your position cannot know what it is like to bear the burden of charity, as you have never felt its weight on your shoulders. I should not have expected you to understand. As discussed, I will be ready to leave at nine. Good night, my lord."

The honorific was a little too much.

She had rarely addressed him by his title, not even upon their contentious first acquaintance, treating him instead as an equal. Employing it now, she sought to affirm his inferiority by paying feudal reverence to his superiority.

The arrow hit its mark.

Recognizing the significance, Hardwicke stared at her blankly for several long moments, the clock by the door loudly ticking away the seconds, before he said, "You think this is about charity."

How superciliously he said it—*charity*, as though describing a minor irritant with which he had to contend, such as a tailcoat that was too tight in the shoulders.

Holding herself stiffly, she confirmed, "Yes."

"Very well," he said. "I will compile a list. Good night."

Verity thanked him, and as he left the room, she wondered why it felt as though she had lost the argument when she had very clearly won.

Chapter Eleven

Friday, June 26
8:54 a.m.

By the time Verity sat down to eat breakfast with Delphine, she had already put in several hours of work, for a good night's sleep continued to elude her. Waking at four-thirty from another unsettling dream, she had availed herself of the chamber pot and found falling back asleep impossible with her argument with Hardwicke rattling around in her head. Accepting the futility, she had climbed out of bed, slipped into her dressing gown and padded downstairs to the study to get an early start. While she was evading a murder attempt and discovering the identity of her father, Twaddle's network had managed to locate the physician who oversaw the care of the boy harmed in Charles Wigsworth's experiments and gather information about the former supervisor's current activities, which seemed to consist almost exclusively of conducting experiments in the attics of his home and courting the good opinion of members of the Royal Society.

The latter pleased her, for it meant he valued his credibility and losing it would hurt him gravely.

Also among the assortment of notes were a half dozen messages describing the recent movements of many of Twaddle's favorites, including the Leaky Fawcett and Her Outrageousness. Although her spies were too clever not to have noticed the precipitous decrease in articles mentioning the Duchess of Kesgrave, they continued to provide detailed accounts of her exploits. Presumably, the dispatches would abate over time.

After establishing the next steps in the Wigsworth investigation, she pulled out the story she had started on prison reform and finished the first draft. Then she made a note to find out how Mrs. Fawcett was dealing with Lady Bentham's openly derisive countdown clock. The Leaky Fawcett would never allow herself to become a figure of fun without attempting to mount a reprisal.

Satisfied with the morning's work, she returned everything to its proper place, straightened the items on the desk, and dashed upstairs to dress for the visit to Lady Abercrombie's home. After going back and forth on the matter in her head, she decided the only way to introduce herself to the countess was as Verity Lark. If she was going to ask the woman to pander seductively to Andrew Brownell for an unspecified amount of time, then she would do it as honestly as possible.

Even so, she took pains with her appearance, tightening her curls and donning a pretty yellow gown. Lady Abercrombie's preference for lovely things was well known, and there was no harm in making an appeal to her senses.

Delphine hailed her efforts as Verity entered the parlor. "I have not seen that dress in a while. It is so flattering. You look as fresh as a daisy."

Verity acknowledged the compliment with a tilt of the head. "That is the plan."

"Have you received word from Hardwicke yet?" Delphine asked as she poured tea, filling her own cup first before moving onto her friend's.

"I have not, no," Verity replied.

Sighing heftily, Delphine returned the teapot to the table and asked what was wrong.

"Nothing at all," Verity replied as she slid the plum cake toward herself and cut a large slice. Then she offered it to Delphine, who declined in favor of eggs and reiterated her question.

"I know something is wrong, so please do not insult me by denying it," Delphine added as she sprinkled salt on her shirred eggs. "I saw Lucy emptying your chamber pot this morning."

Amused, Verity pointed to the hypocrisy of her friend alluding during a meal to the very bodily function for which she had recently reprimanded her friend.

"There is a difference between a mild allusion and a detailed description of a vagrant defiling Mrs. Carey's prized *Dendrobium nobile,* which I am sure you know," Delphine pointed out briskly. "And you will not distract me. Is it your father?"

"*It* is not a thing because nothing is wrong," Verity insisted. "But if there were a thing it would most certainly not be my father. I am not delighted to discover I share parentage with three of the worst men ever to grace society, but it is hardly a blow. We always knew my sire was one sort of villain or another. No decent man would have left me to rot in Fortescue's."

"Your writing, then," Delphine placidly.

With some asperity, Verity replied that she had had a productive morning. "I finished the first draft of Robert

Lark's article calling for prison reform and drew up a list of questions for the physician who treated the boy Wigsworth injured in his— Wait, what do you mean the chamber pot?"

Delphine blinked at her as though baffled by the non sequitur. "Excuse me?"

"You said you know something is wrong because you saw Lucy emptying my chamber pot," Verity said. "How is that indicative of a problem?"

"Most mornings you empty your own chamber pot, and the only time you forget is when you get up before dawn," Delphine explained as she gathered eggs onto her fork. "The only time you get up before dawn is when you can't sleep, and you never sleep well when something is worrying you. Is it the forged antiquities scheme? I imagine after Grint's less than useless visit, you are ready to march down to the customs office in Jeremiah Stubbs's tailored green wool jacket and interview every agent who works there. I am almost tempted to do it myself."

Well, obviously Verity was not, no.

The former member of the 95th Rifles was a poor choice of emissary for a customs office, as he was notoriously belligerent in the face of authority. Mr. Stanley, with his arcane knowledge of naval ships, would be a much more prudent choice or even the Turnip.

"As fascinating as your deductions are, they are wide of the mark," Verity replied evenly as she broke off a piece of plum cake. "I woke up early as a matter of necessity, as I do not expect to have much opportunity to get any work done today."

Despite this reasonable response, Delphine regarded her dubiously as she rested her elbows on the table and dropped her chin into her hands. "It is Hardwicke, then. What did you do?"

Adopting an air of supercilious curiosity, Verity said, "I? What makes you think *I* did something?"

Delphine's patient stare was a study in silent condemnation, and Verity withstood it for a full minute before relenting. "I have done nothing extraordinary. Truly! All I did was ask for an accounting of the expenditures he made on my behalf while I was in prison so that I may reimburse him."

Her friend all but doubled over with laughter. "Oh, yes, nothing indeed. Did he say 'no' or 'hell no'?"

"Neither," Verity replied stiffly. "He agreed to the request and is to present me with a bill today. You may look at it yourself if you don't believe me."

"I do not doubt that he consented to being treated like a shopkeeper," Delphine replied assuredly. "I only wonder how long it took you to browbeat him into submission."

Verity, who bristled at the description, insisted she was in fact treating him like an equal. "Gentlemen settle debts of honor between them without quibbling or making a fuss, and that is exactly what I am doing here. Hardwicke respects that."

"He does, does he?" Delphine murmured, her eyes glinting with unsuppressed humor as Lucy entered the room with a missive.

Swallowing the acerbic reply that rose to her lips, Verity greeted the servant cordially and accepted the message with a grateful smile. Lucy curtsied slightly, brushed a few crumbs from the table, adjusted the position of the plate of eggs, confirmed that the teapot was more than half-full, and left the room.

"Our meeting is at eleven, and Hardwicke will call here thirty minutes before," Verity said coolly, before rising to her feet and begging to be excused. "I shall finish my breakfast in Robert's study, as I have more time than expected to write."

Delphine frowned and implored her friend not to leave. "I

want to hear more about how much Hardwicke enjoys being treated like a tradesman."

Raising her chin as she collected her plate, Verity assured her friend she was not funny, but Delphine, succumbing to stray giggles, insisted she was a little bit funny.

Verity left the room in dignified silence.

※

Friday, June 26
11:05 a.m.

Lady Abercrombie loathed the prince regent.

As Verity examined the countess's Chinese-style drawing room, a gorgeous cacophony of textures, colors, and patterns so evocative of luxury and nature she could almost hear birds chirping, all she could think was that the sumptuous interior was specifically calculated to put the Royal Pavilion to shame. Her ladyship had taken the rich and fanciful elements that made the Brighton palace unique and tailored them to an elegant London establishment. The contrast with the refined home only heightened the exoticism of the design, and it was in that sense of discovery—finding something so strange and opulent in Grosvenor Square—that the pavilion lost its advantage of scale.

If the countess had any respect at all for the prince regent, she would never have dared to challenge him in such an elemental way.

Consequently, she must loathe him.

Or perhaps she merely disliked him a great deal.

Regardless, it was an interesting notion to consider, and Verity wondered what other examples of her ladyship's antipathy she could find if she made an effort to look. If she managed to amass half a dozen, Mr. Twaddle-Thum might publish a catalogue of speculative evidence.

At the very least, the drawing room deserved a warm reappraisal by the gossip, whose original report had been less than effusive. Gaining entry to the home by convincing one of the footmen that an infestation of an obscure but determined pest was imminent, Verity had barely glimpsed the dimly lit room before the butler invited her to leave. In the bright light of day, it was stunning.

The countess was also quite striking, and as she invited her guests to sit down, Verity thought she bore a great resemblance to La Reina.

Not physically.

Lady Abercrombie had cherubic features, all soft lips and rosy cheeks, but her manner was open and inviting, with an effect of seductive dishevelment, as though she had just been tumbled by a handsome groom in the stable and might find a stray piece of hay in her glossy black curls.

Like La Reina, she projected eagerness and ready availability, an impression that was reinforced by how far she tipped her shoulders forward as she lowered to the bergère across from the settee, revealing the deep valley between her breasts.

Fluttering her lashes, the woman owned herself thrilled that Lord Colson had accepted her invitation with such alacrity. "I only issued it on Sunday. Typically, suitors like to feign indifference to my charms for at least a week in a bid to retain the upper hand in our relationship. But I adore enthusiasm and have nothing but admiration for a man who is not afraid to display it. I do not have tea," she added in an abrupt change in topic but not demeanor. The observation was made with the same flirtatious lilt as the others, which was unsurprising, as Lord Colson was an impressive specimen and her ladyship was set in her ways. "I thought champagne was more suitable to the occasion, as I had not anticipated your bringing a friend with you. Miss Lark, is it?"

Although the question did not pertain to Verity's preference in regard to refreshment, she nevertheless replied that a glass of champagne sounded charming. Briefly, she considered adding a breathy thank you in Mrs. Delacour's soft purr.

She decided against it.

Two coquettes in a conversation was intolerable.

"Champagne is charming in every circumstance, even this one," her ladyship said as she summoned her butler, who oversaw the delivery of the ice pail and a trio of glasses. After arranging the items on the table, the servants left the room and the countess lifted the bottle from its bath of ice. Filling the first glass, she continued, "Although I must admit that I do not know what this circumstance is. Your message requesting an appointment as soon as possible was quite intriguing, Lord Colson, especially with its hints of dire repercussions if it could not be arranged. But you made no mention of bringing a beautiful woman with you, one who is my junior by at least a decade, and I cannot decide if I am more intrigued or annoyed. I suspect it is the latter because I do not like the way your companion is looking at me, as though she is assessing my every movement. Ah, there, you see, her eyes just narrowed! Miss Lark is startled. She did not expect me to be astute."

Ostensibly true, the sentiment failed to represent the entire picture and Verity issued a correction, noting that any woman who could mortify the ruler of England with the placement of a bamboo canopy was highly preceptive.

The compliment hit its target as the countess practically simpered with pleasure. "The canopy alone does not do it, for the serpents are necessary for creating the effect. They are based on snakes in Rubens's painting of Medusa. If you are a student of the Dutch master, you will recognize the golden one to the left of her decapitated head. Regardless, your point is well taken, and you are rather discerning yourself if you recognize my drawing room is not mere vanity. And now look—I am intrigued again. Tell me, what terrible thing would have befallen you had I not agreed to this meeting today?"

Hardwicke was supposed to answer.

During the ride to Grosvenor Square, he had requested an opportunity to explain the situation to Lady Abercrombie. It was the option that made the most sense, he claimed, as the countess was already acquainted with him.

The reasoning was specious, to be sure, as the pair's prior meeting had been a fleeting interaction in the drawing room at Kesgrave House, but Verity consented without comment. Hardwicke had the advantage. Despite his reputation as a dissolute second son, he occupied the same social stratum as the countess and knew many of the same people. In that respect, Verity was very much the interloper.

She did not mind interloping.

Indeed, it came quite naturally to her.

But Hardwicke had been brusque with her in the carriage, clearly anticipating a quarrel, and allowing him his preference seemed like the better way to thwart him.

As she waited for him to identify the threat, Verity accepted the glass from her hostess and sipped deeply. Taken aback by its fruity sweetness, she said, "Oh, it is wonderful."

Lady Abercrombie grinned with pleasure. "Isn't it, though? Depriving us of champagne was Boney's gravest sin."

It was a deliberate provocation.

Now that she had met the countess, Verity knew the other woman was not so shallow as to believe the greatest casualty of the Napoleonic Wars was her enjoyment of a refreshing sip. Her ladyship delighted in being perceived as a will-o'-the-wisp.

Verity did not blame her.

It was always to one's benefit to be underestimated.

Hardwicke, placing his own glass on the table, began by asking Lady Abercrombie if she recalled her recent comments about Andrew Brownell.

The countess shivered gracefully, a gesture seemingly designed to draw attention to the delicate refinement of her shoulders. "Goodness, no. I make a habit of expunging him from my mind the moment he rears his irritating head. I trust you have a very good reason for coming into my home and making me think of him."

It was not, Verity thought, an auspicious beginning for Hardwicke's scheme.

Undaunted, he apologized for the unpleasantness and warned her there was much worse to come. "He is determined to kill Miss Lark."

On a lighthearted chortle, Lady Abercrombie said, "No, he is not."

"He has already made one attempt," Hardwicke replied.

But the countess could not be persuaded, for Blandie—and that was how she thought of him in her head, as a bland man with not a single interesting trait to recommend him—had no spine. "He is a cravenly noodle who preys on the weak. The only time he has ever acted with audacity was when he recognized an opportunity to undermine his brothers and responded before he could talk himself out of it. It was he who orchestrated Rufus's mad dash to the Continent, which had him struck from the family bible, and we all saw how ardently he pursued Miss Mattingly after she became engaged to Lewis. He could not bear the thought of his brother having all her lovely money even if he did find her stubby nose and weak chin unappealing. But harming someone like Miss Lark?"

Lady Abercrombie allowed the question to waft in the air

between them as she finished her champagne and refilled her glass. Then she took another sip and apologized to Miss Lark for the offense she was about to give by insisting Verity simply was not worth the bother of murdering. "It would require such a great amount of planning, which is not Blandie's strong suit. As clever as he considers himself, he is actually quite thickheaded. The risk would be great and for what reward? A perverse satisfaction at accomplishing some secret wicked deed? No, that is not Blandie. His defining characteristic is greed, and the only reason he would resolve to kill a nonentity like Miss Lark was if she stood in the way of his inheritance," she said with a rueful glint.

And then her eyes flew open.

She darted a look of sheer amazement at Hardwicke before turning her gaze to Verity, whom she leaned forward to inspect like a jeweler examining a diamond with a magnifying glass. Murmuring almost to herself, she said, "I suppose there is a resemblance, a bit around the eyes and the forehead. But that still does not make sense. Blandie bestirring himself to murder his father's bastard."

Lady Abercrombie pressed her pillowy lips together as she contemplated the mystery. Settling back in her chair, she said, "You *are* illegitimate, are you not, Miss Lark? Frimgallow did not hide you away because of some horrible deformity. I suppose he might have resented the expense of your comeout, but you are presentable and would have acquitted yourself well enough on the Marriage Mart. And keeping you fed, sheltered, and clothed for the rest of your life would have cost him more in the end."

In the pause that followed these thoughts, Verity confirmed her status.

The countess, however, continued as though she had not spoken. "It is no question you are baseborn, and yet you have Blandie in a lather. That is meaningful. He is not the sort to jump at shadows. Could Frimgallow actually intend to put his by-blow in his will? I cannot credit it! And yet he does enjoy tormenting his sons. They annoy him by being so common. He set an example of true depravity and they followed with crude mine swindles and duels. But an illegitimate female—it is bold, it is unexpected, it will set tongues wagging. Frimgallow would like that, especially if it came at the expense of his legitimate offspring, whom he appears to despise. But the family name! He would not tarnish it even to shock the *ton*."

Here, again, she turned an appraising eye on Verity and noted that Lord Colson had taken an interest in her. "An unprecedented event, if I know my Twaddle, and I do. Oh, Twaddle! Yes, that is why your name is familiar to me. Bea mentioned you on Sunday, when I called on her to discuss our country plans and she shooed me out of the house because she had one of her endlessly dull murder investigations to conduct. You have Bea's attention and Lord Colson's support. Ah, so there is the problem: Blandie thinks you're about to marry into one of the oldest families in England and gain just enough respectability to make his father's petulant ramblings an actual threat. You are to be congratulated, Miss Lark, for providing sufficient motivation to convince Blandie to finally live up to his full potential. Frimgallow would be so proud if he knew!"

Delivered with stinging facetiousness, the last idea nonetheless resonated with her ladyship and she asked if they had considered telling Frimgallow about his son's efforts in order to remove the threat. "If he knows his son is so corrupt as to murder his competition to make sure she does not get any part of the estate, then he will be reassured of Blandie's degeneracy and leave him everything. Everybody wins. That is, except you, Miss Lark, if you are in fact hoping to get some of Frimgallow's money."

Verity, who genuinely appreciated the countess's cool

practicality, said she had no interest in the earl's fortune. "But we have passed the juncture where my evading an untimely death is the only acceptable outcome. In his attempt to kill me, Brownell in fact killed someone else."

Lady Abercrombie all but rolled her eyes at this information. "You see! That is what I meant. Conceiving a proper murder plot requires a modicum of intelligence. Whom did he kill by mistake?"

"My neighbor's son-in-law," Verity replied.

Her ladyship nodded knowingly and advised her not to mention the victim in her conversation with Frimgallow, as it would only make Blandie appear ineffectual and bungling. "And you want Frimgallow to believe his son has achieved his full wicked potential."

Verity's patience began to slip at this advice, which was offered sincerely. The notion that the murderer should be held accountable for his crimes seemed to strike the countess as immaterial, and when Verity replied that the need for justice was the more pressing issue, the other woman disagreed.

"The more pressing issue is the threat on your life," Lady Abercrombie insisted. "But you must do what you think is right. I would never dream of trying to dissuade an upstanding citizen from acting in accordance with her personal moral code. In fact, I make it a policy to abstain from all dissuasion. And so I shall let you get to it. Unless there is something else you wish to discuss?" she asked with a curious look at Hardwicke. "Lord Colson, if you are angling for an invitation to my country party at Haverill Hall, then do not give it another thought. You are already on my list. I *had* intended to place your accommodation directly next to mine, as I can think of a no more enjoyable way to spend a week in the summer than a mésalliance, but your affections appear to be engaged elsewhere. If you are hoping to arrange an invitation for Miss Lark, I must disappoint you. I cannot have Frimgallow's by-blow wandering the halls of the Duke of Kesgrave's ancestral home. I am sure you understand."

Verity almost guffawed.

The idea that she should not wander the halls of the Duke of Kesgrave's ancestral home because she was *Frimgallow*'s by-blow was simply the most diverting thing she had ever heard in her entire life.

Truly, nothing even came close.

Hardwicke, impatient with all the folderol, announced that they needed Lady Abercrombie's help in implicating Brownell in Muir's murder—both to ensure Miss Lark's safety and deliver justice for her neighbor. "I respect your lack of interest in following a strict morality and that is precisely why we are here: to propose a decidedly wicked scheme."

"Oh, do tell, Lord Colson," Lady Abercrombie said with a simper of delight as she tilted her shoulders forward again to improve his view of her bosom.

Revealing his profound understanding of his audience, Hardwicke smiled in appreciation and said the plot hinged on her. "You are the linchpin, my lady, and if any aspect of it does not meet with your approval, I hope you will suggest ways we can change it to satisfy your requirements."

The countess told him he may depend on it. "I have never had trouble articulating my needs." Hardwicke began by reminding her of her remarks on Sunday, when she described Brownell as a lecherous puppy who thought of himself as a dangerous rake.

Naturally, she recalled the description, although she wondered if her comment was unfair to puppies in light of the new information. "The little dears are rambunctious, not homicidal."

"You also mentioned that he has never relented in his

pursuit of you despite receiving no encouragement," Hardwicke continued.

"Discouragement only!" her ladyship asserted. "Active and repeated discouragement, which has made him all the more ardent. I keep hoping he will give up like the fox in the tale by Aesop and decide I am too sour for him, but I am a tempting morsel, as legions have attested, and there is something unbearably tantalizing about things we perceive to be just out of our reach. I say 'perceive' because I am many feet above."

"Surely, it is yards," he said.

Although clever enough to know when she was being buttered up, Lady Abercrombie accepted the lavish praise as her due, and Verity decided Hardwicke's plan had a better chance of prospering than she had realized. The countess liked games, and enticing Brownell to his own doom was an excellent diversion.

"Or even miles," Hardwicke said, noting that Brownell's inability to recognize an intellectual superior would be his downfall. "He thinks he is too intelligent to be hoodwinked by a woman, especially one as beautiful as you. He can think only of his own needs, and it is that self-regard we hope to use against him."

Intrigued, her ladyship asked how he planned to do that.

But there was a glimmer in her eye.

She knows, Verity thought. The exact nature of the proposition might escape her, but she had a germ of an idea.

"He wants you to think he is dangerous?" Hardwicke said with blithe confidence. "Very well, you shall find him dangerous."

The countess shivered for dramatic effect, demonstrating how easily she could play the part of a swooning beauty. "Oh, indeed I shall, so dangerous I believe he is capable of murder, so dangerous that I cannot help but tremble in alarm for own safety and feel a frisson of awareness that is as exhilarating as it is terrifying."

"Precisely," Hardwicke said.

"It is a tricky thing, exploiting a man's desire to coerce him into a confession," Lady Abercrombie continued, her expression suddenly serious as she contemplated the particulars of the endeavor. "I shall have to overcome his natural inclination to protect himself, but I do not expect that to be too difficult. I shall gush over how masterful he is being, taking matters into his own hands instead of leaving them to fate—and his father. I can use his father's despotism against him. I could say how wonderful it is that he is finally stepping out of Frimgallow's considerable shadow and how I always knew it would happen. And then I will laugh my most seductive laugh, deep and husky, and bend forward so he can get a proper glimpse of my décolletage. And I will be there, on the settee next to him, so close he can touch me if he reaches out, and then I shall press him for details."

But no sooner had she finished outlining the scene as it unfolded in her imagination than she shook her head and insisted it was all wrong. "If we are to play out a seduction, Lord Colson, then we must play out a seduction! I shall lead him to my bedchamber. He has spent half his life panting to see the inner sanctum, so I shall grant him access and he will be like hot wax in my hand, melting at my touch. By the time I am done with him, he will confess to conspiring to overthrow the monarchy."

Verity, who had been in dozens of noble bedchambers but never by invitation, lauded every one of the countess's ideas. "You have an extraordinary grasp on the assignment, my lady."

"You may be assured I do," her ladyship said, her eyes sparkling with excitement as she raised the champagne to her lips. "Blandie has been pestering me for decades, and I am astonished to discover I am eager for a little retribution. No, not eager. Voracious. I wish to pay him back for every pinch, prod, poke, and squeeze I have been made to endure since I was five and twenty. Do you think he will hang? I do not. Men of his rank never do. The crown loathes a scandal. I expect they shall tuck him away in an asylum."

Having spent time in both Newgate and an asylum, albeit one for orphans, Verity knew they were each awful in their own way. Even so, the former was worse, very, very much worse, and she had little doubt that being confined to the ward in a hospital for the mentally unwell was the superior option.

Did she mind that Brownell would escape the gallows?

No, she did not.

She wanted Brownell to live for a long time with the consequences of killing Mr. Muir and endangering Delphine's life.

"If it is to work, we must figure out how you know of Brownell's wickedness," Hardwicke said. "I thought we might make use of Mr. Twaddle-Thum, who seems to have a preternatural ability to know about the private goings-on of the beau monde. It will not be astonishing if he has somehow caught wind of Brownell's murder plot. We shall drop a word in his ear about our suspicions, and he will write an enticing little item full of hints and allegations. For it to serve its purpose, however, you will need to be able to identify Brownell from Twaddle's description. Can you think of a distinguishing physical feature that you could connect to Brownell without raising his suspicions?"

It was the cornerstone of their entire scheme, and the project would fall apart if the countess could not suggest such a characteristic.

And yet she was too distracted by the effortless certainty with which Hardwicke spoke of passing information to the infamous gossip to offer a suggestion. "By Jove, you know who Twaddle is! How dare you withhold this information from me! Tell me at once! Is it Mrs. Ralston? It has to be Mrs. Ralston. The way she pushes her beak into everyone's business—I cannot believe anyone is *that* nosy. She has to be doing it for nefarious gain. Oh, but is that too obvious? Mrs. Ralston is everyone's first thought, and if I were the most notorious prattler in London, I would ensure I was the person I would least expect," she added softly, almost to herself, before gasping and staring at them in utter stupefaction. "Never say it is Vera Hyde-Clare! If it is Clara's wretched ninny of a sister-in-law, then I shall shoot myself right now and be done with it, for I cannot live in a world where Vera Hyde-Clare is a phantom who floats gently among the *ton*, gathering our most private secrets. You *must* put me out of my misery at once, Lord Colson, and swear on everything you hold dear that Vera Hyde-Clare is not Mr. Twaddle-Thum."

Solemnly, Hardwicke replied that he could not.

Yelping in horror, Lady Abercrombie threw her hand against her chest, as though to calm her racing heart, and looked up to the heavens, which in this case consisted of swaths of scarlet silk and golden serpents.

"Neither can I say that it *is* Mrs. Hyde-Clare," he continued smoothly. "I do not know who Mr. Twaddle-Thum is. All I can tell you is that in my espionage work for the Alien Office, I managed to pass information to him through what appeared to be a network of his associates. I suppose any one of the men with whom I met in the back alleys of St. Giles and Saffron Hill could have been Twaddle, but the truth was never revealed to me. I was merely proposing now to send word through this assortment."

Although this explanation sounded compelling to Verity, her ladyship looked at Hardwicke askance, seemingly incapable of allowing her intense dismay to be assuaged. To her credit, she could not have proposed a more unlikely candidate than the Duchess of Kesgrave's aunt. The woman was a nerve-ridden muttonhead who could not speak a single sentence without immediately amending it or retracting it altogether, and the notion that she was the covert mastermind behind some of society's most shocking revelations tickled Verity to no end.

"But you would not tell me either way," Lady Abercrombie said, scowling. "All you spies with your codes of honor and sworn allegiances. It is quite vexing, you know."

Hardwicke refrained from comment.

"Very well, then, handsome," she said with a hint of impatience. "You do not need a distinguishing physical feature. Simply describe Blandie as an Adonis with blond hair and dark brooding eyes, and his vanity will do the rest. Trust me. When I tell him I knew such a perfect specimen could only be Blandie, he won't doubt it for a second."

In this, Verity was content to trust her. "That will do nicely, thank you."

Satisfied, the countess moved onto other matters, asking how many guests she should expect to entertain on the night in question. "There is you, Miss Lark, and Lord Colson. Who else? Are we inviting a Runner or two to witness the confession? I suggest we invite a magistrate to simplify the process and spare me the obligation of having to go before one to give evidence. I could suggest a few names, as I do have my favorites, but I wonder if it is better that I do not have a hand in it to make sure he is impartial."

Hardwicke assured her he already had a magistrate in mind.

"So the count is four, not including myself and Blandie," the countess replied with a pensive moue. "I wonder what I shall provide as refreshments. Champagne feels too frivolous. As much as I will relish the sight of a man being carted off in chains, one should not celebrate it. What do we think of port? It is still sweet but without the bubbles, so it is more serious. But what do I pair it with? Typically, when I am entertaining in my boudoir, I serve something frothy, but I think cheese would be better in this case. I do not want to ask the staff to prepare anything particularly complex or they will begin to suspect high pranks are afoot. No, it is best to keep it simple. Tell me, Miss Lark, what do you think of cream cheese on toast? I know Stilton is much more in fashion, but it does have an odor."

Verity, who could not decide if the query was flippant or sincere, insisted that the situation did not require refreshments. "It is an ambush, not a social call."

"It is both!" her ladyship chirped, worrying about the snide report Twaddle would inevitably produce if she allowed her guests to languish without a collation or drinks. "Do not tell me he won't find out. Lord Colson himself just informed us that he has a network of spies, and I am now very much convinced my own butler is among them. Twaddle adores food, which I am sure you have noticed as well, Miss Lark. Just consider how lovingly he detailed Bea's fondness for rout cakes. It would be mortifying if it was not so appetizing."

Oh, but it *was* mortifying to recall those items now, not just because she owed her very freedom to the duchess but also because the writing itself was beneath her usual quality. Although generally wary of adverbs, she had allowed her own contempt for the subject to overcome her natural aversion, and contemplating the excesses of those articles, she found it almost impossible not to physically recoil, especially when the countess cited them as further proof that Vera Hyde-Clare might be Twaddle.

"It is precisely her level of triviality to describe grains of sugar," she added, drawing her brows together, still bedeviled by the idea. "But to oversee a network of spies? She could not manage the upbringing of a lone niece and can barely control her own daughter. It is not she. I am sure of it."

And yet!

Having placed that excessively loud bee in Lady Abercrombie's bonnet, Hardwicke suggested they leave and allow the countess to return to her day. "Thank you again for agreeing to meet with us on such short notice. Once I know Mr. Twaddle-Thum will publish the story as discussed, we will settle the timing. Ideally, we would do it two nights hence."

Naturally, the countess had an appointment on Sunday night—theater with Mr. Cuthbert. "But it is no matter! I will rearrange my schedule as needed. The sooner we can box Blandie up, the sooner Miss Lark can stop fearing for her life. I do hope he does not contrive to finish the job before we meet again. I should be exceedingly put out if I have to extract two confessions of murder. Somehow I know it will be more than twice the work."

On this cheerful thought, the countess announced that she had to take her lion cub for a walk, as the darling little lamb had been cooped up in the house all day, and although there were no words in the English language more calculated to induce Verity to hide in the shrub outside the house, she bid her ladyship good day and allowed Hardwicke to escort her to the carriage.

Chapter Twelve

※

Friday, June 26
12:56 p.m.

When Hardwicke asked to speak with Verity alone in her study, she did not expect him to offer suggestions for how to write Twaddle's account of Mr. Muir's murder. She had been slyly alluding to society and its members for more than eight years and had no use for friendly advice for how to disguise a subject's identity.

She was not some rustic from the provinces inserting dashes for letters: On Wednesday, Mr. B_ _ _ _ _ _ dusted cyanide of potassium on top of a lovely tin of chocolate puffs and went about his murderous business.

Verity had assumed he was going to give her the list of his expenses.

A man of his word, he would not renege on a promise.

She had intended to broach the subject in the carriage, but both journeys had been consumed with strategy: there, how to entice the countess into helping; back, how to restrain the countess from helping too much.

Now that she had met Lady Abercrombie, Verity was confident her ladyship would be able to seduce a confession from Brownell, and her only concern was the size of the audience the woman would require for her performance. Verity would not be surprised to arrive to the bedchamber at the appointed hour and find the theater critic for *The Times* tucked behind one of the curtains.

Although diverted by these musings, especially her description of Charles Hill's favorable review in *The Promoter* praising the audacity of the setting ("Placing the action in a site specific to the action is a bold new innovation that other productions would be wise to adopt"), Hardwicke insisted she was worrying about nothing. The countess, he said, had struck him as sensible and astute, at which point she reminded him of the woman's pet lion cub.

Naturally, he had no reply.

The mention of the subject's pet lion cub was a reliable way to end any debate.

Verity would have asked for an accounting then, but the carriage arrived at number twenty-six and she immediately disembarked to give Delphine a report of their meeting with the countess. She knew her friend would be waiting on tenterhooks, and an unnecessary delay would be unkind.

Indeed, Delphine met them at the door and noted how very long they had been gone. "When you did not return right away, I knew her ladyship was receptive to the plan. Tell me, did she require much persuading? And do not forget to include a comprehensive description of her drawing room in your reply."

Readily, Verity complied with this instruction and was amused when Delphine's only remark was to ask if the countess was hoping to be cast as Titania in Drury Lane's upcoming production of *A Midsummer Night's Dream*.

"I expect it is one of only a few venues she would deem

worthy of her talents," Verity said with a teasing glance at Hardwicke.

In response, he requested the opportunity to speak privately.

Now, having endured several minutes of helpful suggestions with a placid expression, Verity opened her mouth to interrupt the litany. Before she could utter a single objection, however, he apologized for not complying with her request earlier. "I wanted to make sure we gave the Brownell affair our full attention, but as you appear to have Twaddle's column well in hand, we may proceed with other business," he said, pulling a document from his pocket. "You will see I arranged the information by category: All the gratuities are gathered together and the bribes and the fees and so on."

Well, obviously, *so on* gave her pause.

Gratuities, bribes, fees—this assortment would seem to cover all the various types of expenses, and yet he had devised a vague fourth group that could encompass anything. Cautiously unfolding the paper, she saw that her suspicion was correct: Hardwicke had over-complied.

Although her sojourn in Newgate had lasted barely three days, he had compiled a list that seemed to contain one item for every hour of her confinement. Determined not to embarrass herself by actually counting the number of lines, she thought there were five dozen in total, maybe even six. The first payment, described as a gratuity to an urchin outside of the prison who watched his horse for ten minutes, was for one pence. The second expenditure was for two pence, also a gratuity to an urchin, this time for twenty minutes of guard duty.

And so it continued down the list, the amount inching upward with the minutes.

The tip section was followed by bribes, which were significantly higher.

Not a single one was less than three pounds.

The fees were dearer still and comprised the largest portion.

As her eyes moved along the page, Verity realized she was not reading the work of a tranquil man. Hardwicke was irate.

He was seething with fury and having a tantrum on page.

Every item on the list was a provocation.

She was supposed to feel silly or absurd or defensive.

Or angry.

Perhaps he wanted her to fume at the blatant mockery of a perfectly reasonable request so that he would have leave to respond in kind.

She would not oblige.

He might have lost his temper, but she would keep a tight rein on hers.

Consequently, she pointed to a charge of seven pounds in the middle of the page and calmly asked what it was for.

Hardwicke leaned forward to read the item, then explained it was for his father's time. "As you may recall, he wrote a letter to the Lord Mayor of London on your behalf, and quantifying his value per minute based on his income and responsibilities, I arrived at that sum. To ensure the greatest accuracy, I calculated in intervals of fifteen seconds, but if you fear that might have resulted in an unfortunate occurrence of rounding down, I can do the computation again using a five-second interval."

No, my lord, let us do it in one-second intervals, as though we are counting grains of sand on the beach, Verity thought, amused by the heavy-handedness of his ploy. "A fifteen-second interval is precisely what I would have recommended had my opinion been sought. And recalculating would be so time-consuming, you would have to add another line for your own time."

"That is on the bottom," he said.

Startled, she looked up.

"Among the miscellaneous items," he added blandly.

"How clever," she murmured.

And Verity meant it.

Having intended her comment to be bitingly satiric, she was disconcerted to discover she had not been sardonic enough.

"It is also where I put the cost of my horse's shoe repair," he replied, directing her attention to another line near the bottom edge. "Shadow threw a shoe while I was returning from my meeting with the warden and I knew you would want me to include it. Every last farthing, you said, and as I have repeatedly made clear, my only desire is to please you."

Oh, yes, very clever indeed, she thought, as a tingle of awareness shivered through her and her heart hitched. He had made that as clear as glass in many delightful ways, and to turn it against her now with this mannered display of excessive solicitousness was diabolical.

But he had always been the superior tactician.

It was the thing about him that annoyed her the most.

"You will see I included the ink for my father's letters in this section," he said, noting the expenditure was directly below the entry for the shoe repair. "I debated whether it belonged alongside fees for several minutes before deciding it fit better here. And you must not worry that I failed to account for my indecisiveness. That is the line following the ink."

The ink, she noted, was two pence, which was astronomically high in the context of writing a single letter.

No, Hardwicke had used the plural.

As if confirming, he said, "My father wrote several drafts. If you are wondering why two bottles of ink were used, that is why. He composed three versions of the request to the lord mayor before the wording satisfied him. He wrote a thank you note as well, but it was concise and pro forma. It used little ink."

Although his ability to know exactly what she was thinking seemed magical, its explanation was far more mundane: He had literally pointed it out to her. He knew she would be struck by the price of ink because the price of ink was striking.

The only way to go through that much ink in the composition of a few brief lines would be by knocking over a bottle and spilling its contents on the blotter.

Or using a wildly exotic color such as purple.

To be sure, the Marquess of Ware did neither, and Hardwicke had simply inflated the price to goad her into complaining about the exorbitance.

Verity refused to comply.

Holding her tongue, she fixed an insipid smile on her face, which he purposefully mistook for confusion. "Ah, perhaps this presentation is too haphazard. Shall we sit down and go through the document line by line? Lucy can bring us a fresh pot of tea and we can take our time perusing it—time that I shall add to the tally if you wish."

How smug he was!

Every aspect of his demeanor was consideration and mild curiosity, the classic butter-would-not-melt-in-his-mouth look, and it was the obliteration of all traces of superiority that was superiority itself.

His technique was superb.

The Turnip could not fumble a package more convincingly.

It was only to be expected, of course, as he was a professional spy whose government had relied on his skillful duplicity to aid in the war effort, but his extensive experience did not make it any less galling.

In many ways, it heightened it because she was also a

professional. Her experience was just as extensive if not more so because she had been refining her spy craft for decades. He had only entered the game in the past few years.

Sweetly, she thanked him for his kind offer but said she would look over the document privately. "Only as a matter of course. I am confident everything is in order."

"Do take as long as you need," he replied with encouragement as he lowered himself into one of the armchairs at the desk. "I do not mind waiting."

Verity's simper deepened. "I am sure you have more important things to do."

"None more important than this," he replied portentously.

It was a mark of his wrath that he was willing to waste even more time on this petulant exercise, an indication of how little he understood the situation he himself had created. Intending to render her ridiculous, he had only turned himself into the picture of a sullen child.

Smothering her amusement, Verity sat at the desk and said, "You must do as you feel is necessary. I trust it goes without saying that we shall add this waiting time to your total. It would be a shame to keep such an accurate accounting and get sloppy at the end."

"I noted the time I sat down," he replied coolly. "We are in the second minute now."

Despite a nearly overwhelming urge to sneer, she lauded his thoroughness.

Hardwicke swore he was just as eager as she to resolve the situation. "The prospect of a large financial imbalance between us is excruciating to me. I want nothing between us, Verity," he added, his eyes, a baffling mix of blue and green, darkening with earnestness as her heart jolted again.

She resented how deftly he seduced her with words, how easily he could unsettle her with statements as ardent as they were casual. He did it so well, murmur gorgeous bon mots that caused her limbs to tremble, and yet they were just words. All his pledges of patience and understanding, and at the first disagreement he indulged a fit of temper.

"That is why I am content to sit here while you review the expenditures," he continued. "You shall approve them and pay me the money. Then the business will be done, and we will never have to speak of it again."

Suddenly, it all made sense.

No wonder Hardwicke was willing to waste hours calculating minutes and measuring ink bottles—he wanted to humiliate her.

Matter-of-factly, as though merely assessing the weather, she said, "You expect to leave here today with one hundred and seventy-eight pounds."

"One hundred seventy-eight pounds, four shillings, one groat, and two farthings," he corrected mildly, scooting forward in his seat to point at the number at the bottom of the page, which he had underlined twice. "I trust you will let me know if any of the amounts seem out of line to you. Out of respect for your request that I provide a figure as accurate as possible, I used the most recent year's account to figure out my father's worth per minute, but we can pick another year. I believe 1813 was an excessively dry spring and a good portion of the crops failed. I can summon my father's steward to advise us on the least optimal year. He has already pulled the records, as I informed him of the possibility before coming here today."

Astonished, Verity could no longer contain her disgust and exclaimed, "For God's sake, Hardwicke, you cannot be this petty!"

"Petty?" he echoed with a confused air, as though encountering a novel concept for the first time. "I am treating the situation with all the specificity it demands. You described the money I spent to ensure your safety and welfare while incarcerated in the worst prison in England as a debt of honor. As you know, debts of honor are to be paid immediately. Should I expect a bank draft, or will you dash off to the Continent to escape your creditors?"

"How dare you!" Verity snarled, darting to her feet. "How dare you come into *my* home and laugh at me?"

Quietly, he denied it. "No, Verity, I do not find this remotely funny."

His calm further incensed, for it was proof that he had won.

He had presented his absurd list with this very outcome in mind: her stomping around the room in a frenzy of whitehot rage while he watched her coolly from a chair.

To stop her hands from shaking, she slammed her palms onto the surface of the desk and leaned toward him as she jeered, "All of this nonsense: your father's time, your time, the steward's time, the horse's time. All of it is just you having a tantrum because you did not like something I said. I make one simple request, and you take a pet. Good God, you are no better than a spoiled child!"

"*I* take a pet," Hardwicke said softly.

But now Verity could hear it, the anger simmering beneath the surface, and she was not surprised when he rose to his feet and pressed his own hands to the desk. Mere inches away, his eyes were a bewildering dark blue.

Hotly, he repeated it. "*I* take a pet. You are the one who is in a prickly huff because I dared to expend some of my considerable resources on your behalf. You are right, Verity, it *is* all nonsense. The idea that the money means anything. The idea that I would notice how many pounds I spent, let alone farthings and pence. The idea that I would not happily bankrupt the entire marquessate to keep you safe. How dare *you* throw that back in my face by asking for an account?"

Verity did not want to hear it.

A marquessate for her—no, no, no, no.

If she could, she would press her hands against her ears to block out the words that were coming next.

Instead, she smiled and chided him gently. "Do not be absurd, Hardwicke, you have nieces, who will require sizable dowries if they are to find decent husbands. And given how free the earl is with his favors, the countryside is likely littered with his by-blows. If you are looking for a worthy cause on which to expend your considerable resources, I would suggest finding his children and settling them in comfortable homes."

But it was a mistake.

The irreverent reply—it was a retreat and he knew it.

Her entire body strained with the compulsion to pull back physically, but she remained where she was, palms against the desk, her face inches from his, because the ignominy of actually withdrawing in defeat would destroy her.

"It is not about the money," he said gently.

And the gentleness cut deeper than any sword.

He knew a skittish creature when he saw one.

"It was never about the money. The debt you seek to settle has nothing to do with pounds or pence," he said. "I saw your face when you found out my father sent a message to the lord mayor on your behalf. You could not have been more terrified if a volcano erupted beneath your feet. And the terror is of me, Verity. It scares you to the bone to realize my faith in you is inviolate. Nothing could shake it, and asking my father for a favor is the least of what I would do."

He was right, yes, but also wrong.

The pistol was in her hand.

There was the Wraithe, dead by gunshot wound and Verity Lark clutching the murder weapon.

Doubt was the only rational response.

Perhaps not sustained doubt.

Perhaps only fleeting doubt.

But *some* doubt.

And yet Hardwicke had embroiled the Marquess of Ware in her affairs without even a moment's hesitation because his faith in her was fixed.

It never wavered, and in return she could barely muster trust.

The corpse, the gun—she had no idea what she would have thought.

At the very least, she would have had questions, and she was not abashed to admit it. The circumstances were damning, and it was impossible to know how a person would behave in a given situation. If events aligned in a particular way, then anything was possible.

And that was the gulf between them, a yawning chasm so deep Verity felt as though she would drown in its depths.

It was a disquieting sensation, and unable to hold her body still, she straightened her posture and stepped away from the desk. Then she adjusted the position of the chair before arranging a quartet of quills in a neat line and moving the ink a few inches.

She was fidgeting again.

Goddamn it.

Verity dropped her arms to her sides and leaned her shoulders against the bookcase that pressed against the far wall of the room. Hardwicke watched her with mild interest, his own hands clasped behind his back.

Trying to communicate something of the consuming inexplicability of the situation, she said, "You have known me for little more than a month."

Oh, but her attempt at clarity fell horribly flat, making everything worse.

Because his reply was devastating: "It took little more than a week."

Her heart thudded to a halt.

She did not want any of this ... this ... this thing, this fascination, this devouring need. It had been there from the beginning. The panic that had swept through her on that morning when he visited her at home and called her the most astoundingly competent female he had ever met—it was a premonition. In the depth of his teal eyes, in the pause before he asked her to giggle, she had divined the whole.

Driven by a desire to beg him to stop making breathtaking declarations, she took a mental step back and with a composure she did not yet feel, tried to explain why an honest accounting of expenses was important to her. "Money is the only part of the debt I can touch. Money is the only part of the debt I can quantify. Money is the only part of the debt I can satisfy. Everything else is ephemera."

"Not ephemeral," he said, smiling faintly despite the earnest tone. "Intangible."

Fear fluttered in her belly as she allowed the distinction. "All right, intangible."

Having gained the concession, Hardwicke examined her silently for several seconds, and Verity resented the cool way he appraised her. The steadiness of his gaze spoke to the pervasiveness of his calm, and there she was, a wild thing with a racing heart and bared teeth.

It gave him the advantage.

In the battle between their wills, he had emerged as the victor.

But he was not content to savor his triumph.

Oh, no, he had to make her feel it keenly by immediately conceding the ground to her.

Now that he had driven her to a frenzy of anger, it was so easy for him to calmly allow that he had failed to consider what the debt might mean to her. "It is precisely as you said: I took a pet. But only because the notion of your owing me for actions taken to preserve my own sanity is madness. Your safety and welfare were my top concerns, but every action I took was to keep myself moving forward so that I would not succumb to terror. Tossing coins at anyone who could help me was central to that project. That said, if you still require it, I will revise the list and present you with a more reasonable tally. I will confess that I got a little carried away with the original."

The unexpected graciousness of the concession further undermined her composure, for it lent a persuasive sincerity to his remarks. He seemed genuinely eager to be reasonable, to acknowledge the validity of her perspective, to put her ego above his own, all of which was further proof that he would not rest until she was dust at his feet. Storming the citadel was not enough for him.

Grappling to seem unmoved by the turmoil roiling inside her, she raised an eyebrow with sardonic curiosity and said, "A little?"

Hardwicke grinned, either fooled by her poise or determined to appear fooled by it. "My father's steward was utterly dumbfounded when I requested all the crop reports for the past decade. He was dying to ask why but could not bring himself to be so openly impertinent. Instead, he will come up with some way to mention it in passing to my father, who will then seek an explanation."

At the mention of the Marquess of Ware, Verity flinched, and seeing her response, Hardwicke rushed to assure her that nothing had changed. "The plan remains the same. I do not have your daybook so I cannot say definitely what the schedule is, but I believe we are due for a fishing expedition followed by a hot-air balloon launch. Obviously, the ponds at Hampstead Heath have not gone anywhere, but I suspect the balloon is miles away by now. Nevertheless, the general principle of stasis holds."

But no, that was not true, for everything had changed again.

Verity felt at once tethered and unfettered.

She wanted to submit to her feelings for him while keeping them in check, to allow an exuberant sanguinity to exist side by side with the cautious cynicism that had always guided her steps.

The two endeavors were incompatible, and although she was too clever to permit competing impulses, she nevertheless yearned for a way to reconcile them. She wanted both to hurl herself at Hardwicke completely *and* hold a measure of herself back.

Hardwicke walked toward her as he proposed an alternative activity: a presentation of a new type of watering hose at the Royal Horticultural Society. "It promises to be interesting, especially if it actually improves on the current design. In that case, I would relish an opportunity to buy one for my mother. Her birthday is next month, and I have yet to purchase her a gift. As a matter of course, I like to select presents a week or two in advance in case something goes awry."

If you need details to trust me, then I will give you every detail I have.

The consistency of his pursuit did not surprise her. An experienced campaigner, he knew the value of steadfast determination, and Verity, whose own tenacity had been commended and cursed in turn by her friends, found herself deeply unnerved by his persistence.

Already, she wanted him more than her next breath.

What else was left?

Dismayed by the answer, she said the demonstration at

the Royal Horticultural Society sounded intriguing and she would check her daybook to confirm her availability.

❦

Friday, June 26
2:14 p.m.

Mr. Jenkinson would never dare to contradict a magistrate.

Raised by a man who had worked as a clerk in the Court of the Chancery for twenty-five years, he had nothing but respect for the wheels of justice, however slowly they turned. Deciding who should stand trial for a crime and who should walk free was a daunting responsibility, and if a magistrate should momentarily shrink from the weight of the obligation, Jenkinson would offer no reproof.

But to refuse to enter into a conversation about the prospective guilt of a suspect—Mr. Jenkinson had only stinging disdain for any member of the judiciary whose commitment to his duty was so lacking.

Hepworth swore it was a matter of propriety!

Using the seductive allure of a beautiful woman to coerce a confession out of a member of the peerage was an insupportable violation of decorum.

Verity, sporting Mr. Jenkinson's bushy eyebrows and generous middle, asked if it was perhaps not a greater breach of etiquette to allow a murderer to kill again. "I'm not saying it is!" she rushed to add in a burly baritone. "I am merely seeking your opinion, your honor."

Morton Hepworth, a stipendiary judge who staffed the Great Marlborough Street office, scowled at the query, rightfully recognizing it as impertinent.

Mr. Jenkinson might scruple to contradict a magistrate,

but he had no rule against needling one, especially when he was being as dense as a mule.

Hardwicke, having chosen the court in Great Marlborough Street because of its proximity to Lady Abercrombie's residence, did not see fit to argue with Hepworth.

The judge was not the only magistrate in London.

Indeed, he was not the only magistrate in the building; the office had three.

Hardwicke, rising to his feet, complimented Hepworth on the moral clarity of his position. "It is refreshing to meet a man who can distinguish between right and wrong with such certainty."

Hepworth, who shared this opinion of himself, readily nodded. Although of average height, he cut an imposing figure in his black robes and bob wig with frizzed sides, and Verity could picture him on the bench, rendering decisions. Currently, they were in a private chamber to the left of the courtroom, an austere sanctum with multipaned windows, dark paneling, and a coved ceiling.

Escorting them to the door, he emphasized the importance of following a more conventional course to justice. "If the gentleman in question poses a significant threat to this woman, as you claim, then you should hire an inquiry agent to gather evidence. Return to me with proof in hand, and I won't hesitate to issue a warrant for his arrest as well as give him a stern talking-to. I am a fervent believer that women should not be wantonly killed. But, please, no more dishonest manipulations. A man's weakness must not be used against him. It is appalling."

Although curious to learn his stance on the discriminate murder of women, Verity complied with the warning look Hardwicke darted in her direction and refrained from comment, which was, she decided as they stepped outside, probably for the best.

Never let it be said that Mr. Jenkinson called a sitting magistrate a numbskull.

◈

Friday, June 26
4:27 p.m.

Fortunately, Ernest Kilby had no moral objection to their scheme.

If a man was so prurient as to allow himself to be led around by his base desires, then far be it for the magistrate to protect him from the consequences of his actions. England's prisons were full of facile men who were not clever enough to conduct themselves properly in civilized society, which was precisely the way Kilby liked it. The more simpletons who were confined to jail cells, the fewer were left to wander the streets and cause havoc by upsetting the horses or bumping into buckets or splashing mud on one's trousers.

Furthermore, Kilby admired Lady Abercrombie's nobility in subjecting herself to the attentions of a murderer to ensure he did not strike again.

Although he had never met the countess, he had read about her exploits in various newspaper reports and one did hear things, especially in Bow Street, which buzzed with activity. He admired the boldness with which she lived her life, and if he thought she was perhaps a little too liberal with her charms, as some of the men on which she was rumored to bestow her favors were young enough to be her son, he appreciated the way she conducted her business openly.

As a magistrate, he valued honest dealing.

To that end, he admitted that part of the plan's appeal was the opportunity to see her ladyship's home. Her taste and discernment were legendary, and if her drawing room was a sight to behold, then he could not begin to conceive the wonders of her bedchamber.

Agreeing to the arrangement, he quickly added that his willingness to witness the scene did not mean he had formed any judgment about the murder suspect's culpability. "Although some aspects of the proceedings will lack the dignity of the courtroom, I will perform my function as though I am sitting on the bench. The evidence must be incontrovertible for me to be swayed. I will not consign—"

Here, he paused and, looking from Verity to Hardwicke, sought to ascertain the identity of the man in question.

"Andrew Brownell," she replied with Jenkinson's mildness.

Kilby recoiled, his shoulders stiffening as his hands clenched, and he took a step backward, as though to put distance between himself and the name. He knocked into a console, sending a silver tray clanging to the floor, and jumped at the clatter. "I apologize for taking up so much of your time, especially after you had to wait almost an hour to see me. It is my fault for not asking for his identity sooner. Based on my experience with Andy... Lord Brownell... I can readily believe he is a murderer. He is nasty and cruel. He tormented me for years at Eton, and I still have the scar on my leg from where he drove a sword into my thigh during a fencing lesson. He claimed the pad must have popped off the tip, but everyone knew he left it off on purpose. Instructors and the headmaster turned a blind eye because they did not care to enrage his father. I am sorry for the situation, especially for the girl whom you say he is determined to kill, but I cannot help you. I will engage in no activity that puts me in his company."

A voice from the doorway begged to disagree.

Startled, Kilby flinched and jumped back anxiously, one foot landing on the edge of the tray, which clanked loudly as it settled again on the tile floor. Pivoting furiously, he rebuked the caller for his intolerable presumption. "This is not a public house but the private chamber of a magistrate judge! You cannot stroll in at your leisure and offer your opinion on a matter that does not concern you. Leave now or I shall have a Runner escort you out."

Kilby's anger was hardly shocking.

The most imposing thing about Daniel Grint was his prominent chin, and the feature was not likely to inspire dread or alarm. Gillray, in his famous caricature of the former head of the Alien Office, gleefully extended the protuberance by several inches, and Kingsley had sneeringly described the feature as monstrously nosy.

As his office carried more weight, he promptly introduced himself as second in command to Lord Sidmouth, the home secretary.

Verity imagined he delighted in saying that—second in command.

It was only possible because his fellow under-secretary had been summarily dismissed for nearly starting a civil war and his replacement had yet to be hired.

Tartly, Kilby said, "I know who Sidmouth is. I do not need you to explain cursory matters of the government. Your position does not give you leave to stride into my chamber and issue orders. You have no authority here!"

Affecting deep confusion over the charge, Grint wrinkled his brow and swore he had issued no orders. "I am sure I requested your assistance. Indeed, I pleaded for it."

Although taken aback by Grint's appearance, Verity was not particularly surprised by it. The under-secretary had a large staff at his disposal and a vested interest in restoring the goodwill he had lost when he refused to help Hardwicke free her from Newgate. It would be easy enough for him to keep abreast of their movements.

Even so, Verity knew they had not been followed.

Together, she and Hardwicke had enough skill to notice when they were being watched.

"Didn't I, Wicke?" Grint added, looking at his associate. "I *begged* to disagree. And I continue to entreat you now, your honor, to reconsider your refusal. I would like to see this matter resolved as quickly as possible, most notably because a woman's life is at stake and as Englishmen we cannot allow a member of the weaker sex to cower in fear while we sit comfortably in our well-appointed chambers. If you search your conscience, I know you will arrive at the same conclusion."

Kilby winced several times during this speech, for its criticism had been quite pointed, and agreed that action must be taken. "But by someone more suited to the task, I think. A man with your resources, Mr. Grint, will have no trouble locating him."

Patently, it was true. There were plenty of magistrates in London, and eventually they would find one who would consent to their scheme. As ludicrous as their proposal was, it was not entirely beyond the bounds. Just three weeks ago, Sir John Piddlehinton hid in a closet to capture a suspected killer in the act of murdering his next victim.

Their plot was almost tame in comparison.

But meeting with additional magistrates came at a cost, delaying the plan's execution and risking exposure. Having failed to anticipate Kilby's prior relationship with the suspect, Verity and Hardwicke would now have to confirm none existed before making their next approach. That would also take time, although considerably less with Grint's assistance.

The under-secretary, however, was disinclined to wait. Impatient with what he perceived as Kilby's cowardice or merely eager to exert his authority, he announced that his considerable resources were currently allocated elsewhere. "If necessary, I can devote them to examining your employment agreement to make sure it does not contain a prohibition against timidity."

Kilby blanched, and Verity thought it was fortunate he had not picked up the salver from the floor because he would have surely dropped it again.

"But that is neither here nor there," Grint asserted confidently. "An Eton man like yourself is not afraid of bullies."

With few avenues open to him, Kilby had no recourse but to agree, and Grint took a step back as Hardwicke reviewed the details of the plan.

Chapter Thirteen

※

Friday, June 26
6:01 p.m.

Delphine, who had previously endorsed the plan featuring Lady Abercrombie, now declared it utterly without merit. "If Grint believes the plot will succeed, then I am forced to conclude it will end in disaster. Any scheme he deems worthwhile must be inherently flawed. I am sorry, but he is too much of a dunderhead for it to be otherwise."

The under-secretary, who was sitting a mere three feet away from her in the parlor at Bethel Street, took no offense at this unkind critique and assured her she did not have to apologize for speaking her mind. "I value an honest assessment."

Raising her chin slightly, she barely acknowledged his presence as she glanced at him out of the corner of her eye and announced that her remark had been directed at Verity and Hardwicke. "They have given considerable time and effort to figuring out how to compel Lord Brownell to confess, and now they must come up with a new idea. It is a blow."

And still Grint remained gracious, allowing that her anger against him was justified. "Your concern for your friend is a credit to you. You were frantic for her safety and wished for someone to swoop in and rescue her. I am sorry that I could not be that person, but the limits of my office are fixed and not open to interpretation. Under no circumstance can I present myself to the governor of the jail and demand the release of a prisoner. I am sure you will comprehend the truth of that as soon as you calm down."

As there were few things more finely calculated to increase Delphine's rage than advising her with placid condescension to lessen it, she could not bring herself to respond to his comments without employing invectives.

Many, many invectives.

Keenly aware that giving free rein to her temper would only extend the interview, she contented herself with darting a waspish grin at him before turning to Verity, who still sported Mr. Jenkinson's bushy eyebrows and rotund belly. "I suggest we revisit the scheme where you dangle yourself enticingly in front of Lord Brownell to induce him to try killing you again. I was too quick to dismiss it."

Verity laughed at her friend's reversal and cautioned her against allowing her contempt for the government official to undermine principles she had held for decades. "He is a sapskull with cotton between his ears, but even a stopped clock is correct twice a day. I am sorry if that sounds too harsh."

Grint assured her it did not.

The comparison to the broken instrument was somewhat cutting, to be sure, but he understood the point she was trying to make.

Verity shook her head at this determined civility and said,

"I was apologizing to Hardwicke. I imagine it is not altogether comfortable to listen to an unfavorable assessment of your character given the length of your association, and I wanted to be respectful of his feelings."

In fact, she did not.

Rather, she enjoyed tweaking Grint's nose.

No fonder of the under-secretary than her friend, she was decidedly annoyed at his presence in her parlor. Having bid him a firm goodbye in front of the building in Bow Street, she had been unprepared to find him standing patiently at her door when she disembarked from the carriage.

Although the insouciance of his pose was meant to suggest he had been waiting for several minutes, she knew it had been only one or two at the most.

She would have demanded he leave, but she wore Mr. Jenkinson's slightly shabby suit and worried about creating a scene. Two men tussling in front of her home would inevitably draw curious onlookers, and she smiled as she imagined the neighbors chattering about Miss Lark's warring beaus.

It had a certain appeal.

Hardwicke, however, had shaken his head and said there was no purpose in fighting the inevitable. "Let us have the conversation and be done."

With a moue of annoyance, Verity admitted him into the house, where Delphine met them in the hallway. She glared pugnaciously at Grint and called for Lucy and Cook to help her toss out the rubbish.

The servants appeared in the corridor with gratifying speed, and Verity smiled at them ruefully as she explained to her friend that Hardwicke suggested they hear the under-secretary out. "He says it is the fastest way to move him along. Let us retire to the parlor. Lucy, we shall not require anything, thank you!"

As soon as they were seated, Grint launched into a laudatory speech extolling the virtues of their plan. Clearly, he had heard most of their conversation with Kilby, if not the whole of it, and repeated many of the details now. Having made his approval known, he turned his attention to Brownell and asked why he wished Miss Lark ill.

The query was met with resounding silence.

Seconds ticked by, each one tolled by the loud clock next to the door, and Delphine's expression grew more and more grim as she stared at the under-secretary. Then she turned to Verity and announced that she could no longer support the scheme.

That exchange had taken place more than ten minutes ago, and Grint showed no signs of leaving. Indeed, he leaned back now in his seat and assured Verity that Hardwicke himself had offered a more stinging assessment of his character on at least one occasion. "Our boat capsized in the channel, and he said several uncharitable things about my mother, more than half of which were entirely unsubstantiated."

Then he smiled to denote he was joking.

"How did you know we were at Bow Street?" Verity asked.

"It was Metcalfe," Hardwicke said, crossing one leg over the other. "He is a thief-taker who trades in information. He was at Bow Street when we arrived, and my presence there was curious enough that he decided to tell Grint about it. Presumably, he is the reason Kilby kept us waiting for forty-five minutes."

The under-secretary unstintingly confirmed it. "He could not have you dashing off before he had a chance to collect his payment. He knows I require proof. But that is all beside the point. We were discussing Brownell's animus against Miss Lark. Why does he want to harm her?"

Blank stares also met this query.

Once again, the ticking clock was the only sound in the room.

After examining her fingernails with mild interest for about a minute, Delphine said to Grint, "And your investigation into John Smith, how is that faring? Have you ascertained a description of him yet from your friends at the customs office or do you remain too timid to press for answers?"

Having wielded the charge of timidity against Kilby to great effect little more than an hour before, Grint showed no alarm at being tarred with the same brush. Calmly, he reminded her that he represented the Home Office. "I must follow protocol."

"Yes, that is right, the *limits* of your office," Delphine noted snidely. "I wonder, Mr. Grint, what purpose you serve if your every action is constrained by rules and protocols. Are you even allowed to be here today? Surely, calling on the home of a suspected criminal is a breach."

Smiling blandly, the under-secretary proposed one use for himself. "I can ensure Brownell faces consequences for murdering Mr. Muir."

Delphine scoffed. "After *we* elicit a confession."

Agreeably, he nodded. "That is generally how our system of justice works."

Unimpressed, Delphine looked at Hardwicke and asked if they had heard enough. "Do say I may summon Lucy and Cook now."

"Heaven forbid!" Grint said with a theatrical shudder before assuring his host that no such aggressive measures were necessary. "I am happy to show myself out—just as soon as I have discovered the resentment Brownell holds against you, Miss Lark. It is a significant piece of the puzzle, and I do not feel comfortable entering into a situation of which I do not have the full picture. Tell me, please, what is the connection? How did you come to meet him?"

"Have I met him?" Verity asked curiously.

Grint leaned forward. "Have you not?"

The clock ticked loudly.

Rising to her feet, Delphine said, "Well, then, we are at an impasse and there is nothing to be done about it. I would say that I am sorry we could not find a way to work together, but I am bound by the limitations of my civility. Perhaps next time! Do forward the information on the customs office if you somehow manage to get it despite your overweening deference."

Although his lips tightened at the dismissal, the undersecretary abided by her request and stood up as well. Wryly, he thanked her for her generous understanding of his position, without which the situation would be untenable.

Delphine simpered.

To Hardwicke, Grint said, "You may keep your secrets. I shall lend my consequence nonetheless. It will do no harm to have reinforcements on hand should Kilby succumb to childhood terror. I trust you will keep me apprised of the details."

Hardwicke agreed to send word as soon as the particulars were settled, and Delphine, taking that as her cue, opened the door to sweep Grint from the room.

※

From the London Daily Gazette
Saturday, June 27

Twaddle Tales
by Mr. Twaddle-Thum

. . .

I am sorry, my darlings, but you must put down your tea.

The report I stand ready to deliver is so shocking and bewildering I cannot say another word unless I am assured of your safety. The prospect of your jerking your hand in astonishment, perhaps to draw it to your chest in an attempt to regain your breath, and splashing yourself with piping hot liquid is intolerable.

Please, dear reader, return the cup to the table for my sake.

Is it down?

Did you push it a few inches away?

Are your smelling salts within easy reach?

Very good, we shall proceed.

Our story begins in the most unlikely of places: a quiet lane in an unfashionable part of town.

Which quiet lane?

That I cannot tell you because all roads lacking the good taste to place themselves in Mayfair look the same to me. Perhaps it was Tilly Road in Medford. Perhaps it was Auster Street in Southwark.

Trust me, my loves, it does not matter in the least.

All you need to know is this lane is home to a man whom we shall call Mr. Unfortunate Soul. On Wednesday, Mr. Soul succumbed to a wretched and immediate death upon swallowing a sort of sweet morsel that you yourself have likely enjoyed dozens of times.

Oh, yes, *do* reach for the smelling salts.

Of course you feel faint.

I feel faint just writing those words.

My heart skipped three beats in terror for you.

But hold steady!

You are safe.

A LARK'S RELEASE

The defect was not in the tasty treats themselves but in the cyanide of potassium that the murderer—yes, I said, murderer—sprinkled on top of them to kill his victim.

It is shocking, I know, and you are probably certain you read that wrong.

Alas not!

I did in fact say *cyanide of potassium*.

It is morning, you have barely opened your eyes, and yet here I am asking you to contemplate complex scientific formulations.

Do not consent!

Brush past the horror of chemistry to the marginally more agreeable thought of Mr. Soul's death, which was mercifully short. In this way, his killer was kind.

In every other way, he was cruel.

And the cruelest cut—Mr. Soul was not the intended victim. He was poisoned by mistake, like a second at a dawn appointment catching his death from a bullet that darts off its course.

So who should be dead in his stead?

It is impossible to say.

Nobody knows!

Well, not *nobody* nobody.

I have heard some rumblings but am reluctant to share them because they do not make sense.

How so?

Consider this: They concern an illegitimate sister whom our villain fears will steal his inheritance. An insignificant by-blow receiving the keys to the kingdom—it is so preposterous I cannot credit it. Not even Gloucester allowed his affection for Edmund to corrupt his good sense so thoroughly.

As for the murderer himself, I cannot credit that information either, for the description supplied to me is of a blond man with beautifully shaped lips, dark brooding eyes, and a well-sculpted form.

A specimen that handsome a villain?

No, he must be pure of heart!

Even so, my darlings, it would probably be wise to exercise a little extra caution for the time being and refuse all Adonises bearing sweets.

Sunday, June 28
8:16 p.m.

Kilby was disappointed by the tasteful décor in the Countess of Abercrombie's bedchamber, which was swathed in shades of cream and blue. Having gawked with slack-jawed astonishment at the sumptuous fantasia of her drawing room, he had anticipated a spectacle twice as wondrous.

To be sure, he had not pictured a merry-go-round to the right of her bed, but a canopy resembling a carnival tent would not have been out of place.

Noting his expression, her ladyship laughed in throaty amusement and consoled the magistrate by informing him he was not the first man to have that reaction. "Here, *I* am the star attraction."

Glassy-eyed, Kilby managed to nod.

The countess's smile widened as she urged her visitors to step deeper into the room. "Come, let me give you the tour of your hiding spots before I leave," she said, gesturing to a leather folding screen in the far right corner. Decorated with birds and blossoms, it would provide excellent coverage. "There are two stools behind there so that you may make yourselves comfortable."

Verity, inspecting the space, decided it would do quite well.

Next, her ladyship pulled back one of the drapes and noted they were made out of a velvet, which was not ideal in the current circumstance, as the heavy material muffled sound. "Do not ask me how I know that because I do not have time to tell you the story, but suffice to say that a man of Lord Pudsey's age and experience should have known better than to taunt a lion cub with a joint of mutton."

Letting the curtain drop back into place, the countess pointed to the settee in front of the windows and identified it as her favorite location, as it provided the best vantage. "I think this is where you should be, Mr. Kilby, as you are the most important person in the room. I would be desolate if I went through all this bother of seducing Blandie and you did not hear every word."

Gratified by the attention, Kilby owned himself delighted by the suggestion and he slipped into the space to confirm its suitability. Once he was tucked comfortably behind the settee, he called out, "Can you see me?"

Her ladyship assured him she could not.

"Then it is settled," Kilby said with a satisfied air. "I shall hide behind the sofa."

Presenting the last option, the countess pointed to a generous chair in the corner opposite the screen. "I had it carried in from the dressing room, and it quite obviously does not belong here, as it is the only item in the room that is green—and such a bright shade at that! But I am confident Blandie will not notice. Indeed, if he has the presence of mind to critique the decor, then it is safe to say that our plan has already failed."

It was, Verity thought, an astute assessment.

Kilby, whose anxiety at confronting his old school nemesis had lessened the longer he was in the presence of Lady Abercrombie, insisted it would not come to that. "You are sure to succeed, and we shall have Sir Andy in a jail cell by midnight."

Although inclined to bask in the magistrate's admiration, the countess could not allow herself to linger another minute more. A quarter hour before she had received word that Brownell had arrived at the Red Lantern, which was her preferred hunting ground.

To be sure, she could woo Blandie anywhere.

They could be standing on the refuse-strewn bank of the Thames during low tide, and all she would have to do was wink and crook her finger.

But at the gaming hell, where his pockets were soon to be a great deal lighter, was the optimal location. The more money he lost, the more wine he drank and the more pliable he became.

"I expect to be back around ten," her ladyship said confidently as she paused in the doorway. "There is the new issue of *Ackerman's Repository* in the dressing room as well as a deck of cards and several books. Do make yourself at home while you wait. I had my housekeeper arrange for sandwiches, and there is a fresh pot of tea. I would advise you all to take to your hiding spots at nine-thirty in case we return early. I have been known to amaze even myself."

The countess swept from the room, and as Verity closed the door behind her, Grint suggested they play whist for sixpence a point.

Kilby agreed but only if they lowered the stakes to a penny.

Sunday, June 28
10:18 p.m.

Twaddling was waiting.

It was the ability to hold oneself still in expectation of an event that might happen in a few minutes or a few hours or not at all.

Typically, it involved discomfort.

Rarely, did one Twaddle on a settee in a room of a pleasing temperature.

More frequently, one had to squeeze inside a crate or a wardrobe or a laundry hamper where the air quickly grew hot and stale. Keeping to a single position for any length of time was physically onerous. Muscles ached, limbs grew numb, and the desire to move for the sake of change was excruciating.

It was not as complex a skill as donning a convincing disguise or creating a believable persona, but it was just as crucial to the success of the *London Daily Gazette*'s most popular gossip.

Waiting in Lady Abercrombie's bedchamber for her to return with Brownell was a relatively comfortable affair. Tucked behind the commodious armchair in the corner, she had enough room to shift around without knocking into the furniture or bumping against the wall, and she had several positions to choose from: crossing her legs, pulling her knees toward her chest, leaning back. There was a steady flow of cool air in her corner, ensuring the space did not grow warm.

There were drawbacks, of course.

The floorboards were hard and splintered in places from wear. A large sliver of wood had driven itself into her hand, and although she extracted it from her palm with a minimum of fuss, several droplets of blood trickled onto her dress. The light was too dim for her to see the damage, and all she could do was hope the red splatter did not mar the lovely silk of her gown.

It was precisely the sort of vibrant pistachio Mrs. Delacour would wear to a garden party, and as she had adopted the widow's vivaciousness that day in Hyde Park when Brownell spotted her talking to Goldhawk, she had decided it was in her best interest to continue with that character.

As soon as Brownell confessed to trying to kill her, Verity would spring out from behind the chair, screech in terror, and have a fit of vapors.

Perhaps she would faint.

The important thing was for Brownell not to realize that she presented an actual threat to him. Hardwicke, Grint, and Kilby would handle the serious aspects of the arrest, and she would remain a bon vivant who understood only that her life was endangered by forces beyond her control. She had settled on the tactic as the best way to discourage the family's interest in her. Realizing she was a frivolous pea widgeon, Frimgallow would cease tormenting his son with empty threats, and she would be allowed to fade softly from the story. Brownell would be taken to Newgate on the charge of murdering Muir.

Verity Lark need not have anything else to do with it.

At least, that was her hope.

In practice, events could unfold very differently.

She would have to wait and see.

Ah, yes, waiting again, she thought dryly, tilting her body to the left to relieve the pressure on her tailbone, which had grown numb in the interval since they had taken to their hiding spots. Despite Lady Abercrombie's confident assertion that she would return by ten, the hour had chimed on the clock about fifteen minutes ago. Either the assignment was taking longer than expected or she was well on her way to failing.

If the case was the latter, then they would have to try again.

Verity doubted the countess would sustain interest in an extended campaign, but she would be amenable to a second attempt.

Kilby, however, might bow out.

The excitement of the evening was almost too much for him to bear, and he had thrown himself behind the settee with gusto, settling onto his knees so that he could look over the back. Verity had watched in dread as he practiced peering, his sandy-colored head popping up over the sofa by several inches, and she had proposed they swap. The armchair provided a glimpse of the bed. It was just a narrow slice—the bottom right corner—but the view was unimpeded and presented little risk of discovery.

Kilby adamantly refused, unwilling to leave the location Lady Abercrombie had specifically designated for him. Hardwicke, sharing her concern, enumerated the many advantages of the screen, including the convenient stool and the prospect of company during the interminable interlude, but the magistrate would not consider it. Accepting defeat, Hardwicke disappeared behind the lacquered panels with Grint and everyone settled in for the wait, even Kilby. Despite her concerns, the judge had been as quiet as a church mouse, and she hoped the longer-than-expected interlude had dampened some of his enthusiasm.

※

Sunday, June 28
10:31 p.m.

The first thing Verity heard was Lady Abercrombie's breathy laughter.

A tingle of delight, the sound wafted faintly into the room, carrying a whisper of seduction, and Verity felt her muscles loosen with relief at the countess's obvious success. The woman would not be tittering flirtatiously if she had failed in her mission.

She had not doubted it for a minute—her ladyship, that was.

From the moment the countess had consented to help—and promptly began tailoring their plan to her preferences—she had known she would be able to lead Brownell on a merry chase.

What had she said?

He will be like hot wax in my hand, melting at my touch.

Another laugh drifted into the bedchamber, slightly more girlish than the last, and Verity noted that the sound had drawn closer.

The couple was either in the corridor or just outside the door.

In the next second or two, they would enter.

Carefully, Verity shifted positions, swinging her legs to the side of her body and leaning slightly forward so she could look around the edge of the chair. In the gentle light of the glowing candles, she could see the smooth blue counterpane on the bottom corner of the bed. At the other end, near the headboard, the silk coverlet had been drawn back invitingly, as though the bedchamber were in a constant state of readiness.

It was, Verity thought, a trifle overdone, and if she were Brownell, she would find the way the scene seemed to be set so precisely more than a little disconcerting.

Lady Abercrombie, however, swore he would not notice. "A man has to have some awareness of himself to question how others perceive him, and I promise you, Blandie has none of that. Other people are merely admiring mirrors into which he peers to make sure his cravat is straight."

Having no countervailing theory to offer, Verity deferred to the countess's superior understanding of the target, which had so far been on the mark. Aside from overestimating how little time it would take to lure Brownell to her home, she had been correct in her calculations, and Verity felt her confidence in the plan's chance of succeeding increase.

A floorboard creaked, indicating that the couple had entered the room, and just as Verity heard another squeak, her ladyship trilled lightly and said with husky admiration, "Ah, you deliciously naughty man. Do that again."

Silence followed as Brownell complied, and Verity, her anxiety about Kilby returning, hoped he had the good sense not to suddenly dart his head up to watch. She imagined the countess waving frantically at him to get down as Brownell pressed heated kisses against her neck.

Lady Abercrombie sighed, and Verity heard a soft thud as Brownell threw himself onto the mattress, his stocking-clad feet dancing into and then out of view. She saw the bed dip again as the countess joined him and then detected the dreamy rustle of silk.

Was that Brownell removing her dress?

Verity had to assume so, especially when her ladyship let out a little growl of impatience, unimpressed, it would seem, with his efforts to disrobe her with grace.

Nevertheless, he persisted in his goal, eventually removing the offending garment and tossing it onto the floor. The countess, affecting appreciation for his efforts, laughed again and called him wicked.

All but crowing, Brownell affirmed her gratifying estimation of his character.

As most seductions were long, drawn-out affairs, Verity

adjusted her legs again, sliding them in front of her as she pressed her back against the wall. She listened as Lady Abercrombie fawned over Brownell's manliness and gushed over his masterfulness. In a lilting coo, she owned herself thrilled by his decisiveness.

And then she stated it plainly: "It is the hint of danger that arouses me, knowing that you tried to poison your own half sister."

Verity straightened up at once, her muscles tightening in anticipation as she braced for Brownell's fervent denial. A charge of murder was a charge of murder no matter how lasciviously it was made.

And yet no disavowal was issued.

Brownell did not say anything at all, and Verity was left to assume he had put his mouth to another use, one that struck him in the moment as more urgent.

Or perhaps silence was his tactic.

An accusation so outrageous did not deserve the dignity of a reply.

Set on her course, her ladyship moaned enticingly and marveled at his virility in not even making a token repudiation. Any other man, she purred, would have told her she was mistaken. "But you are not like the other men I have known. You know who you are and do not shrink from it. I find that wildly arousing."

Ah, that did it.

Naturally, it did.

All a man really wanted from a woman was confirmation of his greatness.

It was as the countess said: Reflect him back to himself with his cravat straight.

"She was making trouble for me, and I wanted her gone," Brownell said, his voice hoarse with desire and slightly muffled. "It was as simple as that."

Oh, but it was not simple, for murder was a bold stroke, a fearsome audacity, and Lady Abercrombie whimpered in need, as though her very bones were melting, and she tossed encomiums at him like rose petals: important, consequential, superior.

Every one hit its mark, petting his ego with so much finesse that he readily admitted to everything: yes, he had tried to kill the girl; yes, he had killed a man by mistake; yes, he intended to try again. He had arranged for a poisoned bottle of wine to be delivered to her house the next morning from the warden of Newgate. "He is sorry for her wrongful imprisonment and eager to curry favor with the Marquess of Ware. I gave him the bottle myself as well as the letter to include in the packaging advising the chit to raise a glass at once to the intoxicating rush of freedom."

That is it, Verity thought, rising to a crouch, her shoulders still tucked beneath the back of the chair as she waited for the countess to give her signal. They had everything they needed to arrest Brownell. The murder confession was more than enough to imprison him in Newgate until he could be tried by a jury of his peers, but the addition of physical evidence—the poisoned wine bottle, the handwritten letter—made the case against him ironclad. Verity was certain the confectioner could be persuaded to give testimony against him now that it would no longer simply be her word against his. Plus, there was the source of the cyanide of potassium. With Brownell in prison, the threat would be gone and Castleheart would have enough time to find the jeweler who had sold it to him.

Brownell was sunk.

But he did not know that yet.

He still thought a decades-old desire was about to be satisfied, and with arrogance and excitement and confidence in his tone, he said, "As you yourself noted, my dear, I am a man of action, and now I must act!"

Offered with glee, it nevertheless sounded like a threat to Verity, who expected a tussle or a howl of distress to follow. Instead, she heard a faint grunt and then the countess's clear if slightly bored voice as she said, "I trust that is sufficient."

Chapter Fourteen

❦

Sunday, June 28
11:01 p.m

Sneeringly, Brownell said, "What in God's name do you—"

But he broke off as Kilby appeared behind the settee.

More baffled than angry now, he stared at the magistrate dumbly, then at Verity as she stepped around the armchair.

Matter-of-factly, Lady Abercrombie made the introductions as she fetched a dressing gown from a chair near her vanity. "This gentleman is Ernest Kilby, he is a magistrate with Bow Street. It is he who shall be overseeing your arraignment and detention. If you have any objections or questions, do present them to him, as my part of the endeavor has concluded," she said, slipping a red dressing gown over her simple chemise and tying it loosely at the waist.

Brownell's expression did not alter.

He still appeared flummoxed.

But slowly he began to move, sliding his legs off the bed, finding his cravat in the folds of the counterpane.

Drawing her fingers through her hair to fluff her curls, many of which had flattened during the romp in the bed, Lady Abercrombie continued. "The woman is Verity Lark. I know you know *of* Miss Lark, but I do not believe you have met her. She was quite put out by your efforts to end her life—I understand the neighbor you inadvertently poisoned was a dear friend—and sought my help. Behind you, previously hiding behind that lacquered screen, are Lord Colson Hardwicke, whose interest in this matter is already known to you, and Daniel Grint, an under-secretary in the Home Office. I have no idea how he is connected to this business but assume it has something to do with a general remit to maintain peace and order in our fair land. If you must know more, then you should ask him."

Although Brownell's fists clutched the neckcloth so tightly the tips of his fingers turned white, he did not seem particularly troubled by this information, not even as Hardwicke and Grint stepped around the bed to join them. Indeed, he regarded the two men thoughtfully, and Verity wondered if he was trying to decide what sway his father might have with Sidmouth. Frimgallow was not without his influence. He was an extremely wealthy landowner, and money was power.

It made problems disappear.

Unfortunately for Brownell, it would not work its magic on *this* problem.

It might have if Kilby had been the sole witness to the confession. Despite the stiffness of his resolve now, the magistrate would most likely have crumbled like a stale biscuit if both Brownell and his father applied pressure. Even Grint might have weighed the merits of pursuing justice against possible damage to his career. But Hardwicke, who carried his own authority, would not be cowed by a pair of bullies, and her ladyship would cheerfully regale the beau monde with details of the shocking encounter for years to come. And Verity herself was not without power. With her access to the *London Daily Gazette*'s extensive readership, she could ensure that all of London chattered about an unequal justice system that allowed men of fortune and breeding to walk away from their crimes while the poor and common suffered for theirs.

Brownell's expression remained pensive as Lady Abercrombie picked up a small porcelain bottle from her vanity, removed the stopper, and gently dabbed perfume behind her ears. A scent of orange blossom and coriander wafted across the room.

Perhaps he had decided that silence was his best defense.

Protestations of innocence would be ignored, and threats of intimidation would be cited as further evidence of his guilt.

"Well, then, I am off," the countess announced with blithe indifference to the scene still unfolding in her bedchamber. "Cuthbert is waiting downstairs to join me for a quiet supper *entre nous*. My chef has prepared a delightful little feast of oysters and braised beefsteaks, and I have asked my butler to open a bottle of my finest champagne. I deserve it, don't I, after this evening's work. I am confident everything is in hand, but if you require anything, do ring for help and the servants will provide assistance. Please try to be gone by midnight, as I have other plans for this room."

Then she bid them adieu and swept from the bedchamber.

It was, Verity thought, a stunning exit.

Brownell appeared to agree, and despite the urgency of his situation and the betrayal by which he had arrived there, he watched Lady Abercrombie saunter away with an expression of intense longing. Then he turned to Kilby and warned him that he really did not want to involve himself further in the uproar.

"It is a private matter among family," he added with calm composure. "You understand private matters among family, as your father killed himself in the study after certain financial irregularities with his parishioners came to light. It would be a shame if all that wretchedness got stirred up again. There was some talk about your mother's involvement in the scheme, wasn't there? So many questions left unanswered. I, for one, would not hesitate to ask them again."

Although Kilby raised his chin resolutely, as though impervious to the menace of these words, he took a step back, then another, bumping into the settee and dropping awkwardly onto the cushion.

"One down, two to go," Brownell murmured smoothly, tilting his head slightly to the right to contemplate Hardwicke and Grint next.

Verity did not enter into his calculation, either because he did not consider her worthy of his attention or he wanted to deal with her last.

"Grinty, Grinty," Brownell clucked with tart disapproval as he slid his legs over the edge of the bed to place his feet on the floor. "How far you have fallen. Once you commanded men all over Europe and now you are hiding behind a screen in a harlot's bedchamber. I do not know for whom to be more embarrassed: you for descending to such depths or Sidmouth for thinking you have anything left to offer your country."

Although Delphine had said considerably worse things to the under-secretary without piercing his mask of bland equanimity, Grint flinched at this insult and turned to address a comment to Hardwicke. As the government official began to speak, Brownell leaped to his feet, and wielding the cravat like a garrote, wound it around Verity's neck and pulled tightly, collapsing her windpipe.

She gasped.

Wrenching her shoulders frantically, she clawed at the cloth constricting her throat, desperate to free herself as her lungs ached to draw air.

It was how Mrs. Delacour would respond to the threat.

By contrast, Verity Lark had read Brownell's intention in the swerve of his body and actually bent forward to allow him to more easily strangle her. As he was three inches shorter than her, he would not have the right leverage to pull it taut enough to cause significant damage.

And his movements were slow.

In his mind, the deadly maneuver might have been performed swiftly and surely, but in reality the cravat had caught on her chin and he had to adjust his stance to properly tighten the cloth.

At any time during the execution, Verity could have either evaded or disarmed him.

A step to the side.

An elbow to his kidney.

It had struck her as more prudent, however, to permit him some measure of success—to allow him a single moment of glorious triumph, yes, because she relished the extra dose of disappointment when he failed to escape, but also as additional proof of his iniquity. A confession of murder was persuasive, as was an announcement of intent to try again, especially when substantiated with a bottle of adulterated wine and testimony from the warden, but both paled in comparison to a murder attempt made directly in front of the eyes of a judge and an important government official.

That was evidence that could not be denied.

Brownell could make the ridiculous claim that he had tripped when standing and the strip of cloth inadvertently wound itself around the victim's neck, but nobody would give the assertion the time of day.

But he did not understand this yet.

Brownell thought freedom was within his grasp because he lacked the ability to conceive a complicated plot or account for unexpected contingencies. All he could see was the step immediately in front of him, and how he was actually going to extricate himself from the murder charge had not yet occurred to him. His only thought was of leaving—the room, that was. He had no plan for exiting the building, announcing that he would allow the chit to go as soon as he had crossed the threshold of the bedchamber as long as nobody followed him.

As Brownell spoke, Kilby struggled to rise to his feet, his efforts seemingly hampered by some remembered trauma. Fleetingly, Verity wondered if his father had hanged himself in that study, and Grint turned to look at Hardwicke as if to abide by his response while Hardwicke glared at Verity.

Impatiently, she realized.

He knew precisely what she was doing and thought the charade had gone on long enough. It was time to end it.

Obligingly, Verity lifted her foot, which was encased in a thick-soled boot, and slammed it down on Brownell's stocking-clad one. He yowled in agony, his grip tightening unbearably as his entire body clenched in pain, then loosening as he hopped up and down.

Verity screamed as well, shrieks of terror that were higher, louder, and more sustained than her assailant's, then she crumpled onto the settee with a pathetic whimper. A highly distressed Kilby gently petted her hand and murmured, "There, there, Miss Lark," and Verity allowed him the liberty because Mrs. Delacour would have been greatly comforted by his consideration. Calming her down also seemed to have a beneficial effect on Kilby's own nerves, and by the time she had judged a sufficient interval for a fit of vapors to have passed, his own equanimity had been restored.

While her face had been buried in a cushion, Hardwicke had taken Brownell in hand, wrenching his wrists behind his body and binding them together with cord. Although Brownell winced at the tautness of the restraints, the sting paled in comparison to the throbbing in his foot, and seething down at Verity, he snarled, "She broke my foot! The bitch broke my foot!"

Such language!

Verity shrunk from the harsh expression of his fury, and Kilby, offended on her behalf, rose majestically to his feet and ordered the miscreant to Bow Street at once. "He must be locked up for the safety of all women in the city! I shall deal with his father if he dares to lodge a complaint," he said confidently before darting a beseeching look at Grint, as he himself could not be expected to march the prisoner to the carriage.

Acceding to the role without complaint, the under-secretary took possession of Brownell from Hardwicke and turned him toward the doorway. Brownell fumed at the brutality, swearing he could not walk a single step on his broken foot, and Grint helpfully suggested he should try to hop instead. With a hateful glower, Brownell gingerly lowered his weight onto his injured foot and lumbered forward with a limp. He moved slowly, laboriously, with an exaggerated affect, each ponderous step an almost unachievable effort, and as he reached the threshold, an accomplishment measured in minutes, not seconds, he turned back to yell at Kilby, "My shoes, you monster! Get me my shoes!"

Dismayed, the magistrate scurried back into the room to fetch the black pumps, which had been thrust to opposite corners of the bed. Clutching them to his chest, he dashed out again and found himself angrily rebuffed when he tried to hand them to their owner, whose gait grew heavier and more plodding.

Brownell's flair for a dramatic exit rivaled the countess's, Verity noted wryly, calculating that it would take the procession at least ten minutes to reach the door—or slightly longer if they stopped to allow the prisoner to don footwear before stepping outside. Content to wait until they were gone before leaving herself, Verity pressed her head against the back of the settee, and Hardwicke, either sharing this opinion or simply following her lead, sat down next to her. Loosely, he linked his fingers with hers.

"It is an utter delight watching you work," he said softly. "Brownell's handling of the cravat was so clumsy, I thought for sure you were going to have to wrap it around your own neck."

Of course he had noticed.

Hardwicke and his eye for detail.

But it was not just that: The maneuver was so poorly executed, he would have had to be blind to miss it or as distracted as Kilby.

"He managed it well enough in the end," she said graciously, tilting her head to the left to contemplate his profile: the aquiline nose, the strong jaw, the graceful forehead.

His lips twisted into a faint smile as he said, "Yes, but only after you kindly moved your chin out of the way."

It was impossible not to find Brownell's astonishing incompetence funny.

Nonchalantly admitting to murder merely to advance his romantic prospects!

If Verity had not witnessed the event herself, she would have dismissed it as fustian, and yet it was all of a piece with his original scheme, which suffered from the same defect: a lack of imagination. Brownell was incapable of conceiving any outcome that did not align with his intended goal. Raised in wealth and splendor, he had been insulated from the consequences of his failures, which had become an alien concept.

It was to her advantage, she knew, for a more meticulous murderer would have succeeded in ending her life before she even realized she was under threat.

And yet she could not be grateful for an ineptness that resulted in the death of an innocent man who had absolutely nothing to do with the situation.

Poor Mr. Muir, scuffling with the wrong shrub at the wrong moment.

"As he was so determined to incriminate himself further, I felt it was churlish to withhold my assistance," she replied mildly.

Hardwicke nodded and tightened his grip on her hand as he promised her Brownell would not escape accountability. "There is too much evidence against him, especially with the bottle of poisoned wine, which Grint will have in his possession before the hour is out. But the display at the end put him beyond the pale. He cannot deny as fantasy or braggadocio something we all witnessed with our own eyes. Despite Frimgallow's undisguised contempt for his progeny, I cannot believe he will calmly accept the apprehension and imprisonment of his eldest son. He will issue either a threat or a bribe to convince you to recant your testimony, and I think it behooves us to preempt such an attempt by making clear the lay of the land. I know you generally hold Grint in contempt, but in this he can be useful by ensuring Frimgallow understands that you have the full support of the Home Office. Brownell will most likely not hang because avoiding a trial is in the best interest of the crown, but deportation to New South Wales is a fate worse than death for a man of his ilk."

Verity appreciated that he did not delineate the relationships.

Frimgallow was not her father.

Brownell was not her brother.

Blood meant nothing.

Nobody knew that better than she.

And yet she could not stop from applying the labels silently: One half brother prevented a massacre; one half brother murdered Mrs. Paisley's son-in-law.

It was a stark difference, and although Verity attributed the distinction to parentage, it was La Reina's sweeping indifference to motherhood that contributed to the duke's decency, not whatever positive qualities she happened to possess.

The tragedy of Andrew Brownell's life was that his father took an interest in his upbringing, and because the thought stirred pity in her heart, she resolutely focused her mind on something else. As they were sitting in the Countess of Abercrombie's bedchamber, she complimented Hardwicke on devising an excellent plan, one in which she herself had had little faith. "You were right to trust her. She is not quite the bit of fluff I had believed her to be. She is just as frivolous, to be sure, but there is a resolutely practical core to her, and I can say sincerely and without quibbling that you had the better idea. Thank you for suggesting it."

Amusement sparkled in the depths of his teal eyes as he said, "And yet somehow you still managed to fend off an attack on your life."

Although Verity scoffed at his attempt to cast the mild tussle as an assault, she nevertheless asked him to refrain from mentioning the confrontation to Delphine. "The notion that I allowed him to strangle me would upset her dreadfully, and she would not believe me when I swore he moved so slowly even a snail would have been able to defend itself. She will call me overconfident and fret about what I will do next time."

Hardwicke, agreeing to the request, asked if there were other details he should avoid, and Verity insisted that he must otherwise be unsparing in his account. Delphine and Freddie deserved to know every aspect of Brownell's downfall, however small.

"Even the moment her ladyship grew impatient with Brownell's pains to remove her gown?" he asked, making no effort to hide his mirth.

"Oh, especially that," Verity replied as the clock chimed the half hour, and deciding they had allowed the trio enough time to get to Grint's carriage, she rose to go home.

※

Monday, June 29
8:12 a.m.

The Earl of Frimgallow owed poor Mr. Muir's family financial compensation.

Delphine was adamant about it.

"Now that Lord Brownell has confessed to the killing, there can be no refusal," she continued as Lucy placed a fresh pot of water on the table next to a plate of muffins before straightening the butter knife and leaving the room. "Lord Frimgallow must be convinced to provide an annuity to Mrs. Muir so that she can raise her fatherless children in the security of which his own son cruelly deprived them. It is the only decent thing to do."

Finding nothing remotely funny about the newly widowed woman's situation, Verity nevertheless smiled sardonically as she repeated the word *decent* as though tasting something unfamiliar on her tongue. "With everything we know about

Frimgallow, I am astonished you can think of that concept in conjunction with him. There is nothing more calculated to spur him to do the opposite than an appeal to his sense of decency. You would have better luck threatening him with a lawsuit if he so much as dares to consider giving one farthing to the Muirs to ease his guilty conscience."

Struck by the idea, Delphine furrowed her brow and murmured, "The family would sooner starve than accept his blood money and so on and so forth. Yes, I see your point and agree it is the better tack to take. It might even work. Thank you, dear. I shall send a missive to the Dowager Duchess of Kesgrave as soon as we finish eating."

Although Verity displayed no visible reaction to this startling non sequitur, anxiety fluttered in her stomach at the prospect of further contact with the duke's family. The obligation of giving his wife firing instruction was so unnerving, Verity had yet to send the required missive thanking the duchess for her assistance and arranging a time for the first lesson, and she could conceive of no reason why they had to correspond with the grandmother as well. "I am not sure I understand how the dowager entered our conversation."

"Well, someone has to put our plan into action, and she is the only logical choice," Delphine explained in an excessively reasonable tone—and then had the temerity to calmly and sparingly butter her muffin as though she had not just made an extraordinary statement.

Provoking creature!

Alas, knowing she was being goaded was not enough to persuade Verity to resist the bait. "I can take care of it easily enough. I have several solicitor disguises that are well suited for the task. Mr. Hawley, for example, is an avid and generous soul who would eagerly represent the interests of a young widow free of charge."

Firmly, Delphine said, "No, it won't do."

"Merriweather, then," Verity said, undaunted by the setback. "He is a crusty old codger who would take a grandfatherly interest in Mrs. Muir. He retired two years ago at the insistence of his children but likes to keep a hand in the game. Lawyering is more enjoyable at his age because the opposition consistently underestimates him."

"You may propose every persona in your arsenal and still it won't fadge," Delphine said with a hint of annoyance. "You are not meeting your father under any disguise. If he seeks out a meeting with you, Verity Lark née Mary Price, then we will have a round table to discuss the best way to handle it. But you are not dressing up in one of your ridiculous outfits and introducing yourself as George Hogarth."

Obviously, not, no, for Hogarth was a purveyor of precious gemstones and would be of little help in the situation.

But her friend's point was well taken.

Verity disagreed with it but was sensible enough to respect Delphine's caution. Frimgallow could not be trusted under any circumstance, and there was no benefit to them in risking the exposure of any of their secrets to him. Anything Verity could do could be arranged by other means.

Perhaps so, but the Dowager Duchess of Kesgrave?

It was an unfathomable choice.

As an alternative, Verity suggested Hardwicke.

Popping a piece of muffin into her mouth, Delphine raised an eyebrow in cynical amusement and said, "Hardwicke? Really? You believe he can be in the same room as the man who raised Brownell and not want to throttle him within five minutes? Who else do you have in mind? Perhaps Freddie, who would not even last five minutes before hurtling invectives at Frimgallow for leaving you to fester in Fortescue's and clobbering him on the head. Grint would never do because he cannot be entrusted with any significant responsibility, and I believe you would die of mortification if we asked the Duke of Kesgrave or his wife for the favor. As far as I can tell, that leaves the dowager, who is perfect. She already knows of the relationship, is acquainted with the earl, would be grateful to do you a service to lessen her remorse, has the appropriate emotional distance from the situation not to allow her feelings to influence the encounter, and is thoroughly terrifying in her own way."

It was a cogent argument.

Verity could deny none of it.

And yet knowing that did not make the pill any less bitter.

"I will send her a letter today," Verity said with an air of resignation. Nevertheless, it was for the best, as it would force her to write to the duchess as well. It was unlike her to be so cowardly about a responsibility or so cavalier about an obligation.

Delphine would not allow it. "You already have more than enough to keep you occupied, starting with Lady Bentham's countdown clock, which has entered its final days. She is drawing a much larger crowd now, thanks to several improvements she made per Twaddle's suggestion. According to Mags, the brass band is excellent. And then there is the customs office, which you vowed to visit as soon as the business with Brownell was resolved. In contrast, I have only some gardening and menu planning to do, leaving me plenty of time to write to her grace. And I will merely touch on the request, as the majority of the explanation would be better made in person. Cyanide-laden chocolate puffs and Lady Abercrombie's outré bedroom performance require some context to understand. As we have already discussed your busy schedule for the day, I shall invite her to tea tomorrow or the next day unless you have further objections."

Verity did not—at least, none that were reasonable—and

consented to the plan. As much as she disliked the prospect of hosting the septuagenarian, she had to concede that her friend was correct: Several aspects of the recent episode sounded highly implausible if not outright impossible.

Pleased, Delphine thanked her for being so agreeable, then urged Verity not to remain at the table on her account. "You finished your eggs ten minutes ago and I am lingering over muffins. I know you are champing at the bit to get on with your work."

In fact, Verity was.

Finding an outfit that suited her morning plans presented a quandary, and she had yet to decide what she should wear. The flower seller disguise she had donned for her previous visit to Lady Bentham's countdown had served her well, allowing her to interview her fellow spectators without drawing undue attention to herself. The pretty dress, however, would be a disadvantage if she decided to conduct surveillance of the customs office before approaching it. In that circumstance, a plain, dull-colored suit was ideal for fading into the background.

Nobody noticed an office clerk.

Perhaps a female laborer, then, one who was on the wrong side of forty and dressed in a frumpy apron and mob cap.

Older women were almost always overlooked.

Although these considerations were somewhat pressing, Verity leaned back in her chair and assured her friend she was in no hurry to rush off. After an apprehensive few days, she was genuinely grateful for the quiet morning and the opportunity to enjoy a restful breakfast without worrying about a murderous relative plotting her demise. She knew the business had been wearying on Delphine as well, and refilling her teacup, she selected a muffin for herself and slathered it with butter.

Chapter Fifteen

Monday, June 29
9:15 a.m.

Lady Bentham had very much taken Mr. Twaddle-Thum's advice to heart.

The countdown spectacle, which had been more of a presentation than a performance, had undergone a significant revision. In place of the reedy violin struck by a butler were two trumpets, a trombone, a clarinet, and a snare drum. The quintet played a lively tune as three footmen deposited a pendulum clock on the doorstep. With its solid wooden case, the instrument had to weigh at least a hundred pounds, but the servants moved it with ease. As soon as the clock was in position, the band stopped and the butler, now sporting the regalia of a town crier, including a tricorn hat with a standing brim, declared, "Hear ye, hear ye," before announcing that three days remained before Prince Adriano left the country, permanently dashing Mrs. Fawcett's hopes of a royal son-in-law.

A rousing cheer met the proclamation, and Lady

Bentham, who had offered only an elegant curtsy last time, smiled warmly at the audience. Then she waved goodbye and disappeared inside her house as the band began to play again. The footmen, struggling with the weight of the clock, lifted it just high enough to carry it over the threshold, and Verity pictured them dropping it on the marble floor inside with a loud bong.

All in all, it was a very fine display, Verity thought, observing that the crowd lingered now to enjoy the music. Even the neighbors, a species generally known for growing irritated with anything that had the potential to disturb its comfort, appeared delighted with the exhibition. Several sat at their windows and listened.

As Lady Bentham's Park Lane address was among the most exclusive in Mayfair, many of its inhabitants were prominent members of the *ton*, and Verity took note of their names to include in her next column, which would be highly admiring.

Any subject who was happy to take direction from the infamous gossip deserved a positive review.

Monday, June 29
12:45 p.m.

The Customs office was neither here nor there.

Owing to a catastrophically timed fire that destroyed the Thomas Ripley–designed building only six months after the first stone had been laid for its replacement, the department was currently without a home. Various administrators worked in an assortment of offices, all of which were in the same general vicinity of the Tower but spread out over several blocks. The temporary arrangement would have made finding

Roger Tillet particularly difficult if Hardwicke had not already discovered he reported to an office in Lower Thames Street.

Verity did not know where exactly in the imposing white edifice the agent worked, but precision was not central to her project, which entailed making as much noise as possible.

Agent Tillet's intense mortification would take care of the rest.

Approaching the entry, she assumed an air of unconstrained distress, her hands shaking as she struggled to open the doors. Once inside, she called for Mr. Tillet, her tone growing increasingly insistent as he failed to emerge from any one of the dozen doorways that lined the corridor.

Presumably, that meant she would find him on the first floor.

Climbing the staircase, she cried out again, her voice cracking with apprehension as she began to shout at the top of her lungs, tears dropping in earnest as her frenzy deepened. She sniffled and blew her nose with comical force into her handkerchief. Verity was halfway down the corridor when the official appeared, a surly expression on his face as he looked around impatiently for the source of the noise.

"Oh, thank God!" she cried breathlessly as she ran the rest of the way, her hands clutching his left arm as she begged him to help her. "You must, Mr. Tillet, you simply must! I am at my wit's end and terrified and do not know where else to turn."

The agent did not appreciate being handled and tugged his arm free of her grasp. "Madam, I do not know what you think—"

Verity shrieked her name, insisting that he must remember her. "It was only a few days ago. You came to my house looking for a missing artifact from the British Museum and I insisted it was all a terrible mistake. You must remember! You searched my house high and low for a little cat statue? I really thought it was a mistake, but now I know the truth and you must help me! You were so strong and capable, so important! And yet kind and patient. You were the first person I thought of when I discovered the truth. Oh, do say you will help me. Please!" she pleaded, a fresh storm of tears overwhelming her. She dabbed frantically at her cheeks with the handkerchief, which did little to stem the flow, and then she wailed in anguish. "I don't know what I will do if you can't help me!"

Although Tillet winced at the piercing sound, his expression softened with recognition and he urged her to try to calm herself. "This is highly unusual, Miss Lark."

Naturally, Verity knew it, and her wretchedness deepened as she apologized for seeking him out. "It is just that I did not know what to do. I did not know what else I could do," she said, her voice growing shriller with each word.

Endeavoring to prevent another outburst, Tillet pressed a finger to his lips and urged her to follow him into the room. "I cannot help you, Miss Lark, if you do not compose yourself," he added with a self-conscious glance at the other occupants in the room. They were six in total, all men dressed similarly to him, and despite the fracas in the doorway, they kept their eyes focused resolutely down at their tables, determined to avoid any interaction with the hysterical woman. "Your tears are not helping."

Verity's only response was a hiccup.

Tillet snapped, "Miss Lark, I really must insist!"

Whispering now, as though afraid to speak normally lest she emit another screech of despair, she said, "I am sorry. I am so sorry to bother you. Truly, Mr. Tillet. You were kind to me, and I hate the thought of causing you any inconvenience. But you are the only one who can help me. Please! You must!"

As her entreaties teetered on shrill again, he led her to a

corner of the room and told her to sit down on a three-legged stool. "That will have to satisfy, as I can't offer any other courtesies. We are not set up to receive visitors."

The room was indeed spare, and Verity wondered how closely it resembled their previous office. The former Custom House had lacked ornamentation, possessing a dignified severity that most critics of architectures decried as uninspired, and she imagined the interior was likewise austere. Presumably, the quarters were also cramped, necessitating the need for the move in the first place.

"I am fine," Verity said, her breath catching in her throat to indicate she was in fact the very opposite of fine. "Please, Mr. Tillet, you must help me. You are the only one who can."

Scowling, the agent said, "So you have mentioned several times now. That being the case, I sincerely doubt there is anything I can do to assist you. But I suppose you should tell probably me what the bother is."

Poor Mr. Tillet, he sounded so aggrieved!

Cautiously, Verity asked if he remembered her. "I live at twenty-six Bethel Street with my brother, Mr. Robert Lark, and my companion, Miss Delphine Drayton. You called on Tuesday and searched my house to find a little cat statue that you claimed was stolen from Montague House. Miss Drayton and I were quite beside ourselves with anxiety."

"Yes, I remember," he said curtly.

"It was a terrifying experience!" she said breathlessly. "But you were so kind to us, especially when you were unable to find the missing figurine. You must understand how very disorienting it was for us to be accused of theft. Miss Drayton and I are mature women well into our spinsterhoods. We live quiet lives and rarely go farther than the fruit market. We could not understand how such a bewildering mistake had been made. And you were equally disconcerted by the error because you were so certain we were criminals."

Tillet conceded the accuracy of the statement. He had acted on intelligence that had been deemed trustworthy by his superior. "I have since been informed that the antiquity in question never left Montague House. It had been misplaced by a member of the cleaning staff. The chief librarian found it in a neighboring room under a table."

Ah, so that was the story Goddard had decided to tell, she noted cynically. A lax custodial staff did not reflect well on his management, but it was better than losing an item in your care without even noticing. "That is a relief for all involved! And it does not surprise me in the least. You see, I have a very wicked uncle, and he is set against me! That is why I am here!"

But Tillet did not see at all. "I am sorry to hear that, Miss Lark, but this is a customs office. I suggest you seek out a solicitor with experience in family disputes."

"It is my wicked uncle who filed the report," she continued as though he had not made this very practical suggestion. "I am certain of it. He visited us yesterday and made all sorts of funning comments about cats and statues because he thinks he is sly and clever, but he isn't. He is just vicious and cruel! You cannot say *twice* in a fifteen-minute conversation that curiosity killed the cat without your listener growing suspicious. He is the one who reported the figurine missing. It was a hoax, which you already knew."

Smoothly he corrected her: A mistake was not a hoax. "If you are upset that you were not issued a formal letter extending our regret for the inconvenience to you or your household, then I am obliged to inform you that the customs office is not in the habit of offering apologies."

Verity shook her head wildly. "No, no, you misunderstand. I need you to tell me about the man who made the complaint. What did he look like?"

"I can't tell you that," he said firmly.

"Oh, but you must!" she implored fervently. "I have to find out if my uncle is behind this terrible thing so that I may know if his campaign against me is escalating. Until now, he has created only nuisance problems. Last month, the wheel on my carriage fell off in the middle of the night, and the month before that my maid of ten years abruptly left my service without an explanation. You see how it is: These events could be misfortune, or they could be intentional. But if you give me the description, then I will know once and for all whether he is doing this to me."

Stiffly, he repeated that he could not give her that information.

Tears welled in Verity's eyes as she asked what would happen to her next.

Sure, Tillet had left without finding the stolen artifact *this time*.

But she could not expect her luck to hold.

And her uncle—he would never stop tormenting her.

It had been like this since the moment her father died.

"Relentless, I tell you," she said on a plaintive wail. "Just everything that is relentless and unbearable. You cannot imagine what it is like, rising morning after morning having no idea what terrible misfortune may befall you. And what makes it worse is nobody believes me! I tell them I am being persecuted by my wicked uncle, and they all swear that no relative would be so repellent as to torture his niece."

And then she keened.

She hated to do it to poor Mr. Tillet, who was already so discomfited by her misery, but she required the description and he remained unwilling to provide it.

He recoiled at the high-pitched squeal and leaned forward as though to quiet her himself. Rather than press his hand against her mouth, he waved it in the air and begged her to regain a semblance of control. "You will get nowhere emitting such a dreadful noise."

In fact, she would get everywhere, as demonstrated a few seconds later, when he promised to introduce her to his supervisor, for it was he who had taken the report from John Smith of Montague House. "I cannot tell you about him because I never met him. But if I introduce you to Mr. Kinsella, you must promise me you will cease all this yowling and howling. This is an office of the customs service, not a nursery, and we require decorum!"

"I will stop!" Verity cried vehemently, brushing away the tears that continued to drip down her cheeks. "You see, I *can* get ahold of myself. I won't say another word without your permission, I swear!"

And then she pressed her lips together tightly to demonstrate.

Tillet eyed her doubtfully for several long seconds, and Verity contemplated the usefulness of smiling tremulously. He was already skittish, and she did not want to send him scurrying from the room in fear of more sobbing. But the additional threat might provide the extra little incentive he needed to make her someone else's problem, hopefully the superior he had mentioned earlier in the conversation.

Verity decided to hold off on the quiver—for now. She could easily turn on the waterworks again, and the agent needed to be convinced of her equanimity. To help in that project, she tilted her eyes downward in a display of appropriate docility.

"I shall talk to Mr. Kinsella," Tillet said, then immediately added that all he could do was present the situation to his supervisor. "If he refuses to speak to you, then all the tears in London will not change his mind."

Ah, but won't they, Verity thought, amused by the challenge.

Her expression was sober, however, when she raised her head and meekly agreed to his terms. Then she issued a dignified thank you.

The restraint she showed in expressing her gratitude seemed to reassure him, and he regarded her with less apprehension as he said, "Very well, wait here."

Recognizing that silence was now to her benefit, she responded with a nod.

Tillet cast another dubious glance in her direction before leaving the room, and Verity kept her chin down as she tried to read the documents on the table nearest her. The top sheet appeared to be the manifest for a ship called the ... she leaned in closer ... *Resolute*.

No, it was the *Resilient*.

Unfamiliar with the name, which indicated it was a merchant vessel, she wondered at its cargo and considered sliding her stool a little closer. The men in the room appeared duly occupied by their own work, and she would need to slide forward only a few inches.

Before Verity had a chance, Tillet returned and announced that Kinsella had given him a description of John Smith to pass along to her: tall, brown hair, brown eyes.

It was almost nothing, which was what she would expect from information conveyed through an intermediary. Years of conducting interviews had honed her ability to elicit details from subjects who did not realize they had retained them, and she knew that if she could put questions directly to Kinsella, she would learn more.

All she had to do was press for the opportunity.

At the same time, she had already pestered Tillet a great deal that morning and there was a point at which a tactic started to lose its effectiveness. She could launch into another fit of weeping but suspected he would respond by sweeping her out the door.

Consequently, she repeated the description under her breath, as if committing the particulars to memory, and then asked if that was all.

"Isn't that enough?" the agent replied testily. "Either you know what your uncle looks like or you do not!"

Now Verity allowed her bottom lip to tremble. "You are right to snap at me. I am a peagoose! I just wanted a description that was as precise as possible so that I can convince my relatives that I am not imagining things. Listening to their criticisms is wearying, but that is my problem, not yours. I am sorry for pestering you with my ninnyish ways. I will leave now. Thank you, Mr. Tillet," she said pathetically.

A lone teardrop hung unsteadily from her lashes before falling forlornly onto her cheek, causing him to sigh with annoyance. Then he spat, "A gap! Mr. Kinsella also mentioned that there was a gap between his front teeth. There, that is everything I know down to the least significant detail. Now you may leave—and quietly, Miss Lark."

Not wishing to anger him further with an immoderate display of gratitude, Verity bowed her head and left without saying another word.

Monday, June 29
2:03 p.m.

As Verity approached number twenty-six, she reviewed her plan for finding the man who had submitted the false report to the customs office. She would begin with Twaddle's network. The description was not as distinctive as she would have liked—in cases of mysterious malefactors, one hoped for a distinguishing feature such as a scar or a birthmark—but it was comprehensive enough to eliminate some portion of the population. She believed the so-called John Smith was involved in the counterfeit antiquities trade in some way, if only tangentially, and would most likely be found prowling the narrow lanes and dark alleyways of Saffron Hill. Twaddle's spies were intimately acquainted with the rookery and would be able to suggest men who met the description.

The list would take some time to compile as information traveled through the newspaper office to protect her identity, and while she waited she would visit Montague House. Without evidence to the contrary, she could not dismiss the possibility that the informer worked in the museum. Just because Goddard was not actively involved in the scheme—on this, Verity trusted Hardwicke's instincts implicitly—did not mean he did not employ men who were. His slipshod supervision had already been noted, and it would not surprise her to discover his most trusted subordinates were hoodwinking him daily.

A man of his character, with his groundless prejudices against women and his flagrant self-regard, frequently lacked the ability to make accurate judgments, and as Verity unlatched the door, she decided she would call in the morning. It would mean postponing her and Hardwicke's fishing expedition, which was not necessarily a bad thing, she thought humorously. Indeed, she could not believe he was serious about the outing and fully expected him to detour to an entirely different destination soon after she climbed into the curricle. They could discuss it later, when he delivered the amended list of expenses, as he had promised to do last night as he was leaving. In the meantime, she would compose an item on Lady Bentham's blossoming sense of pageantry. As the peeress had taken Twaddle's advice to heart last time, maybe she should recommend further improvements and see if they were adopted as well.

Ah, but how to top a brass band?

Circus performers, she thought as she entered the house, picturing a troop of jugglers.

No, acrobats doing somersaults on the pavement directly in front of the steps.

Highly amused, she pictured Lady Bentham's steward's expression as she ordered him to find a rope dancer as well as devise a way to extend a tightrope several feet in the air without harming the portico or the gracious trees lining the road.

It was a daunting assignment indeed.

Tickled by it, Verity envisioned an accompanying illustration showing where to install the bolts.

A diagram—that would be a Twaddle first.

Eager to share the idea with Delphine, she closed the door, but before she could call out a greeting, her friend's voice carried from the other room, "I am in the parlor, darling, as cozy as a darling squirrel."

Smoothly, coolly, as though her heart had not shuddered in her chest before thudding to the bottom of her stomach, Verity said, "That sounds delightful."

Then she slipped off her spencer as she assessed her options.

Oh, yes, my options, she thought scathingly.

She was in a hallway with nothing.

Aside from the garment in her hand, there was a reticule with a torn seam and a salver for letters and calling cards—neither of which could be effectively wielded as a weapon to fend off whoever was menacing Delphine in the parlor.

Because clearly someone was.

As cozy as a darling squirrel!

The only way her friend could be induced to make such a repellent statement was under the threat of death.

It was a warning.

Heeding it, Verity looked again at the reticule and

wondered if she could scrape together enough coins to make it an effective bludgeon.

A reticule bludgeon.

Good God, what a daft idea!

She needed more time to think.

To appear unperturbed, she continued to speak to Delphine in the other room. "It is so chilly out today. I would adore a spot of tea. Would you be a dear and summon Lucy?"

There was Robert's study.

She could run into the room and grab something from there.

The darts!

They were handy little missiles.

But the study was *past* the parlor. If the intruder was standing near the doorway in anticipation of her entrance, then he would surely catch sight of her scurrying by.

Would he attack or wait patiently?

There was no way to know, which made the risk too great.

She needed a weapon now.

"Actually, I am busy at the moment," Delphine called in reply. "With my knitting. I don't want to drop a stitch. You will have to summon help yourself."

Hearing the ripple of fear in her friend's voice, she realized she had no time to lose.

Very well, then, an improvised bludgeon it was.

Digging guineas out of her pocket, she pulled the reticule from its hook and noted its weight with surprise.

Something was already in it.

Encouraged, she untied the strings and found a letter opener.

Of course!

Madame Céleste had cut her finger on it while searching the bookshelves in Niccolo Donizetti's study to find the name of the composition he intended to play at the regent's birthday celebration. Startled by the musician's sudden appearance in the room, she had stuffed the implement into her reticule and sneezed lavishly before launching into a screed against his housekeeper, who had allowed the dust to build up to an intolerable degree.

Although far from ideal, the sharp device was an improvement on the makeshift cudgel and she slipped it under her sleeve. The press of cold silver against her skin was comforting, and assuring herself that everything was under control, she strode across the floor and entered the parlor to find a man bearing a striking resemblance to Andrew Brownell holding a gun to Delphine's head.

Chapter Sixteen

Monday, June 29
3:12 p.m.

Verity swooned.

It was, she thought, the only appropriate response to the situation.

Aged female, lethal weapon, brutal villain, deadly threat—what else was a spinster to do but collapse like a ragdoll on her own parlor floor?

Expecting her to remain conscious and coherent in the face of such overwhelming terror was an insupportable presumption. You may as well demand that the fox sit down to nuncheon with the hound on its heels.

As Verity dropped her head to the floor, she heard Delphine scream and noted how convincingly alarmed she sounded. If she did not know better, she would think her friend genuinely believed she was in a faint.

Next, the man—presumably, Lewis Brownell because the other brother, Rufus, was on the Continent—swore, muttering a string of furious invectives about the uselessness of women in general and her in particular. His voice was rougher than Andrew's, less cultured, and his frame was broader, his hair darker, a sandy color rather than blond but otherwise similar in cut and texture. His clothes were austere, revealing a Corinthian's fondness for simplicity, and his calm grip on the pistol indicated a familiarity with firearms. He would not hesitate to shoot Delphine.

Verity had no intention of provoking him.

He was in charge.

As long as he pressed a gun to her friend's temple, she would affirm his authority and follow his every command and wait for the opening.

And there *would* be an opening.

Sooner or later, he would slip.

Everyone did.

Added to that: He was a Brownell.

Although Lewis *could* be intellectually gifted in ways his brother was not, the possibility struck Verity as doubtful. His very presence in Bethel Street demonstrated a dismaying lack of clear-sightedness. Storming into her parlor in the heat of fury to enact revenge against the woman who had arranged Brownell's incarceration might feel satisfying in the moment but would ultimately end in further disgrace for his family. Brandishing a gun at a pair of helpless spinsters was not good *ton,* even if they were several miles from Mayfair, and the magistrate would be compelled to hear the crime even if he decided it was not worthy of prosecution.

The story would circulate.

Twaddle would see to that.

But first she had to disarm Lewis. The flintlock was double-barreled, which meant he could get off two shots, and with his confident hold, he was unlikely to miss. Her only option, then, was to coax him into lowering his weapon by convincing him it was unnecessary to use so much force with a petrified, helpless female.

To that end, she decided it was almost time to stir. She had been lying on the floor for approximately forty-five seconds and figured another fifteen would firmly establish her bona fides as a milk-and-water miss. As she counted silently, she heard Delphine whimper and Lewis ordered her to stop mewling.

Delphine fell silent.

That is my cue.

Before Verity could moan, however, she was kicked.

A boot, heavy and thick, thrust into her side with so much force she could not draw air.

Dear God, there was a second intruder!

Struggling to regain her breath, she flipped onto her side and pulled her legs to her chest as pain radiated across her chest and pelvis.

"Enough of that," a voice said, male and bored and ... and ...

Amused, she thought in stupefaction as the pain deepened and throbbed.

The man was amused.

He continued: "It was a fine performance, Mary, but now you must stand."

It was a shock, yes, hearing that name, realizing how easily he had seen through her ruse, and she tightened her grasp on her knees to smother the gasp that rose to her throat. She would not give him anything: not a response, not satisfaction.

For as long as possible, Verity Lark would stay curled on the floor in a ball.

Was she afraid?

Oh, yes, there was a tight knot of terror in her belly.

But it paled in comparison to the anger she felt, the rage

that seethed through her limbs as she comprehended the depth of her stupidity. Like a small child who believed a thing ceased to exist the moment she stopped looking at it, she had dismissed her father. In thirty-five years, she had thought of him no more than a handful of times.

And why would she?

He was nothing.

Necessary biological material unworthy of further inspection.

But Frimgallow had paid attention.

If he knew her faint was a feint, then he knew everything.

From Fortescue's to the scullery to Bethel Street, he had kept an eye on her for decades, collecting details that could one day be used against her.

The real information gap was between what he knew and what she didn't.

Not ready to stand, she nevertheless rose to her feet because remaining curled on the floor a second longer displayed a weakness she found unsettling. Stifling a wince of pain, she raised her chin higher to look him in the eye, the man who had sired her, an impressive specimen still, at the age of seventy-four, his posture straight and his height imposing. Openly examining him with amused contempt, she said, "Good afternoon, Father. This is a pleasure I had not anticipated."

Although her greeting was calculated to give maximum offense, he displayed no resentment toward her. Instead, he looked past her to his son standing next to the settee, where Delphine was sitting, and said, "You see: spine and audacity! Mary has no recourse. She is at my mercy. And still she treats me with disdain. A Trojan through and through!"

Lewis smiled tightly, and in the taut curve of his lips, Verity could see his entire relationship with his father, the years of relentless scorn he had endured with increasingly strained goodwill. The solicitor's clerk had said Frimgallow wielded the threat of his illegitimate daughter as a cudgel, bashing his sons over the head with it whenever his annoyance reached a peak, but she saw now it was more like a knife with which he made precise little cuts at regular intervals.

Only in recent weeks, the blade had begun to dig deeper.

"But I am no longer entertained, Mary," Frimgallow continued snappishly, directing his dark-colored gaze at her.

Looking at him, Verity could see no resemblance.

It was there in the height, of course, for he and Lewis were strikingly tall, and standing near them, she had a sense of being among her people. La Reina had always been an alien creature, both in her coquettish personality and tiny frame, and the encomiums most commonly applied to her—pocket Venus, tempting handful—paid tribute to her dainty appeal.

But that was the extent of it.

Lewis looked like his father and both men were handsome in the same anodyne way as Brownell, and their inoffensive attractiveness seemed to underscore the accuracy of Verity's indifference. There *was* nothing interesting about her father.

Except he was threatening Delphine's life and was no longer entertained.

Fair enough.

She was far from amused herself.

Seeking to further convey her scorn, she turned away from him to address Lewis as though he were the authority in the room. "And what about my staff? Are they unharmed?"

He took a moment to answer.

Either disconcerted by the query or the respect conferred by it, he seemed uncertain how to reply and just as he began to explain that the two women were safely restrained in the kitchens, his father told him to shut up.

"You fool! She does not care about the servants!" Frimgallow exclaimed scathingly. "She is trying to distract you.

Now I said I was done playing, Mary, and that means I am done playing. I do not need to know all that transpired last night in Lady Abercrombie's bedchamber to know you did it, and now you are going to undo it. My eldest son and heir will not stand trial or be sent to the gallows. I will not allow you to turn my family into an object of mockery and derision, ridicule and shame. Brownell is an ancient name, respected and revered, and what are you? A bastard who does not know her place, a harlot's issue, an unnecessary *thing* foisted onto the world. I should have drowned you as an infant. I almost did, you know. The woman in charge of that place was more than happy to hand you over to me for a half dozen guineas—no questions asked! But I decided it would be more amusing to watch you struggle to make your way in the world, a lone female, La Reina's baseborn little whelp. It was years before you took on the look of her, and when you did I had you placed in Stechford's house. He was among your mother's most ardent admirers, and I thought for sure he would see her in you, but you evaded his notice."

In fact, she had not.

Verity *thwarted* his notice.

Delphine, who knew a little of her friend's ordeal in Mount Street through the few stories Verity deigned to tell—benign anecdotes cleansed of their horror—started to weep.

Verity was not unmoved by the information.

It was disconcerting, to say the least, to discover the depth of his interest in her, for it underscored the extent of her dereliction in showing none in return. But the revelations themselves meant nothing to her. All her life she had been subjected to forces beyond her control, and it mattered not a whit which hand had directed her fate.

Even the admission that he considered killing her as a baby had no effect on her. It did not undermine her equanimity or awaken a primal fear. She did not suddenly feel as though she had narrowly escaped death or lived her life in the shadow of a horrible event.

Frimgallow wanted to shock her, and the fact that he thought a list of mundane machinations would accomplish that goal revealed how little he actually knew her.

It was a relief.

As tears trickled down Delphine's cheeks and Lewis smirked at her distress, Verity contemplated how to respond. She could stroke the earl's ego by feigning dismay or foil his expectations by appearing untroubled.

The latter, she thought decisively.

He had snapped impatiently at her previous attempt at a distraction, so she offered another. "Fascinating. Do tell me more about my mother's suitors. I know the Duke of Kesgrave was among them. Who else?"

Infuriated by this determined triviality—how dare she lean forward in curiosity when he wanted her to shrink back in fear—he said coldly, "You and I will go to the magistrate's office, where you will tell him it was all a hoax. Everyone knows the Countess of Abercrombie is a depraved strumpet, and entrapping an innocent man with her wiles is just the sort of wanton prank she would find amusing. You will convince the magistrate to release my son and clear my name or Lewis will kill your friend."

To be sure, Verity would not.

Under no circumstance would she leave Delphine alone with an armed man.

She knew pistols.

Pistols had a nasty habit of discharging.

All guns did.

And the idea of her toddling off with dear old pater to visit Kilby—it sounded like an opportunity for her to overpower the septuagenarian, but she knew it would never be that easy. Frimgallow was not stupid. He would have planned for every eventuality, and she did not doubt that before they left the room, he would produce another gun to ensure her compliance. Perhaps he had a burly footman waiting in the carriage.

She had to act now, before she was compelled from the room, and feeling the press of the letter opener against her skin, she identified her best hope: jabbing the implement's edge against Frimgallow's carotid artery and offering his safety in exchange for Delphine's.

Conceptually, the plan had merit.

In practical terms, the likelihood of her overcoming the earl before his son realized what was happening was low. She would have to topple him and apply the blade in one fluid motion, sweeping out her leg to bring him to his knees while simultaneously pulling the knife. If that had any chance of succeeding, she would have to draw closer to him.

How to do that?

Another distraction.

As she was refining her plan, Frimgallow continued to impress upon Verity her friend's vulnerability, noting that Lewis always hit his mark. "Isn't that right, my boy?"

"It is, sir," Lewis replied promptly, his grim demeanor lightening with pleasure at his father's rare display of confidence in his abilities. A cheerful smile swept across his features—the genuine article this time, spreading from ear to ear, revealing all his teeth, including a crooked canine and a missing incisor, and bearing no resemblance to the tight-lipped abomination he had eked out earlier out of a sense of bitter obligation.

Struck by the desperation of his joy, Verity did not immediately grasp the significance of the space. Instead, she focused on his pathetic delight and wondered if she could use his desire for his father's approval against him. Frimgallow had stoked a rivalry between his sons and their baseborn sister their whole lives; it would be an easy thing to exploit. Or maybe the better way to divert Lewis's attention was by garnering more praise for him from his father. He certainly appeared a great deal less threatening with that eager, gap-toothed grin on his face.

And then it struck her: gap-toothed grin!

Lewis was missing one of his incisors, resulting in a space between his teeth, which had been included in the description of John Smith. Tall, brown hair, brown eyes, a gap between teeth—Lewis matched every detail in the account.

Oh, but that was madness!

Lewis Brownell had not stolen an ancient cat figurine from the British Museum only to send it to her house and dispatch a customs agent to arrest her.

What possible reason could he have to go to all that trouble?

It defied sense, especially in light of Brownell's actions: One brother tried to have her arrested for stealing a priceless antiquity while the other brother tried to poison her with a chocolate puff.

Where was the logic?

If it was a two-pronged attack, how did the parts work together?

Confounded, Verity opened her mouth to ask what would happen to Delphine if she failed to convince Kilby it was all a lark. The facile question would allow her more time to understand the brothers' scheme, but she had no sooner thought *brothers' scheme* than she realized there was no collective action among the siblings.

Two plans, not two prongs.

Turning to Frimgallow, she said, "No, he won't shoot. Lewis is not a murderer."

Lewis huffed as though he had just been dealt a heinous insult and angrily swore it was not true. "I will do it! I will shoot!" he barked, pressing the gun against Delphine's temple so hard, her friend cried out in pain, and Verity thought again about pistols and their wretched tendency to discharge despite everyone's good intentions.

Nevertheless, she held her course.

Calmly, she corrected Lewis, noting he had gone to great lengths to remove her without violence. "That is why you took the figurine from the museum, arranged its delivery to my home, and informed the customs house that I had stolen it. You knew that would get me out of the way. Your father would never leave his estate to a criminal, and the reason you knew that was he said that very thing while I was imprisoned there, didn't he? When I was released with the help of my illustrious connections, you began to fear he might actually cut you out of the will. And so the morning after my release from Newgate, you decided to follow me to figure out how to get me out of the way once and for all. That is how you were in Montague House, and when you saw me admiring the statuette, you hatched a scheme to have me sent back to prison —a *nonviolent* scheme. Because you are not capable of murder, unlike your brother."

A vicious hatred washed over Lewis's features at this claim, and the hand holding the pistol shook for the first time since Verity had entered the room. "I *am* capable of murder! I am a cold-hearted killer! I am!" he cried, sounding more like a petulant child than a full-grown adult, and as he spoke, he looked at his father beseechingly, almost pleading with him to believe it.

Suddenly aware of the picture he presented, Lewis took a deep breath before continuing, and although his composure was not fully restored, he was more in control when he insisted that he was not opposed to killing. "What I *am* opposed to, Mary, is a fuss, which is what is typically kicked up when a murder fails to go according to plan, as anyone with half a brain knows. Having you arrested for theft was the better idea—no chaos, no commotion—but when things go awry, I am happy to adapt. To that end, I will remind you that you have your instructions. You should make haste in following them lest I lose my temper, isn't that right, sir?"

Frimgallow agreed. "We have wasted enough time. Let us be off."

Whatever displeasure he took in his son's outburst or the disclosure of competing schemes was restrained in service to the larger goal.

Now was not the time to wrestle with family disputes.

Oh, but it was, Verity thought, seeing an opportunity. Lewis was only one or two taunts away from losing his temper altogether, which she thought was to her benefit.

Yes, he was pointing a gun at Delphine, but he had already pulled it away in his frenzy to yell at Verity. She just had to keep his attention on her to provide her friend with the vital seconds she would need to find safety when Verity tackled the earl.

To do that, all she had to do was apply pressure to Lewis's sorest spot: his rivalry with the brother who stole his betrothed.

Mildly, Verity said, "Far be it for me to judge, as I am merely the intended target of both schemes and have no larger understanding of the issues in play, but it seems to me that Andrew's plan was the cleverer one. Securing cyanide of potassium on a moment's notice is no mean feat and speaks to an ingenuity that—"

Stunned, Verity halted midsentence and looked across the room at Delphine, whose cheeks still glistened with tears. Then she repeated it: "Securing cyanide of potassium on a moment's notice is no mean feat."

But her intonation was different.

Now she imbued the words with surprise and growing comprehension.

So *that* was why Castleheart could not find the source.

"Oh, dear, I misspoke," Verity said with a rueful lilt, casting an apologetic glance at Lewis before looking at Frimgallow. "Securing cyanide of potassium on a moment's notice is not just difficult. It is nearly impossible. Even the research required to figure out how to get it would take a few days at the very least, which means the only reason Andrew was able to concoct a scheme involving the poison so quickly was he already had the substance in his possession."

Delphine gasped, and Verity, glancing briefly at her friend, murmured, "It is so obvious now I don't know how we didn't see it before."

Although she had expected Frimgallow's impatience to increase at this digression, he regarded her with sanguine interest. "You can't help yourself, can you, Mary? It is just game after game after game with you. All these speeches! You think you are doing your friend a favor by coming up with ways to delay our departure. Let me disabuse you of that notion: The longer you make me wait, the more intolerant I become, and although I promised to return Miss Drayton to you alive on the successful completion of our errand, I did not promise to return her unscathed. I trust you understand my meaning. You are an intelligent girl if not quite as smart as you think."

Verity did not hesitate to agree. "If I were truly smart, I would have realized days ago that Andrew already had cyanide of potassium on hand, but I know it now and am left to wonder why he had acquired the deadly poison. And if I were you, Frimgallow, I would ponder it too because clearly the rehabilitated Mary Price was not his original victim. Hmm. Perhaps it was his wife? How is his relationship with Lady Brownell? Are they on mostly good terms? Or did he plan to kill Lewis here? The rumor is Andrew orchestrated the duel that saw Rufus exiled to the Continent. Maybe he had intended for Rufus to be slain in the duel and, having failed in that goal, decided his next effort would be more straightforward."

Jeering at these theories, Lewis said with snide annoyance, "She is playing more juvenile games, sir. She is trying to distract us."

Verity was not, no.

Now she had the bit between her teeth.

The mystery was the thing.

Pursing her lips pensively, she considered other possibilities and asked if his brother engaged in enterprise. "Does he have a business—a genteel one, of course—or a partner with whom he shared responsibilities and profits? Or were you the target, Frimgallow?"

"This is nonsense," Lewis said waspishly. "Andy conducting business! She is spouting nonsense."

Frimgallow, seeming to agree with his son's assessment, twisted his lips in amusement at the suggestion of patricide. "As a brat from an orphanage you cannot know what it means to honor thy father."

Verity could not, no, which she considered a very good thing when the parent in question was he, and she wondered what toll his abuse had taken on his offspring. "All those years of threatening to leave your fortune to a bastard girl. You were just toying with your sons, baiting them, mocking them, and they knew it. You value your name too highly to leave it to a thing you believe is essentially worthless. I've known you for ten minutes now and recognize the truth of that in my soul. But then Brownell sees that bastard girl in Hyde Park in the company of his good friend the Earl of Goldhawk, who informs him that his brother is courting her in earnest, and all of a sudden your son is not so certain what you will do.

The daughter-in-law of the powerful Marquess of Ware is an entirely different beast from a misbegotten cur you can drown in a river. Your blood mingling with that august and ancient family? Brownell can imagine your being swayed by it, and now he is genuinely worried that you will welcome your bastard daughter into the fold. So before the banns can be read, he secures cyanide of potassium to poison you, his father, because dead men are unable to alter their wills."

The argument did not pierce the earl's egotism.

Regarding his sons as an extension of himself, Frimgallow could not conceive of their doing anything without his permission. The notion that they would reject any aspect of his authority or tutelage was simply alien to him, and he continued to smile at Verity's conjecture, congratulating her on having a vivid imagination and swearing he would not claim her even if she married the King of England.

But something about the story resonated with Lewis, who yelled from across the room for her to shut up, his voice loud and piercing and tight with anxiety, and then he moved his arm, shifting the target of the gun from Delphine to her.

Thank God, Verity thought, relieved that her friend was out of the line of fire, and it was only when she shifted her gaze from Delphine to Lewis that she saw the wildness in his eyes and perceived why he was so distraught.

It was both of them.

Pointing at Lewis as he aimed the pistol at her, Verity urged Frimgallow to see what was right in front of his eyes. "Your sons conspired against you. Andrew and Lewis hatched the scheme to kill you together, which I suppose is one sort of fraternal bond, although perhaps not the one you as their father had hoped to foster."

Delphine told her to shut up ("By all that is holy, Verity, *stop talking!*") as Frimgallow yanked her arm and accused her of turning his sons against him ("They have always *honored their father!*"). The harsh tug freed the letter opener, which landed on the wooden plank with a soft thud, drawing Frimgallow's eyes to the floor, and as he looked down, Verity spun sharply on her right heel and hooked her hand around his neck. She grasped his upper arm with her other hand, throwing her weight forward and feeling his body dip backward, and when he bobbled off balance, she swept her left foot under his right. He fell hard, with Verity landing on top of him, and she heard the whiz of the bullet over her head a second before the shatter of glass. Tensing her muscles in expectation of another shot, she grabbed the letter opener, twisted her torso, and hurled the implement across the room, where it lodged in Lewis's shoulder, ensuring that the gun discharged its remaining bullet uselessly into the wall.

Verity heaved in relief as the door swing open, admitting Hardwicke, who bounded into the room to seize the earl by the scruff of his collar just as Delphine conked Lewis over the head with a teapot.

◈

Monday, June 29
3:27 p.m.

Lucy ran into the parlor with a rolling pin held high and a wild look in her eye and, seeing that the villains had been properly apprehended, announced that she was handing in her notice. Having accepted years ago that twenty-six Bethel Street would never be a conventional establishment, she could not ignore the worrying trend of recent weeks. Late-night intruders, murder charges, customs agents, and now men with guns in the kitchens—she could not bring herself to imagine what next month held.

"I will of course stay until you hire my replacement," she added graciously.

Verity, whose shock at Hardwicke's sudden appearance was immediately supplanted by horror at this distressing declaration, leaped to her feet as she implored the maid to reconsider. Stepping over Frimgallow, she said, "You cannot leave us, Lucy. You are like family, is she not, Delphine?"

A glance at her friend, however, revealed that the other woman was not prepared at that moment to discuss mundane staffing concerns. She was staring down at the fragments of broken china scattered on the floor around Lewis's head.

The poor dear was bewildered.

Verity, resolving to give Delphine a few minutes before pressing for an answer, swore to Lucy that Miss Drayton would agree when she was able. "You are invaluable to us, and I will do whatever I can to change your mind. Do you want a raise? Done!"

The maid refused without even ascertaining the nature of the increase.

Oh, dear, Verity thought, momentarily at a loss for how to address a problem that was beyond the reach of money because *no* problem was beyond the reach of money.

And neither was this one, she realized.

It was just a matter of how she allocated the resources.

"I will hire a footman!" she said eagerly.

Lucy's expression did not change, but she lowered the rolling pin.

Encouraged by the show of interest, Verity explained that she been looking at the accounts just the week before and thought she could afford it. "That is what you and Cook would like to help with your labors, isn't it? A footman?"

The maid gave no response.

Verity thought of what else she could offer.

If not money, then power.

"You shall be in charge of him," she continued. "You can assign his duties."

A wrinkle appeared between Lucy's brow as she clutched the rolling pin in both hands. "Carrying up the coal and firewood?"

"Yes," Verity replied.

"Cleaning the privy?" she asked, turning the kitchen implement over in her hands.

"Absolutely."

The maid received this reply with a thoughtful nod and asked about the wicks. "Can I have him trim the wicks as well?"

Frimgallow, whose grumbles had grown increasingly belligerent as the conversation went on, shouted with frustration. "Enough! I cannot bear to listen to this infernal female chatter another minute! Release me!"

Hardwicke complied with his request in the technical sense, loosening his grip on Frimgallow's arm, but he thwarted any attempt the other man might have made to quit the room by pushing him toward the chair. The earl glowered at him darkly while Verity urged him to get comfortable, for nothing could be decided until his son stirred—and it appeared as though Lewis would be unconscious for a good while yet.

Bristling, Frimgallow asked what she meant by *decided*. "There is nothing to be decided. My son and I will leave as soon as he wakes."

Verity assured him he would not. "You will remain until we have come to an understanding."

"Bah!" Frimgallow scoffed.

Pointedly ignoring the interjection, Verity returned to the discussion of domestic affairs and promised Lucy she could assign the maintenance of the lamps to the footman as well.

"Miss Drayton and I rely on your good sense and trust you would dispense his duties wisely and equitably."

Delphine, hearing her name, looked up in surprise and seemed to notice for the first time that Hardwicke was in the room. Baffled, she asked how he had managed to arrive in the nick of time, an observation with which Verity took exception, as they—meaning, she and Delphine—had had matters well in hand before he had stormed into the room.

"You wield a teapot very well, my dear, and might want to keep one on your bedside table for added protection. A tipstaff is not for everyone," Verity said generously. "Hardwicke, however, *did* free Lucy and Cook from their captivity, which was hugely helpful. Speaking of which, where is Cook? I hope she is not in the kitchens preparing tea after her ordeal. If anyone's spirits require fortification, then I shall brew it myself, or, better yet, pour the brandy."

"She is fetching Grint," Hardwicke replied, then added with a sheepish smile that he had asked Lucy to go to Whitehall, and it was that request that had spurred the resignation. "As for my opportune appearance, I entered through the servants' door to present Cook with a recipe for flummery in exchange for the millefruit biscuits she had made the other night and found her and Lucy tied up in the kitchen. I freed them and had just reached the top of the staircase when I heard the first gunshot."

Verity, finding this explanation helpful, promptly added delivering messages to the list of responsibilities for the proposed footman, then begged Lucy to reconsider. "I swear we shall be a perfectly ordinary household from now on. No more midnight intruders, no more deranged callers forcing their way into the house with pistols. We will be as unexceptional as the neighbors."

Frimgallow, who had been muttering under his breath with increasing fury, cursed violently at this description, decrying it as slanderous, which Delphine reluctantly conceded was a fair charge, as they had not *forced* their way into the house. Father and son had presented themselves as polite visitors seeking to calmly discuss Lord Brownell's situation. As a consequence, she had readily admitted them.

"I suppose I should have been more wary, given Frimgallow's reputation," Delphine said with a hefty sigh as she contemplated the porcelain pieces on the floor, then picked up one of the larger shards.

Watching her friend, Verity could not decide which action irritated her more: Delphine blaming herself for a perfectly reasonable assumption—that civilized gentlemen would behave in a civilized manner—or her cleaning up the remains of the shattered teapot only minutes after her own traumatic ordeal. Briskly, she told her to leave the mess for later and suggested she retire to her room for some much-needed rest. "You are distressingly pale, my dear."

Delphine's lips twisted into a humorless smile as she replied that she would go nowhere until they had decided what was to be done about their visitors. "But you are correct: I am in need of reviving and shall pour my own brandy, thank you," she said tartly, smoothly stepping around the fragments as she approached the sideboard, which held several decanters. She selected one and removed the stopper. As she poured the golden liquid, she directed Hardwicke's attention to the clock next to the door, most specifically to the right side of the face, near the number nine. "That is where the first bullet landed. Verity was standing in its path and the only reason it did not lodge itself in her incredibly thick skull was that she happened to drop her letter opener at that precise moment and bent down to retrieve it—the letter opener, I must add, that she had decided at her most Veritiest was an equal match for a gun."

As Verity had heard the ball pass over her head, she knew

it had been a close thing. But it was not *that* close a thing. Delphine's description of events was accurate only to an extent. The implement had slipped out of her sleeve because Frimgallow had grabbed her arm. At the moment Lewis pulled the trigger, she was already in motion.

The bullet was always going to miss her.

Even so, she refrained from defending herself because she knew how it looked from her friend's perspective, and no matter how rigorously she argued that she had been firmly in control of the outcome, Delphine would only point to it as further evidence of Verity's excessive confidence in her own abilities.

Instead, Verity apologized for causing her so much distress.

Alas, this most benign and entirely sincere effort enraged Delphine, who banged the glass on the table so hard half the brandy splashed over the edge. "I said 'darling squirrel'!"

Calmly, Verity agreed. "That is why I grabbed a weapon."

"You were supposed to get help!" Delphine barked furiously. "I literally told you to get help. I said the words: *You will have to summon help yourself.* So what do you do? You saunter into the room with a letter opener tucked into your sleeve."

As Delphine had previously cited the letter opener as the thing that had saved her life, Verity thought this criticism was singularly unjust. Nevertheless, she held her tongue. Her friend was already so upset.

Hardwicke, whose expression had remained impassive as he examined the damage to the clock and calculated the bullet's trajectory himself, agreed that Verity's fondness for throwing herself in the middle of danger was disconcerting and frequently unnecessary. "In this instance, however, you could not have expected her to act in any other way. She was never going to leave the house knowing you were in danger.

She was always going to rush to your rescue, and for my own part, I find I am only relieved that she managed to grab a weapon before doing so. And judging by the way the letter opener is wedged in Lewis's shoulder, I think it's fair to say it served its purpose admirably."

Delphine glared at him balefully as she muttered, "You were supposed to help rein in her worst impulses, not encourage them. We already have Freddie for that."

Although Hardwicke agreed, noting that precise goal was foremost in his mind at all times, he nevertheless insisted it did not apply to this particular circumstance. "Verity's concern for her friends is her best impulse."

Naturally, Verity cringed, for it was mortifying to hear oneself described so mawkishly, an opinion Frimgallow shared, for he moaned as if in pain and begged them to bring back the maid. "Let her list the footman's duties or even a litany of her own responsibilities. Anything is preferable to this treacly prattle."

Although Delphine's color had yet to return to her cheeks, the brandy had served its purpose, restoring her equanimity, and casting a vindictive eye at the earl, she noted that Verity's best quality was in fact her generosity. "She not only gives money to the orphans at Fortescue's but also her time. She is so determined to help the head matron come up with an affordable solution to the roofing problem she has begun reading books on carpentry to see if she could do some of the work herself."

Patently, that was not true. The texts Verity had read on how to ensure the structural integrity of wood beams were only so she could help Mrs. Caffrey hire a skilled carpenter to repair the roof.

As verisimilitude was not central to Delphine's project, she did not allow a minor thing like accuracy dissuade her and she spent the next five minutes subjecting Frimgallow to a list of her friend's finest traits.

In response, he stared stonily, determined to endure the abuse silently, and Verity, noting how his fingers twitched periodically, wondered if he wanted to press his hands against his ears.

Finally, he interrupted to say that Lewis would go to the Continent. "You said we had to decide what happens next. Well, that is the answer: exile to Europe. It is, I believe, the traditional reply to an affair of honor that goes awry."

"An affair of honor?" Hardwicke echoed in mild disgust. "Is that what this is?"

Bridling at the faintly jeering tone, Frimgallow said, "Yes! Mary impugned my honor and sullied my family's name when she used that hussy to lure my son into a trap. It is an act of unspeakable indecency, and I have every right to demand satisfaction."

"Your son murdered an innocent man," Delphine said.

Frimgallow sneered at the sanctimony and swore there was no such thing. "Show me a man who is innocent, and I will show you a boy in leading strings. In regard to Andrew, I shall make no further objection to his imprisonment, although he will not remain in Newgate nor will he be charged with murder. All anyone will know is that he had to withdraw from society for health concerns and I will arrange for him to be confined to Bartleby Hospital in Surrey Heath. Is that all? Have I addressed everything? I believe I have," he said, rising to his feet and showing marginal concern for his son by instructing Hardwicke to escort the unconscious man home when he woke. "Inform him I will call on him in the morning to settle the plans for his removal to the Continent," he said before turning to Verity with a petulant scowl. "I would bid you good day, Mary, but I do not think you deserve even that minor courtesy. It is my hope that the next time we meet you will have learned to respect your betters."

He was imperious indeed, dispensing orders as though commanding his staff, and Verity assumed it was ordinarily effective. He was an important man whose appearance was as daunting as his reputation, and he expected compliance. As Verity knew from her years of Twaddling, the only way to deliver a persuasive performance was to believe it yourself.

Without waiting for agreement, Frimgallow proceeded toward the hallway, and Verity, who was closer to the door, shut it firmly. "You are operating under the mistaken belief that you have power here. Let me clarify: You do not. Brownell will remain in Newgate on the charge of murdering Edmund Muir, and justice will be allowed to take its course. Lewis will be brought before the magistrate for attempting to murder me and Miss Drayton. And you, Frimgallow, will take yourself off to the Continent—after establishing an annuity for Mrs. Muir, whose four children are without a father, thanks to your son's machinations."

"How fierce you are, Mary," he said with snide admiration. "Of all my children, you are the most like me. Your mother's wit, my steel—it is a heady combination. I knew you would be interesting. That is why I did not drown you as a babe: I was curious to see what you would become. But your value to me is at an end. No longer do I find you entertaining. You are only an irritant, and because I do not like irritants, I shall say this just once and then leave: You will abide by our agreement, or I will destroy you. I will take away everything you have and return you to nothing. Remember, I put you in the Stechford's scullery once and I can do it again. Do not test me on this, Mary, because you will regret it."

Verity felt nothing.

He spoke blandly, smoothly, without wrath or rancor, as though the lack of inflection in his tone mirrored his lack of interest in the topic. It was a deft maneuver, for it created a void where the heat of anger should be, and although she could sense the cold emptiness, it did not affect her. It was strange because even as recently as April, the prospect of returning to the scullery, even as only a vague conception, would have terrified her. But the past few months had presented her with a seemingly endless series of challenges, from Twaddle-Sham to Newgate, and his efforts felt paltry in comparison.

Delphine, who was also unimpressed with his speech, trilled with laughter as she repeated his dire threat to destroy Verity. "Oh, dear, Lord Frimgallow, I think you have read one too many Minerva Press novels. Did you take that from *The Castle of Berry Pomeroy*? I swear Father Bertrand says almost the same thing to Matilda."

Frimgallow was too proficient in verbal warfare to respond to the mockery and instead held himself with the same loose grace as always. Calmly, he reissued his warning. "You have been well advised to tread cautiously, Mary. What happens now is on your head. Good day."

But Verity held her spot by the door, refusing to allow him to pass, and reminded him what had caused the contretemps in the first place: her relationship with the Marquess of Ware. "His willingness to intercede on my behalf with the Lord Mayor of London is what convinced your sons that your threats to leave the estate to me might not be so hollow after all. Let me assure you, he remains willing."

It was an empty boast.

The idea that the eminent noble would rise to the defense of La Reina's illegitimate brat was risible. It was one thing for him to accede to his son's request, for it had cost him little.

A letter asking the mayor to consent to a meeting was a nuisance at best.

All the marquess had to do was affix his name and seal.

There was nothing at stake for him.

A refusal did not harm his standing.

But a confrontation with a fellow peer—that carried risk.

If Ware failed to cower the earl, then his reputation would suffer. A man's authority extended only as far as his ability to bend others to his will, and the marquess would never jeopardize his position on behalf of a courtesan's by-blow.

Having made the patently ridiculous claim, however, Verity had no choice but to bolster it. The only way to play a weak hand was by acting as though it were a strong one. "Out of respect and affection for his son, Lord Ware stands ready to do whatever is necessary to ensure my safety, and *he* will destroy *you*. By the time he is done you will be barred from every drawing room in England, and the humiliation will be so great, you will *wish* you were in Stechford's scullery."

The secret to a successful bluff was in its delivery. Make the declaration with enough conviction, and everyone will believe you. It was just another ruse, an alternate form of Twaddling.

And yet Verity found herself swayed by the central conceit of her argument: The marquess loved his son and would take steps to ensure his happiness. Flicking away a fly such as Frimgallow was in fact a minor thing.

Another nuisance.

Did the earl know it?

Verity could not tell.

His face was impassive.

So be it, she thought. Having made one impossibly bold assertion, she might as well make another. "And if you are tempted to try your strength against Ware's—a reasonable impulse, I am sure—know that the Duke of Kesgrave will also intercede on my behalf."

Ah, a flicker!

Frimgallow's cheek twitched.

He is unnerved, Verity thought.

Either peer on his own might be overcome with some effort, but the two together made a formidable pair, and he could not be certain of his success.

Pressing her advantage, she continued, "If you have been following my career as closely as you say, then you know I make no idle threats. Both men would rise to my defense. But perhaps that is not enough to dissuade you, as you are a proud man who is accustomed to getting his way. The notion of being bested by a baseborn whelp is inconceivable, and the sensation in your chest is no doubt unfamiliar. In all likelihood you are mistaking the feeling for rage. It is not. It is impotence, and I would advise you to heed it by accepting my proposal. With all your money, you will live comfortably on the Continent—I understand Paris is lovely under the new king—and you won't have to endure the beau monde's pitying looks as your sons stand trial. I know how much you loathe a scandal. And do recall that through this encounter you learned that your sons planned to poison you with cyanide of potassium. That is another gain for you. All in all, you are the victor of the confrontation. Take your win and be grateful."

As if to endorse this claim, Lewis grunted. Slowly, he raised himself to sitting position and looked around blankly.

"If you are trying to find your pistol, it is on the table," Delphine said helpfully.

Either Frimgallow took Verity's words to heart or the sight of his wakeful son made plain the extent of the problem, for he suddenly owned himself satisfied with the prospect of France. He had dozens of cousins in the Loire Valley, and it had been many years since he had seen them. With that, he bid Verity a curt goodbye and looked expectantly at the door.

Verity darted a glance at Hardwicke, who nodded, and she moved away, allowing him to exit the room. Stepping into the hallway, Frimgallow encountered Grint, and when he tried to slip by the under-secretary, he was detained by Cook, who accused him of attempting to make a daring escape. The resisting earl was returned to the parlor, where the recent conversation was recounted for the newcomers' benefits. Grint, who frowned sharply at the complication presented by Frimgallow and his dutiful son, explained that Sidmouth had not only arranged for Brownell to be transported to a penal colony but also cajoled Lady Abercrombie into keeping more or less mum about her exploit.

"He did this to avoid kicking up an awful fuss," the under-secretary added, darting a weary look at Lewis before sighing heftily. "I suppose we should put him on the ship as well to ensure Sidmouth's efforts are not wasted. Bringing one brother to trial to answer for a crime incited by the other brother's crime risks creating the very commotion his lordship wishes to avoid. I trust you have no objection, Miss Lark?"

The government's eagerness to sweep the ugly incident under the rug was hardly surprising. The murderous Lord Bentham had been granted the courtesy of pleading guilty to a lesser charge for similar reason. Even so, Verity was rankled by it. She wanted Brownell's villainy to be exposed to the world, for him—and, by proxy, Frimgallow—to be held up as an object of ridicule, as the inevitable consequence of rampant cruelty and greed. She wanted them to be the topic on everyone's lips, for their former peers to tut over their downfall disapprovingly as they sipped claret at White's.

But exposing Brownell to public consumption meant exposing herself as well, and as willing as Verity was to sacrifice her own comfort at the altar of justice, she was grateful to avoid it. With her talents and experience, she could have established a new identity with relative ease, but she liked

Bethel Street and the life she had carved out for herself and her little household. She was in no rush to leave.

Before she could respond to Grint's proposal, Frimgallow owned himself satisfied with the arrangement. Discovering Sidmouth's position had a freshly sobering effect on the earl, who perceived now the full weakness of his position.

Nobody was coming to his aid.

No matter!

He was a lord, after all, and well adept at displaying the effete good manners of his class. Accepting the defeat graciously, Frimgallow apologized for cutting his visit short, but he had affairs to put in order before he could remove to the Continent. "If you require anything else from me, I trust you will not hesitate to ask."

Lewis, still dazed from the blow, did not seem to comprehend any of these words, and ten minutes later, when Grint helped him to his feet to take him to Bow Street, he asked why he had not been allowed to leave with his father.

※

Monday, June 29
9:27 p.m.

As Delphine rose to retire to her bedchamber, she reiterated her central thesis for the evening: Grint assisted them in the Brownell matter only in a bid to return to Hardwicke's good graces. Belatedly realizing the difficulty of discharging the duties of his office without the support of his most proficient spy, he had grasped the enormity of his misstep in not helping to free Verity from Newgate—or, at least, not appearing to help free her—and sought to undo the damage by interfering in any number of murder cases.

"*Now* he is not bothered by the tawdriness of revenge and

... and... *and* ritual sacrifice," she added with an air of triumph as she came up with a circumstance sufficiently sordid to illustrate her point.

The fact that the latter did not figure in any of their recent travails, neither the Wraithe's slaying nor Brownell's scheme, eluded Delphine, who had consumed several glasses of wine, first out of relief at emerging unscathed from that afternoon's calamity, then out of necessity as she insisted on discussing Frimgallow's unbearable villainy in placing his daughter in a residence where he knew she would be molested. Despite all the wickedness they had encountered in their various investigations—the Wraithe's rapaciousness, Hottenroth's depravity, Wigsworth's indecency—his eagerness to subject his own child to a sort of mental and physical torture appalled her in a way she had not known possible, and Verity had sought to ease her friend's distress by telling stories from her stay in Mount Street that made her tenure sound like a very great lark.

Sneaking into the Stechford's bedchamber to rub dirt under his fingernails so that he thought he had been digging in the garden in his sleep! Placing chopped earthworms in the pockets of his dressing gown to make him worry about what horrible concoctions he had been brewing in the night!

These efforts convinced nobody—obviously, her years in the scullery were a hideous nightmare—but Delphine and Freddie laughed appreciatively, determined to appear swayed. They knew their anguish served nothing, and when Verity lauded her father for generously not drowning her in a river as a baby, Delphine allowed that Frimgallow had his paternal moments as well.

And then she had changed the topic to her most favorite villain: Grint.

Alas, maligning the under-secretary while consuming copious amounts of excellent Bordeaux was exhausting business, and Delphine yawned again as she designated Freddie chaperone in her absence. "I am trusting you to make sure they behave. I see the way Hardwicke looks at Verity. Very beggar at the feast. Keep an eye on him. He is a wily one. That is why Grint wants him back in his stable. Speaking of, he is sitting awfully close to her right now," she said with a suspicious frown. "Tut! Back to your corner, Lord Colson."

Soberly, Freddie accepted the responsibility, and Delphine swept out of the parlor—after pausing, it must be noted, to make sure his lordship complied with her command.

He did not.

Hardwicke stayed precisely where he was, on the cushion next to Verity, his hand lightly brushing hers, but another yawn overtook Delphine and she merely shook her head in despair.

As she left the room, Freddie followed her a little way to make sure she navigated the stairs safely, then returned to announce his departure. "I will not mind you as though you are small children. You are grown adults and free to conduct yourselves in whatever way you deem appropriate."

Verity grinned at this display of high-mindedness. "You just want to return to the office to begin reporting on the downfall of the house of Brownell."

"Well, naturally, yes," Freddie replied blandly. "Despite Sidmouth's efforts to handle the matter quietly, people will notice the sudden disappearance of Frimgallow and his sons and will begin to speculate wildly if some explanation is not given. I shall provide it. Brownell and Lewis conspired to kill Mr. Muir because he insulted them in Oxford Street and Frimgallow is leaving for the Continent because he cannot bear the humiliation of raising two such petty fellows. It seems oddly fitting that his disgrace come from something so minor when his own sins are egregious."

"Control the narrative," Verity murmured approvingly.

Freddie grinned. "And sell newspapers."

"Both worthy goals," she replied, rising to walk him to the door and sparing a thought for Twaddle.

Frimgallow did not know.

As closely as he had watched Mary Price's progression, he had failed to fully comprehend the breadth of her identity, a conclusion she based on his failure to mention the gossip during their negotiation. Threatening to expose her secret was the only card he could have played and he had kept it off the table.

Presumably, that was because he did not hold it.

Even so, she worried about the prospect, and as she returned to the parlor, she decided to seek Hardwicke's opinion. Entering the room, she began to pose the question, then stopped midsentence when she discovered he was standing by the threshold with a sheet of paper in his hand.

Holding out the document, he said, "Your list, trimmed of all nonsense, as promised."

"Thank you," Verity said as she perused the slip, which contained eight items in two categories: bribes and payments. The total for the former was much in line with what she had anticipated, but she had grossly underestimated how much two nights in the warden's house had cost—owing, she supposed, to the fact that one purchased the room in weekly increments, not daily. "I will examine my accounts and suggest a schedule for repayment, the first installment of which I will give you tomorrow."

She expected him to demur.

He was too observant not to have noticed her surprise at the alarming steepness of the total, and she assumed he would again insist that reimbursement was unnecessary. Deeply offended by the notion of a financial imbalance between them, he would consider it foolish of her to struggle to make ends meet simply to satisfy a debt that did not actually exist, especially in light of the new servant she had promised to hire to appease Lucy.

Verity did not care if it struck him as illogical. She would not relinquish her own obligations to assuage his ego, and although she curved her lips into a pleasant smile, she tensed her shoulders in anticipation of an argument.

But it did not come.

Seeming to comprehend how ardently she opposed his charity, Hardwicke accepted her proposal with an easy nod and said he was happy to accept whatever timetable she proposed.

Inexplicably, she felt a flash of impatience.

His ready agreement was precisely what she sought, and yet she recognized in the insouciant dip of his head the work of a superior tactician. Few things were more effective than a calculated surrender, and in appearing to cede territory, he was in fact holding his army in place. As ever, he remained firmly in control, and any attempt to take issue with his deft maneuvering would undermine her own position by making her appear churlish.

Smoothly, then, she said, "Very good," and returned to the settee. Dropping onto the cushion, she pictured the citadel again, its stone walls strewn around her, and sighed as a wave of weariness descended. Like Delphine, she had had several glasses of wine, and yet she knew the fatigue was more than alcohol-induced exhaustion. She was tired of fighting, and contemplating the rubble, she wondered what would happen if she stopped—if she simply stood amid the wreckage and waved a white flag.

Hardwicke would pounce. A man of his wit and cunning would never pass up an opportunity to exploit a weakness. He would sooner walk away from a gambling table without collecting his winnings.

And yet even as she considered all the ways he would

press his advantage to her detriment, she knew he never would. In all their dealings, he had shown nothing but restraint. Even in the wake of the murder attempt, when she was a mass of quivering desire in his arms, he had held himself in check, ending the madness and recalling her to her senses with a sweet kiss.

Verity could, with very little effort, classify his restraint as yet another tactic—allowing a wild creature to grow accustomed to his scent before seizing control and confining it to a cage—but she could not quite raise herself to that level of cynicism.

Hardwicke did not want to cage her or tame her or bring her to heel.

He wanted to be near her.

Clearly, precisely, he had stated it weeks ago, when she had barely known him: *I want to scheme with you, Verity. I want to scheme with you for hours.*

Everything he had done since then had been in service of this modest goal, and if anyone was playing a complex strategical game, it was Verity herself, for she still could not fathom his fundamental decency. Her affection for him made her vulnerable to his wiles, and the idea that he would not try in some way to use her own feelings against her bewildered her.

How could he resist the immense satisfaction of striding boldly through the citadel in ruin, monarch of all he surveyed?

But this warlike conception of romance was hers, not his.

She was the one who perceived their relationship as an endless series of skirmishes despite having resolved to lay down her arms more than a week ago. And yet it was hardly surprising, given her upbringing, which had been one long battle. Every interaction at Fortescue's had been a contest with two outcomes: If Verity did not win, then she lost. Only a greenhead trusted that the competition was fair, and if she had spent decades putting her thumb on the scale, it was merely to give herself a fighting chance. The notion that she would stand down now, when her heart was at stake, was ludicrous.

But even so, her childhood had not been all Hobbesian struggle and tyrannical rule.

In Freddie and Delphine she had found not only a measure of normalcy but also a countervailing narrative to the Wraithe's almost comedic villainy. Thanks to them, she knew how to love, and if she had not succumbed to infatuation with the same speed or eagerness as Hardwicke, she had nevertheless yielded after what she deemed a reasonable interval of cautious resistance. Despite Delphine's opinion of her as a heedless adventurer, Verity was in fact a prudent creature who weighed every step before she took it, and casting about now for factors to enter into her calculation, she encountered nothing but ephemera.

No, not ephemera, she thought, recalling the amendment Hardwicke had made earlier. They were intangibles—a fair distinction, to be sure, as a lack of corporeality did not necessarily mean an absence of permanence, and yet thoroughly unconvincing.

Because it all *felt* so fleeting: the flash of lust, the spark of affection, the glow of admiration, the warmth of camaraderie. It shimmered gorgeously, like the sun hovering over the horizon, bathing the world in gold before disappearing, and she could not fathom the unbearable presumption of trying to hold on to a sunset.

But Hardwicke did not flinch.

Calmly, unsparingly, confidently, he had declared himself: *It took little more than a week.*

Of course it had devastated her.

It was an astonishing display of faith.

Only not in her, she realized suddenly, but in himself.

He trusted the solidity of his emotions.

For him, none of it was fleeting.

That he could possess any clarity about his feelings in the face of so much desire confounded her. Every time his finger brushed against hers, a dizzying rush swept through her.

The brush of a finger and she melted like snow.

It was unnerving, and in that instant, she saw clearly the arc of her mother's career, for La Reina understood desire: the simulation of it, the manipulation of it, the expression of it.

Verity, in contrast, could discern nothing about it, foundering to identify even its shape.

And there again was Hardwicke, speaking in absolutes, harboring no doubts, seeking favors from his father, welcoming announcements in *The Times*.

His audacity was boundless, and in awe of it, Verity wondered for the first time in her life if she was a coward after all. Flinging herself headlong into a circumstance for which she had taken into account every possible variable did not constitute bravery.

Action in the face of uncertainty—that was courage.

That was faith, she thought.

Determined to display it despite the butterflies beating a storm in her belly, she rose to her feet, tore the list of expenses in half, and hurled herself into his arms.

VERITY LARK RETURNS WITH ANOTHER ADVENTURE SOON!

In the meantime, look for the
Duchess of Kesgrave's latest investigation:
A Pernicious Fabrication.
Available for preorder now.

My Gracious Thanks

Pen a letter to the editor!

Dearest Reader,

A writer's fortune has ever been wracked with peril - and wholly dependent on the benevolence of the reading public.

Reward an intrepid author's valiant toil!

Please let me know what you think of *A Lark's Release* on Amazon or Goodreads!

About the Author

Mistress Lynn Messina is the author of 14 novels of questionable morality, including the *Beatrice Hyde-Clare Mysteries* series and the *Love Takes Root* series of lurid romances.

Aside from writing scandalous fiction to corrupt well-behaved young ladies, Mistress Messina hosts a Socials page where a certain dubious gentleman by the name of Mr. Twaddle-Thum regularly shares scurrilous and certainly false gossip.

Mr. Twaddle-Thum is likewise the author of a worthless little news sheet known as *The Beakeeper*. It prides itself on being filled with nothing but utter tripe and nonsense. It can, however, serve as a remedy for a spot of Sunday afternoon ennui.

Mistress Messina resides in the uppity colonial city of New York with her sons.

Also by Lynn Messina

Verity Lark Mysteries Series

A Lark's Tale

A Lark's Flight

A Lark's Conceit

A Lark's Release

Beatrice Hyde-Clare Mysteries Series

A Brazen Curiosity

A Scandalous Deception

An Infamous Betrayal

A Nefarious Engagement

A Treacherous Performance

A Sinister Establishment

A Boldly Daring Scheme

A Ghastly Spectacle

A Malevolent Connection

An Ominous Explosion

An Extravagant Duplicity

A Vicious Machination

A Pernicious Fabrication

Love Takes Root Series

Miss Fellingham's Rebellion (Prequel)

The Harlow Hoyden

The Other Harlow Girl

The Fellingham Minx

The Bolingbroke Chit

The Impertinent Miss Templeton

Stand Alones

Prejudice and Pride

The Girls' Guide to Dating Zombies

Savvy Girl

Winner Takes All

Little Vampire Women

Never on a Sundae

Troublemaker

Fashionista (Spanish Edition)

Violet Venom's Rules for Life

Henry and the Incredibly Incorrigible, Inconveniently Smart Human

Welcome to the Bea Hive
FUN STUFF FOR BEATRICE HYDE-CLARE FANS

The Bea Tee
Beatrice's favorite three warships not only in the wrong order but also from the wrong time period. (Take that, maritime tradition *and* historical accuracy!)

The Kesgrave Shirt
A tee bearing the Duke of Kesgrave's favorite warships in the order in which they appeared in the Battle of the Nile

Available in mugs too!
See all the options in Lynn's Store.

Printed in Great Britain
by Amazon